DANIELLE:

CHRONICLES OF A SUPERHEROINE

Additional Praise for
Danielle: Chronicles of a Superheroine

Danielle is a modern-day hero for everyone to look up to. A "Wonder Woman" who doesn't need super-strength but rather, her own super brain. Ray's inspiring book makes you think about the small things you can do to better the world and that there are many ways one person can spark change. In a way, we are all Danielle, we have incredible minds and if we decided to use them together, we could really change the world like she does.

—Isabelle Fuhrman, Actress
(*The Hunger Games, Orphan*)

Ray Kurzweil has been my mentor and an inspiration to all those who desire to impact the world at global scale. In Danielle, you will find his teachings and the principles of exponential thinking that are already changing the world for the better. This work is a brilliant combination of fiction and nonfiction, something that has never been done before. A must-read for young people from 10 to 110!

—Peter H. Diamandis, Cofounder (with Ray) of
Singularity University, Cofounder & Chairman of XPRIZE.
New York Times bestselling author of *Abundance* and *Bold*

What do we need for the health and survival of our planet? For every young person to know that they also possess the courage, determination, creativity and intelligence of Danielle. Ray Kurzweil delivers a perspicacious thought experiment combining a poignant work of fiction with a deeply researched nonfiction guide for achieving profound positive change.

—Dean Ornish, M.D., Founder & President of The Preventive Medicine Research Institute; Clinical Professor of Medicine, UCSF. Bestselling author of *The Spectrum* and *Dr. Dean Ornish's Program for Reversing Heart Disease*. First to prove that heart disease and other chronic diseases are reversible by making lifestyle changes.

Ray Kurzweil has been making the world better for countless numbers of people through the power of his ideas and inventions for decades, including giving me and millions of other blind people the ability to read. Now he shares with us a brilliant star, Danielle, who shines a light forward to a future with more peace, more love, and more understanding. Ray inspires each of us to be a Danielle and reach these goals through our gifts, our intelligence and our passion.

—Stevie Wonder

DANIELLE:

CHRONICLES OF A SUPERHEROINE

A Novel by

RAY KURZWEIL

Illustrations by Amy Kurzweil

To be read side by side with two companion books by Ray Kurzweil, *A Chronicle of Ideas: A Guide for Superheroines (and Superheroes)* and *How You Can Be a Danielle*

WordFire Press, LLC
Colorado Springs, Colorado

ISBN: 978-1-61475-639-2

Cover illustration by Amy Kurzweil

Cover design by Janet McDonald and Laksman Frank

Edited by Mia Kleve and Rebecca Moesta

Laksman Frank, Art Director

Published by
WordFire Press, LLC
PO Box 1840
Monument CO 80132

Kevin J. Anderson & Rebecca Moesta, Publishers

WordFire Press Hardcover Edition 2019
Printed in the Republic of Korea

Join our WordFire Press Readers Group and get free books,
sneak previews, updates on new projects, and other giveaways.
Sign up for free at wordfirepress.com

10 9 8 7 6 5 4 3 2 1

Danielle
WATER FOR ZAMBIA
LEAP to LIBERTY
I ♥ PHYSICS
INCLUDE immigrants Now
BE KIND BE SMART
STERN SCHOOL

Contents

To all the Danielles

*Don't let anyone tell you
that you cannot change
the world*

An Alternative Reality:

Any similarities to
—or differences from—
historical figures and events
are purely intentional.

Preface

Ray Kurzweil

In 1955, when I was seven, I recall my grandfather describing his first return trip to Europe, seventeen years after he had fled Hitler in 1938. He had been given the opportunity to handle, with his own hands, Leonardo da Vinci's original notebooks containing descriptions and illustrations of his inventions. He described this experience in reverential terms. Yet these were not documents written by God, but by a human. This was the religion, if you will, I grew up with: the power of human ideas to change the world. This philosophy was personalized: you, Ray, can find those ideas.

To this day, I continue to be convinced of this basic philosophy. No matter what quandaries we face—business problems, health issues, relationship difficulties, the great social and cultural challenges of our time—there exists an idea that will enable us to prevail. We can and must find that idea. And when we find it, we need to implement it.

My mother's mother's mother Regina Stern followed this philosophy. In 1868 she saw girls did not have the opportunity for schooling past ninth grade, so she and her family started the *Stern Schule*, the first school in Europe that provided higher education for girls, going from kindergarten to fourteenth grade (high school and the first two years of college). The idea was met with fierce opposition, and my great-grandmother lectured throughout Europe on why girls should be educated and how to go about it. Her school became influential on the education of girls and women. Her daughter, my grandmother, became an exemplar of her mother's philosophy and became the first woman in Europe to be awarded a PhD in chemistry. She took over the school, and between the two women they ran it for seventy years before fleeing Vienna in the summer of 1938, after Hitler annexed Austria. In 1948, she wrote an autobiography and history of the school titled *One Life Is Not Enough*, presaging my interest in life extension. When I was five she showed me the mechanical typewriter she wrote her book on, which inspired me to become an inventor, but that's another story.

Over the last thirty years, I have come to appreciate an important meta-idea: that the power of ideas to transform the world is itself accelerating. Although people readily agree with this observation when it is simply stated, it is much harder to appreciate its profound implications. Within the next several decades, we will have the opportunity to apply ideas to conquer age-old problems—and introduce a few new ones along the way.

This, then, is Danielle's philosophy. If Danielle's exploits seem remarkable, I would point out that each of her accomplishments are achievements that a person, even a child, can do today. Indeed, young people are already changing the world. The major tech companies—Microsoft, Apple, Google, which together are worth almost two trillion dollars and have indeed transformed the world—were started by students barely over twenty. We see high school kids creating transformative ideas, such as early noninvasive tests for cancer, new approaches to treating Alzheimer's disease, and techniques for reverse-engineering the brains of animals.

Is there a Danielle in the world today? From one perspective, anyone can be a Danielle, at least in part, by having the courage to question the assumptions that limit human imagination to solve problems. The companion book, *How You Can Be a Danielle*, provides guidance for would-be Danielles.

How about a person with the extremely broad range of Danielle's courage and talent? She may not exist, at least not yet. This novel is a thought experiment as to what would happen if there were a Danielle.

However, as I articulate in my nonfiction books, in the decades ahead we are going to merge with the intelligent technology we are creating. This novel explores the impact a single Danielle can have on the world. Now imagine if we all became Danielles. That will happen by 2045.

Ray Kurzweil

This novel should be read side by side with

two nonfiction companion books

by Ray Kurzweil

A Chronicle of Ideas: A Guide for

Superheroines (and Superheroes)

and

How You Can Be a Danielle

It is only ideas that can change the world. The companion book, *A Chronicle of Ideas: A Guide for Superheroines (and Superheroes)* is a nonfiction guide to the scientific, technological, medical, entrepreneurial, political, historical, literary, musical, philosophical, and psychological ideas that animate the world of Danielle, the protagonist of this novel (and my world, too!). Almost three hundred ideas in this novel are tagged with entry numbers which can be read side by side with the entries in this companion book.

How You Can Be a Danielle provides practical ideas for would-be Danielles of all ages that can be implemented right now: how you can help conquer disease, settle conflicts, overcome intolerance, and make this a kinder, more whimsical, more musical world.

DANCING ON QUICKSAND

Please note that the superscripts in the text refer to entry numbers in the nonfiction companion book, A *Chronicle of Ideas: A Guide for Superheroines (and Superheroes)*, which provides my spin (and Danielle's) on the indicated concept.

AGE ZERO AND ONE:
MAYBE SHE'S DIFFERENT

There is one thing stronger than all the armies in the world, and that is an idea whose time has come.

—Victor Hugo

Never give in. Never give in. Never, never, never, never—in nothing, great or small, large or petty—never give in, except to convictions of honour and good sense.

—Winston Churchill

I remember like it was yesterday. Danielle and my dialogue with Colonel Qaddafi. Her challenge to the Madrassa schools. Her confrontation with the Food and Drug Administration. Her arrest. Her taking on the Red Army. The death of her collaborator and soul mate. But I'm getting ahead of myself. Let's start at the beginning.

Hi, I'm Claire. Let me tell you how Danielle came to be my sister. I was six years old and school had ended at two in the afternoon. I was sitting on the dirt floor in the factory—the only afterschool program I ever knew—next to Mum with her sewing machine, playing with my favorite and pretty much only possessions, *Alice's Adventures in Wonderland*,[1] and my guitar. My book was in English, and everyone seemed quite impressed I could read it by myself. My guitar was a small square white box with a round hole. It must have been a wooden crayon box once because it still had the telltale scribblings. Someone had glued on a fingerboard, head, and strings, and it worked surprisingly well. I found it discarded in the factory's trash, and Mum's musician friends fixed the dents and polished out the scratches. It was missing a string and I was still hoping to find it.

I often played and sang for the women in the factory as they sewed button-up blouses and long skirts, which I imagined swaying on the hips of their future owners. Most of the women started smiling whenever I sang for them. I like to think it made their work less dull. Some of them hummed along. Others tapped their feet. I would look out over my "audience" and imagine I was singing in a huge concert hall. In front of me, rows of women at sewing machines, dangling electrical wires, and colorful garments of bold red, blue, green, and white hanging from clothes lines, stretched as far as I could see.

How I loved my music, even back then.

I remember Mum sewing a white dress with blue thread that day. She told me how proud she was of the new song I was playing on my guitar. I can't remember the tune, I had just made it up. Everyone was grinning by the time I finished singing. Several women even paused in their sewing to applaud.

Suddenly the building shook and Mum's cup of coffee fell on me. I cried out as the liquid burned my face. The cup went flying against the sewing machine stand where it smashed into a million pieces. Then the building exploded, the Earth shook, and the ground opened up. I remember thinking that I was like Alice. I found myself falling down the rabbit hole, and I ended up in a totally dark place filled with obstacles— stones, sharp needles, metal gears, buttons flying like bullets, wires, dripping oil, chunks of the walls and ceilings. When I tell this story people assume I must have been terrified, and I suppose I was, but the whole thing was so strange and happened so fast I felt like I'd woken up in my book.

"Mum … where are you …? Mum …?"

No one responded. I didn't panic. I assumed this was some kind of game where I was supposed to find her. I felt around in the dark, pushing things out of my way, at least those objects that would yield to the strength of a six-year-old. I moved from one dark space to another, expecting to see a hookah-smoking caterpillar at any moment.

I didn't realize I was being watched by some man named Richard who'd come to Haiti to help start a school, but quickly shifted to helping with the earthquake rescue operation.[2] He could see me as a blurry image using a special radar that was looking for survivors. Later, he said I "looked like a fetal sonogram." People dismissed the moving image as a trapped dog under the rubble. But as the story goes, Richard disagreed. "No, it's not moving like an animal. That's a small person—probably all alone. We're going to find that child… and if she has no one and nowhere to go … we'll adopt her." People kind of doubt the adoption prediction part of the story now, but I'm sure it's true.

I fell asleep in my Wonderland using ripped clothes as a mattress. There was a large chunk of cement next to me which was a good thing since that's what probably prevented me from being crushed. I was woken by the frantic sounds of local volunteers moving boulders and bricks with their bare hands. When they finally pulled me from the wreckage, people just stared at me in amazement like I must be the Haitian Alice—except I could see this wasn't Wonderland. In the photo I have of my rescue, I'm covered in black soot, wearing shredded clothes, still holding onto my guitar.

"Where's Mum?" I asked.

"Well, let's find out," Richard said. "What's your name?"

"Claire Pierre-Louis."

"That's a lovely name," he told me. I remember him wearing a white T-shirt, which seemed to shine brightly in the midday sun and was only smeared with a few streaks of dirt compared to everything else, which was covered with grime. I recognized the entrance to the factory, which looked like a big barn door, but the rest of the factory was gone.

I find it painful now to think about the following hours—the waiting, the searching, the injured and dazed survivors, seeing all the people who didn't make it.

Finally, a somber Richard answered my question. "Your mum is sitting on your shoulder." I was perplexed at first, but I gradually understood what he meant. I looked down for what seemed like a lifetime, looked at my Mum sitting on my shoulder, and then gave Richard a hug. My mum sits there still.

A few days later, I was still in shock, but I understood Richard's proposal to me. "How about I be your Dad now?"

"Wow, I always wanted a Dad," I replied.

"And Sharon, my wife, could be another Mom. We'll take care of you while you take care of your Mum sitting on your shoulder."

I felt good about this—I figured the more Mums the merrier. I was concerned that Mum on my shoulder wouldn't like it, but she said that she did.

However, some of the local men I knew were not so enthusiastic. "Mèsi pou ede ou, men timoun nan rete isit la ..." *Thanks for your help, but the child stays here. We don't want anybody stealing our children.*

I looked around and saw one of the sewing machine stands lying on its side. It still had three of its legs so I set it straight and climbed up on it avoiding the big gash in the middle.

"But it's what I want!" I blurted out without even thinking. I felt like I was one of those grown-ups I had seen on the factory TV giving a speech, like that guy Mum told me was the most important man in America. "I love everyone. My heart will always be here. And I will be back."

Everyone was shocked at how mature I sounded, including me.

That's how I became Claire Pierre-Louis Calico at the age of six.

We lived in Pasadena, a suburb of Los Angeles, in a wood and glass house that smelled like onions, or at least that's what I can remember. Mom always cooked them in everything. To me, that became the smell of home. And home was also the sight of geraniums inside and outside the house. I loved those flowers. I love them still.

Dad explained to everyone that the house was built by "a guy named Frank Lloyd Wright."[3] He's my favorite architect now. There was a winding stream that you could see from the huge window in the living room. Well, it was a fake stream, but I didn't realize that at the time. It was all rather different from the Cap-Haïtien tenement I was used to. Dad always says a water view is his one requirement for a home.

The one regret he had about the house is that with all the glass walls there wasn't enough wall space for Mom's photos of the family and his art collection, which includes Grandma Hannah's lovely flower paintings.

I had my own room which I decorated with posters of Haiti. There was a picture of a little girl who looked like me writing in her school book using a wooden bench as a desk, a picture of five women carrying baskets full of fruit on their heads, a man wading in the water with flowers of every color by the river bank. Everyone was smiling.

I felt lonely in this big room—I was used to sharing a bed with Mum in a room with three other families. Mum on my shoulder still shared my bed, but she didn't take up as much space as she used to. I enjoyed talking to her each night telling her about my day, but I missed the way her fingers would stroke my forehead and how her body would make the bed sag toward the middle. Instead of feeling lonely, I thought I should be praying to God, thanking him for rescuing me, but Mum said she would take care of that.

Danielle came along the biological way two years later when I was eight. I remember Mom, Dad, and me rushing to the hospital at one in the morning. Mom just put on the fancy black coat she wore to parties over her flannel nightgown. Dad seemed to be ready for this moment and was all dressed and holding the labor bag. I threw my gym outfit on over my pajamas, which looked ridiculous.

When we got to the hospital, I was left in a huge white waiting room with a nurse's assistant. I thought I would go crazy waiting for what I figured would be a long night. I counted the number of large white tiles—there were eight rows of six. I counted them again and again. I timed myself to see how much time I could use up this way, but it was only two minutes for each scan of the forty-eight tiles.

But Danielle, who never hesitated to move ahead when she decided to do something, popped out before I had counted the tiles a hundred times. I was hurried into a room and immediately fell in love.

She was swaddled in a floral blanket and had a full head of dark hair. Mom told me that a newborn's expressions are not intentional, but I could have sworn that her beautiful "o" shaped mouth was telling me how amazing she thought the world was. There was not a whimper or a cry. I remember imagining her as a wise old woman, patiently looking out at the world.

Danielle's precociousness was clear from the get-go.

I remember when she was three months old, she played a looking game with me, her own invention. I'd look at her and she'd quickly look away. Then when I looked away, she would look at me, but when I tried to catch her she'd turn away again. She invariably won, catching me glancing at her. Each time that happened, she broke out in a big smile as if to say, *Gotcha.*

By six months, she had her favorite dolls to whom she was fiercely loyal. She would line them up as if they were her students. Carousels and busy boxes held no interest for her, or, I should say, they interested her for a few minutes and then were cast aside forever.

She loved to play with books of any shape and description. She often sat in the middle of her room on the floor turning the pages, making exaggerated reactions like a mime. Apparently she was mimicking the responses she'd seen Mom, Dad, and me make while reading.

By fifteen months, her book collection had expanded with those stolen from around the house, including some grown-up volumes that were larger than she was. I would try to look over her shoulder to see if there was any correlation between her reactions and what was actually on the page she was looking at, but she would close the book when I came around as if I were trying to sneak a peek at her personal diary.

She almost never cried, but expressed her displeasure by making a mad face. She kept looking through books voraciously and doing her pretend reading, imitating adult reactions, and I kept trying to see exactly what she was reading. This, too, became a game. Once she suddenly turned the book around as if to say, *Okay, nosey, here!* The book was upside down. I wonder to this day if she did that to throw me off.

"Maybe, she's ... different," I heard Mom say to Dad with a furrowed brow one night after dinner. "She doesn't even talk yet." They didn't know I was behind the door that led from the kitchen to the mess room, which is where I always hid when I wanted to listen to them.

"Oh, she's different all right," Dad replied. "But I wouldn't fret about her talking."

"And walking?" Mom added.

"She'll talk when she has something to say," Dad replied.

"And walk when she has someplace to go?" Mom added.

"Exactly."

Danielle liked to fall asleep by curling herself into a tight ball on my lap. I enjoyed this, but it presented a bit of a dilemma if I wanted to do something else. Many nights, I just fell asleep myself with her lying there.

AGE TWO:

DANIELLE IN WONDERLAND

Danielle still didn't talk or walk, although she could crawl faster than most two-year-olds could walk. Nonetheless, it interfered with her social life. Other two-year-olds didn't want to make friends with a girl who still acted like a baby.

Mom found it challenging to find other kids to attend her second birthday party, something that Danielle seemed to be aware of. Mom invited three other kids, cousin James who was one, and the two-year-old twins Rachel and Ryann from next door. Mom put up streamers and balloons, but was not smiling. I remember finding it a bit embarrassing as there wasn't much of a party spirit. Danielle didn't smile either. I tried to engage the kids in games like pin the tail on the donkey, but it was not my most successful party.

⁓ꝋꝋ⁓

"I've asked Dr. Sonis to come over tomorrow," Mom said to Dad that evening in one of their many conversations about Danielle's "differences."

"Well that won't hurt, but I really don't think it's necessary," Dad replied. "Anyway, you're the child psychologist."

"I can't evaluate my own child," Mom said. "Maybe I'm too close to the situation. I just don't know what we should be doing with her."

Most evenings, we ate dinner in the dining room by a panoramic window that overlooked the stream. I was usually assigned to help Mom set the table. Mom took pride in having everything in place before we sat down to eat. My specialty was folding the cloth napkins to look like little mountains. I kind of took these dinners for granted back then, but they're among my fondest memories now.

Dr. Sonis made his visit. I could swear there was a smirk on Danielle's face as she was introduced to him. She quickly pressed him into service, sitting three of her dolls on his knee, putting aprons on them and serving them tea. I was invited to join the party and showed off my napkin folding skills.

The next evening at dinner, I talked with Mom and Dad about *Alice's Adventures in Wonderland*, which was still my favorite book. "The Caterpillar[4] is a really interesting character," I pointed out.

"He gives Alice a hard time, don't you think?" Dad chimed in.

"He gives everyone a hard time," I replied.

Mom smiled at my reply. She once told me that she loved listening to conversations, because it gave her a gauge of how children were developing.

Dad settled in to enjoy our debate. "But his rudeness seems mostly directed at Alice."

"The Caterpillar didn't understand Alice very well when they first met," I replied, "which explains why he was so rude to her."

"Oh, I wouldn't say that," Danielle suddenly said. "He's the know-it-all. Kind of like you, Mom, and Dad. He always seems to say what's coming."

Mom dropped the wooden bowl of berries she was about to serve. A blizzard of blueberries bounced across the table. Most of them ended up in Danielle's and my laps.

Dad gave Mom a look like, *What did I tell you?* and calmly asked Danielle, "So how come he always knows what's going to happen?"

"Cuz he's the one who makes it happen," Danielle declared.

Mom's eyes sparkled with fascination. She still stood there with her mouth agape. No one cleaned up the blueberries.

"What makes you say the Caterpillar is like Mom and Dad?" I asked.

"He's always trying to teach Alice a lesson," Danielle replied. "Like he gives her the mushroom to make her bigger, and she learns that there is more to growing up than just being big."

"Wow, that's quite a message," I said.

Danielle replied, "Well, it's the Cheshire Cat[5] who actually explains it to Alice, but it's the Caterpillar's lesson."

Composing herself, Mom asked, "What about the White Rabbit[6]? Do you like him?"

"Not really," Danielle answered. "He acts kind of like a big shot. He's not very nice to the people who work for him, but he's kind of fake-nice to the even bigger shots, like the Queen of Hearts."[7]

"Good point, darling," Mom replied. "It's not very nice to be fake-nice."

"Yeah," Danielle said. "I read about a guy who called that obsequious."

Tears streamed from Mom's eyes, I couldn't tell for sure if she was happy or sad, but I think it was both.

"What guy?" I asked.

"Oh, I think his name is Ronald. It was in a book called *Wonderland Revisited*."

"Hey, that's my book," I said, "I was wondering where it went."

"It's such a cool word," Danielle added. "Ob-see-quee-us, ob-see-quee-us ... Sounds kind of like what it means."

"That's onomatopoeia,[8] Danielle," Dad replied calmly.

"Obsequious is onomatopoeia?" Danielle asked.

"What Dad means is that obsequious is an example of onomatopoeia, a word that sounds like what it means."

"Oh, okay. So 'onomatopoeia' is not onomatopoeia," Danielle said with a smile.

"I think that's right, Danielle," I replied, "although I've often wondered about that."

"Anyway," Danielle concluded. "Alice is just nice to everyone. I think that's the way we all should be."

Later that evening, when Danielle and I were alone, I asked her, "What else have you been doing in your room? Secret cartwheels?"

Danielle shook her head no.

"You know Mom wants you to walk. I assume you've tried it?"

Again she shook her head.

"Let's try, then."

She took my hand and was able to stand rather easily.

"You must have tried this part, right?" I asked.

She nodded her head yes.

"Hey Dani, you do talk now, remember?"

"Yes, I've tried standing."

"You're pretty good at it… Let's try taking a step. Put one foot forward like this." I demonstrated for her.

Holding my hand, she took a wobbly barefooted step on the white carpet in her room. I got the impression that this was really her first step. She just hadn't wasted time with it before. We slowly walked around the room saying hello to her dolls, and then around again.

"Hello again, fancy meeting you here," we said to each doll with each passing. By this time, her legs were getting shaky.

"That's pretty good for now, Danielle. Let's do some more tomorrow."

We practiced each evening, and a few days later she was walking on her own—still a little tentative, but she had it.

"We just have to figure out how to introduce your new skill to Mom and Dad," I said. Danielle had a plan.

"Thank you, Claire," Danielle said. She gave me a big hug.

The next evening after dinner, I suggested that we all take a walk.

"I'll get the stroller," Mom said.

"No, I'll get it," Danielle said. She did her fast crawl to the hallway.

"Maybe if she didn't crawl so fast—" Mom began to say, but before Mom could finish her sentence, Danielle came out of the closet walking, pushing the stroller in front of her. Mom teared up again and hugged Danielle.

"I guess that's another use for the stroller," Mom said.

"Actually, I don't think we need this anymore," Danielle said, as she pushed the stroller away.

"Maybe we should hold hands," Mom said. And with that we took a very slow stroll toward the park, although it appeared to be Mom who was slowing us down.

The stream that passes by our house goes through the park, and the ducks gather there. People always feed them right next to the *Do Not Feed the Ducks* signs. Danielle took off after one of the ducks, not running exactly, but she seemed to have mastered the art of fast walking.

Danielle threw a rock in the water. The duck then scampered away from the wide part of the stream and toward Danielle. She let out a yell and made a face. The duck started quacking angrily, reversing direction again. She played this little cat and mouse—or Danielle and duck—game with each duck we encountered. Each time Danielle cracked up hysterically. We walked back to the house at an even faster pace than before.

Before Danielle's bedtime, we often got together, like we did when she practiced walking. Some nights I read to her, even though she could read for herself. Sometimes I made up little songs and sang them to her. It was our special time together.

That night, as we were having our goodnight ritual, Danielle suddenly burst into tears.

"Hey, what's the matter, Dani?" I said, but she didn't hear me. Not knowing what else to do, I grabbed her and she hugged me back. I held onto her and gradually her cries softened into a whimper. I continued to hold her until she fell asleep in my arms. I didn't know what the crying was all about at the time, but I think I have a better understanding of it now.

Ever since Danielle was born, Dad had talked about starting a school based on his idea of "learning from doing." He bought a small campus that had a long history as an Episcopal monastery, a brief stint as a country inn when the monastery moved to northern California, and was then abandoned for ten years.

Before Danielle could talk, Mom was not thrilled with the idea. "If you're so interested in education, maybe you could focus on the fact that we have a two-year-old daughter who can't talk," was a typical comment.

Once it became hard to get Dani to stop talking, Mom joined in the school planning. She took responsibility for setting up the counseling department, but took special delight in designing the renovations and landscaping. At home, the walls of the kitchen and hallway were filled with Mom's sketches.

"I should have been a designer," she often said. Danielle was quick to adopt the place as "my school." She took after Mom in the decorating department, building a scale model of Mom's landscaping ideas. Danielle was at the construction site almost every day planting flowers. I usually joined her when my classes were over.

She told me she was in charge of the flowers, and she seemed to have her own very specific plan for their arrangement, a plan she was not open to any input on.

Dad had a little ground-breaking ceremony with the people who contributed some of the money. Danielle was running around like it was her opening, making sure all her flower beds were in good order. Before I knew it, she was dragging Martine Rothblatt,[9] the CEO of United Therapeutics, over to see her flowers.

"It's nice to meet you, Miss …"

"Danielle. Danielle Calico."

"Ah, so you're the precocious daughter."

"Reporting for duty."

"This is a cool design you have here," Martine said, referring to her flowers.

"Yeah, it's the layout for the computer instruction codes in the Analytical Engine.[10] See, these pansies are the op codes and the poppies are the operand addresses."

"Awesome, Danielle," Martine replied. With that she started counting. "Yup, there's forty positions in each row. I don't think I've ever seen a computer made of flowers," she said with a broad smile.

"Yeah, well, it doesn't run."

"The analytical engine didn't run either," Martine noted. "But that didn't stop a brilliant young woman named Ada Lovelace[11] from writing programs for it. She was the daughter of the poet Lord Byron and the world's first computer programmer, even though it would be another century before there were computers you could run programs on. She was a lot like you, but a bit older."

"Yeah, I've read about her, I think she's really cool," Danielle said, as she noticed one of the pansies was out of place. She tried to dig a hole to move it, but the tough Pasadena soil was not budging. Danielle took a serrated spoon that she used in these situations out of a pocket in her pant leg and loosened up the dirt enough for her spade to dig in and move the pansy.

～ℓℓ～

Dad gave a speech to the people assembled in the courtyard for the ground breaking about his idea of kids learning from taking on world challenges. "Whether they succeed or not," Dad said, "they might actually learn something they will remember."

Dad described his inspiration. "I was looking for ways to educate my two daughters, who are here with us today. A couple of years ago, I paid a visit to the European Education History Museum in Vienna and discovered this remarkable school, the 'Stern Schule,'[12] which practiced 'learn by doing.' It was, incidentally, the first school in Europe to provide higher education for girls when it opened in 1868.

"It was founded by a courageous woman, Regina Stern. The idea was very controversial in mid-nineteenth-century Europe and was met with considerable criticism and anger. She bravely lectured throughout Europe on the importance of women's education and how to go about it. It was taken over years later by her daughter, Lillian, who became the first woman in Europe to get a PhD in chemistry. Between these two women, they ran the school for seventy years until they had to abandon it when fleeing Hitler in the summer of 1938. If they had stayed any longer they would not have been able to escape.

"In honor of these two great women," Dad said, "the new school will be named 'The Stern School.'"

With that, we all took turns with the shovel, ceremoniously moving a bit of earth. Dad had brought a small shovel for Danielle to use, but before he could grab it, Danielle was wielding the big shovel with gusto, although she fell over trying to use it. Each of us took a turn—Danielle, Dad, Mom, me, Charlie, and the other kids who had come for the ceremony.

Oh yes, Charlie—we met a few months earlier, when I had just turned ten. His family moved in nearby and he joined my fourth-grade class at the Chandler School. I was still a little uncertain of myself then, and he showed up in my life as this very friendly, accepting person with a big smile. He had wavy red hair which always ended up in front of his eyes. He also came to this country when he was six, having arrived from Ireland with his mom after his dad died of a heart attack. He was tall and lanky and prone to dramatic gestures, like falling into the stream—also a human-made one as there were few natural streams in Pasadena—with his arms spread wide, splashing whoever was with him, which was generally me.

Charlie and I played games in the field during recess, trying to skip stones across the stream. This is very hard to do in moving water, but he was a pro. He'd glance at me whenever he got one to see if I was watching. I always was.

AGE THREE:
A PIG IN MUD

*T*he Stern School held an open house a week after Danielle's third birthday. Most of the classes were in the main building—a stately red brick structure with turrets and stained-glass windows. The dorms were a long white building with evenly spaced Spanish-looking windows on the other side of a big field with California pepper trees, which look like weeping willows. The faux stream wound its way behind the building, and you could hear it babbling when you opened the dorm room windows. It was pretty amazing how much better the place looked just a year after Dad bought the campus.

The open house welcomed 140 students, ranging from six to twelve years old, and their parents. Danielle was like a pig in mud, trying out the different sample classes, as I struggled to keep up with her.

When the school officially opened a few months later, Danielle went there almost every day accompanied by her nanny, Marie, a friendly Latvian woman. Marie was still perfecting her English. Danielle was not shy about correcting her, and Marie, in turn, was teaching Danielle Latvian.

People could always see Danielle coming due to her diminutive size and her distinctive flower dresses, which she picked out herself. It did not take people long to figure out that she had seven dresses, one for each day of the week. Her first stop each day was at her flower beds where she checked on her poppies, pansies, zinnias, and sunflowers. She told people the flower bed was a subroutine for computing factorials.

Danielle had difficulty deciding which classes she liked best, so she just went from one to the next. She was not yet formally enrolled, and the teachers seemed to tolerate her showing up occasionally for each subject. Despite her sporadic attendance at each class, the teachers were eager for her arrival, and would typically spend that hour interacting with Danielle.

"It's when the sideways speed of the little thing equals its inward, speeding up toward the big thing caused by gravity," Danielle said as she walked into the How the Universe Works class, answering the question about how orbits arise.[13] It had apparently stumped the older kids.

"Gertrude feels the girl in the play within the play is making fun of her for marrying so soon after Hamlet's dad died," Danielle responded to a question in the Shakespeare class. The teacher, who claimed to be Shakespeare himself, complete with mustache, beard, curly hair and Elizabethan-era attire, had asked what the famous line "The lady doth protest too much, methinks" meant.

"Any thoughts on the characters in *The Wizard of Oz?*"[14] asked Vivian Sobchack, the teacher of the Cinematic Visions class.

Emma, a sixth grader like me, replied, "I think the girl munchkins are cuter than the boy munchkins."

Danielle piped up, "I think the Tin Man, the Lion, and the Scarecrow are Dorothy's id,[15] super-ego,[16] and ego,[17] respectively."

The kids shook their heads.

"Boy, I'd have to think about that one, Danielle," Mrs. Sobchack replied. "What about Dorothy herself?"

"The redness of her shoes represents growing up. When she clicks her red heels, she accepts that she's a grown up and she's able to go home." That made the sixth graders giggle.

"Those are lovely flowers on your dress, Danielle," Miss Chabon, our art teacher, commented. "What do the flowers mean to you?"

"Well my Mom always has geraniums around the house, and my Grandma Hannah painted flowers. Flowers are kind of like people," Danielle replied.

"How so?" Miss Chabon asked.

"Well, they grow up like people. They're pretty and happy for a while, and then they wilt and fade away."

"Not everyone does that," Miss Chabon replied.

Danielle certainly got the attention of the teachers, not to mention the students, who weren't thrilled to be shown up by a three-year-old.

Maybe this is a good time to explain that Mom and Dad decided to approach parenting a bit differently from most parents. They knew by now how exceptional Danielle was. I was no Danielle, but I was talented, sensible, and mature for my age. Mom said I had exceptional emotional intelligence. Mom and Dad wanted to give us a rich environment and an unusual amount of independence and free choice. They didn't make this decision lightly. They had set aside a modest savings account for each of us, to be used for our education, and they didn't want us to touch it until we were older.

Mom and Dad told us that if they were ever concerned about our choices, they would step in and make adjustments or help us. They thought in Danielle's and my cases this freedom might well help us develop into truly amazing people, and I think they were right. But I'm getting ahead of myself again.

That spring my dreams were coming true. After years of guitar and singing lessons at Stern, tons of auditions I didn't get and a few small ones I did, I was invited to play a solo set at the annual Country Music Association Festival. It was on one of the small side stages—a huge deal given that I was only eleven. Danielle was super excited for me, and our goodnight ritual had expanded to rehearsals, with Danielle playing the audience. She would jump from spot to spot changing her hat and acting like different people—a woman with flowers in her straw hat, a slightly tipsy cowboy, a teen boy with an LA Dodgers' cap, and others. Her dolls got into the act as well.

Charlie and I were both enrolled at Stern from the beginning. One day, while I was sitting by the stream at recess, he stole a kiss on my cheek, burst out laughing, and ran away. I took off after him not entirely sure what I planned to do if I actually caught him, like a dog chasing after a car prepared for anything except actually catching the car. Our kissing game became a ritual. One day while I was chasing him, he stopped short, and I crashed into him and fell down.

He extended a hand and said, "Are you okay?" He graciously helped me up and we exchanged a shy fleeting look. I've always remembered that glance.

The next day he gave me a ring to wear on a ribbon around my neck and made a joke about our playing boyfriend and girlfriend, but I wasn't so sure it was a game.

It was then that I told Mum on my shoulder about my new friend.

"Oh, you've made me very happy," Mum said.

That was not the reaction I had expected. Mum had always cautioned me about boys and men.

"A good man is so very hard to find," Mum added.

"Mum, he's only eleven. I'm only eleven. You're the one always telling me to take it slow."

"Oh, I'm not saying anything about that. You promised to be pure on your wedding day, and that is the right way to live. Some men only have one thing on their minds."

"Ha ha, Mum. It's no different here. Have you seen American billboards? Oh, okay, I guess maybe not."

"Like I've always said, you have to respect yourself and your body. And if you found a man who shows you respect, you've got to hold onto him."

"Charlie's not exactly a man. And how am I supposed to do that anyway?"

"My dear Claire, it is the woman who makes up her mind when it comes to love. Men like to think they're deciding things, but when it comes to love, you've got to make the choice."

"Like what?"

"Choose to hold on and not let go."

"Isn't it kind of soon for that? He's the only boy I've ever really talked to. Even if you think it's my choice, what makes you think I'm ready?"

"I can see it, girl, I can see it. I can see it in your eyes."

"How can you see my eyes when you're sitting on my shoulder?"

"Oh, I see you. You've made up your mind. You just haven't realized it yet."

"Okay, Mum. But this stuff about, you know, being pure … I mean, I know what you're talking about. But it's kind of a mixed message."

"Mixed message?"

"I'm sorry, Mum, that's an American expression. What I mean is you're telling me to stay pure but to throw myself at Charlie."

"Commit yourself to him in your mind. Keep him close as a friend, and soon he'll see what you already know: that your souls are connected."

As I walked into Danielle's room that evening for our goodnight ritual of sharing our day and singing and kissing goodnight, Danielle pointed at me and laughed, repeating in a singsong voice, "Claire has a boyfriend."

"Oh my god, Danielle, were you listening to my conversation with Mum? You're much too young to understand this stuff."

"Why? I do read, you know."

"Yeah, like what?" I asked.

"Let's see, *Pride and Prejudice, Love in the Time of Cholera, Doctor Zhivago*," Danielle offered.

I sighed. "Okay, that's pretty grown-up reading for a three-year-old."

Then she giggled and started her teasing song again. My face burned. I was now sorry I had discussed it with anyone.

AGE FOUR:
NO ONE SEEMED TO NOTICE

A year later there was some criticism of Danielle's unpredictable class schedule, so she decided to just enroll in all the classes I had signed up for. Thus began her interest in physics and biology. She found it remarkable that everyday reality was composed of such intricate mechanisms and that there were machines within machines within machines; people formed from cells, composed of molecules, comprised of atoms, made up from subatomic particles, and broken down into quarks.[18] She started to imagine out loud what would happen if we changed some of those machines.

"Suppose we just combine these nuclei?" she asked during How the Universe Works class.

"I think you'd get a nuclear explosion," said Dr. Kendall, whose curly hair made us think of him as Einstein.

"Whoops," Danielle replied.

"Yes, we'll have to be careful with that one," Dr. Kendall said.

Danielle found history fascinating and started to write stories of times gone by and how they could have turned out differently. Her essay titled "What If?" examined what would have happened if the British had broken up the East India Company[19] before the Boston Tea Party,[20] if the Kuomintang[21] had not allowed Mao to escape with his long march,[22] and if the US had not exploded two atomic bombs in Japan.[23] Miss Livingstone was so excited that she devoted a class to each of Danielle's scenarios.

Danielle wrote and sang her own songs and organized a small choral group, which I joined after some strong lobbying by her at one of our evening tête-à-têtes. She was very keen to join me on the Country Music Association Festival stage. "Your time will come," I told her.

～ℓℓ～

Mom was concerned again about Danielle, this time with her socializing, or lack thereof, outside of school. Mom and I organized her fourth birthday party. We invited the three six-year-old kids from the Stern School. Otherwise I went around the neighborhood—I had to walk a half mile to find five neighbors aged four through six. I could have done that in Cap-Haïti by walking a few dozen yards. Mom also invited Aunt Ellie who was in town from Washington, DC, figuring Danielle might relate better to an adult than her peers.

At the party, Danielle sat on her bed, ready with her pillow. The other kids were swinging away with pillows I had gathered from around the house. A girl named Annie swooped in, hit three kids with her pillow, and danced away to avoid a counterstrike while doing an imitation of Dustin Siever doing a moonwalk, or at least that's how I interpreted it. All the kids apparently thought her moves were hysterical. Except Danielle, who was having difficulty getting into the swing of this activity, so to speak.

But then, wait… Danielle finally got ready to swing her pillow. She hesitated… calculated… then swung.

She actually succeeded in striking the back of Little Miss Moonwalk. But Danielle's target ignored it and no one else appeared to notice. Danielle seemed disheartened as the kids spilled onto the floor and headed out the bedroom door.

That gave me an opportunity to change the activity. "Hey boys and girls, who wants some ice cream pie?" The kids squealed and followed me to the kitchen. I looked back and saw a frustrated Danielle at the back of the line still carrying her pillow.

How did my amazingly confident little sister become so hapless? I wondered.

AGE FIVE:
THE PRICE OF BEING FAIR

Danielle showed up at the foot of our curving staircase of wooden steps holding the wrought-iron banister with one hand and wheeling her Babar the Elephant overnight bag with the other.

"Going somewhere?" Mom asked.

"Uh, I'm off to Include."

"Include?"

"Yeah, the protest to let more people into America. Well, I mean they're already here."

Dad spoke up. "That's 3,000 miles away, Danielle. Are you going by bicycle?"

"Oh, I've got that worked out," Danielle replied. "But I do need you to drop me off at the airport."

"Airport?" Mom replied, her eyebrows rising ever higher.

"Yeah, and sign some forms. It won't take long."

Dad, who was generally good at swinging with Danielle's punches, asked, "What happens then?"

"You hand me off to the United stewardess and she'll deliver me to Aunt Ellie at Reagan National Airport."

"Aunt Ellie, really?" Mom said.

"Why don't we just confirm these arrangements with her?" Dad suggested.

"Oh, I already talked to her about it when she was here for my birthday party."

Danielle's pout displayed her impatience while Dad called Aunt Ellie.

"Okay I'm glad she's talked to you about this, but no, she has not discussed it with us," Dad said into the phone.

"It's the first we've heard of it," Dad said again.

"Were you planning on discussing this with us at all, Miss Calico?" Mom asked as Dad hung up.

"What do you think I'm doing right now?" Danielle replied.

"Your father and I don't think you're quite ready for such an adventure."

Without saying a word or changing her expression, she remained there impassively with her suitcase.

At the end of an animated discussion between Mom and Dad, the resolution was that I would accompany Danielle to Washington, DC.

"No offense to the United stewardesses, but I think your dad and I will be more comfortable if a family member goes with you," Mom said.

Dani shrugged. "Sure, I love to travel with Claire."

We'd just learned about the politics of immigration reform in our citizenship class at Stern, but it hadn't occurred to me to actually pack up and join the protests. This was the first time, but not the last, Danielle's brazen confidence pushed me to contribute to a heroic fight.

"And as an immigrant myself, I would enjoy attending," I responded. "But I can't stay for the whole event, I have to get back for the CMA rehearsals, remember?"

"That's fine," Dad said. "She'll be in good hands with Aunt Ellie once you get her there."

~e l~

Two days later, I was back at dinner with Mom and Dad. The kitchen TV was temporarily moved into the dining room so we could watch the Include coverage. Suddenly a little girl in a pink-flowered dress appeared on the screen.

Oh no, it can't be, I thought to myself.

"Our Washington correspondent has found a very articulate young protestor with something to say."

"Miss, what are you protesting?" the correspondent asked.

"American apartheid," Danielle replied.

"Apartheid,[24] really? What makes you say that?"

"Well, we have two classes of citizens. That's apartheid, just like South Africa had."

"I'm not sure I can agree." The interviewer leaned toward Danielle. "We only have one class of citizens. And the immigrants want to become citizens. How is that two classes of citizens?"

"Those are just words," Danielle said. "What's really going on is that we would never send all of the so-called illegal immigrants back to where they came from. Our country would fall apart. They are part of our economy. So, they get some things—like the doctor will see them in an emergency room and some kids get to go to school. But any one of the families can be picked on and thrown out. They're called illegal, but that's not really honest because we need them. They get some rights but not others. So that's apartheid."

"Interesting. I had not looked at it that way before. So, what do you think we should do about this?"

"Make them official citizens. The first class of citizen."

"Well, the demonstrators here apparently agree with you," the correspondent continued. "People on the other side of this issue say that if we gave millions of undocumented immigrants the official rights of citizens we would have to pay them more and prices would go up."

Danielle looked surprised and confused. I had seen this deer-in-the-headlights look of hers before when her ideas at her Stern School classes had gone awry. She was clearly thinking over what the correspondent had just said.

Finally, Danielle replied with a concerned look, "Yeah, I think that's right. I hadn't thought of that."

There was another long pause, and the correspondent was about to break away, when Danielle added, "I guess that's the price of being fair."

"Well said, miss," the correspondent replied. "And how old are you?"

"Five."

"From the mouths of babes, you heard it here on CNN. Back to you, Anderson."

A few days later, Danielle was back at the dinner table with Mom, Dad, and me. Mom was serving her favorite dessert, blueberries, with a satisfied smile.

"That was a very interesting interview on CNN, Danielle. I haven't heard that logic before. Where did you get it?" Dad asked.

"Nowhere. It's kind of obvious, don't you think?"

"All good ideas are kind of obvious," Dad replied, "once you think of them."

"I was impressed by how well you spoke," Mom said. "Just think, millions of people were watching and listening to you."

"Maybe, but nothing has changed. We didn't accomplish anything."

"Your voice was heard, Danielle," Mom replied. "That's important."

"But no one is listening." She took a bite of blueberries and chewed slowly.

"People *are* listening," I said. "It's a good start. You didn't expect to change everyone's minds in a few days, did you?"

"You can't make a revolution with one television interview or one demonstration," Dad agreed. "It took the Civil War to end slavery."

"Dani compared the class system to South African Apartheid,[25]" I pointed out. "That's a better example. Mandela[26] was in prison for twenty-seven years before it was peacefully overthrown."

"There's got to be a better way," Danielle concluded.

I was almost expecting it that evening when Danielle had a bout of uncontrollable crying.

"Tell me what you're feeling, Danielle."

She didn't answer right away, but then, "I'm walking on a long bridge."

"Really? How long?"

"A million miles."

"Who's on it?"

"No one besides me."

"Where does it go?"

"Nowhere as far as I know."

"What's the point of a bridge that doesn't go anywhere?"

"That is the point."

I had become very good at pacifying her fears with a big hug and we both knew what to do by this time. Mom and Dad had still not noticed.

AGE SIX:
MAKING GOOD USE
OF THE SEWERS

A year later, Danielle was wheeling that same suitcase, but she had covered Babar with stickers of Wally Melson and Vance Gale. Mom was out of breath, having just come in from her run, and met Dani at the foot of the stairs. Dad calmly walked over from his computer in the study. They were used to her independent ways by now. I watched my sister with amusement, although leery of where we might end up this time.

"Danielle, don't you have reports due for school?" Mom asked.

"This is my report," Danielle replied. "I'm reporting for school."

"And where might that be this time?" Dad asked.

"Zambia."[27]

"Really?" Mom wiped perspiration from her forehead as she listened.

Dad seemed to guess immediately why Danielle was going. "Are you bringing a plane full of water?"

I recalled having heard about a great drought in Zambia.[28]

"Oh, I've got you one better than that," Danielle replied.

"If you go now, you'll miss Thanksgiving, Danielle," Mom pointed out. "Can't you put this off a couple of weeks?"

"No, no. The machines are arriving on Wednesday. I have to be there. Anyway, they don't celebrate Thanksgiving. They're concerned with water, not turkeys."

"This is Danielle's way of giving thanks," I offered.

"You say you have machines?" Dad asked.

"Yeah, I have a hundred Slingshot machines[29] arriving."

Dad thought this over. His creased eyebrows relaxed, and a half smile crept over his face. "That's a pretty fine idea, Dani."

"Isn't it? Each machine can provide clean water for a hundred people," Danielle said.

"But where are they going to get the water for the machines to clean?" Mom asked.

"From the sewer," Danielle replied, as if it were obvious.

"Ick," I said.

Mom thought this over. "It sounds unappealing, but I guess that would work."

"This is going to take some organization," Dad said. "You can't just drop-ship these machines. They could be stolen. And people need to be trained to operate them. And someone needs to collect the sewer water on a regular basis."

Danielle's tight-lipped expression seemed to say, *Of course I've thought of all of that.* "Oh, I'm working with a really nice man named Chibesa Bakala."

Mom nervously rubbed her fingers, and looked in Dad's direction.

"Not everyone in Zambia is reliable," Dad said. "There are many war lords and bandits. What do you know about this gentleman?"

"He's definitely not an outlaw. He's the Commissioner of Natural Resources."

"You know they have crooks in the government, too," Mom said, biting her lower lip.

"Yeah, sure, I know that. But not this guy. I checked him out."

"It wouldn't hurt if we found out more about him. What do you say?" Dad said in a mild voice.

"Sure, go ahead."

"You're actually going for this?" Mom whispered to Dad.

"Won't power be a problem, Dani?" Dad asked.

"The country isn't as unstable as people think," Danielle replied. "They just don't have water."

"I didn't mean political power," Dad said. "I meant electricity to operate the machines."

"Oh yeah, I ordered Stirling engines,[30] too. Each one makes enough electricity for one water machine."

"But don't those Stirling engines need fuel?"

"Sewage."

"It looks like we'll be making good use of their sewers!" I commented.

Danielle was well prepared for this interrogation. Mom, on the other hand, paced between the front door and the closet.

Dad asked more questions. "That's about $200,000 of Slingshot and Stirling machines by my calculation. Who is paying for all this, Danielle?"

"I'll have a grant from the World Health Organization."[31]

"You applied for a WHO grant yourself?" Mom asked.

"Yeah, I'm *sure* it'll come through. I mean I've got all their goals covered: Meets a basic unmet need. Minimal ongoing maintenance. Cost effective. Decentralized. There's no way they'll say no. I'll get their official answer soon."

"That's certainly an appropriate place to apply to," Dad admitted. "But you should never place an order before your funding is confirmed."

"He means don't count your chickens before they hatch," I said.

Dani gave us all a determined look. "These chickens *have* to hatch. These people need clean water."

Mom sighed in resignation. "I assume the Zambian government knows you're six years old?"

Danielle glanced away. "I don't think that's come up ..."

Danielle had arranged this great deal on tickets, but the catch was it was all middle seats. On the first leg from LA to JFK, Danielle was in the seat ahead of mine, so I kept seeing her head popping up and looking back at me with a big grin. Dad was in the back of the plane. That flight wasn't too bad, but the red-eye flight to London was a bit more difficult. Dani was doing just fine, curled up in a little ball and sleeping like a baby. I, on the other hand, was up all night in between two overweight guys who seemed to be flirting with each other. I finally offered to change seats with one of them, which they were delighted to do, and that got me an aisle seat, but I still couldn't sleep.

We then had a tight connection in London to catch a small propeller plane to Lusaka.[32] We flew through a rainstorm and the plane bounced around like a ping-pong ball on the surf. Even Dad looked nervous. I alternated between being convinced we were going to crash to using all of my concentration to prevent myself from throwing up. Danielle was smiling like it was an amusement park ride.

As we landed, I could see a big sign that said *Welcome to Zambia* and another sign for Lusaka International Airport with a couple of missing letters. When I stepped off the plane it felt like a sauna, with searing gusts of sand swirling around. We were met by Commissioner Bakala, whom I recognized from his web picture, a heavyset bald man with a round face, a white hat, a black suit, and a smile as big as Danielle's. He had one lanky young assistant dressed in some kind of traditional red robe, who was very eager to please us. He gathered up our bags and held an oversized umbrella to block the swirling sand.

"Ah, very well, Danielle has brought her family. We are greatly honored," Mr. Bakala said in slow, carefully enunciated English.

Dad introduced Danielle.

"Oh, there is a little Danielle?" Mr. Bakala said.

Dani and I gave each other a look, wondering if he understood the situation.

"Perhaps your assistant would like to go with my assistant," Mr. Bakala said to Dad, referring to me.

"No, thank you. Claire is my daughter," Dad explained.

Flustered and embarrassed, the Commissioner replied, "Why, yes, of course."

That, by the way, was not the first time someone had made that mistake. Every time this happened, my whole body burned, but then I'd look into the eyes of my family and remind myself that I belong. I know it, even if not everyone else does.

"And where is Danielle?" Mr. Bakala asked with an expectant expression.

"This *is* Danielle," Dad replied.

"I mean the older Danielle," the Commissioner clarified.

Dad gave him a wry smile. "Oh, there is only one Danielle."

The Commissioner again tried to regain his composure.

The Slingshot machines started arriving at the airport in large wooden crates, but there were no Stirling engines. After some investigation by Commissioner Bakala, it turned out they had been seized by the Zambian Electric Power Commission.

"There are lots of fiefdoms in the government here," Dad explained to Danielle.

"Unlike our government? I'll go talk to the power commissioner then," Danielle declared.

"Dani, you know what we've discussed," Dad counseled. "It always pays to figure out who really makes the decisions and talk to him or her."

"Yes, very good advice," Mr. Bakala noted. "You should listen to your father, Danielle. And I can tell you who that person would be."

Mr. Bakala took Danielle to meet with General Namusunga Lopa, the Chief of the Zambian Armed Forces while Dad and I remained in the background. Dani told me all about their meeting after the fact, and apparently the General was very impressed by such a confident and eloquent child.

We soon got a call from the Power Commissioner with profuse apologies for his misunderstanding. "The Stirling engines are on their way," he reported.

Mr. Bakala organized a group of volunteers in the town square to help Danielle assemble the machines, but they only spoke Nyanja,[33] the principal language of Lusaka. The instructions for setting up the machines were terse and not very clear. Danielle had all the parts for one machine scattered on a concrete plaza, which was getting increasingly hot as the midday sun settled in the sky. The volunteers seemed eager, but were unable to read the English instructions. I handed Danielle parts as they started to put the unit together. She had particular difficulty trying to insert the compressor unit. It took a bit more force than Danielle could muster, and after several attempts, Mr. Bakala was able to get it to click in place. The rest of the assembly went fairly smoothly with the village girls eager to help in assembling the machine.

One of the girls poured the brownish, sour-smelling sewer water into the machine. It started to make a whirring sound, and after a few minutes, out came pure, odorless water! Everyone cheered. We all drank the water from plastic glasses that Mr. Bakala had brought for the occasion and Danielle curtsied for the group.

We were staying in a concrete building on metal beds with straw mattresses, but they were rather comfortable compared to sitting up on the plane. That night I could stretch out for the first time since leaving LA and fell into a deep sleep only to be awakened at the crack of dawn by the high-pitched braying of eight donkeys.

"We have most donkeys working in Africa," Commissioner Bakala proclaimed as I looked out of the window. "We are ready for first field installation."

The volunteers had fashioned rolling carts for two crates, containing one water machine crate and one Stirling engine. Each cart was pulled by one of the donkeys. There were also donkeys with saddles for Danielle, me, Dad, and two of the volunteers.

"We have a problem," Dad said.

Danielle and I gave Dad a questioning look.

"Someone's got to look after the machines in Lusaka," Dad explained. "But I need to go with you two girls."

"Mom will have an answer," Danielle said.

And indeed, she did, as we spoke to Mom in a somewhat static-filled video call.

"I've had the same concern," Mom said. "I already spoke with Uncle Eric, and he's ready to fly in from Chicago. He says it sounds like a worthy cause, and he's happy to volunteer a bit of time and the price of a plane ticket to help out."

Eric is Mom's brother who's had an adventurous history as the manager of a forestry company in Northern Michigan. Both Danielle and I had been regaled with his tales of encounters with grizzly bears, and gangs of lumber thieves.

"That's great. Eric will be fine to watch the machines. I'm glad he's available," Dad said.

"Actually, Richard, I'd be more comfortable to have him go with the girls. You can take care of the machines," Mom replied. "He at least knows something about the forest."

After that exchange, we waited two days for Uncle Eric's arrival.

The two-day donkey ride was breathtaking as we passed a diversity of animals. From my pocket-sized book, *African Wildlife in Pictures*, I was able to identify pelicans, cormorants, herons, egrets, storks, osprey, big and little snakes, all sorts of small animals, antelope, and a pod of hippopotamuses. Feeling vulnerable, I looked intensely for lions, but Eric tried to assure me that he was pretty sure they were on the other side of Zambia at that time of year, and if we did encounter one to just remain calm. While I kept up my lion vigil, Danielle practiced her skills using a guitar simulator on her iPad. I must say that the speed and turns of her riffs were astonishing. On the first night of our two-day donkey trip, we camped out in a grass field under a fantastic quilt of stars we never see in Los Angeles.

We finally arrived in the small village of Sempala,[34] and were met by a welcoming committee of three women in colorful blue and black dresses, and a girl about Danielle's age.

"My name Amukusana. Me you call Amu," the girl said in what was apparently her only English. She smiled as if Danielle was an old, lost friend. Danielle grinned back in kind. She gestured for Danielle to follow her and the two girls ran off giggling around a fat tree. It reminded me of how immediately accepting Charlie had been when I first met him.

"Icimuti," Amu said as she pointed to the tree.

"Tree," Danielle replied. "Dog," Danielle said as she pointed to a village pet.

"Imbwa," Amu replied in her native Bemba.[35]

Danielle tapped Amu's shoulder and then ran away. Amu seemed to catch on quickly. The two girls ran their game of tag around the village, tapping and running, laughing and shrieking.

The volunteers were eager for us to unpack the donkeys and get settled, but I had never seen Danielle play with anyone like this before. I gestured that they should be patient. We let the girls continue their game, while I was given a tour of the town by a tall woman wearing thick eyeglasses and a bright red and yellow blouse.

The houses were single room huts with walls made of reddish brown wooden planks. "Kayimbi," my guide said pointing to a wall, which I gathered was the type of wood. The roofs were pointed and thatched with straw. There were glassless wooden windows you could swing open. Inside were straw mats that served as beds. It looked like one or two families lived in each hut, which was luxurious compared to the brick room that Mum and I had shared with six other families in Haiti.

She showed me a large building with a crudely painted sign that said ANIM L B RN. I looked in, though my guide seemed eager to move on. There appeared to be no animals, but then I heard some scurrying and looked through a wire mesh window to find three chickens. I watched them do three wide circles around their pen. The largest one—I figured he must be in charge—pecked incessantly at the smallest one, who pecked at the one with a missing wing.

I noticed there were no men in the village. I asked my guide about this, but she didn't understand, so I took out my pen and a pad and drew the stick figures for a man and a woman, pointed to the man and gestured "where?" She then made two gestures—showing me her necklace and then imitating someone striking the ground with a pick. I got the idea that the men were off working at a mine somewhere.

44

"Royal suite," were the only English words my guide spoke as she showed me where they apparently intended Danielle and me to sleep. It was a hut like all the others, but it had two beds and featured the only wooden shelves I had seen in the village. I wanted to rest, but I was struck with a sudden concern for Danielle's whereabouts. I tried to ask my guide where the girls were, but she did not understand, so I ran through the village. It was not long before I heard two girls giggling hysterically from one of the huts.

I walked in and there was Danielle with a big grin swinging a woven straw mat. Amu ducked and swung back. I picked up a mat similar to the ones that the girls were wielding and found it was surprisingly heavy and hard. That would not do—I needed to get them some real pillows, and fast. I didn't see any nearby, so I conducted an urgent hunt for pillows in adjacent huts, but this was equally unsuccessful.

I looked up. There, hanging on a clothes line that traversed a dusty lot, were seven colorful blouses. I recalled that there was a pile of hay in the barn.

I'll make my own pillows, I thought. But as I approached the clothes line I realized that I couldn't just take a stranger's clothes. I ran back to our royal suite, grabbed two of my blouses, actually the only two that I had brought, ran back to the barn, filled them with straw, tied the ends with string and the arms to each other, and voilà: two rather colorful makeshift pillows.

I'll always remember Danielle's teary reaction when I presented her with my creations.

Thank you, Claire, she mouthed, grabbing the flowery one. She ran after her new friend with her new pillow, and I tossed Amu the other one. As the pillow fight raged on, I slipped out to stroll through the nighttime village. The darkness was lit with candles and gas lanterns and all was remarkably tranquil despite my lingering lion concern.

When I came back to check on them, the girls were asleep arm in arm in Amu's cot. My blouses had not fared as well as the girls—the fabric was ripped and stained, but I figured my wardrobe had been sacrificed to a good cause.

PART ONE

~ℓℓ~

The next morning Danielle and Amu prepared to put together the two machines while video-recording each step with Danielle's iPad.

"This is the input collection basin," Danielle said, as she removed the first big piece from the water machine crate and placed it on a blanket while Amu held the iPad in video record mode. One by one the pieces ended up on the blanket as Danielle narrated. The girls then put the pieces back in the crate and Danielle recorded Amu taking them out and placing them on the blanket with her own narration in Bemba. Amu seemed to catch on quickly. Both Danielle and I wondered what Amu was actually saying as she took each piece out—we figured it was something like "big fat round bowl" and "long pointy thing."

With my help, Danielle put the pieces together following the same procedure that worked so well in Lusaka, again with Amu video recording. Then Amu took it apart and assembled it with her Bemba narration and a bit of assistance from Danielle. The crowd of women watching us grew, along with anticipation as Amu tightened the last bolt. They followed the same procedure for the Stirling engine, which was much simpler as the motor comes preassembled. To prove that it worked, Danielle was able to illuminate a test light bulb, which got a cheer.

Danielle poured in the sewer water, which was not quite as scary as the foul fluid we used in Lusaka, but had its own strange odor. Danielle allowed Amu the honor of pressing the Start button. The machine jolted into action, but something was wrong. Danielle winced as we heard a grinding sound.

Danielle urgently pressed the Stop button and she and Amu began to disassemble the machine. The women watched with increasing concern. The water had already made its way through the mechanism, so the girls were getting soaked in the pungent liquid, which didn't seem especially hygienic to me, but Danielle and Amu kept pressing ahead. Amu quickly identified the problem—a key assembly bolt had been inserted at an awkward angle.

"Argggh," Danielle wailed as the head of the screw came off in her wrench. She looked forlorn as she realized that the bolt was buried deep in its shaft with no head to turn and no way to access it. Amu and the other women poked at it with spoons and small rocks, but Danielle urged them to stop, concerned it would only make matters worse.

Fifteen minutes later, Amu started jumping up and down and raising her hand suggesting she had a solution, said something in Bemba and ran off.

Danielle just sat there. "Just bringing another collection basin assembly will be too risky," Danielle said to no one in particular. "I'd better bring a whole other water machine."

"That would mean a round trip to Lusaka by donkey," I pointed out.

Dani bit her lip and studied the machine again.

After about a half hour, she started slowly and sullenly taking the other assemblies apart. By the time she got down to the one assembly that was stuck with the jammed bolt, Amu came back, jabbering excitedly. She pointed off in the distance. We looked up but there was nothing to see—just the sun's intense rays dancing on the hot, swirling sand.

But then, like a mirage in the mist, a tall bare-chested man emerged slowly leading a donkey, his image gradually coming into view as he drew closer. He had bright wide eyes and a mustache, and tied onto the donkey was a large ragged suitcase held together with string, along with a giant shiny metal box. Amu ran up to him and they hugged.

"Nsishumba," Amu said pointing to the man and to herself. I quickly realized that Nsishumba was his name and that he was Amu's dad, Nsishumba Mwanza. Danielle curtsied to him, which later became a signature move for her whenever she wanted to show someone deep respect. He strode to his suitcase and took out three necklaces, each consisting of a beautiful woven braid and a pendant of richly colored dark blue lapis lazuli, which he presented to Amu, Danielle, and me.

He took down the shimmering container which was taller than Danielle and unlatched it. Inside was a fantastic array of every sort of tool—wrenches, screwdrivers, saws, hammers, pliers, welding equipment, and strange gadgets I had never seen. Danielle and Amu showed him the problem. He tried a tool that was able to wrap itself around the bolt, but the size was not quite right. He tried many different sizes until finally a grin crept over his face, which was quickly returned by Danielle and Amu. The tool was able to slip inside the sleeve and wrap itself around the bolt.

He turned a knob, tightening the mechanism around the bolt, and then attempted to rotate it, but it wouldn't budge. He kept turning it, with the strain showing on his face and his biceps. Danielle looked concerned that something was going to break. He tried again, but it just wasn't moving.

Finally, Nsishumba gestured that he had an idea. He took out an acetylene torch and heated the bolt for about half a minute. He then pointed to the tool and said a few words in Bemba to his daughter. Amu gingerly turned the tool and lo and behold it now turned easily. Within seconds, the stuck bolt was removed.

But now there was another problem. They had no replacement bolt. Danielle found the head of the bolt that had broken off at the bottom of the water machine and made a gesture indicating that we just needed to connect it back to the bolt shaft. Nsishumba smiled and went back to his treasure trove of tools, this time selecting a small welding machine. But—he held up the plug—he needed an electrical outlet.

Danielle lit up and pointed to the female outlet on the Stirling engine. Nsishumba's eyes widened as this was the first time he had ever seen an electrical outlet in Sempala. He plugged in his welding machine and Danielle started up the engine. The ready light came on. An expression that said *Now we're getting somewhere* was on everyone's faces. In a few more minutes, Amu's dad welded the head back onto the bolt.

Amu inserted it, turning very slowly to make sure it went in straight this time. The two girls put the rest of the assemblies back together taking turns assembling and video recording. Amu had very quickly become an expert on Slingshot machine assembly. She invited her dad to pour in the dirty water. Everyone was silent as Amu gently pushed the Start button. This time, the machine began its gentle purr. Thirty seconds later, crystal clear water poured from the spout into the ceramic bottles the women had ready. There were cheers and tears of joy while Danielle and I shared a satisfied smile. I thought to myself: *A father is a good thing to have.*

On our way back to our royal suite, I stopped to show Danielle the animal barn and the three chickens. Danielle immediately shared my affection for them, giving the big chicken the name Loleck, because she seemed to laugh every time she poked the little chicken. I named that smaller chicken Boleck because she seemed to walk with a bow-legged limp. Boleck picked on the chicken with the broken wing, whom Danielle named Roleck because she would roll across the coop each time Boleck pecked her. Danielle became incensed as Boleck kept picking on Roleck, so Danielle picked up some seeds and, just as Boleck was about to peck Roleck, she threw a seed at her which startled her and prevented the attack. It took a few such interventions for Boleck to get the message, but it seemed to work. Then she saw Loleck headed for Boleck so she used the same strategy. By the time we left the chicken coop, the three chickens were sitting peacefully together. I joked, "We should send you to the Middle East next."

"Great idea, Claire," Danielle replied. "You think I can use the same strategy?"

The next day, Danielle and Amu held master classes for the women on how to use the two machines, while I passed the day wandering around the village. Again and again I saw Danielle rush urgently to the village outhouse.

"Dani, our toilet paper roll is getting dangerously thin. We only brought one. It needs to last until we get back to Lusaka. Or maybe we should start collecting leaves as plan B."

"Thank you, Miss Calico," she responded, as if I were a scolding teacher, "I'll definitely take your concern into consideration."

Our meals were almost all vegetables. Lunch was a stew of tomatoes, cabbage, eggplant, and onions with strong spices. I recognized ginger, paprika, and chili powder, but there were some unidentifiable other flavors in the mix. It was tasty and seemed to agree with my digestive tract, but Danielle's stomach had its own ideas. There was always a dish of cornmeal paste, which was bland but filling. My favorite part of each meal was the compote of fruits which looked strange but tasted like mango, pear, and passion fruit.

Amu came up to me eagerly and shared another English phrase she had learned. "Celebration tonight," she said.

Danielle ran up after Amu and nodded enthusiastically. "It's for the water machine," Danielle explained.

On the walk back to our royal suite, Danielle and I checked in on our new animal friends. Danielle ran up to the chicken coop and curtsied to Loleck with a smile that quickly turned to dismay as she looked inside.

"What's the matter, Dani?"

"Oh my god, Roleck is gone," I said answering my own question. "Boleck must have finally gotten to him."

"Maybe Boleck was mad from my little discipline session," Danielle added.

We stared at the coop hoping Roleck would magically appear.

I started to count the metal loops in the mesh, and that reminded me of counting the white tiles in the hospital when Danielle was born.

"Actually, I don't think Boleck had anything to do with it," Danielle concluded as we morosely left the coop.

As we made our way back to our room I began to fret about something else. The only two blouses I had brought were wrecked so I considered how to spruce up the T-shirt I was wearing. I eyed some wildflowers that I imagined I could attach if only I had some pins. I picked one that I recognized as a "blazing star" from my botany class and tried to insert it in the T-shirt's neck opening but that looked outlandish even before the flower fell apart. *Maybe I can just carry some flowers to make myself look more festive,* I thought.

But when I got to our hut, there, neatly folded on my bed, was a beautiful red, yellow, and orange blouse with images of Zambian fruits and flowers.

"Hey Dani, do you know anything about how this got here?"

She widened her eyes as if to say *Beats me, I have no idea.* But I didn't believe her.

Women in dresses with bold and intricate swirls of red, black and gold were sashaying around the room as we walked in. Danielle wore a light blue skirt with images of a five-pointed white and yellow flower I've seen all over Zambia. Someone must have given it to her as I had not seen it before. A band of four women consisting of three drummers and a marimba player played a song that made me think of the Mad Hatter jumping frenetically around the tea table. A dozen children danced with remarkable synchrony. There were candles on the tables and garlands of flowers hanging from the rafters. I saw only kids and women, with the exception of Nsishumba, who wore a traditional vest that came down to the floor decorated with images of colorful shields.

"Dad go back mine," Amu said sadly but proudly in her improving English. She held up her lapis lazuli pendant to make the point about the mine.

The first course consisted of long pieces of what looked like celery but tastier and crisper, served with a spicy cold dip that tasted like hummus with some sort of crunchy nut in it.

The women serving us lit up, as if something profound was about to happen. They whispered to each other like excited school girls and ran to the neighboring tent—the kitchen—to fetch the next course.

Ceremoniously, they carried out the pièce de résistance of the evening. They looked eagerly at our faces for a reaction to the delicacy they had placed in front of us. Women from the neighboring table, including Amu's mom, came over to our table to catch a glimpse. Apparently, our head table was the only one to get this version of the entrée—a lovely jubilee of rice, corn, tomatoes, and something like eggplant. But at our table, there were also small chunks ... of chicken!

"I told you Boleck wasn't responsible," Danielle whispered in my ear.

"Maybe we can just slip the remnants of our friend into our pockets," she added.

But this proved impossible with the women eagerly watching over our shoulders. Gingerly, we each cut a small piece of chicken into yet smaller pieces and put one in our mouths and swallowed.

Thirty seconds later, Danielle's face turned green and she urgently pointed out of the tent toward the outhouse.

"You go," I said to Danielle, feeling a bit queasy, but thinking I could wait it out. But I couldn't. We both made a beeline for the outhouse. I usually try to resist this urge to purge, but feel better after I admit defeat—I got to the hole in the wooden plank that serves as a toilet barely in time and what little I had eaten came back up the same route it went down. Danielle was not quite as fortunate and threw up all over her skirt.

Exhausted, the two of us lay hand in hand in the outhouse. I thought maybe Danielle would have one of her crying fits, but instead she started to laugh at the incongruity of our situation, taking in the warm air, and closing her eyes.

$$\smile \! e \, e \! \smile$$

"We'd better think about returning to the party, Dani," I said, regaining my wits. Danielle's eyes were closed but she nodded like that would be a good idea.

"Our next problem is cleaning you up," I added, and took Danielle's hand. I led her to the stream, grabbing a towel hanging on a clothes line en route—which I figured would be okay under the circumstances.

"This water is polluted," Danielle noted.

"Right," I replied. "We wouldn't need the water machines if it were drinkable. But it should be okay to clean you up. Just don't drink it."

"Oh god, this is cold," Danielle exclaimed as she waded in. She took off her skirt and we both cleaned it in the water using the big plantain leaves that lined the stream as scrub brushes. Gradually the stains disappeared.

"We just have one problem left," I said as Danielle ran out of the water wrapping herself in the towel.

"Yeah," Danielle responded holding up her dripping wet skirt.

"Dannel! Clear!" we heard a man shouting followed by what was obviously Amu's voice, "We look for you."

"Over here," I answered, and with that Amu and her dad came running around the bend. Amu had her hands on her hips as if to say *Where the heck did you go?* Danielle held up her dripping wet skirt and Nsishumba immediately grasped the problem and held up a finger. I figured that meant he had a solution.

He gestured for us to follow him. Danielle limped along holding the towel around her and lugging her shoes while I carried the skirt.

We were back at the tool chest and the two machines. He took out the acetylene torch that had caused all three of us girls to frown, but he shook his head gesturing that this was only part of the solution. He retrieved a fan from the tool box, plugged it into the Stirling engine (which Amu turned on) and held the fan just past the point of the flame, and voila, a makeshift hot air dryer.

"I hope they didn't save our chicken entrees for us," I whispered to Danielle on our walk back to the party. She grimaced. But my fears were unfounded as they had moved on to dessert. There was a cheer as Amu and Nsishumba returned with the two of us in tow. The dessert was a fruit cake—the first cake we had seen in Sempala. It was the best treat we had had there and we dived into it robustly, much to the delight of our hostesses.

The next morning I was groggily regaining consciousness when Amu burst in exclaiming, "I go Danielle." Danielle was one step behind her resolving any ambiguity in Amu's slowly improving English.

"But there's no donkey for her," I replied, gradually regaining consciousness.

"Two seats!" Amu replied.

"Yeah, well two saddles," Danielle clarified. "We just tried it. And, anyway, we need to edit our instructional videos. There's a showing when we get back to Lusaka that Commissioner Bakala said he would organize."

"And how is Amu going to get back to Sempala?" I queried.

"Eric will take us," Danielle replied. "He has to return two of the donkeys anyway as they belong here."

"Okay, but I don't think you're going to get much video editing done on our trip back," I concluded.

We said our goodbyes. Amu's parents embraced Danielle. Nsishumba was also leaving by donkey with his tool chest and suitcase, but headed to the mine where he worked. Women crowded around the machines and many hands waved to us as our caravan left the village.

It turned out I was wrong about the editing. While I held on for dear life, trying not to fall off my donkey and negotiating with my GI tract, which was definitely not happy with the donkey's gait, the girls busily edited their videos while laughing and even recording additional video segments.

"Make sure you put the third basin screw in straight and turn it slowly," Danielle said as Amu filmed. Then Danielle held the iPad and filmed Amu nodding in agreement with what Danielle had just said. Then they fussed with the video app, inserting the new segment in the right place. Amu was picking up iPad video editing skills to match her rapidly growing proficiency in English. Both girls seemed completely oblivious to the fact that they were riding on a donkey. Dani seemed as relaxed as she would have been sprawled out in our living room in Los Angeles. I was far less relaxed and stayed on the lookout for lions.

"Dani, you're going to run out of battery," I shouted at her.

Danielle held up a satchel. "Five batteries!"

"No wonder your luggage has been so heavy," I replied.

As our caravan approached our inn in Lusaka, Danielle and Amu jumped off their donkey and ran to Dad who waited outside for our arrival. Danielle gave him a big hug and introduced Amu.

"He's got a tool for everything!" Danielle said to Dad about Amu's dad as I caught up with them.

It was a good thing the girls had edited their videos because scarcely an hour after our return to Lusaka a large group of volunteers, both men and women, assembled to watch and learn.

"Shouldn't we vet this?" Dad asked.

"I'll show you five minutes, but there isn't time now to watch the whole thing. You'll see it with the Commissioner."

The screenings were a big success. In the film, after each phase of assembly, Danielle and Amu struck poses to demonstrate the configuration of the levers and pulleys, while a snippet of LaDonna's "Pose" played in the background. They used decals on their arms and legs to show the position of screws and bolts. This generated laughter, but Amu's Bemba version appeared to be even funnier—judging by the response of the mostly female audience. The editing seemed rather professional considering that it had just been completed hours earlier by two six-year-old girls riding on the back of a donkey in the Zambian jungle.

～乙 乙

"There is a little problem, but nothing to worry about," Commissioner Bakala told us. "It appears that thirty of the water machines had been stolen by bandits. We are trying to figure out which police district has jurisdiction. I hope it is not the Muchinga District. There is much corruption there," he added.

"They'll sort this out," Dad counseled. "Our flights are tomorrow, and we really need to get back. I think we've accomplished our mission here."

Danielle just stood there. She and Dad held a familiar staring contest, which Danielle always won.

"Okay, let's find the police commissioner," Dad replied.

The main police station turned out to be only a few blocks away.

"We've been expecting you," the Commissioner greeted us as we entered the station. "We've been looking into this, but the machines do not appear to be in our district. We did intercept one attempt to sell the parts. Apparently, they were trying to get 250,000 *kwacha*."

"That's so inefficient," Danielle exclaimed. "The machines cost us a thousand dollars each and they're selling the parts for forty dollars!"

"Crime is rarely efficient, Danielle," Dad explained. "That's one reason it's a crime."

As we left the station, Dad kept an eye on Danielle, who was staring off into the distance.

"Okay, I'm going to the hotel to pack. Let me know when you're ready to leave," Dad said.

Eric and I stayed with Danielle who just sat looking dismayed but determined at the same time. After a few attempts at suggesting solutions to Danielle, we resolved to just sit with her as late afternoon set in.

Suddenly, a military convoy pulled in to the town square, spreading dust in all directions. A formation of soldiers stepped out of their jeeps and ceremoniously opened the door of an elaborate armed vehicle. Out strode Commander Lopa. Danielle ran up to him and he extended his hand which Danielle shook vigorously.

"Ah, just the person … I wanted you to know that we have declared the missing water machine situation to be a matter of national security. The army has been put in charge of the problem. We have already recovered five of the machines and apprehended several of the bandits. My men …"

"And women," Danielle added.

"Why, yes of course." The commander continued, "They are scouring the nation—trust me, we will find every part of every machine."

Danielle wrapped her arms around him, which seemed to please him.

"We can go now," Danielle whispered to me.

By the time we were ready to leave, several donkey convoys were getting ready to take machines to remote villages, while other machines were being loaded into a jeep to go to a nearby city.

When we got back to Los Angeles, we learned the disposition of Danielle's funding application to the World Health Organization. It had been approved, but only for 70 percent of the cost.

Danielle raised the remaining $60,000 on the crowdfunding site GoFundMe posting funny and poignant videos of her and Amu lecturing the grown-ups on how to assemble the water machines.

"We didn't do much," Danielle said at the dinner table.

"Hey that's an improvement over 'we didn't do *anything*,'" I noted.

"It sounds like thousands of people have clean water now who were drinking contaminated water before," Mom said. "That's something to be proud of, not mope about."

"Danielle is always looking at the glass half empty rather than half full," Dad observed.

Danielle sighed. "By my calculations, the glass is now about one third of one percent full."

"That's a lot, Danielle," Dad countered. "The Talmud[36] says 'whoever saves one life has saved the whole world.'"

She perked up slightly. "The Talmud says that? Okay, but a million people in Zambia are still without clean water."

"Danielle, you can't solve all of this by yourself. Anyway, you've contributed more than just some machines," Dad pointed out.

"Like what? Amu's and my instructional video?"

"You gave them the most valuable thing of all, a good idea," Dad explained. "Others can follow in your footsteps."

"We'll see," Danielle said. "Mao[37] once said he felt he was only moving a few deck chairs around on a sinking ship. He didn't feel he was having much impact."

"Too bad Mao didn't stick to moving deck chairs around," Dad replied. "Impact is not as important as having the right ideas. If one percent of the world did as much as you, there would be no suffering."

Danielle shrugged her shoulders.

"I hear you made a friend, Danielle," Mom said with a smile.

"Yeah, how about that," Danielle replied. "Will miracles never cease?"

"I'd love to meet her."

"Hey, not a problem," Danielle offered. "All you have to do is hop a plane to New York. And then a red-eye to London. Then don't dally in London, because it's a tight connection to the old propeller plane to Lusaka. And you should hope that it's not raining so that the flight isn't too bumpy. You should bring a good nausea medicine, just in case. When you arrive, you need to arrange a donkey caravan, which you can't reserve in advance since they have no phones, let alone Internet.

After that, it's a two-day donkey ride through the jungle to Sempala. Oh, and make sure you have a good guide because Sempala is easy to miss."

"And watch out for lions," I added.

"And if Amukusana's not on a mission to gather swamp or sewer water," Danielle concluded, "then you can say hi."

AGE SEVEN:
BURYING THE EVIDENCE
OF A CRIME

I'll celebrate when I see Amu," Danielle said, rejecting Mom's suggestion of a seventh birthday party. Not wanting another awkward party, Mom backed off.

I was sort of expecting it that night when Danielle had one of her crying fits. I can see them coming because her lower lip curls, her nose becomes scrunched, her eyes half close, her hands start flailing, and she hunches over like an old woman.

"You sort of know how this will work out," I said to Danielle as she sniffled in my arms.

"Sure, but I can't help sinking into this feeling," she said as she regained enough composure to respond.

"The million-mile bridge again?" I asked. She was thinking it over, so I added, "That sounds pretty strenuous."

"Pretty lonely, actually," Danielle responded. "Like a goodbye."

"A goodbye can be followed by a hello."

"There's no hello," Danielle replied, "just goodbye."

"Mom's talking about another visit from Dr. Sonis," I said.

"Oh my god, you told her!" Danielle exclaimed.

"Well, a week ago Mom saw you running to my room with, uhh, some urgency. I had to reassure her that nothing drastic had happened. Dad was there, too, and he said he knew about it."

"Yeah, I think Dad overheard me and we talked about it."

"Oh, thanks for telling me that Dad knows."

She nodded and sniffled. "Yeah, and thanks for telling me about Mom."

"So, what did Dad say?"

"He said he knows about the endless rooms, too."

"Endless rooms?"

"Yeah, well, endless rooms, endless bridge, it's just different metaphors. But he's learned how to be okay with it. He said when you're in one of the rooms, the rest of the world seems like an illusion, but when you're out in the world the eternal succession of empty rooms becomes the dream." Danielle sighed. "I don't think I found that especially comforting. What did Mom say?"

"She said they're panic attacks. Dad has had them, too, but she's disturbed that you're having them at such a young age. I didn't have the heart to mention that these episodes started when you were two."

She was standing at the foot of the staircase again with the rolling suitcase. Those country music stickers had been replaced by scotch-taped pictures of someone I didn't recognize.

"New singer, Dani?" I asked.

"I don't think he sings. Cheng Liu is a physicist."

"He looks pretty young to be a physicist."

"He's ten," Danielle replied. "Well, almost eleven."

"You probably have the only Cheng Liu suitcase in all of North America."

"I think there might be a few in China."

"What sort of physics? Stars and galaxies?"

"Actually, the other end of the size continuum," Danielle replied. "Very little things. You've heard of strings?"

"String theory?[38] Sure."

"Strings are like little spaghettis only much smaller and with zero width," Danielle explained.

"I like fat spaghetti myself," I replied.

Danielle went on as if I hadn't interrupted. "Cheng Liu replaces the strings with what he calls manifolds.[39] Two-dimensional ones are like curved sheets of paper. And three-dimensional ones are like tiny objects bending in the fourth or fifth dimension."

I smiled at her earnest explanation and gave a nod. "Makes sense."

"It makes a lot of sense. I could never understand why string theory was restricted to just one-dimensional objects."

"That does seem pretty limiting."

"Now this research has me wondering, why stop at three dimensions?" Danielle said, a spark of excitement in her eyes. "I mean, if we have the dimensions handy, then why not have four or five dimensional manifolds and beyond?"

"Exactly my sentiment."

"Okay, you'll see," Danielle said.

"I'm sure I will. Where are you off to this time? Antarctica?" I asked, and immediately regretted it, not wanting to give her any ideas.

"I thought maybe I could go with you to CMA."[40]

That was easy. "That's no problem at all."

"And I'd like to perform."

"Uh, well. That's probably doable, too. I'm only allowed to introduce one new singer each year and I was going to introduce Meredith," I said, referring to a Stern School classmate. "But I suppose she can wait until next year. I mean I think you can do it."

"Terrific!" Danielle replied.

"But why don't you talk to Dad about it first," I added.

Danielle frowned.

63

Danielle and Dad discussed the CMA at dinner, with Mom and me listening.

"You know, I've heard you two girls singing for years and you definitely have an amazing talent," Dad said. "But there are a couple of things you should think about."

Danielle turned in Dad's direction and widened her eyes in anticipation.

"First, your sister already told Meredith she could perform this year."

Dani bit her lip. "Go on."

"Second, if you're successful, and I'm sure you would be, it will be as if you've been shot out of a cannon. There will be no turning back."

Danielle returned to eating her peas. I could tell she was thinking over Dad's counsel.

"You know, if Meredith was counting on performing," Danielle conceded, "I don't want to be responsible for bumping her. I can wait."

Dad, Mom, and I shared a relieved look.

⁓ℓℓ⁓

While we were eating Mom's blueberry pie, Danielle had another announcement.

"I got a letter from Amu." She held a piece of paper and handed me an envelope.

"Oh wow, those are beautiful stamps," I said as I passed the envelope to Mom.

"That's wonderful, darling," Mom said. "I know you've been missing your friend."

"Her English is really getting better," Danielle observed.

I was so happy for Dani. "We're all ears. What did she say?"

"She writes 'Dearest Dani, I hope all family happy. I go with Dad to Lusaka for water meeting be there last Tuesday November. Maybe you be there I bring pillars. All love, friend forever, Amukusana.'"

"Pillars?" I asked, knowing the answer as soon as the word left my mouth. "Oh! Pillows!"

Danielle stood and held up the pillow she had been sitting on. "This works out perfectly," she exclaimed. "Claire and I will fly to Lusaka after the CMAs!"

ℓℓ

So, Danielle and I went off to CMA.

I remember kneeling on the stage, checking the microphones while a massive wooden cowboy loomed over me. I motioned for Dani to come over beside me and she ran onto the stage holding her guitar. I pointed out at the vast, empty grassy field. "That's where the fans will be soon. Isn't that exciting?"

She looked at the field and gave a curtsey, as if greeting thousands of fans in the audience. In her enthusiasm, she grabbed the mic and started to sing one of her songs.

Before I knew it, the backup band for the Mountain Boys, who had been tuning their guitars, started jamming along, so I joined in, too. This resulted in a spontaneous fifteen-minute jam that ranged from Alabama blues[41] to Jimi Hendrix.[42] The Mountain Boys folks stared at Danielle, their mouths agape. As she struck the final dramatic chord, a couple of older guys who had listened from the field clapped with wild enthusiasm and their dogs started to howl in response to the clapping.

"That was pretty amazing," I told Danielle that evening. "I mean you were, like, possessed. I've never heard you play quite like that before."

She grinned. "Yeah, I can start my fan club now with two aging hippies and three hound dogs."

"You gotta start somewhere. And, hey, there's nothing wrong with aging hippies."

ℓℓ

Our propeller plane landed in Lusaka. We had good weather this time, which made all the difference in the world. Our plans to connect with Amu were pretty sketchy given that the only way to communicate with her was by letters that took a week to deliver. Danielle's plan was to find out where the water meeting was once we got to our inn in Lusaka. I thought that "water meeting" was a bit vague, but she wasn't concerned about it.

We were back in the stifling heat of the Lusaka airport. As we gathered our luggage, we were met as planned by Uncle Eric, who had been looking after the water program. Danielle gave him a hug, then paused. Something was wrong.

"Where's Amu?" she asked.

"She's fine," Eric said. "She just wasn't feeling well enough for the ride." Eric gave Danielle a note.

"Not worry, dearest Danielle. Little sick. Amu good quick. All my love, Amukusana."

I recognized the look of alarm in Danielle's eyes.

"She's really ..." Eric started to say, but Danielle cut him off.

"Uncle Eric, you're coming with me," Danielle ordered. "And Claire, dearest sister, please get two donkeys, one for Eric and one for you and me. We're going to Sempala."

"I'm not sharing a donkey, dearest sister."

"Three donkeys then."

"They're not always available," Eric cautioned.

"Eric, please just come with me. Claire will get the donkeys." I knew enough not to counter Danielle in her urgent problem-solving mode.

"Oh, and give me the printer," she added. "It's in your luggage."

"What do you need with that?"

"It will help with communication."

"What are you communicating?"

"I'll explain later. Please focus on the donkeys."

Danielle didn't want to stop to sleep so we went thirty-six hours straight on the donkeys. The diverse display of animals in our midst did not seem quite as vibrant as they had the last time, and the carpet of stars only served to illuminate my lion patrol.

We finally arrived in Sempala, and Danielle ran frantically to Amu's hut, with me just steps behind her. A few of the women recognized us and gave us animated waves. Amu was lying there, asleep, drenched in perspiration, two women sitting by her bed.

Danielle had learned enough Bemba to ask them where Amu's mom was. The women told her that she was seeking a nurse, but the answer was delivered with a look of resignation that said *We don't expect this mission to succeed.* Danielle gave Amu a hug which left Dani's T-shirt dripping wet. Amu opened her eyes and gave us a weak smile.

Danielle pulled out a mercury thermometer and stuck it in Amu's mouth along with her fingers to prevent Amu from biting down.

"102°," I read off the thermometer.

Danielle then produced several devices from her knapsack. She had Amu bite on a rubber ball while she stuck a metal scraper into her throat and within a few seconds had the sample she needed. Out came several bottles with different colored liquids, and another tool to carve up the sample. One by one she put small samples into the bottles and mixed various preparations.

"She doesn't have malaria," Danielle declared after about twenty minutes. Other conclusions followed. "Negative for typhoid … Negative for dengue and yellow fever. I do think it's viral, however."

The women tending the water machine hugged me each time I went to fetch water for Amu. We had now been up for about forty-eight hours and Danielle finally fell asleep holding Amu's hand. I accepted one of the women's offer to share her bed. I don't think anybody slept very well, with Amu wheezing and gasping for breath.

The next morning, I went to fetch more water and when I returned Danielle was holding the thermometer for me to read.

"103°."

The day after that was worse. Amu was in and out of consciousness. When she was awake, she just panted and moaned.

As I came back with water the next morning:

"105°."

"We have to get a nurse," I said in a panicked voice.

"Good luck with that." Danielle sounded surprisingly calm.

"We still have to try," I said.

She nodded. "I'll stay with Amu."

I ran out of the hut and tried to ask for help, but had difficulty explaining my request, as there was no entry for nurse or doctor in my English-Bemba dictionary. I did find the word "hospital," but when I said the word Cipatâla to the kind ladies by the water machine, they sighed and pointed far in the distance. "Mufulira," they said.

I ran to the donkey station and caught Uncle Eric as he was grooming the largest one.

"Uncle Eric, we need to get Amu to a doctor or nurse immediately. She is sinking—or I should say her temperature is soaring. I understand there's a hospital in Mufulira."

"Actually, I already looked that up. It's twenty-four hours away without stopping," he replied. "I don't think Amu could make a trip like that."

"Then we have to go fetch help and bring someone back here."

"We can try, Claire," Eric replied, "but that's a very small hospital, and they're not exactly on standby to make house calls. And isn't Amu's mom trying to find a nurse?"

"We have to try, too," I said. "I'll be ready to leave in ten minutes."

I ran to tell Danielle the plan, as fast as my feet could carry me.

But when I entered the hut, Amu was sitting up, smiling, and the color back in her face. Danielle handed me the thermometer.

"Oh my god, 99°!" I exclaimed. "It's a miracle!"

"Miracle of modern medicine," Danielle said.

"Medicine?" I asked.

"Ribavirin,"[43] Danielle replied. "It's a strong broad-spectrum antiviral, effective against Rift Valley Fever, which is what I think she has—probably from a mosquito. Ribavirin has a good track record in swampy areas like Sempala."

"How did you get that? Isn't it a prescription drug?" I asked.

She glanced away. "We'll discuss that later. I think Amu needs some fresh air."

Danielle helped Amu up, and she walked shakily and slowly out of the hut with Danielle holding her hand. The two girls took a slow walk to the stream, visited the water machine, got a drink of water for Amu, and then came back to the hut.

We stayed the night again in Amu's hut, only this time the girls talked for several hours, helping each other with their English and Bemba respectively. Amu walked slowly to her suitcase and opened it. There were the two small pillows she had planned to bring to Lusaka. They had a very gentle pillow fight and fell asleep arm in arm.

This made me think of Charlie, and I started to miss him.

One of the donkeys was ill, so I ended up sharing a donkey with Danielle on the trip back. I got the front saddle and it was not as uncomfortable as I feared. As it turned out, this was a good thing, since I was easily within reach when Danielle had one of her crying fits, as twilight set on the first day of our voyage back to Lusaka.

"You seem to time these well," I said. "I mean you don't seem to get panic attacks when you're engaged in a crisis."

That seemed to distract Danielle momentarily from her crying. "I'm glad crises are good for something."

"Well maybe. But did you ever think that you might seek crises to protect you from your panic attacks?" I added.

"Thanks, Claire, I'll be sure to mention that to Dr. Freud the next time I see him."

"Does Dr. Freud make house calls?"

"Okay, Dr. Sonis, then."

At our usual resting spot between Sempala and Lusaka, we snuck away from Uncle Eric to find a spot in the grass to gaze at the stars. I had been too distressed to enjoy them on our donkey ride to Sempala.

I finally had a chance to ask Danielle about the medicine. "Okay, so how did you get your hands on Ribavirin? That *is* a prescription drug, right?"

"I just gave the prescription to the druggist—that's why I needed the printer."

"What prescription?"

"Right here," Danielle said, unfolding a wrinkled piece of paper from her vest pocket.

"This is a prescription for your nose drops."

"Yeah, my Nyanja is a little uncertain, so I may have made a few mistakes translating it."

"I see. And they just handed this drug to a seven-year-old?"

"No, no, to Uncle Eric. He was the grown-up."

"And he didn't notice your, uh, translation errors?"

"Turns out his Nyanja is a lot rustier than his Bemba."

"And how did you know that Ribavirin was the right drug?"

"I got the ones I thought might be needed."

"Ones?"

"Yeah, let's see," Danielle said as she took her supplies from her knapsack. "Oseltamivir and Zanamivir for additional antivirals, and Amoxicillin, Ciprofloxacin, and Erythromycin for antibiotics." The labels were all in Nyanja.

"And they gave you, er, Uncle Eric, all these drugs with one prescription?"

"Well, one at each pharmacy we went to."

I shook my head in amazement. "What else do you have in there?" I reached into her knapsack. "Syringes of blood?" I asked.

"That's Amu's blood—I needed to run some additional diagnostics. Otherwise how would I know what drug to use?"

"Yes, of course," I replied. "And where did you get all of this medical knowledge?"

"I do read, remember?"

"Good point. You never did stick to age appropriate literature," I replied. "So, tell me, in your extensive reading, have you ever studied Zambian prison conditions?"

Danielle responded with her typical silent defiance. "Do you think I did the wrong thing?" she finally answered. "I mean, Amu wouldn't have survived much longer with such a high fever."

It was my turn to be silent for a long time. "I think you did the right thing, Danielle. I just don't know how long we can survive with you always doing the right thing. You know, we might want to get rid of this stuff before we go through airport security in Lusaka."

She gave me a knowing look, and took a small fold-up shovel out of her knapsack.

"Boy, you really thought of everything," I said.

"You know they could actually use these medications in Zambia," I added.

"Right," Danielle replied. "We'll just get rid of the paraphernalia. We can leave the medicines in a paper bag by the front door of the hospital near the airport."

And so, by the light of the moon, we took turns digging a deep hole to bury the evidence of Danielle's crime.

AGE EIGHT:

I'LL BE BACK SHORTLY...
AS A GIRL

D anielle's eighth birthday party was off to a slow start until Annie—
little Miss Moonwalk from Danielle's fourth birthday party—got
a beep on her cell phone alerting her to a message. She passed her
phone around. Apparently, someone had put a video of Danielle's
impromptu jam session with the Mountain Boys backup band from
earlier in the year on YouTube. Annie's excitement was rather
satisfying. The kids gathered around her cell phone gasping and
pointing. Everyone exclaimed at Danielle's guitar riff around 1:34. We
cheered as the number of views passed a million.

It was five million by the end of the party.

In the days that followed, invitations for Danielle to headline
concerts and to appear on national talk shows poured in. She turned
them all down, saying she was saving her debut for CMA. I remember
Mom seemed sad, which matched my own feeling of mourning at the
passing of an era in Danielle's childhood. I had expected Danielle to be
excited, but she wasn't smiling either.

For the next three weeks Mom, Dad and I took turns bringing Danielle's meals to her room as she practiced around the clock with her instruments—keyboards, violins, guitars, mandolins, banjos, and harmonicas—along with microphones, amplifiers, and speakers scattered across her bed and floor.

"Can I help you?" I heard Mom say as she greeted three polite, if scraggly, young men at the door.

"Yes, ma'am, I'm Elliot," said a man in a leather hat and brown corduroy jacket.

"Tony," said a man with a goatee and blue denim shirt with gold buttons.

"I'm Ben," said a man in a black T-shirt with a white skull and bones, and carrying an electric guitar that reflected the sunlight streaming in from the skylight.

"We're here to play with Danielle," Elliot added. I laughed to myself at this greeting from guys four times Danielle's age, as Mom looked perplexed.

"Hey, Mom, those are the guys from the Mountain Boys," I heard Danielle yell from upstairs, the first words she had said in at least a day.

"You must be Claire," Elliot said as he climbed the stairs to Danielle's room.

"Uh, maybe," I replied. "And you're Wally Melson? No wait, he's not expected until next week."

"Do I look that old?" Elliot replied. "Amazing sister you have."

"Yeah, that's for sure."

The guys went into Danielle's room and her door slammed shut again. Mom promptly went upstairs and opened the door.

Minutes later Danielle stuck her head out. "Claire, could you join us?" It seemed my skills as a chaperone were overshadowing my musical skills.

⁓ℓℓ⁓

"I'd like to introduce to you another talented young girl from my school. She writes all her own songs and she is my good friend ..."

Thus far the words had been the exact same ones I'd used every year at CMA—albeit on much smaller stages than this one—to introduce a singer from the Stern School, a different one each year. But this time I stopped, and people started to wonder, *Why has she stopped talking?* Of course, that had been my plan.

I looked around and couldn't see to the end of the immense crowd. The huge wooden guitar hung over my head and I had a passing image of it crashing down on me. You could hear a pin drop as the multitude waited. I noticed eager faces in the first few rows. I felt tears well up in my eyes and had trouble blurting out the end of my sentence,

"—and my sister!"

The crowd went wild—they had been waiting for this moment. The power of the crowd was frightening, a feeling I had not experienced before. There was a delay, and then Danielle, wearing a black cowboy hat with a silver band and light blue jeans embroidered with a single white rose, sauntered to the center of the stage, seemingly unfazed.

"Boy, you're all friendly," Danielle told the still cheering crowd. "But maybe you should wait until you've actually heard me sing."

Elliot, Ben, and Tony came out to more cheers.

Accompanied by the guys and herself on guitar, banjo, harmonica, and fiddle, Danielle went on to sing a killer set that combined bluegrass and blues with riffs that wandered into heavy metal. I was shocked at how low-pitched her voice sounded, and it quickly became apparent that all her songs were from a man's perspective, convincingly mimicking men's voices and moves ...

a young guy who couldn't wait to get out of town (Danielle raised her hat to a bus parked at the side of the stage);

a man who falls for a girl he meets on the bus (Danielle eyed a girl in the front row);

a man looking back wistfully on his life (Danielle raised her eyes to the sky):

> *Clutching images*
> *Memories dimmed*
> *Minutes become years*

Drifting in dreams
Of her coming back
I'm waiting still

Danielle sent a preplanned tweet while she was singing, informing listeners that the only sound modification she was using was to lower her pitch by two octaves.[44] After forty minutes, she told the massive crowd that she would be back shortly and, after the thunderous applause died down just a bit, she added, "as a girl."

Ten minutes later, she again took the stage. This time she wore pink cowboy boots, a sparkly yellow ribbon in her hair, and a dark pink dress that came down to just above her knees printed with images of large yellow sunflowers. She was a girl now.

I'm a bird from afar
Resting wings
On your shoulder
Searching a silent sea
For sweetness in your glance

She ended her set and the roar of the crowd went on so long that Danielle ran out of gestures to acknowledge her new acclaim. Danielle yelled over her newly minted fans, "Please welcome back my lovely sister," as she introduced her encore. I have to admit to having been overwhelmed by the crowd as I walked out. I was her sole accompaniment as she sang her final song.[45]

Why, why don't you come out and play
I need you to say
It'll be all right
Alone lying in tangled posing,
Love unfolding
Before your eyes tonight
Before your eyes tonight

As an impromptu security contingent guided us to a waiting car, holding back the surging crowd, a reporter broke through and asked me whether Danielle was really as talented as she seemed. This made me cry as I replied, "You have no idea."

That evening, Danielle confided in me that she was relieved she didn't forget her lines. "That was my terror. Focusing on that, I didn't think too much about ..."

"About fifty million people watching you?" I finished Danielle's sentence.

"There were only fifty thousand people there," Danielle replied.

"Plus television and live feeds," I corrected.

"Oh yeah, that."

"I'm proud of you, but I can't help but think about what Dad said."

"About my being shot out of a cannon?"

"Exactly."

"Yeah, I've been thinking about that."

The next morning there was an unprecedented concert report above the fold on the front page of *The New York Times*: Danielle with the headline, *She Came, She Sang, She Conquered.*

Danielle and I ate breakfast in the motel cafe while urgent requests for Danielle to appear immediately on every talk show filled my inbox imploring me to intervene, since she was ignoring her email.

Looking out the window, I saw three police cars with whirling lights and a police cordon holding back a throng of fans.

"I think you need an agent to sort all this out. I don't know how you're going to do all these talk shows."

"They aren't going anywhere," Danielle replied. "I haven't seen Amu for six months. This would be a good time ..."

"Oh my, Dani, what if the press followed you to Sempala?"

"You mean follow *us*—I wasn't planning on going alone."

"That's not so simple. We have to arrange flights and donkeys, and we don't know exactly where Amu is."

"So, CMA was simple?"

"Good point, but I don't know if Mom and Dad are going to go for this."

Get serious, Danielle's look said.

So, for the next few hours I worked on plane reservations and reported my progress. "I got tickets through to Lusaka, not great seats…"

Dani shrugged. "Yeah, what else is new?"

"There's one thing new: now that I'm sixteen I can go without an adult dropping me off, but we'll have to get an adult to hand you off to the flight attendants."

"Elliot, Tony, or Ben would be happy to do that," Danielle replied.

I turned my laptop screen toward her. "Hey, look there's a donkey service now with a website, lusakadonkey4u.zm, and an email address so I emailed them."

"That's progress," Danielle said.

We noticed a man dressed in a stylish black corduroy suit standing behind us.

"Going somewhere, ladies?" he asked.

Danielle gave him a smirk.

He seemed to get the message and responded, "Allow me to introduce myself. Mike Kline of Columbus Records."

Danielle raised her eyebrows.

"How did you get past the security cordon?" I asked.

"They know me," came the response.

"Makes sense," Danielle said.

"There's no reason to book a flight," Mike said. "My plane is a few miles from here. Why don't I fly you where you need to go? And we can talk about your career, uh, careers."

"We'll have to check with our parents," I said.

"Yes, of course. And by the way, where are we going?"

"Oh, to Sempala," Danielle replied."

"Not a problem," Mike said smoothly as he looked up Sempala on Google maps.

"Oklahoma?"

"No, not that Sempala," I replied. "It's in Zambia."

Mike searched for Zambia.

"Yes, in Africa," I added.

Mike replied quickly and took the news in stride, "Hmm, not a problem. We can refuel in Kenya." He did some more searching. "Uh, I don't see an airport in Sempala."

"Actually, if you just get us as far as Lusaka, that will be fine," Danielle said.

Mike finally located Sempala. "I see. Well, I can arrange a helicopter in Lusaka. It can make the trip to Sempala in a few hours from there."

"Sounds like a plan!" Danielle exclaimed.

～ℓℓ～

"Oh my, great to see you, but what are you doing here?" Danielle said to Aunt Ellie, who showed up unexpectedly as we were boarding Mike's plane.

"Your mom felt that it was a bit too cozy with you two girls and a record company executive on a big plane," Ellie said.

Ellie turned to me and said in an aside, "You know what they say, sex, drugs, and rock 'n roll, and all that."

"Hey, I heard that," Danielle said. "Besides this is country music."

"Same difference," Ellie said.

This was by far the most comfortable trip we'd taken to Sempala. There were full beds on Mike's private jet and we slept twelve hours en route to Lusaka.

The helicopter then whisked us to Sempala while Danielle and Mike talked business. It was hard for me to hear all of their conversation against the loud noise of the helicopter, but it sounded like Danielle agreed to be represented by Columbus Records. If Columbus was good enough for LaDonna and Baylor Sweet, I figured Danielle was in good hands.

We saw a crowd of people, large by Sempala standards, gathered by the field as our helicopter touched down. I wondered if they had ever seen a helicopter before. As the rotors slowed down, Danielle spotted Amu and ran out to her, with me a few steps behind.

I could see Danielle's crestfallen expression when Amu bowed down to her. That was not the greeting that Danielle—or I—had expected.

Danielle got down on one knee beside her friend. "You don't need to ..." Danielle implored.

Amu seemed to take that as a criticism, burst out crying, and ran away.

"I guess she's heard ..." Danielle said to me. "I'm King Midas[46] now. It's kind of hard to explain to her that I don't want her to be my subject, or my fan ...."

"A fan is okay," I said. "I'm your fan."

"Well, you better not bow down to me," Danielle replied. "I don't know Bemba well enough to explain it to Amu. I was trying to ..."

"Look, why don't you just cut through all of that. Use a Gordian solution."

"Like for the Gordian knot[47]? I, uh, don't have a sword handy."

"You don't need a sword. Use the language of love."

A little light seemed to turn on in Danielle's eyes.

"Gotcha," she replied, and took off like a deer in Amu's direction.

Amu had gone over the bridge, but Danielle took a shortcut through the dirty water in the stream. She stumbled and was carried downstream by the rushing water. Alarmed, I splashed into the water behind her, but Danielle managed to catch her stride, and swam to the shallow water on the other side, while I stopped just short of the deep part. The white orchids on Danielle's skirt looked wilted as she emerged from the stream, dripping wet.

Danielle caught up to Amu and threw her arms around her friend pinning Amu's arms down, and when Danielle didn't let go, Amu nuzzled her head into Danielle's shoulder. Danielle let go and Amu initiated the next hug, seeming to squeeze even tighter. My suggestion seemed to have worked, and the two girls walked off hand in hand.

"You had more success than King Midas," I said as Danielle and I settled in for the night in the royal suite. Amu had gone to sleep with her mom. Aunt Ellie was in the next cabin.

"There's still a problem," Danielle said.

"With your ... star status?" I asked.

"We've gotten past that.... I hope. I think it's Amu's Dad."

"Is he sick?"

"She's not saying. But every time I bring him up, she looks away and says he's fine."

"So maybe he is."

"It's a forlorn gaze ..."

"She probably misses him. He's gone for long periods of time."

"Claire, all the other dads are back from the mine."

"He might be earning some overtime," I suggested.

"I think it's more like he's earning a dollar a day at the prison."

"Prison?"

"Yeah, I was reading about the lapis lazuli mine culture here. There are gangs that prey on solo workers and steal their day's stones. If they're caught, the police just arrest everyone involved; they don't even try to sort out who's actually responsible."

"That's kind of a big leap from Amu not looking you in the eye when you bring up her Dad."

"How else am I supposed to reach conclusions, Claire? That's the only scenario that makes sense."

The next morning, I joined Danielle, who was wearing her one fairly formal dress—the white one with a ruffled lace collar and pendant-shaped blue lapis lazuli flowers—to pay a visit to General Lopa, who greeted us with outstretched arms.

"Ah, my favorite girls from America. What troubles do you bring me today?" he said warily.

"Thank you, General, it's my friend Amukusana."

The general leaned back in his leather chair and placed his hands on his desk. I noticed their deep lines which matched the carvings in the massive wooden desktop. "Amukusana Mwanza?"

"Yes, well, actually it's her dad," Danielle replied.

The general raised his eyebrows, waiting for Danielle to provide more information.

"He's been arrested."

The general responded with a troubled stare.

"But it wasn't his fault," Danielle continued. "He was attacked by a gang … one of the Kabimba gangs … I think."

I gave her a perplexed look.

Danielle acknowledged my concern and then stared intently at the general who was lost in thought, contemplating what Danielle had said.

I had a vision of Danielle and me sitting together at the far end of a rather long and drooping branch.

After a few minutes, he finally appeared to have a plan, and opened one of the ornate carved drawers in his desk and took out a directory with dog-eared yellow pages. He painstakingly leafed through it, and then dialed a number on one of the five old-fashioned rotary phones on his desk.

We heard a ring at the other end and then a voice. There was an animated discussion in Bemba that Danielle appeared to be understanding better than I. This was followed by silence, and then more discussion with the general shaking his head from left to right.

"No record of a Mr. Mwanza, I'm afraid."

We all sat there quietly until Danielle had another idea.

"He may have been at a different lapis lazuli mine when he was arrested, a very small one, the Kafubu mine, right at the eastern-most tip of Zambia, near Mzuzu in Malawi…."

"That's a five-day donkey trip from Sempala," the general interjected. Nonetheless, he cocked his head, "Maybe …"

"Yes, that's it!" Danielle concluded.

He again went through his directory and dialed a second number. This was followed by another animated phone discussion.

"He wants to talk to you," General Lopa said as he handed the phone handset to Danielle. "He speaks English. Well, sort of."

"Hello, this is Danielle." She listened attentively as the police commissioner spoke at length. I could only hear Danielle's side of the conversation, which was mostly silence.

"Yes Mr. Mwanza was minding his own business…."

"Yes, his stones were stolen at gunpoint…."

"Yes, but …"

"But you don't know who started the fight?"

"Right, but there's no evidence ..."

"The other guy has a record, does he not?"

"Well then. So obviously the other guy started it...."

I gave Danielle another perplexed look.

She mouthed the word, "Later."

The conversation continued in this vein for quite a while.

"Yes, yes, father of the water girl," Danielle added. This part of the conversation now began to sound encouraging.

"Yes, Amukusana. Her dad, right ..."

Finally, Danielle concluded, "Ah, that is very good. Yes, very good. Amukusana thanks you. And I thank you."

The general raised his hand, and Danielle added, "And General Lopa thanks you."

Danielle offered the phone handset back to the general, but then quickly rescinded.

"Oh, there's one more thing," Danielle added. "Please don't tell Mr. Mwanza that I had anything to do with his release."

Danielle continued to listen while nodding. She turned to us and said, "He says that will be no problem, it would be hard to explain anyway."

As we left, Danielle gave the general a Danielle signature hug, which he seemed to appreciate.

On our walk back to Sempala, I asked Danielle how she knew all these things.

"Think about it, Claire. I mean it was clear the other guy was the perpetrator, wasn't it? So, it was unlikely to have been the first time. That meant that Nsishumba's attacker had probably gotten in trouble before. The rest of it kind of falls in place from there."

"Any other miracles up your sleeve today, little sister?" I asked.

"Well, the mine has already fired him."

"How do you know that?"

"Well, what do you think?"

"Yes, I suppose that makes sense, but they'll hire him back now that he's been cleared?"

"Oh, I don't think so. The mine knows the police can't figure out the truth of these skirmishes. There are dozens of men for each position.

They don't want possible troublemakers. They'll just stay clear of anyone involved in an incident. And no other mine will hire him either. Amu's family was just barely hanging on with that income."

"You seem to know a lot about the Zambian mines."

"I can show you my references."

"That's okay, I trust your insight," I said. "But I think you should discuss this with Dad."

Danielle gave me a frustrated look.

We walked back to Sempala, passing thick meadows of blue and yellow spring flowers. Danielle was lost in thought, while I was again preoccupied with lions and noted many places they could be hiding.

As we approached the outskirts of Sempala, Amu came running and gave us both a tight embrace.

"Dad, he getting home," Amu said, her English improving each time we saw her. Danielle returned her hug and the two girls went off arm in arm, but I still felt something heavy in the dust they kicked up behind them.

When Danielle returned to our royal suite, we spoke to Dad, gathering around her satellite phone speaker. We could barely hear over the static. Danielle explained Amu's dad's presumed predicament.

"It depends on what you want, Dani," Dad said after Danielle had explained the situation. "A loyal subject or a smart, independent friend?"

"You know the answer to that, Dad."

"That's why I asked it."

Danielle understood Dad's advice, but she was not very happy with it.

"Sometimes the hardest thing," I said, "is doing nothing—especially for you."

"Are we ready to leave Sempala, Danielle?"

"Not so fast, I think there's going to be a problem with the helicopter."

"You're an expert on helicopters now?"

"It's not the helicopter. It's the owner of the helicopter."

"Mike?"

"Yeah, well, Columbus Records."

"They don't really own the helicopter and they need to return it?" I asked.

"No, it's their helicopter, all right. And the helicopter is fine. But I read the contract."

"The helicopter contract?"

"No, my recording contract."

"And?"

"Well they get 70% of the proceeds. And there's a long list of deductions from my 30%, like marketing and promotion, all of which they control."

"I think that's pretty standard, Danielle. It's not easy to get a contract from Columbus."

"So, what are they doing for their seventy percent? Downloading an MP3 file?[48] I can do that in 30 lines of code."

"I think there's more to it than that, Danielle. Like promotion."

"Which I'm also supposed to pay for. And I'm doing it anyway. They didn't have anything to do with my CMA performance."

"Yeah, that's true, my inbox is still overrun with appearance requests for you."

"My point then."

"I do think they know what they're doing. I mean that's who the best artists go with."

With that comment, I lost Danielle's attention. She opened her C++ compiler.[49]

An hour later, Danielle piped up, "Hey sis, bring up CR3 on your computer."

"CR3?"

"It's the Wi-Fi signal from Mike's helicopter."

"So, we're stealing his Wi-Fi now?"

"He won't notice. Now go to DanielleWorld.com."

Up came a page with Danielle's signature victory smile. I recalled seeing that same smile in between airline rows on our flight from New York to Lusaka two years earlier.

Download Danielle's new hit single: "Come Out and Play," the page read in big red letters.

I clicked on *Press Here* and an animation of a Rube Goldberg machine was displayed as the song downloaded. Seconds later, Danielle's song started to play.

"Easy as pie," Danielle exclaimed. "I wonder where that expression comes from," she continued. "It makes little sense."

"I guess it means easy as baking a pie."

"Baking a pie isn't so easy. This was a lot easier," Danielle replied.

"That's true of a lot of expressions, like 'run it up the flagpole.' Language is full of metaphors."

"Actually, that one makes a bit more sense," Danielle said.

I had done a report on expressions and their origins, so I added, "George Orwell[50] described clichés as dead metaphors."

"Dead because they've been used so much?" She asked. "Then maybe we should get our wisdom from clichés."

"Anyway, I was saying that I think there's more to running a music company than writing thirty lines of code."

"Yeah, like what? Promotion? I'm doing that. Brand development? Got that covered. Concert gigs and merchandise? I can hire an agent who will take only 15 percent to book gigs. Same with merchandise."

"It's time-consuming to run a company, Danielle."

"There's time for everything, Claire. And, anyway, this work will qualify for projects for several classes, like graphic arts, business, and programming."

"I see you have it all figured out."

"Except how we're going to get back home," Danielle said.

In the end, we did end up getting a ride home on Mike's helicopter and jet.

"I'm not going to strand three young girls in the middle of Africa," was one of the few things he said to us on our trip home.

Aunt Ellie smiled at being referred to as a young girl.

While Danielle was sleeping on the plane, curled up in a ball still wearing her white dress with pink petunias, he added, "Your sister is amazingly gifted, but what she has in singing talent she lacks in maturity. You should prevail on her while the getting is good. We'll promote you both. Anyway, she already agreed."

I saw a little smirk flash by on Danielle's face. Apparently, she had overheard this little exchange.

Danielle continued her coding during the flight. "I have the free sample site coded. The personal library part is ..."

"Personal library?"

"Yeah, where each person stores their songs, the free samples and the songs they've bought ..."

"I see."

"The library's tricky, but I'm making progress."

"That's good. You're going to handle credit cards and PayPal?"

"I think I'll need a consultant for that. But I've got a guy in Poland...."

"Poland?"

"Yes, he comes highly recommended."

Back at home, Danielle's room overflowed with racks of computers—to handle the volume of downloads she expected—and recording gear. She was holed up writing code around the clock, interrupted only by visits from Elliot, Tony, and Ben to record more tracks, and meeting the financial needs of her new business.

"Dearest sister Claire, I have the opportunity of a lifetime for you."

"Why don't you just ask for my help?"

"But this *is* an opportunity. I'm valuing the business at only two million dollars, it will be worth a hundred times that in a month. I'm figuring a million downloads a week. The costs are minimal. I'm going to sign up other artists, like Meredith at school. And the price to earnings ratio should be very high in today's market."

"I'm glad you have all that figured out."

"You have control of your savings account now that you're sixteen."

"Yeah, Mom was furious at Dad about that. Well, it's about $50K."

"Perfect. That's twenty-five percent of what I need."

"You need two hundred thousand dollars? Your projects are escalating."

"It's all for the e-commerce part of the site. I can do everything else myself. But the transaction stuff, it's too much for me to read into right now. Well, I could get it from the other Stern School kids."

"Actually," I replied, "it does sound like a good investment."

For the next two weeks, Danielle locked herself in her room dressed in a grey flannel nightgown with yellow daffodils. It was frayed and small on her and reminded me of a younger Danielle. She had worn it since she was four. Mom and I took turns bringing meals to her room which she ate while continuing to code. I was her alpha tester.[51] I confirmed that the basic promotion and downloading features seemed to be working. Elliot, Tony, and Ben continued coming over to record tracks with Danielle. Her room was filled with computer equipment, so my room became the recording studio.

Problems with Danielle's plan became evident at our family dinner that evening, the first that she had joined in several weeks. No one commented on my napkin mountains.

"The lawsuit from Columbus came in this morning," Dad announced.

"They're suing an eight-year-old?" I exclaimed.

"I did sign the contract," Danielle said, "but you never countersigned, did you Dad?"

"No, I didn't," Dad replied, "but they're suing because you're inducing their other artists to break their contracts."

"She's still only eight," I pointed out.

"Right, that's why they're suing Mom and me."

"And two nice gentlemen from the Securities and Exchange Commission[52] stopped by this morning," Mom added. "They pointed out that the Stern School kids you've been soliciting for investments are not qualified investors for an exemption from registration. At eight to twelve years old, they're underage, for one thing."

"Well, while you're listing problems," Danielle said, "the software that my Polish consultant sent doesn't work at all, and he seems to have disappeared."

"With your two hundred thousand dollars?" Mom asked.

Dani nodded.

"All of it?" I asked with alarm.

"Uh, well, yeah," Danielle confirmed.

Mom closed her eyes. "At least they'll feed us in jail."

That kind of ended our dinner conversation. Danielle returned to her room and slammed the door.

After another three weeks of Mom and me bringing Danielle's meals to her room, Danielle rejoined us for dinner. This time she was smiling.

She set up her notebook computer on the dining room table and with a ceremonial flourish, pressed the enter key.

Danielle Music Launched flashed across the screen.

Within seconds, we saw another message: *Paid Download, JKJones, initiated.* A second later, another message appeared: *JKJones download successfully completed.* We all clapped at Danielle Music's first online sale, and Danielle beamed.

Five minutes went by and nothing happened. Mom started to serve the salad. Then we saw a second download message.

"Something is the matter," Danielle said.

Mom rolled her eyes, as if to say, *I'll say,* and *I told you so,* and *We're doomed.*

For the next week, Danielle was again secluded in her room. I enjoyed having Mom's and Dad's attention and recalled our dinners together before Danielle came along. The unspoken focus, however, was on Danielle.

Finally, she joined us for dinner again.

"The good news is I think I've found the problem," Danielle announced. "The bad news is that I've lost a million orders."

Mom gave her a quizzical look.

Danielle then worked forty-eight hours straight and finally collapsed on the floor curled into her sleeping ball position. Mom and I gently lifted her into her bed.

My computer started beeping madly. I opened it and discovered that orders for *my* songs on Danielle Music were going through the roof. Mom, Dad, and I watched my computer as Danielle slept for sixteen hours. My orders reached a hundred thousand dollars.

Finally, Danielle woke up and placidly joined us for dinner. Mom, Dad, and I stared at her.

"Don't you want to look at your computer, Danielle?" I finally said.

She walked over to her computer and took in the information tipping her head back and forth.

"It looks like I'm back up to a million orders," she said.

"That's wonderful sweetheart," Mom said, looking a bit dazed.

"Plus another million," Danielle added.

~ℓℓ~

"They've backed down," Martine Rothblatt said, coming in our front door the next morning.

"I'm not surprised," Danielle replied. "Are you?"

"Actually, yes," Martine replied. "But your suggestion that we threaten to cut off our support for their streaming[53] spinoff 'if they didn't stop picking on an eight-year-old girl' seems to have worked."

"Did you get a chance to look at Revoy's resumé? I think he'll make a great CEO," Martine continued.

"Yeah, Peter Revoy looks cool," Danielle replied. "But I had Chief Operating Officer[54] in mind. I'll be the CEO."

"Are you going to have time to run a company with all of your third-grade responsibilities?"

Danielle smirked.

"Okay, COO for Revoy will be fine," Martine concluded. "I was thinking six percent of the stock."

"At this point," Danielle pointed out, "there'll be tax complications to give him founders stock. We already have two million dollars of revenue in our first day. We can offer incentive stock options.[55] Although the Black Scholes value[56] is significant, it would be a tax-free transaction and he would still preserve his long-term capital gains treatment."[57]

Impressed, Martine replied, "That'll work."

"But I was thinking one and a quarter percent," Danielle said.

"How about five? He has an outstanding track record."

"One and a half," Danielle countered.

"Four percent?" Martine asked.

"Very well. We'll make it one and three quarters percent," Danielle concluded.

"All right," Martine acknowledged, "and I was thinking forty percent for my thirty-million-dollar Series A investment?"[58]

Danielle chuckled. "Ha, who says you don't have a sense of humor? I was thinking ten percent."

"You're pretty funny, too," Martine countered. "Make it thirty percent."

"I think eleven will be good," Danielle replied.

"I can agree to twenty-five percent, but that's my final offer," Martine countered.

Danielle smiled again and said, "All, right we'll settle at twelve percent. And it will be a simple preferred[59] with no ratchet downside protection."[60]

"If you insist, Danielle."

"Perfect, that's exactly the valuation I had promised my sister."

"I like the way you negotiate, Danielle," Martine concluded. "I think you will make a very good CEO."

"Well, I'm going to need the money for our water project. And I have a few other things in mind," Danielle said.

"Yes, I certainly support that," Martine replied.

"Oh, and I forgot to mention," Danielle said, "the Mountain Boys and SuzAnn Chimes have joined Danielle Music."

"Yes, I heard," Martine replied. "And I brought you today's *New York Times*." She opened it and we all huddled around the paper. There was a picture of Danielle, typing on her computer, taking up half the width of the page, this time with the headline *She Sang, She Programmed, She Conquered the Music Business.*

AGE NINE:

BE KIND. BE SMART.

*T*hen it was Danielle's birthday again. I couldn't believe she was already nine. We had a low-key family dinner. Danielle beamed, but she quickly shared that it was not because of her birthday.

"I got my first email from Amu," Danielle announced triumphantly. "And her English has gotten pretty good."

"We're all ears," I replied.

"Here goes. 'My dearest Dani, I go to Lusaka with Mom for water show. I tell how screws work. They give me job to teach how to use screws and other stuff. They call me picture of program. Mom has job too. She take me around Zambia. I have teacher go with teach me English and other subject. Dad has job too taking machines by truck and donkey. And fixing. We are moving to Lusaka. They have Internet at café. With much love, your friend forever, Amukusana.'"

"I can see why you're excited, darling," Mom replied. "That's wonderful news."

Dad's eyes blazed. "Yes, there was an announcement this morning of a new UN program to install 400 water machines in Zambia," he said. "You see how your idea is growing? How full is the glass now?"

"Four percent," Danielle replied.

PART ONE

A few months later, Danielle and I appeared together on *The Look*, our first time on the show. We both hugged the hostesses although they seemed especially eager for their Danielle-hugs, which apparently had become a much-coveted experience.

Sandra Winters shared she had important news not even Danielle had heard. "Oh, it's good news," she said, in case anyone became anxious about this unusual announcement. "It's from Washington, DC. The National Science Foundation Certificate of Merit in Physics is going to Danielle for her n-dimensional membrane thesis which has expanded String Theory."

Dani caught my eye and mouthed, "Oh, for *that?*" surprised they were making a fuss about her fourth-grade science paper. Hearty applause followed, and Danielle faced the audience and gave a deep curtsey to the floor—her flowing flowery yellow sundress spreading out in all directions, in what was becoming a signature move.

I had heard of Danielle's membrane project, but hadn't given it much attention. She had tried explaining it to me several times and while I had understood each thing she said, I would have been at a loss to explain it to someone else. Back home, Danielle gave me a printout of Cheng Liu's whitepaper *Strings Are Manifolds*. She knows I prefer to read long documents on paper.

"My idea is based on Liu's. I just went a step further from his two- and three-dimensional manifolds and extended them to n-dimensions."

"Yeah I remember you mentioning this a couple of years ago. N dimensions?"

"Read this, too," Danielle said handing me an old crumpled book titled *Flatland*,[61] about two-dimensional creatures in a two-dimensional world who have difficulty comprehending what a three-dimensional world would be like.

"Then just apply my n-dimensional membranes to so-called quantum probability fields.[62] Actually, calling them probability fields is just another anthropomorphization,"[63] she said laughing.

"I see," I said smiling weakly. I had never been good at physics jokes and figured I should wind down this discussion while I was ahead.

She picked up the Liu whitepaper again. "This one is really good. Definitely read this before you read my class paper again." Noticing that I was not entirely enthusiastic about reading a manuscript of mostly formulas, Danielle handed me another Liu essay. "Here, you might like this, too. It's quite inspiring. And there's no math. *A 5,000 Year Destiny* is Liu's manifesto for democracy in China and includes the stories of the movement he helped to found."

I was impressed that Liu was only thirteen, but then remembered that Danielle was even younger. Weighed down with documents and a book, I made my retreat.

～ℓℓ～

"This stock capitalization of Danielle Music shows you with only seven percent of the stock. I thought you had ten times that?" I asked Danielle during Fireside, which is what we called our bedtime chats even though there was no fire.

"I gave ninety percent of my stock to my foundation," Danielle explained. "That's why I negotiated so hard."

"You have a foundation?"

"Yeah. Danielle," she said.

"The Danielle Foundation?"

"No, just Danielle. Why use three words when you can use just one? Organization names should be concise. We don't say 'Google Search Corporation' or even just 'Google, Inc.,' we just say 'Google.'"

"Won't there be confusion between Danielle the foundation and Danielle the girl?"

"Is that a problem?"

"I suppose not."

"Okay, then."

"And what's your foundation going to do?" I asked.

"Well, we already matched the UN water program in Zambia."

"We? Is that the royal we?"

"Ha. So, it is."

"So how full is the glass now?"

"That would make it eight percent."

"Getting up there. What sort of things are you going to focus on?"

"Danielle's motto is 'Be Kind. Be Smart,'" Danielle said.

"That's clever."

"Yeah, a lot of foundations have noble or 'kind' goals, but they're not effective," Danielle explained. "Unlike a company that has to justify its strategies with actual revenue, foundations often think they can just rest on benevolent aims."

"Yes, I've often thought that."

"Or think of social philosophies," Danielle said. "Communism was based on a 'kind' goal: 'from each according to his ability, to each according to his need.'[64] Now what could be wrong with that? But it wasn't smart. Forced collectivism[65] resulted in the worst catastrophe of the twentieth century, except perhaps for Hitler's 'final solution.'"[66]

"That makes me think of Kant,"[67] I replied. "We were just reading him in Moral Distinctions. He said that a good will is sufficient for right action."

"You know what they say about the road to hell." Danielle pointed out. "I think Kant would have changed his mind if he had seen the communist revolution."

"John Stuart Mill[68] had a different view," I said. "He argued that the end results are more important than the motives or intentions."

"I think you need both," Danielle replied.

"Okay I like it," I concluded. "Be Kind, Be Smart."

AGE TEN:

SORRY ABOUT BLOWING UP YOUR CAR WITH YOU IN IT

Since the Stern School's motto was "Learn by Doing," Dad always encouraged class assignments to be directed at real world problems.

Annie had collected 20,000 books in Spanish and English and sent them to native Indian children in Mexico. She worked with another classmate, Sam, who became interested in the question of why the Mayan civilization[69] in Mexico collapsed so suddenly in the ninth century. The native Indians that Annie communicated with were their descendants. The Mayan cities were all abandoned more than a thousand years ago in just a few decades. Sam had a thesis that it had to do with a viral infection and found evidence in preserved bones he examined in a Mexican museum. His paper in *The American Journal of Archaeology* generated a record number of letters to the editor.

Charlie negotiated a sister school relationship with a high school in India, sending them art supplies along with his paintings. In return, we got back hundreds of student paintings which Charlie and I hung around campus.

Meredith, who had her CMA debut the previous year, got invited to open for SuzAnn Chimes.

For my high school senior year social studies class, I organized a meeting between Libyan government officials and leading democracy advocates. I called my project "A Leap to Liberty for Libya."[70] Danielle and I were always fond of alliteration.

Danielle, who was then 10, wanted to come along, but the security team said they only had the bandwidth to look after one of us. She seemed very frustrated as I left, which I chalked up to her being left out. Apparently, there was more to it than that.

The conference did not go well. Tarek Mohan, one of the participants and a leading dissident, was uncomfortably outspoken in accusing the government of kidnappings, torture, and murders. When desks and chairs were thrown and windows broken, the democracy advocates hurriedly fled the building.

I was quickly whisked away by my security detail.

I was hiding with my security team in a remote part of Libya in a small stone building, when who should show up but Danielle with Uncle Eric and more guards in tow.

"Oh my god," I exclaimed, "how did you ...?"

"Danielle has small planes now," she started to explain. "But we can go over that later. Look at this." She handed me her iPad, open to a breaking story:

```
Outspoken Libyan Dissident Tarak Mohan
Sought by Libyan Government Assassination
     Squads After Aborted Conference
```

I was heartbroken. Danielle calmly explained, "You can't just convene a peace conference without first changing the facts on the ground. That's a sure way to blow things up."

"It wasn't a peace conference," I clarified. Danielle put her arm around my shoulder, noting that the conference had succeeded in galvanizing support for democracy throughout Libya. "There's been latent hatred for Qaddafi,[71] but the population hearing the stories of his abusive policies and tactics at the conference, such as the killing of dissidents and their families and brutal imprisonments, and the open discussion of democracy, has changed everything. The assassination squad is very upsetting," she added, "but it's also an opportunity! The government is making a profound error in picking a fight."

Danielle, who knew many of the social media leaders in Libya, had largely mastered Arabic, which I had only dabbled in. I had opened the conference with a few carefully practiced lines in Arabic, but my actual understanding was slim. Over the next several days, Danielle struck up friendships and alliances with hundreds of dissidents across Libya. Before I knew it, she had organized a communication network for opponents to the government while locking the government out.

"Maybe we've done enough," I told her, concerned that she was going too far.

"I don't think it's an option to quit now," Danielle responded. "The government's already launched an aggressive program of attack and is targeting everyone you've met with."

"My friends?" I said.

"Yes, exactly."

"I was just trying to create a bridge of discussion, Dani."

"Well, we talked about the bridge, road, or whatever to hell," Danielle said.

"I thought your bridge went nowhere," I said.

"Yeah, well, that's a different bridge."

A few days later, the government responded to my aborted conference by shutting down the centrally controlled servers which provided Internet coverage for the country. Fortunately, Danielle was prepared for this and turned on clandestine servers she already had in place. She had set up dozens of iPads in a command center in the desert. I felt like we were sitting at the controls of an airplane that we were flying in, but I dared not touch.

Danielle had no such hesitation. "We have to launch this plan now while we still have communications," she said.

I felt that Danielle's debut at the CMA Festival had launched her into the stratosphere, and she now was soaring to a higher orbit. I had given up trying to slow her down.

"Is that what all these trucks are for?" I asked.

"We need to pre-position some things."

"Things?"

"Well mostly, signal interceptors.[72] A lot of their electronics are not on the Internet, so I need to access their local area networks.[73] Team A will drive them into the city. I would have preferred less bulky transportation, but the trucks were all we could scrounge up."

"When are they leaving?"

"A few have left already. The rest should leave now but some of the trucks aren't working. These three won't start. That one starts but then chokes up after a minute. Those..."

"I see the problem," I responded.

Danielle downloaded some of the service manuals and was reading them, but having been up for thirty hours, she finally passed out on the straw mats that had been set up for us. I changed into my flannel nightgown and joined her. Danielle was just curled up in her flower dress.

Six hours later she woke up startled, flew off of the mat and ran outside. "Claire, half the trucks are gone. They must have been stolen!" I quickly changed back into my jeans and "Leap to Liberty" sweatshirt and followed her.

It felt like a windy sauna outside the tent. With the swirling sand in my eyes, I had a fleeting thought to scour the few scraggly palm trees for a hidden lion but quickly realized they were not indigenous to this part of Libya.

I ran past several trucks and turned the bend, and who did I find there embracing Danielle but Amu. And beyond them was Amu's dad Nsishumba with his shirt off, sweating in the hot Libyan sun, bent over the chassis of one of the truck's engines.

"Dad fix trucks!" Amu said excitedly.

"How did they know?" I asked Danielle.

"I sent her an email," Danielle explained.

"And they took a donkey caravan here from Zambia?"

"The water program now has a small bush plane. Nsishumba flew it here."

~ℓℓ~

We watched one of the pre-position missions on our growing iPad command station in the desert for an anxious fourteen hours, waiting for them to execute their assignment. The first task—setting up several hidden signal interceptors for the government's tank command local area network—was completed. Each display monitored the surrounding area. Suddenly Danielle was alarmed by a coordinated movement of people who were not on the team.

"Trojan horse in blue, 1:30, twenty yards!" She alerted the mission commander of the trap, but it was too late. Our team fought a rear-guard battle and she was able to direct them to commandeer a docked passenger ferry to escape into the Mediterranean Sea. They ended up in Tunisia where they were arrested, but fortunately not by the Qaddafi forces.

"Well, at least we pre-positioned the most critical assets," Danielle concluded.

Other teams reported in and Danielle declared that we should turn in for the night. As we were getting ready to switch off the lights, Dad appeared on Skype.

"Danielle, your Mom and I feel you've done very well. But, it's gone beyond what Miss Crutcher imagined."

"And your parents," Mom added.

"You mean, Claire's social studies teacher?" Danielle asked.

"Yes, we think you should focus more now on your science class. You got an A on your last paper," Dad said.

"Yes, darling," Mom piped in. "You've both been gone a long time. Dad's a bit more sanguine, but this doesn't seem safe to me. And we'd love having you both home this weekend. I thought we could all do something together."

"I'd love to," Danielle replied, "but that's kind of like telling a woman in labor to put off that baby project, that she's got higher priority things to do."

"You're kind of young to be having any kind of labor pains," Mom told her.

"I'm not nine anymore you know! I'm double digits now. Anyway," Danielle added, "that's why we're hidden behind these iPads here in the desert. Hey Mom, Dad, I gotta run—need to send out tomorrow's code list. I miss you. Love you. We'll visit again tomorrow."

∼ℓℓ∽

Danielle and I disguised ourselves and slipped into the insurgent controlled area. She was immediately recognized. The rebels were her fans.

"I download all Danielle song from website," said a thin young man who seemed to be a commander.

The conversation quickly segued to strategy and tactics. "You're using standard res for Google Earth? You can't guide medium-range munitions with that!" Danielle told them. "Here, use this link, download a patch called Hi Res Earth Patch 3. I wrote it this morning."

They quickly discovered that they wanted and needed her input on every decision.

∼ℓℓ∽

Several days later, Qaddafi ordered all of his tanks, planes, and helicopters to pursue the rebels, including Danielle and me.

We returned to our command station in the desert which Danielle had expanded to 100 iPads serving as terminals, with Microsoft Kinect motion-sensing game controllers[74] for quick user control. I wore green fatigues, which I thought appropriate for the occasion, but Danielle was still wearing her red sundress with yellow daisies and combat boots with rubber soles.

"Oh my god, there's a leak!" Danielle exclaimed.

"Someone leaked our position!?" I responded in alarm.

"No, no, a memory leak,"[75] Danielle clarified.

"Memory leak?"

"Yeah, one of my Java functions is failing to release the memory blocks it requisitioned, so the memory usage keeps expanding until it blows up," Danielle explained.

"So maybe we should step away from the iPads?" I asked.

"It's not a hardware problem. It's a software bug. When the storage cache blows up, the computer crashes."

"And this means?" I inquired gingerly.

"Here, let me show you how to get around it, dear sister."

Danielle showed me how to monitor the amount of available memory and how to reload all of the system software and applications before the memory leak crashed the computer. This then became my job. The only problem was I had to do this for a hundred iPads. And when I got through all hundred, I had to start over again. And again.

"Can't you automate this, Danielle?"

"Well, yeah, I could automate it or even fix it but there's no time for that. Our engagement is beginning now."

So, I went madly from iPad to iPad doing my memory-leak-fix procedure. After doing this several thousand times, I could do it in my sleep. And after continuing this for forty hours, that's exactly what I felt like I was doing.

The government tanks traveled about a hundred yards, then halted. The software viruses Danielle had programmed and hacked into the tank operating systems had come to life.

The government planes took off, but once they were airborne, all controls went dead and the planes went into a tailspin. We heard the pilots screaming through the iPad control station. At the last second, Danielle snapped her hand in front of a Kinect controller, and the pilots' controls went live again. Danielle then spoke to each pilot by name.

"Hi there, Adama, this is Danielle. Sorry about the disruption. I would appreciate your following my instructions carefully, so we can avoid any more, uh, interruptions...."

"Danielle from US?"

"Yes, from Los Angeles. Where are you from?"

"Tripoli. I do not believe it is really Danielle I see on TV."

"Yeah, well, one and the same. What's your favorite Danielle song?"

"Daisies in the Desert."

She sang:

> *Endless rolling hills*
> *Of whiiite, a yellow flower*
> *Do my eyes deceive me?*
> *Have I have been away from you soooo long ...*

"Danielle! Praise Allah. It is really you! I am at your service, Commander Danielle. Please tell me what is it? Your wish?"

She ordered him to bomb the government storehouses of weapons and described where they were, which he promptly and efficiently carried out.

With one pilot after another, Danielle took over each plane's controls remotely from our iPad command station in the dessert. Some, like Adama, were fans of Danielle and secretly hated Qaddafi. They enthusiastically cooperated with her orders. Others were persuaded simply by the fact that she could turn off the plane's controls at will.

With Danielle controlling the regime's tanks and planes, the rebel forces overran Tripoli and a special commando force Danielle had set up infiltrated Qaddafi's compound and took him prisoner. The commandos were under instructions from Danielle to capture him alive if at all possible.

Our commando car with the imprisoned Qaddafi was followed by three government cars loyal to Qaddafi who did not realize their leader was actually in the car they were chasing. They chased the commando car and tried to corner it. Danielle tapped one of the iPad monitors, and instantly twenty iPads burst alive with the chase scene, encircling us like

a 360-degree virtusphere. The sound was deafening, and the gritty commandos looked like they were sitting in my lap.

She shouted urgent orders to the driver of the commando car to take a specific route that went over the explosives one of her original pre-positioning teams had planted in the street for remote activation. "Left on Busayf, three blocks, right on Qaddafi Drive." At the correct moment, she chopped the air aggressively with her hand. This motion was picked up by the wireless Kinect controller, which in turn activated the appropriate set of pre-positioned explosives. One by one she derailed the government cars pursuing the rebel car with Qaddafi in it. She was careful to activate the explosives at precise moments so as to send the government drivers into parked cars and plate glass windows along the side of the street, rather than killing them.

"Danielle, you missed!" one of the rebel soldiers exclaimed.

Danielle replied, "Yes, exactly as I planned."

⁓ℓℓ⁓

"That was like taking candy from a baby," Danielle confided in me after Qaddafi's arrest.

"Sure, taking candy from a baby *is* easy. The hard part is dealing with the baby's friends and relatives," I warned.

"He won't have friends after we meet with him," Danielle responded.

"And the relatives?"

"They've all fled."

"He does have cronies, Danielle."

"He *had* cronies. Now that he's in custody, they'll all disappear into the woodwork. They'll be like, Colonel Qaddafi? Never met the guy."

⁓ℓℓ⁓

"Ah, the Calico girls; just who I wanted to meet," Qaddafi said in English as we walked in.

We were in a small walk-up apartment on the outskirts of Tripoli. Rebel soldiers stood guard.

"The feeling is definitely mutual," I responded, pleased that I was able to say something suitable.

"Did you write the Niger Passageway Manifesto?" Danielle asked.

"Yes, I wrote it and issued it. It is directed at the rats who have abandoned the ship of Libya and asks simply that they return to their proper roles in society in peace and solidarity."

Danielle calmly clarified, as she shuffled papers as if to tidy up the files, "It also says here to destroy the rats mercilessly by drowning, asphyxiation, burning, the chopping off of hands, feet, and heads."

"Wait, that's supposed to be in the Bani Walid Directive," a suddenly bewildered Qaddafi muttered.

"A directive you didn't write?" Danielle said. "But you just said you wrote the Niger Passageway Manifesto."

"No, no, I had nothing to do with it."

"But that's not what you just said," Danielle replied earnestly.

Danielle then gave him a look that would become a Danielle signature expression. She gazed at Qaddafi with a serious, penetrating, and pitying look that indicated she had nothing further to add to the exchange.

Danielle hacked into the government-run radio and television and aired her interview with Qaddafi, which linked him directly to the government's brutal treatment of the Libyan people. The remaining government resistance crumbled.

With the rebel victory, Danielle visited the hospitalized government agents who had driven the cars pursuing the commando car with the captured Qaddafi.

"Sorry about blowing up your car with you in it," Danielle said bashfully to one of the drivers.

"Actually, it was extraordinarily kind of you to even think about my safety under the circumstances. You have my eternal gratitude," came the reply.

That evening, I went back to our command center and there was no Danielle. Before I got a chance to worry, one of our comrades, a friendly, older man in an ill-fitting grey suit, smiled at me, and gestured to follow him. Khalid, my head of security in Libya, nodded that this was okay. I heard music not unlike that at the Sempala celebration coming from the tent ahead. As we squeezed through the fabric flap door, I saw makeshift instruments—a drum made of an empty diesel fuel can and an improvised string instrument that reminded me of my guitar in Haiti. And there was Danielle, her arms around two of the rebels. They were all laughing.

"What's that you're drinking, dear sister?" I asked with some suspicion.

In between giggles, Danielle said, "Oh, just some Libyan apple juice!"

"Libyan apple juice?" I grabbed it from her and tasted it. It was indeed apple juice.

"Ha ha, you didn't trust me," she said, touching her right thumb to her nose while wiggling the other four fingers in my direction.

I could only catch occasional words of conversation, but I joined the party anyway. We laughed and danced until the sun came up. My favorite was a Libyan line dance with intricate swinging and skipping.

The next day, we again Skyped with Dad who was still in LA. I could see the edge of the patio and stream that flows down below.

"That was nice work, you two. And Danielle, the reverse aviation worm[76] was the most impressive."

"There was more than one," she said. "But Dad, I didn't know about the firewall[77] tap you put up. We needed to patch some of the aviation bots and, well, it complicated matters."

"Hmmm, I'm sorry about that. It would have alerted me if things got out of hand."

"And the security team would have whisked us away on the Blue Star Jet?" Danielle said.

"Exactly," Dad replied. "Anyway, it doesn't seem to have caused too much difficulty. But I do need to protect my daughters. You know how your mom feels about this, and safety's not negotiable when it comes to these class assignments."

The success of the revolution left the government in disarray, if we could properly call it a government anymore. There were endless disputes of all sizes. A big one was merging the militias into one national armed service. A small argument that became quite contentious was whether to repair a traffic light leading to Tripoli's city square. The light apparently had always had strong opposition as it appeared to exacerbate the morning commute. Danielle suggested a gradual program for the militias to turn in their weapons, and suggested a more intelligent traffic light that would take the direction of traffic into consideration. She offered to program it herself. When Danielle offered a proposal, it settled matters, at least for the time being.

"You seem to have become the de facto leader of Libya," I pointed out at one of our Fireside chats.

"Yeah, it's easy to fill a vacuum. They listen to me now, but they know I'm not staying long. And the more uncompromising leaders are just biding their time until I leave."

"Yes, I thought that could be a problem," I replied.

"We'll have to leave some semblance of a democratically elected government before we go," Danielle said.

Danielle—the foundation—helped set up a communication infrastructure with national free Internet and reliable television service. Danielle—the girl—organized teachers from around Libya to give online classes in every subject and at every level up through grade twelve. Classes of students around the country gathered around the tablets Danielle the foundation had rushed in.

"Danielle TV," seen around the world on cable and the Web, started to broadcast several hours a day of her comings and goings, speeches, meetings, and concerts. Danielle focused much of her energy on reconciliation and the nascent development of democratic institutions. Meanwhile, I read stories to the kids of Libya via Danielle TV broadcast, including *A Leap to Liberty*, which I had just written about the revolution.

A six-year-old girl from Tripoli who lost her parents to government violence approached me.

"You look just like my mom. Can you adopt me?"

"How about I be your godmother instead?" I suggested. "I'll make sure everything goes well for you, but I'm not quite old enough to adopt you."

"You and Danielle can run the revolution but not be my mom?" the girl asked.

"I guess that's part of the problem," I answered. "We're pretty tied up with trying to turn the revolution into a government at the moment."

"What's a government?"

"I'll explain it to you," I replied, taking her hand and leading her on a walk through a Tripoli park, which was still littered with stalled tanks.

Within a few days I arranged for a Libyan couple to adopt her, and I checked in with her frequently.

Danielle spent time with political and business leaders, asking them penetrating questions on Danielle TV. She wanted the people of Libya to evaluate them. In one of her many televised sessions, she met with William Silverstone, the CEO of the Libyan Oil company which was foreign owned. In a sweetheart deal with the previous government, the company had been pocketing all of the profits from the country's oil production, except for kickbacks to Qaddafi and his regime. Danielle still needed their expertise, so she was not prepared to send them on their way completely, but in a televised session she presented him with a new contract that radically changed the profit sharing and controls between the company and Libya. She gave Silverstone two hours to sign the agreement, warning him that if he didn't, she would implement plan B, which would be to seize and nationalize all of the company's assets in Libya.

"There is no legal justification for this," he protested. "We will file immediate petitions with the courts to reverse any such action."

"You mean those courts?" she said, waving to two nearby justices of the court wearing black and white robes. They smiled and waved back to Danielle. "Do you want the two hours or should we just conclude this meeting now?"

"I'll make good use of the two hours," came the nervous reply.

After an hour and forty-five minutes Silverstone presented Danielle with a marked-up draft of her proposed agreement in both print and digital forms.

She asked politely for an explanation of how the MS Word mark-ups worked, as if she had never seen the MS Word mark-up feature before.

"That's very clever," Danielle told Silverstone as she looked over the changes. "So, Word lets me see everything that has been changed, and with what words."

"Exactly," Silverstone answered.

Smiling, Danielle said, "You know I like being organized, don't you?"

"Why of course, that's the mark of a good executive," Silverstone replied.

"I agree. I have a new filing system that works really well. As I always say, a place for everything, and everything in its place." While she was saying this, she tore up the print version of the modified contract that Silverstone had modified into tiny pieces. With a flourish she threw a handful at a fan which lifted the scraps into the air where they showered down like confetti on Danielle and Silverstone.

Danielle blew away some pieces that landed on her nose and lips. "Now, as I was saying, I would greatly appreciate if you would sign this contract." She placed two copies of the original unmodified version in front of him. "Time is getting short—there are only ten minutes left before I will have to go to plan B." At that moment, the commander of the new government's Armed Forces, dressed in a crisp military uniform complete with medals, stepped forward next to Danielle.

"I don't have the authority to sign this," Silverstone stammered. "I would have to get permission from the management committee of the board."

"You really are between a rock and a hard place," Danielle said sympathetically. "Let me give you some advice. I think you'll have an easier time explaining why you took it upon yourself to make a quick but necessary executive decision as opposed to explaining how you lost all of these oil wells. And I have two decorative pens we can keep as souvenirs."

Silverstone, who was now sweating profusely in the hot Libyan sun, his white button-down shirt drenched, grabbed hesitantly for one of the pens. He signed both copies of the agreement. Danielle did the same.

"It has been a pleasure doing business with you," Danielle said.

"Yes, well I hope so; I may be coming to you for a job."

⁓ℓℓ⁓

After a brief Fireside chat, Danielle and I settled in for the night at our compound in Tripoli. She climbed into my bunk and threw herself into my arms crying hysterically. She held on for dear life. I sensed that the thing to do was just to hold her and defer any discussion.

Eventually she straightened up, sniffling. She was now only whimpering, saying, "Thank you, Claire, everything is okay."

"Yes, it is, Dani, but what was going on this time in that little head of yours?"

"I was in a vast space with no light. A never-ending voyage with no way to the exit."

"Hmm," I replied. "Bridge, connected rooms, voyage, I see a common thread here."

"You weren't there," Danielle went on. "Mom and Dad weren't there. I was just walking forever in the shadows. Abandoned." she concluded.

I held her until we fell asleep. I dreamed that I ventured gingerly into the realm of Danielle's eternal extent, and in the very dim light of that containment I saw sewing machines, dresses, bricks and boulders, wires, and shrouded figures. I awoke startled, but managed not to wake up Danielle. I lay there shaken for the rest of the night while she softly snored.

⁓ℓℓ⁓

The next morning, we walked into the center of Tripoli and had breakfast on a veranda. "Look at that woman chasing after her two girls," Danielle said. "Makes me think of Mom. She won't take her eyes off them."

"Which one is you?" I asked with a smile.

"The sniffling one with the tissue," she replied. "I miss Mom and Dad."

"It's been a while since we've been home, like a couple of months," I noted.

"Let's do it," Danielle exclaimed. "And let's surprise them."

As we walked back to our room, Danielle skipped in front of me and I remembered her tears the previous night. I thought maybe this was my destiny, to be Danielle's confidante, to remember her stories, to comfort her during long, scary walks through shaded mazes, journeys I dared not take myself.

The reunion with Mom and Dad was emotional. We went to Danielle's favorite restaurant in Los Angeles to celebrate, but Mom was wistful. "Maybe you can stay in LA for a time," Mom said hoping to keep Danielle in one place for at least a little while.

"Sure, Mom, but there's still a lot to do in Libya," Danielle responded.

Mom did not look convinced.

Sleeping in my bed was comforting, but I began to realize that I was spending less and less time at home.

On our way back to Libya, we made a one day stop in New York City.

"Why Brooklyn?" I asked Danielle.

"It's the key to my whole class project."

"Brooklyn is the key to the Middle East?"

"It's the final key, the last piece of the puzzle."

"If you say so, Dani." We smiled at each other.

There she met, in one of her televised encounters (as most of her endeavors were now becoming) with Rabbi Schneerson,[78] the "Rebbe" of the Lubavitch[79] organization. It was very influential on the religious wing of Israeli politics, although this dynasty of Hasidic[80] Rebbes was headquartered in the Crown Heights neighborhood of Brooklyn, and named for a Polish-Lithuanian village. He was a short, gentle man with a full, white beard and an infectious smile. The meeting took place in his cramped office, which was lined with shelves of centuries-old Hebrew volumes and an ornate carved menorah.

Danielle spoke to the Rebbe. "Moshiach[81] revealed the primacy of the word of"—here she gestured with her open hand and face toward heaven instead of speaking the name of God—"in contrast with the idolatry of the golden calf."[82]

The Rebbe smiled, but corrected Danielle. "The Moshiach has not yet appeared, but yes, he surely will do that when he assumes his role."

Danielle continued, "Ah yes, of course. So, from this day forward, we establish the transcendence of words over material objects. Words symbolize ideas that humans can share with each other, even if these thoughts derive from…" The Rebbe and Danielle gestured toward the heavens.

The Rebbe responded, "Everything derives from…" and they again gestured together toward the sky.

"It started with the apple," Danielle observed. "The fruit of knowledge[83] which gave us understanding and responsibility—"

"—and shame," the Rebbe completed her thought.

They continued like this for three hours speaking in Talmudic metaphors and the Rebbe was profoundly impressed with her deep understanding and wisdom.

"This is a sacred and wise child," Rabbi Schneerson said bidding Danielle goodbye. "We should follow closely what she has to say."

We then stopped off at Lincoln Center[84] for a jazz concert. I played the drums while she played both the piano and saxophone simultaneously using a Danielle Finger Glide. This was an invention of hers in which the expressive movements of her right hand and fingers intercepting laser lights were translated into the sounds of the saxophone, while she continued to perform on the piano with her left hand.

She called her concert "Prime Jazz," which seemed innocuous enough. Right before the concert, she sent a tweet to her billion followers. *I wonder how long it will take to figure out. I would guess 20 min.*

The online discussion started out along the lines of *Figure out what?* All over social media and the Twittersphere, people quickly decided that it had something to do with the concert, and probably the title.

Once she started the concert, it took fifteen minutes for a consensus to be reached, beating Danielle's estimate.

I tried to be conservative. Virtuous wisdom of crowds,[85] she tweeted later.

The question was: What is unique about the jazz pieces that Danielle is performing?

The answer was that instead of the numerator of the time signatures being the usual powers of 2 (that is, 2, 4, 8, 16, for example 4/4) that are always used in jazz; Danielle was using prime numbers[86] (that is 3, 5, 7, 11, 13, for example 13/8). Danielle had played several short pieces at the beginning of the concert, so the more astute listeners could catch on quickly to this pioneering pattern.

"You seem more comfortable in front of thousands, or even millions of fans, than you do with a handful of friends," I pointed out to Danielle backstage.

"Yeah, I'm comfortable being one on one," she replied.

"One on one?"

"A crowd is like a friend. It has a distinct personality and communicates just like a single person."

"I'm sure the adulation doesn't hurt," I added.

"I'm afraid it's addictive," Danielle replied.

Danielle was now up to about ten hours per day of televised encounters, concerts, and other performances. Almost all of her substantive gatherings were shown online in real time. There was ample online dialog about the pros and cons of doing this, such as the difficulty of making secret side agreements on the one hand, but the added transparency of her interactions with world leaders on the other. Given Danielle's ability to think on her feet, the advantages appeared to have a significant edge.

We were now both on Life Bits[87] around the clock, although this was not publicly revealed. Video transmissions from our contact lens cameras were fully recorded and stored privately in the Cloud. This had been cleared by our legal team as it was set up, so that none of the information would be made publicly available without the permission of the people in the scene. Most of Danielle's meetings took place online anyway.

Mom was not so sanguine about this.

"There are computer breaches every day," Mom said at one of our rare family dinners. "You hacked into Qaddafi's computer, remember?"

"Yeah, well," Danielle replied. "Our security is a lot better than his was."

"What about all the people you surreptitiously record?" Mom asked.

"We're not going to release any videos without people's permission," Danielle said.

"Unless your Life Bits are hacked."

Danielle gave her a stubborn look. "Not going to happen."

We returned to Libya and Danielle continued her nation building.

"We must retain the cultural traditions of the tribes, but with a tolerance that transcends tribal differences," said Professor Tillisi, chairman of the Political Science Department at the University of Tripoli, in an extensive online discussion with Danielle.

Danielle argued for a policy of liberal immigration, citing the strength of the United States from its immigrant history. "Let diverse and talented people flow into Libya from every corner of the globe. Let us build a harmonious society of all the world's peoples right here," she said in a speech to the nation.

Danielle privately trusted me with her feelings about the subtlest things. She was amazingly confident about consequential things, but got upset at the furrowing of a brow or the hint of a pursed lip of doubt. She tried not to show these reactions until we were together.

"No, the majority leader doesn't think you're ugly, Dani."

"So why was he smirking?"

"I think he was having trouble keeping up with you."

"Didn't I make myself clear enough?"

"Oh, I think you were perfectly clear."

We would carry on this exchange until Danielle was a little less uncomfortable with whatever it was that she was obsessing about. It seemed no one else was able to put these matters into perspective for her. Every time I resolved one of Danielle's minor crises, I saw how I was the one who knew which words could soothe her.

AGE ELEVEN:
NEVER AGAIN

One day in spring, while relaxing with Danielle on our favorite veranda in Libya, I received a handwritten card from King Abdullah[88] of Saudi Arabia,[89] hand-delivered by an aide. I thought it was going to be a birthday card for my nineteenth birthday, but it was an invitation to a meeting.

"Are you coming with me?" I asked Danielle.

"It doesn't look like I'm invited."

"I always go with *you*. Aren't you curious what this is about?" I asked.

"I'm sure I'll find out soon enough."

I met privately with the King two days later. He wore flowing white robes, a white head covering which also served as a kind of scarf, a black felt circle on his head, and a golden sash, all of which were regal but understated. He projected solemnity and sadness, as if he'd resigned himself to some unfortunate situation.

"I have become a Daniellite," he confided.

"A Daniellite?" I had never heard this term before. It had an interesting ring to it, and I kind of understood what he meant. *I'm a Daniellite, too,* I thought to myself.

The King continued, "Despite my position as King, I do not have the power and skill—and now, entering the autumn days of my reign, the energy—to navigate my country toward the new world values that Danielle embodies."

He went on to plead with me that Danielle come to Saudi Arabia and work with him as his special royal advisor, assuring me that she would have his strong support for her ideas.

I found it funny that he thought I had a role in such decisions, and was the proper person to put this request through. I attempted to clarify a few questions.

"So, is this a real position recognized in Saudi law?"

"I can assure you, Miss Calico, and Danielle, that all necessary changes will be made."

I suppose that's one advantage of being King, I thought, although I wondered if he was really prepared for Danielle's concepts and goals.

I made the brief trip back to Libya and reported to my sister.

"Yeah, it sounds like I could squeeze it in," Danielle commented.

"You seem to be taking this in stride," I replied. "I mean these Arabian kings are always asking Jewish teenage girls to guide their countries."

Smiling, Danielle said, "Is your emphasis more on Jewish or teenage? And by the way, I'm still eleven."

"I keep forgetting, but it's true you don't look like a teenager."

"Yet," Danielle clarified.

"Actually," I said, "my emphasis was on *girl.*"

Danielle flew to Saudi Arabia for a televised summit with the King. She wore a white gown that reached to the ground and she covered her head and arms with a shawl of the same color. As a statement of her own signature fashion preference, there was a blue six-pointed star-shaped flower on the dress near her right shoulder.

"We'll get to Saudi fashion," she protested to me later. "I have more important issues to start with."

"That flower … a hyacinth?" I asked her.

"Exactly, the symbol of spring," Danielle replied.

After some mutually admiring words, and without missing a beat, she told the King that she did not want him to be surprised by her program.

"I will want a strong constitutional government with a largely symbolic national monarchy much like England has. The trillion-dollar sovereign funds[90] should be clearly managed by an independent government agency. Well, you guys can keep a few billion dollars; we'll have to work out the details.

"The government funding of Madrassa schools[91] can continue, but the schools should provide a modern liberal education including all of the world's religions and the theme of 'many paths to the truth.' I would like you and the government to join our program to advance women's and children's rights. Female Genital Mutilation[92] will be banned and the prohibition enforced with a major educational and cultural program to move Saudi society away from this practice."

The King responded with just a hint of surprise, "If anyone can actually carry out these changes, it would be you." The two agreed to move forward.

Before we left Libya, the command post in the desert that Danielle had put together during the rebellion became an official national monument. The iPads were still in place and there was a bronze statue of Danielle in a dramatic pose chopping the air near the Kinect controller she had used. There were also statues of our fellow Libyan rebel leaders operating the controls. I was there, too, hovering over the iPads doing my memory leak thing.

While Danielle started her Saudi gig, I prepared for my annual visit to Haiti. I was glad to go alone that time. When Charlie went with me, it reminded them I was now part of a white family.

Charlie was a recognized artist by then and had ideas about four- and five-dimensional art which he said were based on Danielle's membranes.

You experienced them in a virtual reality environment where vibrating three-dimensional images responded in turn to your own movement in the virtual environment. Even subtle motions of a finger or your nose had fascinating effects. He was working with a toy company on an interactive environment for children, so there were invariably kids around when we visited with each other.

We had just become "lavaliered," basically an old-fashioned engagement to be engaged. Charlie made the pendant from my favorite of his creations and it hung from a gold chain around my right ankle.

"You sure you're going to be okay? I mean I won't be there to protect you," Charlie worried as we walked through a Los Angeles park before I left for Haiti.

"I'll have some real security this time," I assured him.

"I get some great inspiration for my installations on those trips," he added.

"Yeah, I get inspired, too, for my stories," I replied.

"I'll miss you," he concluded.

I turned my head to the ground and then looked up to meet his eyes.

And although I love when Danielle comes with me on my annual trips to Haiti, it can be difficult for my own projects because of the attention she attracts. When I go alone it is my little world. I have no official title, but the media has dubbed me "the princess of Haiti." When I turned eighteen, the most prominent Haitian blog wrote "we should update that now to Queen Claire."

Of course, I never left either Charlie or Dani completely behind. Most of the questions I got from the press were not about Haiti, but about my activities with Danielle in Africa and the Middle East. And as for Charlie, I thought of him when I used his immersive art software with the televised third grade class I taught for a day.

I was especially proud of the Cholera-Free Ceremony we held celebrating my Cholera [93] Initiative, marking that there had been no cases in Haiti during that past year. Twelve years earlier when I was rescued from the earthquake, cholera in Haiti had been epidemic.

I rejoined Danielle in Saudi Arabia, and once we were alone, she fluttered like an injured bird into my arms. I understood by then what this was about. Well, I still didn't *fully* understand it, but I was prepared. She had been on her own without a close friend or confidante for more than a week. I'd actually understand better if I was the one who needed this comfort, but Danielle's dark room of disaster and desertion is not a place I allow myself to go.

As her sobs subsided, she whimpered, "You got here in the nick of time. I held out as long as I could."

"What about your new buddy?" I teased.

"You mean the King?"

"Yes, although I suppose if you hugged him like this it might give people the wrong idea."

"Not to mention him," Danielle added.

I thought again about my fortune as my sister's cry pillow. I seemed to be able to soothe her, and each time I did, I'd try to remember exactly what I said that moved her. After we spoke, I'd retreat and write it all down.

Danielle's partnership with the King went more smoothly than many critics had predicted. The King issued edicts to enact support for her economic and political changes. Her immense popularity helped seed the social and cultural changes, but six months was not nearly enough time to reverse traditions that went back centuries.

"This isn't working," Danielle commented to me on the FGM (female genital mutilation) part of her program.

"I wouldn't say that. You've anchored a stake in the ground. You've raised the issue, and Saudi Arabia isn't the heart of the problem anyway. There's been more progress on this in the past two months than in the previous ten years."

"Yeah, that's great," she responded. "Tell that to the girl about to undergo the, uh, ceremony. I think the time has come for me to deliver this speech."

"What speech?"

"I showed it to you a year ago. I wrote it for fifth grade composition class, remember? I was waiting for the right timing, which I think is now. I just need the right setting. You're right, it's not just a Saudi issue."

A week later, Danielle gave her first address to the United Nations General Assembly,[94] taking the King's Saudi Arabian spot, which he had passed on to her for this session.

I sat in the first row of the stately General Assembly Hall. Danielle stepped to the podium, which had a magnificent golden structure behind it that reminded me of a menorah. Danielle was intent, confident.

"Let us mark today an emancipation proclamation on behalf of girls. It is said that you can measure the character of a society by how it treats its weakest members. Considering the history of how humanity has treated young females, we should be ashamed for our civilization. It wasn't so long ago that we bound girls' feet so that walking was excruciating. Today, parts of the world put a premium on the birth of boys, so girls are left at poor orphanages—or worse. In other parts of the world we invade and destroy the most personal spaces of girls' bodies. And these are just the official crimes. Add to that the pervasive abuse that goes on behind closed doors. What other species does this to its young female members?

"Let us discuss female genital mutilation. Or can we? Why does this widespread, horrific practice get so little attention? Because the topic of maiming young girls is too distressing to talk about in polite company, much less in public. FGM involves such intimate matters that it feels too inappropriate to describe, making it virtually impossible to discuss."

Danielle paused at this point and there was discernible discomfort among the delegates who shifted in their seats, coughed, and otherwise made their unease audible. Danielle remained silent and let this display continue for two minutes although it seemed much longer at the time. This effectively made her point.

When this reaction died down, she continued. "Some call this practice 'female circumcision,'[95] but that is a grotesque distortion of language. The proper comparison to male anatomy would be called female *castration*. Even aside from the sexual aspects, the pain and degradation of FGM is too heartbreaking to describe. This cruel custom must be ended once and for all.

"So where are the so-called feminist organizations in all this? Why don't we hear more of their voices raised against these vile forms of child and female abuse?"

She went on to call on girls to "do whatever you need to do to confront and end the annihilation of your inalienable rights."

It was this last line that got the strongest reaction and the most push back. Critics wrote that she was asking girls to violently confront traditions with nothing to back them up. An editorial in *The New York Times* read, "Danielle's challenge will make things worse and lead to tragedies. She is leading young girls to slaughter."

Danielle was unmoved by this line of commentary and responded firmly and politely to an almost constant barrage of denigration. She was instead disappointed in herself for having pulled her punches with regard to American feminist organizations.

"I thought you were pretty strong in your criticism," I pointed out.

"Not really," Danielle responded. "The inaction of the many feminist organizations makes them complicit in these crimes."

It was hard for me to tell whether Danielle's impatience reflected her deep commitment to justice, or her immaturity, or both. She was rarely moved by appeals to Realpolitik.[96] She asked me to convey a back-channel ultimatum to the National Organization for Women[97] to get fully behind her initiative or else she would release what she had originally planned to say in her speech.

I was glad, actually, that she asked me to communicate her thoughts since it would give me an opportunity to express them with a modicum of diplomacy. In my meeting with the NOW president in her Washington, DC office, I explained that Danielle was not satisfied with her own censure of their organization, and that she had soft-pedaled her message to give them an opportunity to change their position while saving face.

"That was soft-pedaling?" she asked me, raising her eyebrows.

Without answering her rhetorical question, I explained that Danielle felt strongly about the issues she had raised. "You have to admit that FGM and China's one child policy haven't been high-priority issues for NOW."

"We've stated that we categorically oppose FGM and one child,"[98] she said.

"That's just lip service, Danielle says," I pointedly replied.

She responded, "We appreciate that these are important concerns, but we are not really set up to be effective for these types of global issues."

Here I used a technique I learned from watching Danielle and glared back at her with a look of incredulity as if to say, *That's an answer?* This only works if done at the right time, I've found; it gives your interlocutor a chance to consider the weakness in their argument.

We had a bit of a staring contest. She finally broke the silence, "Very well. We do need to do a lot more. Let me work on this."

With that, we parted. Two days later, the NOW president delivered a major address to a Washington, DC audience, covered live by news networks, including Danielle TV. She echoed Danielle's words and thanked her for her leadership. She acknowledged a failure of imagination on the part of her organization and affiliated groups. She concluded, "We have been much too respectful of the exigencies of traditions and have lost perspective on the requirements of justice for all. Justice is, after all, why NOW exists. I look forward to Danielle's continued guidance."

The sandstorm had barely settled on Danielle's public dustup with NOW when the headline that I had been dreading flashed on our screens. *Girl, nine, shoots and kills her father.*

The back current of censure for Danielle's call to action at the UN became a veritable explosion. *Danielle leads violent putsch of gun-packing tykes,* and *Better wear a bullet-proof vest when tucking your daughter in,* were among the more civil condemnations that dominated the press and blogosphere. Tweets were more blunt, such as *Arrest Danielle for murder.*

"Sometimes you get criticism when you move forward," Danielle calmly told me in our Fireside that night. Security was especially tight at her performance that evening in New York, but it couldn't prevent people from screaming "killer," "assassin," and more colorful epithets as she walked on stage. She tried to sing over the shouting, but finally walked off the stage and canceled the show. "It was just a concert," she said, but the tears in her eyes betrayed her reaction.

Meanwhile, I read everything I could about the incident and something didn't add up. Danielle and I met with our American security team. The principal investigator summarized what we knew about the case.

"The girl is in juvenile custody. Mrs. Adams has made a statement of shock at her daughter's action. The mom is the breadwinner, working as a chef's assistant. The police were called several times to respond to arguments between Mr. and Mrs. Adams, but nothing panned out. Oh, and he was actually the step-dad."

"Step-dad, huh?" Danielle took note.

Danielle dug into the dossiers the forensic team had presented and declared that she planned to interview the mom on Danielle TV.

"You sure you want to throw gasoline on a raging fire?" the PI asked.

"I don't recall asking you for public relations advice," Danielle responded icily.

Surprisingly, Mrs. Adams readily replied that she would be happy to speak with Danielle. Within hours, the two of them were talking, watched by an audience of tens of millions of people. They talked amicably about Lisa, the young girl. The mom was clearly distraught that her little girl was in detention and was deeply worried about when and whether she was going to get her back.

"You miss Stan?" Danielle asked casually as if she was talking about her husband having gone on a business trip.

The mom was at a loss for words. Her look was hard to describe. There was anger, but it did not seem directed at Danielle. Mixed in was a deep sorrow, but it did not seem to be for her departed husband.

They sat quietly and somberly. Suddenly, as if a dam had exploded, the woman broke down with a huge cry and made an almost otherworldly sound. She fell from her chair and knelt shakily. Danielle watched quietly and sympathetically.

"He was a monster!" she finally managed to say between cries of anguish. "I was a weakling. I failed to protect my daughter."

"He abused you both?" Danielle asked.

The mom nodded.

Danielle paused and added, "Well it's good riddance then, I say."

"But it should have been me pulling that trigger. I can't tell you how many times I thought of grabbing the gun."

"So, he was threatening you with it?" Danielle asked.

"When he wasn't hitting me with it," came the response.

"It's not so easy to grab a gun in those circumstances," Danielle pointed out.

"Lisa managed it," the Mom responded.

"Well, thank god for that," Danielle said.

The woman smiled for the first time, breaking the gloom that had permeated the dialogue thus far.

"You know, I don't think you've fully absorbed that he is gone. I think that it's just becoming clear to you now," Danielle said reassuringly, putting her hand on the woman's shoulder. "You don't need to be afraid anymore."

The mom nodded.

They had a prolonged hug and the meeting was over.

I wouldn't say that the interview completely ended disparagement over Danielle's call to young girls to defend their rights, but the public relations crisis was over and press and blogger attention shifted to how the police had missed the signs that this guy was a menace. A political cartoon in the Washington Post showed Lisa spinning a gun around her finger with the police portrayed as mice looking on in awe.

The shooting was ruled self-defense, and Lisa and her mom were reunited. Quietly, Danielle assigned a security team to look after them for a period of time, lest they attract the wrong kind of attention.

We returned to Saudi Arabia.

In the final weeks of her Saudi gig Danielle presided over a democratic election with multiple parties.

"I don't know how much real power this new government will have," Danielle confided. Her skepticism was shared by the western press.

"It's a start," I offered. "You've set a direction."

"I hope they stay on it," Danielle responded.

Danielle paid a state visit to Israel and met with Prime Minister Netanyahu[99] to encourage him to recognize and support the new Saudi government.

"What is a nice Jewish girl from Los Angeles doing running Saudi Arabia?" he asked her.

"I'm not exactly running it," she replied.

"Looks like that to me."

"Oh? Well, what is a nice engineer from MIT doing running Israel?"

"Ha, have you seen my coalition? You have more influence on Saudi Arabia than I do on Israel."

They continued a discussion they had started a year earlier at the United Nations about a peace agreement between Israel and the Arab and Persian worlds.

Danielle and I paid a visit to Yad Vashem,[100] Israel's Holocaust[101] museum and memorial. We wore long black dresses, Danielle's first public appearance in a dress with one white flower. We were both moved beyond tears as, together, we placed fifteen stones by the Eternal Flame,[102] representing the 15 million people of all faiths who had perished. It is not a Jewish custom to place flowers to commemorate the dead. The tradition is to use stones rather than flowers, since stones more closely reflect the permanence of the soul. After composing herself, Danielle stood beneath the giant dome of images of victims at the Hall of Remembrance[103] and shared her thoughts to a world audience.

"As the first member of the Government of Saudi Arabia to visit Yad Vashem, I want to convey the sorrow, comfort and condolence of the Saudi people to those who suffered the ineffable losses of the Shoah[104] and who suffer it still. And as a Jewish girl growing up in the wake of such a catastrophe, I feel an unreachable duty of remembrance.

"A few minutes ago, in the Hall of Names,[105] I watched a woman who, sixty years later, is still mourning the loss of her infant son. I tried to grasp the loss of that child with my own emotional arms, but failed. How, then, can I hope to grasp the loss of millions of children, parents, and grandparents from all walks of life? How do we even begin to remember the sufferers of such devastation and the bereavement of those left behind? This memorial is a noble, righteous, and heartrending start, but it is a journey without end.

"What can we say about God in the light of such evil? I am certainly not the first to ask this question. How do we reconcile the perfection of God with the reality of this unhealable wound? Was God too weak, too distracted, too diverted to counter the wickedness of human hatred on such a scale? Is there some mysterious plan in which such anguish leads to a benevolent resolution in the end? Can we even say that God exists in light of the Shoah?

"Perhaps with greater experience I will gain greater wisdom, but I look at it this way: The mother mourning her son is expressing pure love that transcends time and space. Her child lives on in that love. If there were no love there would be no mourning, so we can say that mourning is the price of love.

"If the love of a mother for a single child is unbounded, then we can say that the light emanating from the remembrance of this calamity is an infinite eruption of love. God is that love.

"Death is an eternal tragedy, whether it stems from hatred or from indifference. The Shoah resulted from both. When Hannah Arendt[106] went to interview Adolf Eichmann,[107] the architect of the Holocaust, she expected to descend into the bowels of human loathing. Instead she encountered an ordinary and prosaic bureaucrat whose malevolence resulted from his failure to question the values in his midst. The Shoah resulted at least in part from this failure of critical thinking, from this 'banality of evil,'[108] to quote her deservedly famous phrase.

"God is love. And love begat the world. And the world evolved intelligence. And with intelligence we created morality. We are the moral creatures, so overcoming suffering is *our* charge, *our* goal and we should seek to make it our destiny.

"Thus, God works through us. The Shoah was, therefore, our failure. Although we can never hope to cleanse this stain nor heal this wound, what we can and must do is commit ourselves to ensuring that the expression of such hatred will happen …

—*never again.*"[109]

Rabbi Schneerson came to Israel for his first trip outside Brooklyn (and in defiance of his own vow to not go to Israel until the arrival of the Messiah) in order to support Danielle's peace initiative. This development, which Danielle had anticipated, transformed the political dynamic. The religious right now supported Danielle's peace proposal due to a personal and spiritual loyalty to her. And although the various Chassidic rabbis are competitive, they all rallied around Rabbi Schneerson's commitment to her peace initiative. The political left in Israel had supported Danielle's peace proposal from the beginning. The centrist and central right parties, such as Kadima[110] and Likud,[111] found themselves boxed in on the right and left.

Danielle's peace proposal was different from the consensus proposals advanced by President Clinton and others after him. It started with the notion that the Arab countries should embrace Israel gratefully rather than begrudgingly. They should accept its existence, which they had not previously done. The agreement was to explicitly address this core ideological perspective.

"Your expectation with regard to Israel," Danielle told Palestine[112] and other Arab countries, "will be a self-fulfilling prophecy. Treat her as an enemy and that is what she will be. Treat her as a friend, and you will have none better."

To Israel, her advice was more practical: specifically, to prevent terrorism by relying on modern security methods such as Terahertz frequency[113] monitoring and microbot swarm[114] defenses, rather than continue with the twentieth century security concepts of geography and firepower. "Terahertz scanning,"[115] Danielle explained, "can see terrorist threats from hundreds of yards away without being detected and without harm to humans."

The situation was complicated by the new Arab democratization movement which had resulted in outspoken censure of Israel from many quarters rather than the predictable and sterile repetitions of anti-Israeli slogans of the old tyrannies. Danielle quoted Churchill[116] in

speeches and blog posts to reassure the Israeli public about the thousand new voices that were emanating from the Arab street, "democracy is the worst possible form of government … except for all of those others."

"Ultimately any peace that is fashioned between democracies will be far more durable," she counseled. "Outspoken critical voices are essentially positive—people can voice their grievances rather than blowing things up."

Danielle was insistent that I read my stories about Zambia and Libya to the Israeli and Palestinian children, and we experimented with classes mixing both together. The kids were fascinated with my lion patrol, and all the sundry places I imagined they were hiding, even though I never saw one.

"You know, I really cannot tell these kids apart," I said to Danielle in our nightly chat.

"Yeah, I know what you mean," Danielle replied, "not until they open their mouths do their languages, accents, and stories of their experiences give them away. The kids are more influential on their parents than the other way around, so this is really very helpful, Claire. And I especially like your stories."

"Well, you're still a kid yourself, you know," I replied.

Danielle was opposed to forcibly moving or closing settlements.

"The new borders between Israel and Palestine will be specified in the agreement," she said in a speech to the Knesset.[117] "If an Israeli settlement wants to stay in Palestine, then so be it."

Although the initial reaction on both sides was that this would be a guarantee of continued strife, the Palestinian Speaker of the Parliament surprised the Israeli negotiators by saying, "We welcome the Israeli settlers to stay. We'll protect them. This is the new attitude that Danielle has asked of us."

Israel's response was that they had better do so, but in the end the agreement was accepted. The right of Palestinians to return to Israel proper was finessed with the acceptance of immigration to Israel by the original inhabitants of Israel proper who could document their situation, as well as payments from Israel and the Quartet[118] to others with less persuasive documentation.

After an intensive week of diplomacy, an agreement was forged, and a signing ceremony quickly arranged. The new Palestinian nation asked

Danielle to be their advisor. This went a long way in quieting Israeli fears.

Middle Eastern presidents and prime ministers and kings—some now constitutional monarchs—arrived to sign the agreement, along with heads of state from around the world. Danielle was given the honor of being the first to sign.

The Nobel Peace Prize[119] committee made an unusually fast decision, and their representative showed up at the ceremony with a letter announcing that Danielle had been awarded the Nobel Peace Prize.

~ℓℓ~

I watched Danielle on Life Bits from my room in Tel Aviv later that week: "I think my work is done here," Rabbi Schneerson told Danielle in a private meeting.

"Indeed, it is," Danielle replied. "You have my humblest gratitude. Your contribution was irreplaceable."

"Each of us is irreplaceable," the Rebbe replied. "As is each leaf and each blade of grass in the miraculous creation of…"

Danielle and the Rebbe gestured together to the heavens.

"People were surprised to see you," Danielle told him.

"Yes, it is true that I said I wouldn't come to the Holy Land until we could proclaim certain destined events, but the Talmud teaches us that we must always give ultimate priority to alleviating the suffering amongst us. I saw an opportunity to contribute to a more welcoming world for the Moshiach's arrival."

"A little spring cleaning then," Danielle noted.

"Yes, a blossoming of love and understanding," the Rebbe confirmed.

"Thanks be to…" Danielle concluded, and she and the Rebbe again gestured to the heavens.

~ℓℓ~

At a press conference, Danielle revealed that her Middle Eastern mission had been an assignment for her social studies class and that she had received a B+ for the course. Danielle's teacher for this class was our dad and the fact that she did not get an A generated widespread consternation. Danielle defended the grade citing escalating tension between Shiites[120] and Sunnis,[121] the continuing war in Syria, the emergence of new Sunni terrorist groups,[122] and the fact that the whole process took longer than she had anticipated.

A reporter asked her if there would be a party to celebrate the end of decades of hostilities between many Arabs and Jews.

"Oh, there'll be a party all right," Dani assured them, but she refused to say when or where.

"Any ideas, Claire?" Danielle later asked me apropos of the celebration.

"That's unlike you, Dani. Surely, you have a dozen ideas."

"We had fun with Bady and Mohi…"

"Ha ha, Dani, more Libyan apple juice? I think we need to include more people this time."

Three days later, Danielle and I along with Elliot, Tony, and Ben started playing her original dance songs—okay I had a few, too—on a makeshift stage in a large empty field in Hyde Park,[123] London. We played for no one and everyone. Danielle wore an especially bright yellow dress with roses and lilies of all colors. I had on jeans and a blue flannel shirt. We were not exactly fashion coordinated. Our security team provided instant surveillance using Terahertz scanning. Artificial intelligence[124] analyzed the images and security officers looked at anything the software found suspicious. People streamed wildly into the field and started dancing in a flash mob[125] celebration.

Squares around the world—Times Square in New York City, Plaza Mayor in Madrid, Plaza de Mayo in Buenos Aires, Zocalo in Mexico City, Tiananmen Square[126] in Beijing, and many others—were instantly converted into dance festivals. Traffic was diverted, and people streamed in to watch, listen, and dance to live coverage of our unannounced concert on huge screens.

Apparently, police departments around the world were not forewarned about the party, but were nonetheless able to smoothly handle the sudden massive crowds with help from Danielle teams by using the same scanning and software analysis that we were using in Hyde Park. Many others watched on their varied displays. I sweated completely through my flannel shirt by the end.

An estimated two billion people participated and danced in our instant two-hour celebration.

⁓ℓℓ⁓

"Most disturbing," Premier Dingxiang Zhongfa said to Déwei Guo, his deputy premier, just as our festivities ended. Zhongfa wore a slightly crumpled grey Mao jacket[127] and matching cap. Guo wore a perfectly pressed black Western-style suit with a white shirt and blue tie with thin red stripes. I wasn't aware of this conversation at the time, but Danielle and I received Guo's own Life Bits video of it several years later.

"How so?" Guo asked.

"She organized more than a half million Chinese to pack Tiananmen Square and a hundred million more throughout the country in the space of thirty minutes. No one has ever done that in the history of China. The last person to fill Tiananmen Square with that many people was Mao, and that took two months of planning."

"It was just a concert—music and dancing."

"A concert today, but perhaps something else tomorrow. Where did you say she was from?"

"Los Angeles. America," Guo replied.

"So, she just waltzes in here," Zhongfa said, "and organizes a hundred million Chinese people instantly—that is a grave concern."

"Actually," Guo replied, "she was in London at the time. She has never been to China."

"Imagine if she were to actually come here," Zhongfa said with disquiet.

"There is no indication that she has an interest in China," Guo pointed out.

"Oh really?" Zhongfa replied. "Then what was that repartee with 'all you guys and gals in Tiananmen Square' about? She managed to hold an extensive conversation with half million of our people—*in Chinese*. She had them in the palm of her hand. No Chinese leader has been able to do that; not since Mao."

"We've avoided charismatic leadership[128] since then due to the, uh, excesses of that era," Guo replied.

"It seems to me that she has an interest in China," Zhongfa observed.

"It seemed to be just banter," Guo replied. "I listened intently to see if there were any political implications."

"Organizing a tenth of the Chinese people with almost no notice is inherently political. Within minutes, there were expansive computer displays and speaker systems appearing out of nowhere in the square and all through the country. You know that's illegal?"

"Yes, we noticed that."

"It was hard to miss."

"But the people were packed so tight," Guo pointed out, "the police couldn't get to them, and anyway it would have triggered a revolution had they attempted to remove them."

"My point then," Zhongfa said.

"I have to say, some of what she says makes sense," Guo replied.

"That troubles me all the more," Zhongfa concluded. "We'll have to keep an eagle's eye out for this young lady."

PART TWO:

BOUNDING THE GREAT WALL

AGE TWELVE:
A HIDDEN DANCE OF PAIRS

Danielle and I visited our parents at our home in Pasadena and after some hugs, she and Dad became engrossed in a topic that Danielle had returned to: the nature of reality inside subatomic particles. I'll quote Danielle here, but don't ask me to explain it.

"We can see the footprint of a hidden variable[129] inside the n-dimensional membranes. If we could measure it consistently from different points in the field, it would remove the probabilistic nature of quantum mechanics.[130] I have some ideas about setting up a falsifiable experiment[131] but I need to design a rather small measurement tool. But if we did that, we'd be integrating the hidden variable with the collapse of the wave function[132] that occurs in the presence of an observer."[133]

I watched the conversation from my bedroom on the Life Bits Share[134] function which records every moment of our lives in video. This was a new feature of our Life Bits system that opened up our video streams to our parents and each other, which our IT Security Department went nuts about. "It's hard enough to keep this secure when storing the data, but if there's transmission, the potential for intrusion multiplies a hundredfold," they told us.

Danielle worked on the privacy issue herself and implemented a quantum encryption code[135] that she was happy with although IT was still nervous. "No security is perfect," she said. "We'll just have to take the chance that someone may listen in on our sister-gossip."

"There's someone I'd like you to meet who can shed some light on the hidden variable." Dad led Danielle into the living room where, unbeknownst to her, the young astrophysicist prodigy Cheng Liu was waiting.

Although Liu is his family name, he uses it as a first name in western circles. Right after his birth, his parents left their rural village in China where they worked as farmers and became factory laborers in the Guangdong region. Liu quickly distinguished himself as a student and did pioneering work expanding string theory to manifolds of two or three dimensions. The government organized a research institute based on Liu's ideas. He was the de facto chief scientist, although at fifteen he was too young to have an official title.

At the same time, he gradually became the public symbol of the nascent pro-democracy movement. This caused significant consternation and ultimately resulted in the institute easing him out under government pressure.

Of course, Danielle knew who he was. She had been an ardent fan of his since she was seven, but this was their first meeting. Danielle had watched countless hours of 3D videos of Liu, but this was different. He was actually there and responding to her. Later on, Danielle told me it was like encountering a unicorn. One with wings. A unicorn flying around the room. He was shorter than she had expected, and friendlier and happier.

Danielle wore white ballet slippers, a bow in her hair, and a light blue dress sprinkled with deep blue morning glory flowers with white star centers. She immediately curtsied deeply, as she does whenever she meets someone she profoundly admires or respects for the traditions they symbolize.

"I'll just leave the two of you to get to know one another," Dad said as he quietly left the room. Danielle was so completely focused on Liu that she didn't even notice Dad leaving.

Liu, dressed in an argyle cashmere sweater, also knelt and bowed to her. She bowed at the same time and they bumped heads on the way down. Both burst out laughing. As they tried to stand, Danielle's hair got caught in Liu's glasses which he was holding in his right hand, causing her to fall. Liu tried to catch Dani, but ended up falling over her.

"I think we're two entangled membranes,"[136] Danielle said as they tried to separate themselves, "definitely not strings."

"Ah, yes," Liu replied hesitatingly. "I think we're disentangled now."

"I'm not so sure about that," Danielle replied.

There was an awkward stillness, which Liu broke. "Do you really think we can extend membranes beyond three dimensions?"

"Why stop at three? I mean, we have the dimensions available."

"Most of them are tightly curled,"[137] Liu countered.

"If you are *within* a dimension, you don't notice the curl," Danielle explained.

"Good point, Danielle."

Danielle changed the subject. "Zhongfa seems to be weakening."

"I'd have to agree with you," Liu replied, "although that does not seem to be the common wisdom."

"There's an opportunity now," Danielle ventured. "Don't you think?"

As Danielle spoke about China's future, I noticed a slight fidget in her fingers, and I even caught her checking out her reflection in the mirrored glass of Dad's shuttered bookcases. It was strange to see her show even the slightest hint of nerves—except of course for when she falls apart completely. I wondered if Liu noticed, too.

Finally, Dad rejoined them. "I see the two of you getting along."

"Ah, yes, I was just leaving," Liu said.

Liu showed up every afternoon to continue his conversations with Danielle. I was reminded of when Elliot, Tony, and Ben started showing up to play music with Danielle.

After a month, Danielle let me watch another such encounter on Life Bits.

The two of them just sat there quietly. After what seemed like an eternity, and almost in a whisper, Danielle broke the hush, saying "You know, aside from my family, I've never been with anyone I could be silent with. And we've just met."

"It does feel like we've known each other a very long time," Liu whispered back.

They smiled at each other. "You know I based my membrane theory on your manifolds," Danielle said. They talked about manifolds and membranes and Danielle's new ideas on hidden variables.

"Like when two entangled particles meet, like when matter and antimatter[138] collide, they become one again. A hidden dance of pairs[139] that is invisible, undetectable except for their intrinsic, inseparable oneness. Always apart. Always together. Two sides of the same whole," Danielle said.

"Yes, that works," Liu replied hesitatingly.

"And the whole universe vibrates in merriment," Danielle said.

"Yes, it's very possible," Liu replied. "There could be other entangled particles[140] far away."

"Like little children," Danielle continued.

Trying to transition the conversation, Liu brought up his Institute. "It's not exactly my institute anymore."

"You may not work there physically now, but none of the scientists will dare take a step, scientifically or politically, without checking with you," Danielle countered.

"That may be true, but how did you know that, Danielle?" Liu asked quizzically.

"I need to keep up on these things."

"Yes, of course you do."

Neither of them spoke for a while and Liu kept readjusting his sitting position.

Danielle broke the silence. "Entanglement is a bond that transcends time and space. The two particles could be a million miles apart and it is still as if they are one."

"That's right," Liu said nervously. "You've always been a very quick study, Danielle, in more ways than one."

"We can only move at the speed of light."[141]

"Are you sure about that?"

"Well, because of Heisenberg's Uncertainty Principle,[142] we can't measure exact speed or location. Actual measurements will reflect a Gaussian distribution[143] around the speed of light. So, some will appear to be going ever so slightly faster," Danielle pointed out.

"Good point. I hadn't thought of that."

"Am I too fast, Liu? Am I faster than you?" Danielle asked.

"No," Liu replied, "maybe slower, but I have a problem that you don't have."

Danielle stared at Liu wistfully, and finally said, "Yes I understand. I'm twelve."

"You're no ordinary twelve-year-old girl," Liu interrupted.

Danielle laughed. "No twelve-year-old girl is ordinary."

"You know what I mean, Danielle."

"My sister found true love at the age of ten. So, you could say I'm slow," Danielle noted.

"Yes," Liu said, "but hers was with another ten-year-old. We're nearly four years apart. There's half a lifetime between twelve and almost sixteen."

"Well, about a third of a lifetime in my case," Danielle replied. "Anyway, it worked out pretty well. Claire and Charlie are still going strong. Love has no age, no limit, and no death."

"That's very poetic."

"Yeah, well, John Galsworthy[144] said it," Danielle replied.

"It's a nice quote to have handy," Liu said.

"He also said 'Beginnings are always messy,'" Danielle added.

"That's true of most every beginning I can think of," Liu said.

Danielle bit her lip. "In my experience, when a goal is rooted in love and transcendence, there is always a way around any obstacle."

"Who said that?" Liu asked.

"Oh, I just made it up myself."

Liu looked down at the floor, and there was more silence.

"I'm sorry to make you uncomfortable," Danielle offered. "Just tell me you don't like me and I'll leave you alone."

There was another long pause. Liu replied, "I can't tell you that."

Danielle smiled. "That's the most romantic double negative I've ever heard!"

There was another pause. "Okay, then, I've got the solution, Danielle."

She looked intently at him.

"I'll just wait for you."

"You mean we'll wait for each other," Danielle responded.

"Yeah, right," Liu said.

Danielle looked up, raised her eyebrows, and she replied playfully, "So ... how long are we going to wait? Until I'm thirteen? In the Jewish tradition I'd be a woman then."

They blushed. "I think a thirteen-year-old girl and a guy who's almost seventeen is even more of a problem."

"How about sixteen then?" Danielle countered. "I hear that's the age of consent."

Liu replied, "We're not really talking about *that*, are we? I mean you've taken a vow of chastity until marriage, haven't you? At least that's what I've read."

"Eighteen?" she asked in a soft voice.

"That's getting there," Liu replied. "An eighteen-year-old girl can choose whomever she likes."

"Eighteen-year-old *woman*, I think is the correct term," Danielle noted.

"It may not qualify as the biggest scandal to hit the *National Enquirer*," Liu said, "but a public relationship would undergo scrutiny given our leadership roles. People would consider eighteen too young for that kind of responsibility."

"Ah, yes, the burdens of leadership," Danielle said with a touch of sarcasm. "We have to set a good example."

"So, what do you suggest, Danielle?"

"I've been making suggestions. How about we wait until I'm fifty-two? That's forty years from now, the amount of time Moses[145] waited to see the Promised Land."[146]

"But he never got to see it," Liu pointed out.

"Yes, good point," Danielle replied.

Liu suggested, "Why don't we wait until you're twenty-one?"

"You're going to wait nine years for me?" Danielle asked.

"And you for me?"

"What about …" Danielle began, perhaps realizing how long nine years really was.

"We'll want to make some rules, I guess," Liu offered.

"Right. The rules are: no rules. I expect that you'll want to date other girls, or, uh, women."

"And the same for you. You should date other boys, or men, when you get to that point. And if you should fall in love, so be it. You should pursue that love."

"If you can say that, you must not really care about me," Danielle said.

"Or I care too much and want you to be happy, whatever it takes. If after nine years, you feel with the benefit of hindsight that you and I aren't right for each other, then you should send me on my way. It will be an honor just to remain your friend."

"That's very romantic, Liu."

"That makes me think of something else," Liu said. "It would not make sense to avoid touching each other but then to engage in romantic talk."

"You mean like we're doing now?" Danielle asked.

"Yes, well, our understanding needs to last for nine years, so we're getting a running start," Liu pointed out.

"Let's call romantic talk 'RT,' and we can call each other on it," Danielle suggested.

"Okay, I think we have two rules now," Liu concluded.

A couple of days later I came home to find pieces of fabric and ribbon scattered all around Danielle's room. She was sitting on her bed.

"It's a complete mess," Danielle exclaimed, pointing to a doll she was making.

"This is—" I started to say.

"—yes, a Danielle doll," Danielle finished my thought.

"Okay, that's nice," I replied. Then I noticed a doll of a smiling Chinese boy. "This is Liu?"

"Yeah, he gave it to me."

"He made it?"

"No. He got it from a handmade doll shop that his aunt owns."

"I see. Your, uh, Danielle doll isn't too bad."

"Yeah, if I want to scare him away."

Danielle and I stayed up half the night finishing her doll. The face needed a lot of work, so my drawing skills came in handy.

The next day, Mom, who was not entirely enthusiastic about Danielle's new friendship, had a little discussion with Dad. I didn't have Life Bits on this one, but Mom told me about it later.

"What kind of father fixes up his twelve-year-old daughter with a boy several years older?" Mom said pointedly.

"It wasn't a fix-up, I just introduced them."

"You're arguing with me about semantics? What difference do those words make? She fell head over heels for the boy."

Dad paused for a few moments trying to find the right words to explain the situation, or at least his role in it. "You know they were going to meet, and soon. There was no stopping it. She started reading his writings when she was six, and she's read everything he's ever written multiple times, including every blog post. There's every reason to believe that he's done the same with her writings. Her physics project is an extension of his work. And they're both democracy pioneers. How did you think you were going to stop them from meeting?"

"I'm not suggesting stopping anything. We could have let nature take its course and hope that she would proceed responsibly."

Dad said, "I guess I felt that if they met here we would have more—"

"—control of the situation?" Mom suggested, finishing Dad's sentence.

"Did you say control?" Dad said laughing heartily. "Control Danielle? Now there's an oxymoron! I'd have more luck guiding the North Wind. No, I'm thinking of a more subtle form of influence, to … uh … as you say, proceed responsibly."

"I suppose I'm more concerned about Master Liu," Mom added. "I mean, what do we know about him?"

"Cheng Liu, I can vouch for. His intentions and behavior come from a deeply honorable place few people can truly understand."

"Really? I sure hope you know what you're doing," Mom said.

"Actually, I have no idea what I'm doing. My only instinct is to protect our girls."

Meanwhile, Danielle worked on a cure for cancer as an extra credit project for her biology class. She used the method Dad always talks about. "Imagine yourself giving a speech in the future," Dad says. "Imagine you are explaining your solution and how it works. What would you be saying? What would you have to say? Work backwards from there."

"Well I would have to say," Danielle spoke to her future audience, for which I was the stand-in, "that I solved the problem of the asymptoting logarithmic response curve[147] of pathogen count to total dosage in the following way." She was referring to a pernicious phenomenon that had thwarted cancer research for decades. "When a population of pathogens such as cancer cells is exposed to an anti-pathogenic agent, a plot of the fraction of the surviving population of pathogens as seen on a logarithmic scale[148] will decline in a straight line—meaning exponential decline—going from one hundred percent to ten percent to one percent to a tenth of a percent and so on, but instead of continuing to oblivion, the curve levels off usually at something like one in a million or one in a hundred million of the original population.

"Then after a period of time, the population goes back up to 100 percent or beyond, again in a straight line on the logarithmic scale (meaning exponential growth) with a different slope.

"The reason for this is obvious: The pathogen has evolved around the attack. Or to put it another way, there is genetic variation in the population of cancer cells due to DNA replication errors.[149] The one cell per million or hundred million that has a genetic 'error' enables it to survive the attack. Therefore, its descendants are all immune to the toxin.

"The only way to address this is with a cocktail hitting the enemy several different ways at the same time so that it does not have time to evolve around the attack, kind of like a karate combination of multiple punches combined with a drop kick to the heart, all at about the same time.

"But the problem with cancer goes beyond this phenomenon. Even a cocktail[150] for killing cancer cells would not be sufficient unless the progenitor cell—the cancer stem cell[151] that produces the cancer cells in the first place—is also destroyed. For the same reason, we will need a cocktail for that, as well. And the patient needs to survive both cocktails."

That's as far as Danielle got with her imaginary speech.

"Go on," I prompted.

"Sorry, Claire, I didn't get very far."

"You seem to have a pretty complete statement of the problem."

"Yes, I suppose we can't solve a problem until we can state it."

"And as far as I can see," I added, "no one else has ever done that before with cancer."

Later in the year, after Danielle had been working on her cancer project for several months, I was nominated for a Sundance Film Festival[152] Award for Best Screenplay for a movie called *Liberté*, a true story about a secret society of teenage girls in Paris during the French Revolution.[153] These girls took the ideas of democracy and liberty very seriously and worked behind the scenes to save a community of artists from the excesses of the revolution by hiding them in secret compartments they built in abandoned buildings. I based my screenplay on a story that had been buried in the archives of the Sorbonne. And tonight was *my* night—the first time I had ever been nominated for a significant prize.

I did help Danielle get dressed in a silver dress that shone in the light and flowed to the ground. It had red flowers, each one different. I asked her what the flowers were, and she texted me a link to a compilation of autumn flowers of California. We both agreed that it made more sense for her to wear a variation of her signature look than to wear a little girl version of a grown-up dress. I helped her with her mascara and lipstick, which she wanted to be understated. She helped me get ready, as well, or tried to, but I must say this was one area she was not an expert in.

I was up against some tough competition, specifically a movie called *Passing Passion* written by Adolpho Cayetano, based on Cayetano's immensely popular amorous novel of the same name, which had been translated into English by his wife Adelita. It had already been announced that Cayetano and his wife would share the Nobel Prize for literature for the Spanish and English versions of the book. This remarkable shared Nobel literature prize recognized Adelita's unusually adept translation and the long, intricate, supremely poetic, and sensuous sentences in the book. *Passing Passion* was so popular and admired it was favored to win. Many had called the book the best romantic novel of the past century.

Danielle, Charlie, and I sat together at a table with Jackie Rock and a woman I didn't recognize. Danielle and Charlie cheered exuberantly when my name was called as a nominee. But as I expected, Cayetano won.

"This is indeed a brilliant book," Cayetano said in his acceptance remarks.

He waited for a few moments, and added, "You know how we Spaniards can be. Juan Belmonte[154] was not very shy about his bullfighting skills. And surely you remember Salvador Dali."[155]

The audience applauded his acknowledgment that his opening comment was a bit hubristic and allowing that he deserved to be prideful.

"You definitely had my vote, Claire. Cayetano is rather full of himself. The Institute seems to be confusing arrogance with talent," Danielle offered as we walked to Jackie Rock's after party.

"I was happy to have been nominated."

"Yes, that's quite an achievement."

"I don't mind having lost to *Passing Passion*, Danielle. It's actually a rather brilliant book."

"Yeah, I agree with you there, but I liked *Liberté* a lot more. It reminded me of our escapades together."

"You've read Passing Passion?"

"Oh sure, I've read all of Cayetano's books."

"Isn't that a bit of a grown-up reading list for a twelve-year-old?"

"Twelve and a half," Danielle replied with a smile. "Besides, many of the intelligence briefings we've read are not exactly PG."

"After reading about the world according to Cayetano," I asked, "how do you feel now about our vows?"

"I feel better about them," Danielle replied.

"You mean it makes you want to avoid the messy situations that Cayetano's characters get into?"

"No, not exactly. I don't mind messy. I just feel that reading about these experiences is as good as actually having them," she said. "I'd say that encounters we have through reading are actually better because we're more reflective and less likely to get carried away, like Cayetano's characters do."

"Hmmm, I'm not sure everyone would agree with you. I mean if that were true, why are people so eager to get into these situations in, uh, real life?"

"I guess they're not very good readers," Danielle replied.

"Or maybe," I added, "they're not reading works by very good writers."

"Yeah, writers like you, Claire."

"I mean, that's the goal of literature, isn't it?" I clarified. "To transport you to another time and place. To put you in someone else's shoes. To see through their eyes. To feel through their skin. To live in their home. And under their sky."

Danielle and I took off our shoes which were killing our feet and held hands as we entered the party.

Between urgent calls with Peter Revoy, her Danielle Music Chief Operating Officer, Danielle returned to her cancer project. She also continued her imaginary speech about how she overcame the exponential asymptote problem that has plagued every other cancer treatment, with me acting as imaginary audience in her bedroom back at home. This reminded me of when the three-year-old Danielle was my imaginary audience when I practiced for CMA.

"I figured that an effective cocktail would combine orthogonal approaches[156] because otherwise one genetic change in the pathogen will defeat multiple parts of the cocktail. I was able to combine three existing agents that destroy cancer cells using very different pathways. Evolving around these diverse mechanisms is essentially impossible. This also streamlines regulation as there is existing experience with each agent.

"But I also needed to address the cancer stem cell. It has a completely different biochemistry and uses different reproductive enzymes[157] so it needs a completely different cocktail. Moreover, there is tension between the needs of the anti-cancer cocktail and the anti-cancer stem cell cocktail. Cancer stem cells thrive in anaerobic conditions,[158] that is without oxygen, exactly the conditions that chemotherapy drugs[159] create to kill eukaryotic cancer cells.[160] This is a principal reason that cancer returns.

"Ultimately, I found three orthogonal approaches to destroying cancer stem cells. But now the problem is that since all of the experience in the so-called war on cancer has been in attacking cancer cells and not cancer stem cells, none of these drugs has any record and none are approved. Although the FDA[161] does not explicitly ban cocktails, the rules make it all but impossible to actually put a cocktail through approval in a reasonable timeframe. The procedure is supposed to be that each drug has to be put through on its own, whereas none of the drugs may in fact work by themselves. Even if they do, the whole process would take much too long."

"I have a question," I piped up.

"Yes, you there in the last row," Danielle replied.

"But the AIDS cocktail[162] got through," I asked.

"Ah yes, it got through all right," Danielle answered her interrogator. "Since the AIDS activists were already orphaned from society and were allied with like-minded doctors and lawyers and knew exactly what they wanted, they rammed it through with very forceful political, legal, and extralegal tactics. If only the cancer patients were as alienated and aggressive, they might succeed, too. Instead most are passive, thankful for whatever tired and expensive crumbs the regulatory system will toss their way.

"I'll have to reword that," Danielle said as an aside, "so I'm not insulting cancer patients."

After many more imaginary speeches and a few actual experiments, Danielle had her two cocktails. She arranged to test them in China, Cambodia, and Haiti, given the impossibility of conducting useful trials in the US. I coordinated the Haitian experiments.

Even Haiti let us test only on the sickest patients, but one by one people on the edge of death were pulled into remission.

Six months later the results were holding and microscopic analyses, including extremely sensitive blood marker tests Danielle had devised, indicated total remission for ninety-eight percent of the thousands of patients she had tested.

She presented her results, which created a stir and an immediate worldwide demand for the treatment, especially for those critically ill patients who didn't have time to wait for further corroboration. One country after another approved the Danielle cancer treatment with varying degrees of liberalism as to who was allowed to get them.

The US Food and Drug Administration, however, refused to budge from its usual rigid procedures, which would take years, especially since the treatment involved not one but two cocktails. After discussing the matter with Dad and me, she decided on a Gordian knot solution.

She began distributing the treatment kits in the United States without any government approval to any medical provider willing to be trained in their use and to prescribe them. Outraged, the FDA declared the activity blatantly illegal and warned that there would be arrests if it continued.

The Medical Director of the Mayo Clinic,[163] a strong supporter of the Danielle Cancer Protocol, arranged a public meeting at their Jacksonville, Florida hospital during which Danielle ceremoniously presented him with a box of the kits. It was bigger than she was.

They were both arrested.

This was of course covered by Danielle TV, and her usual viewership of a hundred million viewers quickly grew to over a billion. Danielle was taken to a juvenile detention center which was part of a federal prison complex that also housed men and women.

It was no accident that the warden of the prison was an ardent Daniellite. He permitted her entire entourage—which included me, Mom and Dad, plus extensive security, audio/visual, and press contingents—to go in with her as guests. The world watched as she and I were given a tour of the prison by the warden.

The inmates decorated their bunks with letters, photos, and drawings. In the women's section I noticed a drawing, apparently by a child, of a woman with wings flying out of the prison courtyard. Danielle spoke with the inmates at length, probing them for their stories, so the public heard the narratives behind the faces of her new friends.

"Twenty years, really?" Danielle asked John, a prisoner. "What did you do, hijack a plane?"

"No, I was just selling marijuana."

"That's hard to believe," Danielle replied.

"Let me tell you what happened," John explained. "My school was full of overworked teachers and overstressed police. There was more for me to learn outside its walls, or so I thought, so I dropped out. I needed money and took the easy way out. I started dealing, and one day, the perfect storm hit. My supplier accidentally provided me with twice the amount we agreed on. I was going to return the extra, but my arrest came before I had the chance, so I was over the threshold for being a large distributor. And I had a knife in my back pocket."

"That's awful," Danielle said.

"Awful, yes," I commented, "but not surprising. We were just discussing in Social Histories class how the number of incarcerated people has vastly and steadily shot up since the 1970s. And black men like John are five times more likely to be arrested on a drug offense, even though the prevalence of drug use among black and white men is virtually the same."

"And when you've been in prison once," John added, "it's not too long before you're back here again."

ℓℓ

"I love your new outfit, Dani," I commented on her orange jumpsuit. "Did you pick that out yourself?"

"Actually, there was a choice. There was a yellow one, but it was even bigger on me than this one."

"No flower prints?"

"Maybe we can paint them on."

Which we did. Danielle had brought yellow paint and a brush into prison with her—planning to spruce up her prison garb with a yellow bird of paradise.

That evening, still clad in her jumpsuit, she performed an hour-long concert backed by Elliot, Tony, and Ben on guitars and drums and myself on mandolin. The concert took place in the large recreation courtyard and was attended by all of the prisoners—men and women, as well as the children from the juvenile detention center. It was the first time they had all been together. The inmates were wildly enthusiastic, and the world audience reached two billion people for her concert.

"What flower is that?" asked a man with several missing front teeth who was seated in the first row.

Danielle sang, paraphrasing Oliver Wendell Holmes:[164]

With hues from heaven so freshly born,
With burning star and flaming band,
Kindling all the sunset land,
It's the starry flower of liberty

She sang of loneliness:

Waking from a wintry sleep
With the storms cloud parted
Where is my heart?

And she sang of freedom:

Embracing the mist
With Our bodies
And a leap
To the other side

The next day, the largest demonstration in American history took place, with five million people descending on Washington and many millions more in other American cities, as well as cities around the world.

Signs and banners read, Free Danielle, Mr. President: Another 1500 People Dead Today From Cancer, and Hey Hey FDA, How Many People Did You Kill Today?

Danielle addressed the worldwide protest from the prison.

President Obama[165] was furious with his administration for stumbling into this situation. "We can't take on Danielle, that's crazy," he told his attorney general. "Get her out of that prison immediately."

In her cell Danielle commented on the offer she had just received from the administration. "Clemency, huh?"

"I guess you seem like a needy case," I responded.

"I don't think there's anything I need clemency for," Danielle said, handing the letter back to the warden. She didn't rip it up as she didn't want to show disrespect to the warden.

The administration tried other means, such as providing bail or even dropping the charges, but they all required Danielle's and our family's cooperation. We refused all cooperation unless the law under which she was arrested was revoked and rewritten, and she had already provided the draft of a new law to do exactly that. She also demanded that the head of the FDA and the Secretary of Health and Human Services be replaced immediately with people she had identified.

This caused the Attorney General to revert to an aggressive strategy and ordered the warden to be fired for gross dereliction of duty, but the order was refused by the chain of command between him and the warden. They were all Daniellites, too.

ℓℓ

"Loved when you sang 'Twenty Years Apart' last night. I've only got six months, but it seems like twenty years," Danielle's bunk mate, Roxanne, said.

Danielle smiled and asked, "So what are you doing here?"

"Oh, I fell in with these girls—each one was nice, but we were mean when we got together. We broke some windows and messed up some walls. Well, my friend Mary got off; Charlotte and Sandi are down the corridor, but I don't want to see them."

Liu showed up at the prison for a private meeting with Danielle. I watched on Life Bits Share. Our Life Bits technology had just been expanded so the view was not only from Danielle's or my eyes but from tiny cameras in the vicinity. So, if I were watching Danielle's Life Bits, I could now see Danielle herself, not just her point of view.

"I took the foundation jet immediately upon hearing the news. You looked great on TV, but how are you holding up?" Liu asked.

"So, I looked great on TV, huh, but not so good now with you?"

Danielle did look disheveled, her raven hair ragged. But her eyes shone with an inner light of conviction. Her face was red.

"You are always radiant to me," Liu said.

"Ah ha, RT!" Danielle exclaimed.

"We've never done a great job of avoiding that, Danielle. But this must be traumatic…"

"It's fine, really. Everything is going smoothly, just as we planned."

"You know getting arrested and stuff like that is not always so straightforward," Liu cautioned.

"Come on, this is America, not Libya before the revolution, or, uh, China."

"Has anyone hurt or threatened you?"

"I'm a VIP prisoner, and anyway Gerald and his team are down the hall," Danielle said referring to her security detail. "Most prisoners here are lucky if even one other prisoner looks out for them, and I've got my whole security team."

"I know everything went down as you had mapped out, but I couldn't bear anything happening to you."

"You know if you don't stop all this RT, I'm going to give you a big sloppy kiss and then you'll be sorry."

They reverted to sitting together silently, as they often did when they ran out of things to say—which happened frequently, given all of the restrictions they had put on their time together.

"We could talk about muons?"[166] Danielle suggested sheepishly.

"I don't think I would be of much use on the subject at the moment as I've been up for two days," Liu replied.

"I hear muon neutrinos can go faster than the speed of light," Danielle noted.

"Like us, Danielle?"

They went back to their mutual meditation with their eyes wide open.

ℓℓ

Meanwhile, the demonstrations persisted and grew, prodding Congress to quickly pass legislation implementing Danielle's recommended changes to the FDA charter with a veto-proof margin.

Years later in Hillary Clinton's[167] memoir, this conversation came to light. "How did we get in this corner?" the president asked his secretary of state.

"You took your eye off the ball, sir."

"So what do you recommend?"

"Don't stand on pride. Just do what she's asking. You'll be friends again, privately and publicly. I have assurances that she'll quickly repair the damage. You're on the wrong side of history at the moment, but she has provided a bridge to the other side."

The president sent word he would abide by her demands and he took Air Force One to Jacksonville to escort her from the prison. She curtsied deeply when the president showed up and gave him a tour of the prison while introducing him to several model inmates.

"That clemency thing you offered? Well, here's a guy you should do it for," Danielle told the president, introducing him to John.

As the dust settled, blame for the incident centered on the departed officials. Deflecting blame away from the president was part of Danielle's plan as she wanted him to be reelected as a lame duck. That would suit her future plans.

The president did grant clemency to John and others whom Danielle recommended, and implemented changes to the prison system that she and the Jacksonville warden suggested, such as access to online courses and email for well-behaved prisoners.

Once John was released, we heard he went on to start an organization that lobbied for prison reform.

The cancer cure held up. Although some observers continued to express reservations until more time went by, Danielle demonstrated new ultra-sensitive cancer tests which showed the original cancers had been completely destroyed and were not going through the usual initial steps of growing back at a microscopic level.

"Yes, I'd like you on the board," I overheard Danielle say from the hallway outside her room at home. She was talking to Martine Rothblatt, inviting her to be part of another new Danielle company, Danielle Stem Cell. "But we don't need investment capital this time," Danielle said. "You can have one percent for the board position. Since the company already has significant value, I'm afraid they will have to be nonstatutory stock options.[168] And yes, I'm doing the same thing with Danielle," Danielle said, referring to giving ninety percent of her stock to her foundation.

The Nobel Prize guy showed up again.

"You're too young to be so blasé about these things, Danielle," I said after she got word that she won a Nobel Prize in medicine for her cancer work.

"I know I should enjoy this more, Claire, but my mind is obsessed with the next tribulation."

"You should take a moment to savor a job well done."

Danielle folded her hands in her lap and twiddled her thumbs. "So just how long is a moment?"

I'LL BREAK ITS LEGS IF I HAVE TO

Danielle and I had a week together in Pasadena before she left for China on her thirteenth birthday. I was surprised at how she was starting to mature physically, though she managed to hide it from the public.

I was watching on Life Bits Share as she arrived in Tianjin to meet up with Liu. They sat together in a public park and she swept into his arms weeping. Liu did not know what the crying was about, but held her and tried his best to comfort her. After about twenty minutes her crying gradually subsided.

"Is something the matter, Danielle?"

"No, nothing at all, why do you ask?"

"It just seemed like the thing to say."

"Okay, I'm sorry. It was just one of my anxiety attacks. Not a big deal at all."

"I didn't know about that. I guess I'm still learning about you."

"Yeah, well, I try not to have them when you're around. But it's nothing. I just need to hold someone for a while and it goes away."

"That could be awkward, depending on who you're with. I mean it would have been interesting if it happened when you were meeting with William Silverstone or King Abdullah."

"Interesting like the old Chinese curse, may you live in interesting times? Claire has made the same observation."

"If you ask me, I think you were just angling for a hug," Liu said.

"Definitely, that was it. I'm still trying to get you in trouble."

"So seriously, Danielle, how long have you been getting these, uh, panic attacks?"

"Hmm, since I was two."

"That's when you started to speak."

"Yes. I should go silent again."

"What exactly were you feeling?"

"Just the usual, you know. My chest gets tight. I can't breathe. I'm shaking. My stomach is exploding. I feel the walls, floor, and ceiling closing in on me."

"Like the garbage disposal scene in *Star Wars*?"[169]

"Exactly like that, Liu."

"Maybe you're finding your assignments too demanding."

"I'm not so unusual like that. Most kids find their schoolwork stressful."

"You do have interesting projects, Danielle."

"Actually, I think these tasks protect me from my sense of abandonment. I get distracted by thinking them through."

"I can relate to that," Liu replied.

～ℓℓ～

Danielle and Liu went back to sitting with their hands folded in their laps, occasionally talking about whether quantum events are really indeterminate.

I must say he was pretty good at comforting her. He seemed to know just what to do. Dani's unrelationship was providing another cry pillow.

Before they said goodbye, Liu urged Danielle to get more involved with issues of Chinese society.

"We could really use your help. Party Chairman Zhao has been supportive, probably the first chairman sympathetic to our cause. The prospects for moving to democracy have never been brighter."

They decided she would attempt to settle the Tibet question[170] as a way of familiarizing herself with Chinese politics. She had a successful meeting with Chairman Zhao, and together they went to convene with President Hu[171] who was much more cautious. She told Hu that they had a unique but time-limited opportunity to reach an agreement with the Dalai Lama.[172]

"Once he's gone," Danielle pointed out, "there will be no one who has the moral or political authority to agree to a settlement."

President Hu was moved by her argument about the fragility of the opportunity, so he supported Danielle reaching out to the Dalai Lama. This actually proved to be the more difficult encounter. Their session, broadcast on Danielle TV, took place in a beautiful Buddhist monastery in upstate New York. It was a delicate white building with an eight-sided structure for the second floor, with five windows on each of the five sides. On top of that was a turret with a gold dome. The Dalai Lama sat on a small ornate stage while Danielle sat on a rug on the floor in front of him.

His idea for autonomy, even though it fell short of the independence demanded by younger, more impatient Tibetan leaders in exile, would not fly, Danielle told him. The reality was that Tibetans had become a minority in Tibet.

The Dalai Lama responded by patiently describing the history of Tibet's de facto independence for the first half of the twentieth century, the ill-fated Seventeen-Point Agreement[173] between the Tibetan government and the People's Republic, the systematic repression of Tibetan culture, the brutal suppression of the 1959 uprising,[174] and the forced mass immigration of Han Chinese[175] into Tibet.

"There was supposed to be a 'one country, two systems' policy,[176] but these promises were short lived," the Dalai Lama told Danielle while the world watched and listened.

"Your Holiness, I don't take issue with your recounting of history, and people can debate endlessly whether the current situation of ethnic balance in Tibet was engineered intentionally or is the unintended byproduct of other agendas, or a bit of both, but the reality of the Han majority cannot be ignored.

"I have a different proposal," Danielle continued. "One that is perhaps more ambitious, but reflects the worldwide consensus for how

this type of ethnic issue should be resolved. The idea is to have full religious and cultural freedom in Tibet. If you are indeed not advocating independence for Tibet—which I don't think I could deliver, and in any event, you would then have a country that is still dominated by non-Tibetans—then I think this is the only answer."

The meeting ended inconclusively. That evening, the Dalai Lama assembled with younger Tibetan leaders who were outraged by Danielle pressing them to drop their autonomy demand. They wanted to move the other way and declare Tibet's full independence from Beijing.

In the midst of this unsettled situation, Danielle shuttled back to Beijing. She was able to arrange for a conference between President Hu, the Dalai Lama, Chairman Zhao, Liu, and herself.

Meanwhile an epic struggle was developing in China. On one side were Liu's pro-democracy supporters and the growing corps of Chinese Daniellites. On the other side were conservatives who believed that only anarchy would come from implementing Western democratic ideas and that this was to be avoided at all costs.

At the same time, demonstrations organized by young Tibetan activists broke out in American cities, including New York, indirectly criticizing the Dalai Lama but directly and harshly criticizing Danielle. There was shoving and broken store windows in a Tibetan neighborhood in Jackson Heights, Queens.

Danielle proceeded with the summit. Disturbed and disappointed by the discord among his own ranks, the Dalai Lama surprised the world by embracing Danielle's call for religious freedom in Tibet and dropping his advocacy of autonomy. The session appeared to go well, but in the background, out of sight of the media, the conflict in China was taking a toll, including disappearances, suppression of demonstrations, and arrests. I monitored the response of different Chinese constituencies and became increasingly uneasy about what I was hearing. Danielle called upon her supporters to keep protests peaceful.

A massive Chinese demonstration broke out in Tiananmen Square supporting the Tibetan protestors, and calling for general religious and political freedom. In what appeared to be a looming moment of historical déjà vu, Red Army tanks headed for the demonstrators.

However, President Hu, whose style strongly preferred trying to defuse conflicts quietly and out of the limelight, did not want to leave a Tiananmen Square II as his legacy. At the last moment, he overruled the Commander of the Red Army[177] and ordered all tanks to return to their bases. With Chairman Zhao's blessing, he approved the tentative agreement Danielle had proposed in the meeting with the Dalai Lama. Religious freedom for Tibetan Buddhism[178] was declared in Tibet. The demonstrators dispersed.

Danielle and Liu saw this as a foot in the door. Recognition of freedom of religion in Tibet was likely to spread to other parts of China and to other freedoms. Of course, their opponents saw it the same way, but were far less enthusiastic about the implications.

Having now worked together, Danielle and Liu spent more time alone. They ended each of their working sessions by sitting together on the floor.

"I like this part of our get-togethers. It's like meditation," Liu pointed out.

"It's like kissing," Danielle countered.

"RT, Danielle!"

"Okay, okay, it was just a metaphor."

"All language is metaphorical, Danielle."

Awakening from the trance of a mutual reflection session, Danielle exclaimed, "You know, the hidden variable is like a gear, and because of the limitation of state information in a quantum field,[179] we should be able to read the gear position by taking multiple readings in time and space of the field."

"Whoa. Let's step through that, uh, one quantum[180] at a time."

This started a long conversation on how to design a falsifiable experiment to confirm the hidden quantum variable.[181]

They finally left the study, where they had been alone together all day and night, and rejoined their entourages on the main office floor of

Liu's institute, like two kids sneaking back home in the first light of morning.

Several months later, Danielle was home with me in Pasadena while Liu stayed in a nearby hotel in Pasadena. The Tibetan agreement was holding, and Danielle focused on manifolds. I was writing my book on Danielle's and my adventures together during her early life.

Liu asked to come over to visit Danielle in her room. She beamed as he walked in, but Liu's somber expression did not match her glow. She sensed something was wrong and felt immediately thunderstruck. She found herself slipping into her endless dark room, and feared that she was having one of her attacks.

"We need to talk, Danielle," Liu said solemnly.

She realized that this time her panic did not originate in her mind alone. Something was actually happening here. She sensed what it was.

"I don't think we should continue seeing each other as we are doing."

Danielle's mind raced. She had never contemplated actually hearing the words that she had just heard, but they confirmed her worst fear from only seconds earlier. Her eyes spoke of something precious and irreplaceable having just slipped through her fingers. She seemed to be thinking, *Why is this happening? I can argue against this,* but she couldn't speak.

I learned later that Liu was overwhelmed by Danielle's strong silent reaction. He'd had a whole speech in mind, with explanations and comforting things he had planned to say, but it all seemed irrelevant in the moment.

Neither Danielle nor Liu were able to say a word. After a few minutes of agonizing silence, Liu seemed to feel there was no alternative but for him to just slip away. He thought of taking her hand and squeezing it as a final gesture, but it seemed like the wrong thing to do, so he simply left.

He called me to tell me what had just happened. I had not been on Life Bits Share, but from the details Liu shared in the call and the tone of his voice, I felt almost as devastated as Danielle must have been. Later I learned he had things in mind to say to me, too, but apparently nothing felt appropriate, so all I got was a brief, stark call.

I rushed to Danielle's room. She was still sitting there distraught, not crying exactly, but gripped by a private agony. I cycled through some things I could say, but decided to just take her hand. We just sat that way for hours until we both fell asleep in her bed.

ll

The next morning, Danielle's face had a serious and determined expression. She didn't have her usual lighthearted step and sense of humor, but at least she was moving.

"So, I have this design for the hidden variable measurement," she said.

"Can we talk about what happened last night?"

"No, no," Danielle replied. "There's nothing to discuss. We need to talk about the hidden variable."

I went along with this, figuring I'd hear more about the previous evening soon enough. "I can't say that I fully understand these formulas, but if you measure the hidden variable, then it's not hidden anymore? You'd have to call it something else."

"It's very indirect," Danielle replied.

"That's true of most measurements in physics,[182] isn't that right, Danielle?"

"Okay, I'll have to give that some thought," Danielle said.

Over the next several weeks I was able to help Danielle organize the equipment she needed, including gaining access to the CERN accelerator.[183]

"Liu wants us to focus on the hidden variable," Danielle said in her only comment on the change in her relationship with Liu.

"Hidden variable, that seems appropriate," I replied. Danielle frowned.

Danielle conducted the experiment that she and Liu had designed and indeed, she confirmed the existence of the hidden variable. But this "gear" mechanism inside a particle revealed another multi-dimensional field[184] that has a probabilistic element,[185] so the indeterminate nature of quantum mechanics[186] was preserved—at least that was my understanding of it. Nonetheless, Danielle and Liu, despite their severed alliance, had advanced the understanding of nature at an even finer scale.

～ℓℓ～

Six months later, Danielle was awakened with disturbing news. Both Chairman Zhao and Cheng Liu had been arrested. The agreement with Tibet and the Dalai Lama had not yet been suspended, but was put under review.

Stunned, Dani told me that she intended to travel to the prison to speak to Liu.

"That may be dangerous," I said. "And you haven't seen Liu since, well, you know. Are you really prepared for that?"

"It's strictly business, Claire," she replied. "We still have jobs to do here. As for safety, I have that under control."

"Whatever you say, dearest sister, but I'm coming with you."

～ℓℓ～

Liu was very circumspect as Danielle was led into his cell. He had multiple reasons to feel sheepish about being in her presence.

"We have to stop meeting like this," Liu said, but quickly realized it was not funny and Danielle was not smiling. Even so, Liu continued to try to lighten the tone. "Everything is going according to plan; isn't that what you said to me when I visited you in prison?"

"That was true then, but it is not true now," Danielle responded firmly, "and the warden of this prison is no follower of mine or yours." Danielle continued in an even more solemn tone, "I have some information that you need to know. The pro-party forces are just waiting for you to escape, and have made it easy for you to do so. Then they plan to capture you and kill you."

"I'll have to be careful about that, won't I?" Liu responded.

Danielle was very dissatisfied with the lack of seriousness in his response. She was now down on her knees and betraying her commitment to herself. "You have to promise me that you won't escape, and that you will tell your followers not to rescue you."

Liu stared back at Danielle. She lay prostrate and crying by his foot.

"Promise me, I beg you."

"Okay, Danielle, okay, I promise."

Danielle pulled herself together, not at all pleased with her emotional display.

"You seem to like to cry at the feet of dissidents," Liu said.

Danielle was not amused and didn't believe Liu's promise to her.

"Can we talk privately?" Liu asked.

I signaled that I would be happy to leave the two of them alone, but Danielle responded, "I think we're done here."

She ordered Regiment Four, one of the contingents of special operations forces who had secretly pledged loyalty to her, to clandestinely guard Liu in the prison and prevent any possible escape plan by his supporters or otherwise.

We got a call from Dad, who said he wanted to talk about the situation in China. She hadn't told Dad about the status of her unrelationship with Liu, and I had been sworn to secrecy about it. She felt that she had screwed up because Dad generally didn't interfere with her class projects.

"There's going to be a meeting of the 205 members of the Central Committee of the Communist Party[187] next week to elect a new chairman now that Zhao is out of the picture. That new chairman will have to be you, otherwise you will be banished and Liu will be in grave danger," Dad said in a grim voice.

"I only have twenty-three supporters on the committee, that's not enough."

"I know," Dad said. "That's why we're having this difficulty."

Danielle grasped for straws. "I can press the regional Daniellite committees."

"That's not going to do it, Danielle. We have no choice but to raise the priority level to nine."

The priority level was a system that Dad, Danielle, and I had put in place so that we could activate very rapid action by Daniellites in emergency situations. Most of Danielle's initiatives ranked between level four and seven, rarely getting to eight. Level ten is considered almost theoretical and would refer to an existential risk threatening all of humanity. The Libyan revolution got up to level 8.2, which was the highest level Danielle had experienced up to that time. She realized that painful compromises would inevitably need to be made at level nine. Danielle was astonished and upset.

"Dad, I never thought it would come to this."

It took only minutes for word of the new priority level to spread to the millions of Daniellites in China. The tremendous surge of activity took a great diversity of creative forms including demonstrations, lobbying, seductions, blackmail, and fistfights. Danielle admonished her supporters to keep their activities nonviolent, and for the time being that seemed to be holding.

Although the Communist Party[188] conservatives had certainly become aware of the extraordinarily high priority level set by Danielle, they were overwhelmed with the results.

Danielle's tally of her support on the committee rose to seventy-eight.

"I only need a plurality of the committee," Danielle told Dad. "Maybe that's enough."

"No, it's still short by at least six votes. Premier Dingxiang Zhongfa has eighty-three votes according to the tally I've just received."

Danielle and Dad raised the priority level again, first to 9.1 and finally 9.15. This activated the three leading crime families in China, who started to detain Zhongfa supporters. No communications between Daniellite forces and the crime families would ever surface. In fact, there were none, but they seemed to know exactly what to do. The crime families were apparently eager for Danielle-style democracy as it would provide them more freedom of action.

Danielle squeaked out a plurality by two votes, but there was an immediate outcry and court filings complaining of suspicious detentions of Zhongfa supporters.

She realized that her position was fragile and could unravel at any moment, but she counted on an old tradition of the Chinese Communist Party to be their downfall. In keeping with their myth of infallibility it had always been their custom that once a candidate achieved a plurality of the Central Committee, another vote was taken and virtually everyone was expected to support that candidate. This presumably showed that all of the members were wise because almost all thought the same way. Although it was already 3:00 AM, Danielle insisted that the follow-up vote be taken immediately.

The Zhongfa forces wanted to delay the vote so they could consolidate their complaint and invalidate the first one before taking a second, and hopefully arrest Danielle and her supporters for illegal interference. Danielle objected to delaying the vote, but Zhongfa got a quick decision by the Administrative Subcommittee, which turned out to be stacked with Zhongfa appointees. They voted to suspend the first vote and to investigate Zhongfa's charges against Danielle. Zhongfa himself called for Danielle's arrest.

The next day the Tibet agreement was suspended, and Danielle received an urgent 3D video call from Mom and Dad insisting that we both flee immediately. More alarmingly, our back channels to Liu, which I had been in charge of, were no longer working. We received a message from Regiment Four that they had lost control of Liu and did not know where he was.

We went back to Los Angeles. "You've started a movement, darling," Mom told Danielle, trying to comfort her.

"These things don't always go in a straight line," Dad added. "Sometimes we need to let fate walk its own path."

"Can't say that I've ever seen either of you do that," Danielle responded. "Anyway, with my friends and colleagues detained or missing, I'm not going to let fate take any strolls on my watch. I'll break its legs if I have to."

AGE FOURTEEN:
AN UNRELENTING FINALITY

Danielle, Ms. Rothblatt is waiting for you," Mom yelled from the living room. I think we were all glad to see her because we needed some distraction from the China situation.

Martine was casual, wearing jeans and a blue Danielle Music T-shirt. The shirt had a white outline of the outer contour of Dani's face, her wry smile visible above a white rose.

Martine seemed agitated and cut right to the chase. "Your COOs are desperate for some of your attention, Danielle. The artist expansion has stalled. Baylor Sweet won't budge. And as for DSC, it's great that we're giving away the cancer kits in Africa, but we're cash flow negative and running out of money."

For the next week, Danielle threw herself into her companies. With her country music expansion blocked, she decided to focus on new indie artists.[189] She finished up her own studio album, which itself was more indie than country.

She had a big grin as she joined Mom, Dad, and me for dinner.

"You look like the cat who ate the canary," I said.

"Well, all this talk about calcifications in the artery,"[190] Danielle exclaimed. "Like it's just some crystal collecting calcium deposits."

We all raised our eyebrows waiting for her to finish her thought.

"Well, it's bone! Fetal bone!"[191]

"Uh, that's interesting," I said.

"So, it's a fetal organ[192] growing inappropriately in a mature person," Dad commented.

Danielle smiled. Dad seemed to be getting it.

"And that means …?" Danielle prompted.

"It's caused by the same stem cell that causes cancer?" Dad ventured tentatively.

"Exactly!" Danielle said.

"You mean the same cocktail should work for atherosclerosis?"[193] I asked.

"Do people who get the Danielle treatment also have less atherosclerosis?" Mom asked.

"Good question, Mom. We have noticed some reduction," Danielle responded. "But for this to really work we need to deliver it in a different way, given the pressures involved in the arteries and the hardness of the plaque compared to tumors."

"I think it's enough of a lead to float a bond offer,[194] don't you?" Danielle added.

We were all relieved at Danielle's diversion. But each night, at around two or three AM, Danielle came into my room crying. Only half awake, I'd haphazardly throw my arms around her and fall back asleep, which, apparently, she did, too, because I usually found her sprawled out in my bed the next morning.

This went on for several weeks while Danielle worked on her heart disease treatment, new album, and indie music initiative. She also checked regularly on China, but things seemed to have quieted down. Too quiet it seemed.

One afternoon I walked into the living room. Mom had already set the table. I thought about how many years it had been since I made my napkin mountains.

CNN was on.

"We interrupt the CNN sports roundup to bring you this breaking news. Several democracy dissidents including Cheng Liu were killed today during a prison break in Tianjin, where they had been held by the government. Details at the top of the hour."

I felt like someone had bashed me in the face with an iron anvil. I fell to my knees and broke down sobbing. Mom came running to the living room.

Mom's look of horror served to ask me what had happened.

"Liu …" I couldn't get the words out.

Mom looked at the TV, and the text crawl at the bottom of the screen delivered the rest of the message.

Mom's face broke into agony. She joined me on the floor and grabbed my hand.

I don't know how long we sat on the floor in shock. Our grief was interrupted by the same distressed thought.

"Oh my god, where is Danielle!" Mom exclaimed. We both looked up at her room. The door was closed. "I don't know how to tell her," Mom added.

"If she doesn't already know," I responded. Our worry for Danielle eclipsed our own anguish, although I cannot say that this provided any relief.

We both walked quietly up the stairs. I turned the doorknob to her room and opened the door.

I found the curtains drawn and there was Danielle sitting on her knees by her bed as if praying, a position I had never seen her in before. She had put on the black dress she wore when we visited Yad Vashem.

Mom and I looked at each other. Danielle knew.

Mom, Dad, and I took turns holding Danielle's hand as she maintained her vigil by her bed.

"You have to eat. A hunger strike is not going to help anything," I whispered to her.

I didn't like the way that came out, but Danielle didn't react. She didn't seem to react to anything any of us said.

Finally, I took matters into my own hands. I fed her mashed potatoes and apple sauce with a spoon. I figured it wouldn't require much cooperation on her part. She wouldn't need to chew, just swallow. My plan seemed to work although the food got on her face and on her dress. Still, she ate. Mom wiped off her face and Dad and I lifted her into her bed. Dad left the room as Mom and I took her dress off. She rolled up into a ball and fell asleep.

The next morning by the time I came in she had put her black dress back on and was again sitting by her bed. I got my first return communication from her since the news. She pointed to her computer and then went back to her praying position. On the screen was an email from Liu's sister Jian, which I read aloud.

"My dearest Danielle. We are devastated, as I know you are. Yesterday we struggled, but were filled with hope and entertained dreams of what tomorrow might bring. Our world has now collapsed into a million pieces. We do not have the strength to pick them up, so we just lie here amongst the splinters of our sorrow. Your attending the funeral would bring us great comfort, but I am sorry to say that it is too dangerous for you to come. You must stay away, or the same thing will happen to you. The government has returned Cheng's body to us. I have attached a picture of his open coffin, but please do not open it if it will bring you too much pain. I pray that we can see you again when safety, and dare I say hope, have returned. With much love, Jian Liu."

Two days later, Amu showed up with her dad at the front door. We visited with Nsishumba in the living room while Amu went into Danielle's darkened bedroom. I peered into the room and saw Amu sitting on the floor beside Danielle in the same praying position. At dinner time, she helped me feed Danielle.

"The Zambian glass is now ninety-five percent full," Nsishumba offered in his improved English, as he joined us for dinner while

Danielle and Amu stayed in Danielle's room.

"That was Danielle's expression," I said.

"Oh, I know that very well; Amu quotes it all the time. The African glass is about four percent full. But we have big plans. Or I should say Amu has big plans."

"Amu is running the program?" I asked.

"Essentially, yes. There's an official United Nations commissioner, but, yes, my daughter, she is calling the shots."

Amu and her dad stayed four days. Danielle did stand up to hug Amu goodbye, and said "Thank you."

A week later, I led her by the hand to the dinner table where she solemnly joined Mom, Dad, and me. Danielle didn't say anything. We were not a lot more talkative—what little conversation we had consisted of discussing the logistics of serving the meal.

Jian Liu came on TV and I turned down the volume as I didn't want any further disturbances for Danielle. Jian spoke about her memories of her brother and the enduring sadness of her family.

A week later, I heard a commotion in Danielle's room and quickly went in.

"Where is he?" Danielle cried.

"Who? Liu?" I asked.

"Liu the doll. The doll. Where is it? It's gone," she said with tears welling up in her eyes.

Her other dolls were scattered all over the floor. Some had been ripped.

I overheard Mom and Dad talking about Danielle.

"Her behavior is not normal," Mom said.

"She's grieving," Dad replied.

"But this is not normal grieving behavior."

"So, what exactly is normal grieving behavior?" Dad asked. "Especially when you were in love with the person and think you're partly responsible for his death?"

"But she's not responsible," Mom said. "She needs to understand that."

"I think she understands the situation," he said.

"I can't handle this myself," Mom said. "She needs her therapist."

"Good luck getting her to go."

"Then I'll have Dr. Sonis come here."

"Good luck with Danielle on that, too."

ℓℓ

Dr. Sonis came over. Danielle wouldn't come out of her room. He was hesitant to enter, but Mom practically pushed him in. Then thinking of the propriety of the situation, she pushed me in, too.

"I'm sorry to interrupt you, but—," Dr. Sonis said in a hesitating voice.

"Oh, I was expecting you," Danielle replied. "You can sit on that chair. Just throw those dolls to the floor."

"I see a lot of them are on the floor already," Dr. Sonis replied.

"So, tell me," Danielle said. "What part of the neocortex[195] was Freud[196] referring to when he talked about the unconscious?"[197]

"I don't think we knew about the neocortex a hundred years ago," Dr. Sonis replied.

"Well what region are we talking about now?"

"I'm not sure; I'd have to look into that....."

"Due to the plasticity of the neocortex,"[198] Danielle continued, "I don't think we can identify meaningful regions of the frontal cortex. Most of it is unconscious anyway."

"Actually, Danielle, I was hoping to understand what happened to your dolls."

"Oh, really? Is that what you like to talk about when you barge into the bedroom of a fourteen-year-old girl when she is in bed?"

"Hey, Danielle, that's why *I'm* here," I said.

"Yeah, well I thought it was a good line," Danielle grumbled.

"I think I see a flash of the old Danielle returning," Dr. Sonis commented.

ℓℓ

"My god, how can you say that!" Danielle was having a conversation with Dad in her room. I had just walked up the stairs, and stopped to listen.

"That's the thing about death," she continued. "There's an unrelenting finality to it."

Dad finally responded, "I don't know, Danielle. Maybe you will realize his dream and that will serve as a testament to your love. And your shared mission."

She did not respond.

"I'm worried about your mom," Dad added.

"Why? Is she upset about Liu, too?"

"Well, she is, but she's even more upset about you."

I glanced into her room and saw Danielle looking down at the floor.

"Maybe the old Danielle could pretend to show up," Dad suggested.

"Mom, do you know anything about the doll?" I asked.

"Doll? You mean Danielle's Chinese doll?"

"Yeah, Mom, Danielle's Liu doll. Do you know where it is?"

"Yes. It was all grey, so I sent it to the cleaner."

"Mom! Don't you think it would have been a good idea to have run that by Danielle?"

"She hasn't exactly been communicating lately. I thought it would please her."

I grabbed the cleaner receipt from her and drove urgently to the dry cleaner. I soon realized that it was likely to be closed given that it was a Sunday, and indeed, I found that to be the case when I arrived.

I called Charlie's cell phone from the parking lot. "You know Heather, Mr. Greyson's daughter, right? Well, I need to reach her right away, actually her father."

"You have a, uh, cleaning emergency, Claire?"

"Yes, exactly. I can explain later, but please, just text me her number."

"I have an old number. I tried to text her a month ago and it didn't work," Charlie replied, "but I do have their address."

So, I picked up Charlie and we paid a visit to Mr. Greyson's house. There were balloons at the entrance, and a big sign with an arrow that said, "Party in backyard."

"Thanks so much for coming to my birthday," Heather exclaimed as we walked into the backyard. She seemed perplexed, realizing, perhaps, that we had not been invited.

"Happy birthday, Heather," Charlie said, "but we're actually here on a cleaning mission."

"Cleaning?"

"Yeah, it's a bit of an emergency. Is your Dad around?"

Heather frowned and pointed to a picnic table by an apple tree. "He's cutting my cake."

Mr. Greyson looked up, annoyed. "Medical emergency, huh?" he exclaimed, as we attempted to explain the urgency of our situation. "I don't think I've had a cleaning emergency before. You sent a vital piece of medical equipment to the cleaner?"

"Yeah, that's about the size of it," Charlie responded.

With a frustrated expression, Mr. Greyson handed the cake knife to Mrs. Greyson and said, "I'll be right back."

We followed Mr. Greyson out of the backyard and ignored the annoyed expressions of Heather and her friends. We followed his car.

When we got to the dry-cleaning store, Mr. Greyson looked up the item in his computer. "It's still in the staging area, so I can't identify which bag it's in. We'll just have to go through all the bags from here to the conveyer belt. What exactly does it look like?"

"Well, uh," I replied, "it's a device about this big with a cloth covering."

"Look," Mr. Greyson, replied, "I don't usually do this, but I have to get back to Heather's party. Why don't you find it and let yourself out. The door will lock as you leave."

After Charlie and I went through about ten bags, we estimated it would take us twenty hours to go through them all. So, we texted our Stern School classmates, inviting them to an impromptu doll-finding party.

There wasn't much in the way of refreshments, but a few of the kids brought sodas. They were perplexed with the mission, but knowing that Danielle was in a distressed state they all appeared to be taking it seriously. We showed them a picture of the doll on my cell phone.

A couple of the girls found negligees in the bags, put them on over their T-shirts, and started doing a mock fashion show.

"Meredith, Annie, I don't think that's very hygienic," I said. "Besides, we're going to get everything mixed up. By the way, congratulations on your country music tour, Meredith."

"Uh, thanks," Meredith replied with a grin.

"And, Sam, congrats on those Yale professors corroborating your virus thesis on the Mayan collapse."

"I have to admit, that was cool," Sam said.

Our party labored on for two more hours. We were getting near the end of the bags and I was worried that the doll was lost.

But then, Annie exclaimed, "Is this it?!"

Danielle beamed that evening as I returned her Liu doll. It was still grey. She sat it on her white rocking chair, which was decorated with pictures of Liu and physics equations, and rolled herself into a ball on my lap as I sewed her torn dolls. I thought it was just like when she was two, but a definite improvement over my having to feed her like a baby a few weeks earlier.

"You look so peaceful, Danielle," I whispered in her ear.

"Equanimous,"[199] Danielle replied.

Oh my god, I thought. This *is* like when she was two.

"Equanimous," I replied. "That's a very nice word."

"Yeah, another example," Danielle said.

Another example, another example. I madly raced through my memory, trying to figure out what she was talking about. I gave up. "Another example?"

"Yeah, of onomatopoeia," she explained.

"Oh right." She *was* continuing our conversation from when she was two!

"That's funny, Danielle. This whole situation was already reminding me of when you were two. You rolled up on my lap. You also blurted out an unexpected reply. Talking about onomatopoeia ...”

Danielle now rolled over on her back. "Baader-Meinhof,"[200] she said.

"Now there's a phrase I haven't heard of."

"Well then, you're bound to hear it again very soon."

She elaborated, "It's when you encounter something new, and then you find it comes up again and again; that's the Baader-Meinhof phenomenon."

"I'm not sure that fits, Danielle. I mean I think of you as two years old all the time."

"Thanks. That old?"

I suppressed a smile. "Well, two one moment, a hundred and two the next."

"Great, no wonder Liu had dumped me."

"I think I do see the old Danielle returning."

Danielle replied, "Yeah? Well, Dad asked her to pretend to make an appearance."

"That's very nice of the old Danielle, but you know it was Mom who Dad had in mind for that reunion."

Danielle responded by staring in my direction.

"You're also making me think of something else you said. Much more recently."

Danielle widened her eyes.

"Mourning is the price of love."

A week later, Danielle was again at the foot of the steps with her roller bag, a bigger one now, but still with Liu stickers. Tears welled up in Mom's eyes.

"I'm glad to see you up and about, Danielle. But can't you be up and about the house, not the world?"

"Love you both, Mom, Dad, you know where to reach me," Danielle said as she announced that she was leaving for Taiwan.

"You know, you can monitor the situation just as well from here," Dad implored.

Danielle's mouth set in a stubborn line. "I may need to return to the mainland on very short notice."

"That's what I'm worried about," Dad responded. "And being in Taiwan will itself be provocative."

"Some things can't be helped," Danielle replied.

"Claire, will you please go with your sister?" Mom added. "You can at least make sure she eats."

"And what about—" Dad began.

"Yes, my security team is going with me, too. And Claire's always welcome to come along. But do either of you have any blood oaths laying around? They might be handy just about now."

"You mean ones that we haven't already used?" Dad asked, raising a skeptical eyebrow.

"Hey, I don't mind drinking from the same well twice," Danielle said.

Dad sighed. "I'll see what I can do."

Danielle and I holed up in a small hotel in the Zhongzheng District of Taipei with a view across the street of the Chiang Kai-shek[201] Memorial Hall, a stately blue and white structure with a traditional Chinese octagonal roof. The red blossoms reminded me of Danielle's flower computer when she was three. To pass the time, I wandered over there each day. The large bronze statue of Chiang Kai-shek made me think of Liu. The inscription by Chiang Kai-shek's head read "The purpose of life is to improve the general life of humanity. The meaning of life is to create and sustain subsequent lives in the universe." I thought Liu would have approved.

The weeks dragged by and the messages from Liu's former supporters were confusing. "These communications are just fragments, I'm really not following this. I must be losing it," Danielle told me.

"No one wants to be too clear," I responded. "I think we need another run through," I added, referring to the concert we planned to give that evening. It was to be an online concert from a Taipei music studio so no one would know we were transmitting from Taiwan. We practiced, but Danielle was distracted.

In the middle of the concert, messages streamed in stating a battle had just erupted on the mainland, which alarmed Danielle. Although we managed to get through half of the concert, she told me that we would have to skip the rest of our set, and she retreated quickly to our dressing room in the studio with me running behind. We didn't appear for an encore or follow-up bow.

"It's clearly the activists devoted to Liu's memory. This is their signature watermark," Danielle told me. "It seems to be a battle of software viruses. I can't tell who they are fighting, but it does not take much imagination to figure that out."

"And the Red Army?" I asked.

"Looks like they are still maintaining their lotus position. Here, check this out." Danielle showed me a draft of a virus she intended to send out.

After looking at Danielle's handiwork for about ten minutes, I responded, "The code looks sound, but you'd better be careful that it helps the right side."

That night, both of us had difficulty sleeping. In the middle of the night, a message came in directed to me, so I decoded it.

It was somewhat cryptic: "Now Like P, fourth loc, Lone Blue and White Bundle."

I was somewhat reluctant to share it with Danielle, as I sensed it might cause her to launch in a new and possibly dangerous direction, but I felt I had no choice. "I'm not sure Dad will be happy about this. Besides, I don't think we can consider it reliable."

"Yeah, the reliability is hard to assess," Danielle replied. "It has a priority 'Like' the current one which is still 9.15 and thus is imploring us to go immediately. Location 4 is you-know-where in Shanghai."

"It would be dangerous to go there, Dani."

"Well, what else is new? Are you coming, or am I going alone?"

"Why did this come in to me?" I asked. "It was already triple encrypted with 200-bit keys."[202]

"Just another layer of obfuscation."

We showed up at a hidden room behind the kitchen of a small dim sum restaurant in Shanghai, and to our delight, we were met by former Chairman Zhao.

"Wow, when and how did you get released?" I asked.

"No time," Zhao said as he led us through a warren of small hallways covered with cheap simulated wood paneling to another cramped room. Zhao asked me to wait behind while he and Danielle walked down one hallway. A guard let them through a narrow door and then closed it behind them.

I heard a scream; I was sure it was Danielle, but I had never heard her scream like that before.

I found myself flying toward the door. I distinctly remember thinking that even though it was indeed my legs carrying me down the hallway, I was flying like a cruise missile. Had I actually been able to think through the situation, I would have done exactly the same thing, but there had been no thought involved. I was just a projectile on automatic pilot hurtling down the corridor toward my sister's cry. I thought to myself how remarkable it was that I was actually having these thoughts when my entire being was focused on getting to my sister.

I was an unstoppable force encountering an immovable object: the guard at the door. I simply crashed through him; the door sprang open, and we both ended up tumbling onto the floor of the room.

I looked up.

And I, too, screamed.

AGE FIFTEEN:
CHAIRGIRL

I looked up and there standing next to Danielle and Zhao …
was Liu!

Tears streamed down Danielle's face.

Liu looked sheepish.

As for myself, I was back in *Alice's Adventures in Wonderland*. I was six years old. Falling down the rabbit hole with the Cheshire Cat sitting on Liu's shoulder.

I shook myself back to reality.

Liu hugged Danielle and then me. I could see a million questions bubbling up in Danielle's eyes.

"I guess you're not dead," Danielle said in a deadpan voice as she composed herself.

"We do need to stop meeting like this," Liu said trying to lighten the tone.

"Maybe if you stopped getting into trouble," Danielle replied.

"I've been trying to get out of trouble. That's why I'm here."

"I thought we agreed," Danielle said, "that you were not going to escape. You promised."

"There wasn't much choice, Danielle. Let's just say that the prison doesn't exist anymore."

"The message contained information only you were supposed to know," Danielle replied. "'Lone Blue and White Bundle' seemed like it had to be you, but of course that seemed impossible. I mean, no one except my family knows about the doll."

"Claire knows?"

"Of course."

"And much of the ninth grade at the Stern School now knows," I added.

"You still have the doll?" Liu asked plaintively.

"Oh, I don't know. It's somewhere, I think, Los Angeles maybe," Danielle answered.

"By the way, that virus you sent was rather useful," Liu said, "but it didn't really know where to go; we had to help it along."

"I figured it wouldn't do much harm," Danielle responded, "until someone with authorization pointed it in the right direction."

"So, your death," I piped in, "was just a ruse?"

"Exactly," Liu answered.

"Whose?" I asked.

"The government, of course," Liu replied. "I heard about my 'death' while I was still in prison. Jian and the rest of my family had been arrested. The message to you, Danielle, was fake, and the interview with Jian was all staged. They had to film about fifty takes before they got one where they felt Jian was convincing. I was desperate to let you know I was alive, but there were threats of dire consequences if I succeeded in doing so. My coded message was the best I could do."

Danielle looked joyful and sad at the same time, an expression I had never seen before. "I guess they were hoping to crush the opposition."

"But the opposite was achieved," Zhao said. "I was aware of your counsel for Liu not to escape, but it became clear to us that a more radical faction had decided to make their ruse a reality. We acted while we still had time."

"And your family?" I asked.

"They are all safe now as well," Liu responded. "Rescued by Regiment Four."

"That photograph of your open coffin?" I asked. "We had image experts examine it. They said it was authentic."

"Yes," Liu responded, "it was all very competently done."

⁓ℓℓ⌒

"Zhao?" I said, turning to him, "Can I speak with you privately?" My intention was to leave Danielle and Liu alone, although this proved awkward as I didn't really have anything private to discuss with Zhao. I just asked him how Liu was doing which resulted in confusion as to why I had pulled him to another room.

But I did manage to give Danielle and Liu fifteen minutes alone. When I returned Danielle was looking down at the floor. She caught my eye and very subtly shook her head no.

⁓ℓℓ⌒

"I'll explain more later," Liu continued, "but we need to strike while the iron is hot. Zhongfa is, um, distracted at the moment."

"Distracted? Where? With what?"

"You know not to ask questions like that, Danielle," Zhao cautioned, "but I really don't know the answers myself. I suspect he will be released once you set the priority below 9.15. In the meantime, I've been able to get your arrest warrant quashed and the first vote reinstated."

"You know what I've asked: all demonstrations, all expressions are to remain nonviolent," Danielle said.

"Why of course," Zhao responded.

"Detentions are not exactly peaceful."

"Well, yes, we all agree."

"So, I want him released immediately."

"But we don't know anything about it," Zhao insisted.

"That's not entirely satisfactory," Danielle replied. "And there was really no evidence against me."

"Exactly," Liu said. "We need to press immediately for the second vote before any more furniture crashes to the floor."

"I can't seem to shake the guy," Danielle confided to me as we traveled to Beijing for a convening of the Central Committee that Zhao was quickly organizing.

"You're like an estranged couple with babies to look after," I responded.

"Babies, huh?"

"Yeah, there's the quantum membrane baby. And Liu's 5,000-year Chinese destiny baby that you've also adopted."

"So, adopted babies, then."

"Adopted?" I said in an objecting tone. "Is there a difference?"

"Hey, you were the one who used the word, Claire."

Mum caught my eye from the edge of my shoulder. I thought of her often, but had not spoken to her for a year now. She raised her eyebrows as if to say, *Danielle is right.*

We arrived in Beijing and were rushed straight to the meeting. I was designated to press for a follow up vote. Zhongfa's supporters, even though Zhongfa himself was still mysteriously missing, pushed for a delay in order to conduct further investigations, including the reason for Zhongfa's detention.

Zhongfa's irregular forces showed up menacingly and surrounded the Central Committee building, but they were met by Regiment Four. An uneasy standoff took place.

The Zhongfa caucus again argued for the Administrative Sub-committee to vote on the procedure, but Danielle did not fall for that course of action this time. She got the floor of the full Central Committee and read the committee rules which clearly directed this decision on procedure to the Secretary of Rules and Order. We knew the Secretary was a Daniellite, and indeed his decision was in our favor.

The second vote for chairman took place, and in keeping with tradition, Danielle received 199 votes out of 205. Since the margin was no longer dependent on just a few votes, all investigations and court claims were thrown out. Danielle lowered the situation priority level to seven, and the detainees, including Zhongfa, were released.

Danielle had been elected chairman of the Communist Party of China.[203]

"The title of 'chairman' isn't really appropriate for me," Danielle said in her brief acceptance speech. "Neither is chairwoman as I'm only fifteen. Some people have suggested I just be called 'chair,' but I am not a piece of furniture. So please refer to me as 'chairgirl,' chairgirl of the Communist Party of China."

Danielle's picture, in which she wore a red dress with small gold roses, beamed around the world with the word "Chairgirl!" She'd tried for a stern expression to match the usual look we had seen for these sorts of pictures, but it was not very convincing.

A few days later, Danielle delivered a major address to the Chinese nation upon her induction into office. She sported a new set of braces on her teeth. She declared that she would be the last "Chair anything" of the Communist Party as a party, that she planned to reorganize the 80 million members into a national service organization with no political role. And the nation would move toward democracy.

"That was clever," I commented to Danielle during our Fireside that evening.

"Yes, it would have been impossible to simply disband the party. We don't need 80 million disaffected members. So I gave them a new mission."

"A pretty good one," I concluded.

As we prepared for a concert in Tiananmen Square, the guy from Stockholm showed up accompanied by Liu. He asked if he could have a brief public audience with her and Liu before she started her concert. We both knew immediately what it was about. She was uncomfortable standing next to Liu, but she managed a wan smile when the gentleman from Stockholm announced that she and Liu would share a Nobel Prize in physics for their advance in understanding the hidden variable in quantum mechanics.

"I think the membrane baby has reached its terrible twos," Danielle complained to me later.

"Oh, I know ex-couples with much more dysfunctional relationships than the two of you," I responded.

"Well, I'll appreciate your continuing to be my liaison."

So, this appeared to be my role now. In addition to still being her cry pillow, I became Danielle's ambassador to Cheng Liu. Maybe I could get Danielle to be my ambassador to Charlie, I thought to myself laughing. Actually, that would not have been a great idea—he still played the kissing game with me in an ironic grown up kind of way. As kids, we ran as fast as we could. As adults, it became more of a practiced dance. Neither of us would have appreciated a stand in.

A few months later, Danielle presided over the first direct election of the Chinese president. Unlike the historically secretive deliberations of the Chinese Communist Party, the plans and negotiations for the election were all televised on Danielle TV, and many other stations and online outlets in China and around the world.

With the election process under way, Danielle moderated a televised debate between the leading candidates. She asked the first candidate, Han Zheng, a friendly and portly former mayor of Shanghai, what he would do as president.

"It is said," he began, "that politicians will articulate what they are intent on expressing rather than answer direct questions, so let me follow in that tradition and share what is actually on my mind." He fumbled and brought out a document from his jacket pocket. "I have here a draft of an amendment to permit you specifically, Danielle, to be president, a one-person exception to the age and nationality requirements for Chinese president. We just passed amendments to permit this election, so why not one more? You should be the first democratically elected president of China, and I will do whatever it takes to make that happen."

Danielle managed a tight but sweet smile as she does when she wins awards or receives a compliment. The other candidates, except one, stood and applauded Zheng's proposal, as did about half of the studio audience. The one who did not stand was Pinyin Shaoqi, son of Liu Shaoqi, the labor organizer who helped the communists come to power in the late 1940s.

The ovation continued, and the pressure was on Danielle to say something. "I am deeply honored and humbled by your confidence in me."

There was a long pause. "Let me think about it. And while I do that, why don't we continue with the debate. Mayor Zheng," Danielle continued, "if, for some reason, you were not the next president of China, what would your advice be to the person who is?"

Zheng stood and smiled, "My advice will be to you, Danielle, as our first elected president," he began. "It will be to adopt business-friendly policies, to emphasize green environmental policies, and to promote the five freedoms."

Danielle went from candidate to candidate, and again, the attention was on her. "There seem to be a few people in this room who would like to see me run for president," she said. "I don't think that constitutes a majority of 1.4 billion people. So why don't we hold a referendum asking if I should run. If that passes and if the amendment goes through, then I, too, will be a candidate."

It did not take long for the amendment and referendum hurdles to be cleared. The major parties, with the exception of the Labor Party, voted to nominate her. She reached out to them, explaining that her pro-business policies would benefit factory workers and that she would strengthen worker protections and provide expanded health insurance. But she didn't press too hard on this, as she and I agreed that having an effective opposition party would be beneficial.

It became a two-person race, Danielle versus Pinyin Shaoqi. Danielle led in early polls 60 to 40 percent, as a result of widespread appreciation for Danielle's role in bringing democracy to China. The Labor Party's primary argument was that the president of China should actually be

Chinese. No one seemed overly concerned about her being only fifteen years old.

Danielle called for a series of national debates, but Shaoqi agreed to only one. She took a break from active campaigning to brush up on her Chinese and did around-the-clock practice sessions with her coaches.

Although diminutive, Danielle looked elegant and confident at the debate, wearing a floor-length red dress with a purple peony at her left shoulder. It had been the national flower of China before the communists came to power. Shaoqi was dressed in his usual black suit, white shirt, and red tie.

Danielle only needed a draw, and she seemed to be holding her own with five minutes to go. But then, my English translation feed quoted Danielle as saying, "Chinese history is decidedly tedious."

I heard a shudder from the studio audience and the Twittersphere exploded with hostile comments. "*Labor is correct, we need a leader who does not insult China,*" was the trending tweet.

Danielle seemed perplexed and tried to recover, but it was time for the closing comments and she ran out of time.

"I mixed up lengthy and tedious," Danielle confided to me that evening. "They're pretty close in Mandarin.[204] I was trying to allude to China's long and noble history, but I should have vetted that phrase more."

"Zhōngguó lìshǐ quèshí hěn fáwèi," Danielle's offending comment saturated the Chinese media. Her explanation about having confused two words only highlighted Labor's point about her not understanding Chinese culture. The polls quickly flipped, with Danielle running three percent behind.

"It's true I'm not an expert on the Chinese language," Danielle said to a meeting of her campaign management. "But Shaoqi is no expert on democracy. We'll have to fight fire with fire."

"We cannot trust our future to the ignorant citizens," recorded from a Shaoqi speech to the National Communist Party Congress three years earlier, became the highlight of Danielle's final saturation ad campaign, all in Chinese of course. This was followed by Danielle's voice in perfectly enunciated Mandarin, "Do you think it is a good idea to trust the future of democracy in China to this person?" The ad ended with an old recording of Shaoqi saying, "One person, one vote, will be the ruin of China."

The ad campaign managed to bring the polls to a dead heat on the eve of the election. Danielle seemed remarkably tranquil that night in our Beijing hotel room and curled up in a ball in my lap, something she had not done for a year.

"Huì shì zěnyàng, huì," Danielle said to me.

I looked down at her. "Meaning?"

"Que sera, sera." Danielle said with a smile.

"You're mixing metaphors," I said.

"Languages, actually," Danielle replied.

The next day brought victory. Danielle won 52 to 48 percent.

"I must say, that's a more convincing victory than the usual 99.8 percent vote by the National People's Congress," Danielle said during her acceptance remarks.

At age fifteen, she became China's first democratically elected president.

"The population problem is a myth," she said, announcing in her presidential acceptance address that she was dispensing with the one child rule. "Try taking a train trip across China. One sees vast swaths of unused and lightly used land. There is plenty of room for people. With new technologies, such as nano-based solar energy production,[205] decentralized water purification cells,[206] vertical agriculture,[207] and three-dimensional printing[208] of building modules,[209] we have all the resources we need for an expanded population."

"And the one child policy," she continued, "has been a catastrophe for girls."

AGE SIXTEEN:
BEST MALE SINGER

Danielle's tenure as president of China started smoothly enough, so she was able to devote some attention to her businesses, which were definitely helped by the publicity she was getting.

One of Danielle's new indie artists, Michael Matthews, was attracting attention with the latest imbroglio manufactured by the online tabloids. He had reportedly cheated on his starlet girlfriend, Cynthia Kale, who dumped him a week before he was going to take her to the Grammys. He'd been nominated for Best New Artist. Each day's news focused on the latest singer or actress he had asked to be his date for the award show, each of whom publicly turned him down. Each day's lead photo was of some other female star giving Matthews the thumbs down.

"I'll get a date for the Grammys, you'll see," ran a headline on *Slate*. And she'll be the prettiest girl at the show.

The widely anticipated day arrived. Michael got out of his limousine with a wide smile. His hair was combed up to look like wings. He wore a grey tuxedo with a black bowtie, a black handkerchief, and black sneakers with two-inch platforms. A large retinue of paparazzi met him as he slammed the door of his white stretch limousine.

"Oh, wait, I almost forgot," he said. He turned back to the limo and opened the door for his mystery date.

And out of the limousine she came.

It was Danielle! She had not even been expected to appear at the Grammys that year, given her new job as president of China.

But this was not the Danielle that people had been used to seeing. Gone were the braces, the colorful childlike flower dresses, and the sweet hair styles. She wore a revealing black and white Christian Dior[210] gown with red satin trim and see-through lace. The low neckline and high heels were two firsts for Danielle. Her hair was cut pixie-short with sharply defined bangs.

She had not left the flowers behind completely; there was a discreet white and yellow iris over her left breast. The iris was quickly identified by a blogger as copied from a Georgia O'Keeffe[211] painting.

Photographers abandoned the other stars and fell over each other to snap photos of Danielle. These pictures appeared seconds later on news websites with the headline "Butterfly Takes Wing!"

Although I had been using Life Bits Share sparingly, this I had to see, especially since we'd spent the afternoon getting ready together. Danielle and I planned to meet up after the red carpet and sit together for the show.

Apparently, one of the stars left at the altar, so to speak, as all of the photographers rushed to shoot Danielle's picture, was Baylor Sweet. She was promoting her new album. Her initial reaction to being deserted was surprise and a hint of dismay, but she smiled when she saw Danielle.

Danielle saw a tweet about this incident and sought out Baylor in the auditorium and apologized.

"Really, no apology needed. All you did was get out of the car. You deserve every bit of the attention. And that's a stunning dress, by the way," Baylor said.

"I appreciate that," Danielle responded. "Thank you so much. Your dress is beautiful, too, but I rained on it and on you. Why don't you join me?"

Danielle had already announced she would not accept Grammy awards in the major categories she had won previously as she had won

so many of them in the previous eight years. But there was a category she had not previously been nominated for: Best Male Singer.

Some of the male nominees weren't happy about this. Danielle left it to me to make the argument.

"Why shouldn't gals be allowed to compete for this category, or any category? Hey, the guys are welcome to compete for Best Female Singer. Anyway, gender is not always so clear," I told *Variety*.

Danielle responded to the controversy with a tweet: *Read Martine Rothblatt's book The Apartheid of Sex.*[212]

When Danielle's name was read as one of the nominees, there was cheering and laughter as she put on a cowboy hat and pasted a mustache under her nose.

She won and accepted her award, still wearing her mustache and fussing with her dress. "I guess I'm not really used to a dress like this," she said. "These things are dangerous!"

She skipped the usual slew of parties and went to a small restaurant that had been cleared for Danielle and her date.

"You know I didn't cheat on Cynthia," Michael said.

"I knew that," Danielle replied, "I did check it out. We're going to have to work on your public relations."

"That would be good," Michael replied. "You know, this is a first for me."

"First?"

"Well, it's the first time I've dated the Best Male Singer."

"I see. Have you ever dated the president of China before?"

"Oh, I do that all the time," Michael replied.

Danielle smiled.

Michael brought Danielle home at about 3:00 AM surrounded by a contingent of Chinese and American secret service cars.

"I did kiss Michael goodnight," she shared with me after she came in. "Well, actually, he kissed me, but I didn't stop him."

I broke out in an unrestrained smile. "Yes, I noticed," I replied.

"Ha, so you were watching; Life Bits Share should really tell me when you're doing that."

"Yeah, we've asked for that feature. So ... how was it?"

"Couldn't you tell?"

"You had your eyes closed. You seemed into it."

"Actually, it was pretty amazing, so much more intense than I ever imagined. I may have to rethink my idea that reading about things is as good as doing them."

"Ha ha," I responded. "We'll have to study that carefully. You know, try things both ways. Are you going to see him again?"

"Maybe. He'll have to come to China."

"I'm sure that can be arranged," I replied. "You've got a thousand airplanes at your disposal."

"Well, if he can't come to China, I can always read about it," Danielle said.

"Read about it?"

"In my journal. I include fantasies in there also."

"Didn't you just say that reading is not quite the same?"

Danielle raised her eyebrows, then turned toward the stairs, heading to bed, I presumed.

"You know, you can check in on me on Share, too," I added, as she walked upstairs.

"I think about it, but then each day is over before I get the chance," Danielle replied.

"I know you're busy—"

She interjected, "But I did watch Charlie propose—that was not to be missed."

"That I'm engaged is our little secret," I said.

"I'll add it to the list," Danielle replied.

"I don't think we would want to write out that list, Danielle," I said. "But I'm glad you insisted that I ask Charlie if you could watch us."

"Yeah, well," Danielle said, "you felt it would be okay if I just watched without him knowing. But that would not have been a good idea at all."

"I don't know what I was thinking. But as it is, he still doesn't realize we knew he was going to propose that night. He'd flip out."

"So how did he manage to fit a whole painting inside a fortune cookie?" Danielle asked.

"It was on an exquisitely thin film which he rolled up and then curled the roll around itself. And it was a rather big cookie."

"It's really a beautiful portrait of you."

"It's flattering, all right," I said. "I love how Charlie is kneeling down presenting me with the ring. Mum was ecstatic."

"You should frame it."

"Yes, I'm doing exactly that. It's certainly not going back in that cookie."

ⅇℓ

Danielle moved to Zhongnanhai,[213] a palace complex dating back to the Ming Dynasty[214] in 1406 when the Emperor moved the Chinese capital to Beijing. Liu lived about a mile away in a condominium on Wangfujing Street near the Forbidden City.[215] Charlie and I had separate rooms in Zhongnanhai.

This started a period of dating for Danielle with young men from China and around the world. She approached the activity as if it were a sociology experiment. She even wrote a class paper on her dating experiences. She didn't submit it, claiming it wasn't very good, but I think she felt it too revealing.

"Are all boys so timid?" she asked me one night during our Fireside in my room at the palace.

"Only when they're dating the president of China."

"That's definitely getting in the way," Danielle said. "Although I don't have much to compare it to. And the security doesn't help matters any."

"Still, Danielle, you're getting to meet a variety of nice young men. Even under normal circumstances, one's first dates are always a little constrained, if not ridiculous. Someone will break through, you'll see. Remember what you always say about transcendence."

"You know it's interesting," Danielle mused, "how boys approach the end of the evening and the kiss goodnight. Some act like it is part of some script. Some try to artfully segue to a romantic topic. Some try to warm me up by putting their arm around me."

"Or all of the above," I said. "All I have to say is if they have the courage to kiss the president of China on the lips, they can't be all that bashful. Is there something more you want, Danielle?"

"Well, none of them really try to go, uh, you know, further than a kiss," Danielle clarified.

"Do you want to go further than a kiss?"

"Well, uh, no," Danielle replied. "But I have to say there are different factions in my mind on that subject."

"So, you'd turn a guy down if he tried to go further?" I asked.

"I suppose so."

"So, you want guys to try and then you want to turn them down?"

"Well, I don't want to turn guys down."

"But that's your intention?" I asked.

"I suppose."

"But you still want guys to try?"

"Hmmm."

"Maybe that's why they're not trying," I said.

"My society of mind[216] is bickering on that one, too," Danielle explained.

"I'm glad I have only one guy to worry about," I replied.

"You know, the physical part isn't the main thing in my mind. I'm lonely when I go out with these guys," Danielle said.

"You're probably missing Liu."

"I miss what I thought we had. The conversations. The feeling of ease."

"You'll find love again, Danielle. You're only sixteen."

"No, no. It's gone. I'll never find love like that."

"That's what love is like, Dani. When you have it, you have the world. And when it's gone, you feel like love just doesn't exist and never did. But it will happen again, trust me."

"What do you know about it, Claire? You met one guy. You fell in love. You two are still in love and always will be."

"It's true. I've never lost a lover."

"Or an unlover, in my case. But it's not going to happen. It's impossible. I'm fine. I have you. I have Mom and Dad. I have plenty of things to occupy my mind."

✏ ✏

Danielle gave Liu the title of Secretary of Institutional Development, which translated to advancing the democratic foundations of China, human rights, and civil liberties. It was not a very well thought out position, but Liu had been deeply influential without a formal position, so he thrived in this role. And I was Danielle's ambassador to Liu.

Her primary concern as president was losing China's ability to make nimble decisions as it moved to more democratic institutions. She did not want China burdened with an oppressive bureaucracy, which has been a huge challenge for India's democracy. Although there was tension among China's 56 ethnic groups, it was nothing compared to India's Hindu-Muslim conflict[217] and the still-stifling caste system.[218] She worked extensively on achieving harmony among the various groups, and sent Liu and me to reach understandings with the Uyghur Muslim separatists[219] in northwestern China's Xinjiang region.

She supported entrepreneurship especially among emerging technology businesses, resulting in a dozen "silicon valleys"[220] springing up around China. She streamlined regulations while developing a highly paid regulatory bureaucracy that was relatively resistant to corruption. She established a bill of rights for workers that was strongly opposed by the pro-business parties who had been her strongest supporters.

GDP growth rates rose from seven to nine percent. Major strides were made in air and water quality. Beijing didn't have a smog[221] alert for four months. As China moved increasingly to an intellectual-property-based economy, she emphasized the importance of China itself respecting IP protection.[222]

"So far, so good," I commented to Danielle on her progress.

AGE SEVENTEEN:
CHINESE DEMOCRACY MUST HAVE CHINESE FEATURES

I'm afraid that the honeymoon has come to an end," Danielle commented as I entered her office. "Our old nemeses are up to their old tricks."

"Democracy must adopt the right principles and policies which all candidates must commit to," Zhongfa said to a small audience of carefully selected supporters in Tiananmen Square in one of his many nationally televised speeches as the Minister of the Election Commission. *We cannot allow the democratic process to go in a direction that ignores our socialist values. Chinese democracy must have Chinese features,* my real-time translation read.

Danielle, Liu, Zhao, and I sat in her presidential office, watching Zhongfa's speech on our retina displays. The National Service Corps, formerly the Chinese Communist Party, which was responsible for running elections, were barring candidates that Zhongfa and his cohorts deemed unsuitable. Some candidates who had attempted to ignore the new rules had been arrested.

"Very unfortunate," Zhao commented as we watched.

"Yeah, it was a mistake giving the National Service Corps this responsibility," Danielle said.

"You had to give them something to do," Zhao commented.

"And we couldn't reasonably expect such a deeply ingrained totalitarian[223] institution to understand democracy," Liu pointed out.

"Authoritarian[224] I think is a better description," Danielle clarified. "The communists have not been totalitarian since Deng Xiaoping[225] came to power."

"Look, there's no going back, Danielle," Zhao said. "Anyway, who else was going to take this responsibility?"

"I think the only approach now is that I'm going to have to distract them with other assignments," Danielle said.

"Distract the former Chinese Communist Party from something other than the levers of power? Good luck with that one," Zhao commented.

"What might that be, Danielle?" I asked.

"I think you'll want to stay away from education," Liu said. "That's even more dangerous than elections."

"Well, there's fixing potholes!" Zhao suggested.

"Or making the trains run on time,"[226] I said, alluding to Mussolini[227] in the early 1940s.

Everyone laughed.

"Actually, an economic role does make sense," Danielle said. "The former Party embraced the special economic zones, which was a liberating move. Look at the remarkable success of Shanghai.[228] Why not have the Corps spread these zones to the rural areas? That could increase economic growth while discouraging migration to the cities."

"I like that," Zhao concluded.

I decided to lead a "learn by doing"[229] revolution in Chinese education, but many student-run projects ran into conflicts. A high school class in Tianjin built a rocket and planned to send it into orbit. The rocket's small head cone contained an experiment intended to determine how rice would grow in a weightless condition. The local police seized their rocket and arrested the students for violating a fireworks ordinance. Danielle had to intervene to get them released.

A junior high school play showing Mao with adoring young women was condemned by the Local Service Corps as dishonoring national history. Mao was still a national icon and any implied criticism of him struck a very sensitive nerve.

A group of college entrepreneurs demonstrated their GetAround system that could bypass Cycorp, the still-nationally-controlled messaging system. Zhongfa and the National Service Corps obtained a court order shutting GetAround down and threatening criminal sanctions. Danielle managed to stop the criminal investigation but GetAround was nonetheless disbanded.

"At least the fight now is with words," Liu counseled in a 3D video conference with Danielle.

"Yes, we've moved beyond Mao's 'power coming from the barrel of a gun,'"[230] Zhao replied, who was with Danielle and me in her office.

"On the other hand," Danielle countered, "threatening criminal sanctions is an organized form of violence."

TODAY WILL END
THREE DAYS FROM NOW

Danielle and I stole away to Los Angeles so I could finally marry Charlie. Everyone was impressed that we had been able to keep our engagement a secret and hide the wedding from the paparazzi, which was a blessing. Charlie really wanted to avoid the media circus our wedding would have become. It was a beautiful private ceremony with a hundred guests, not one of whom had spilled the beans about their invitations. It was a happy time for us all to be together and to expand our family, although Charlie had already been a big part of it.

With Liu absent, we had to tell Mom and Dad what was going on—or *not* going on—with their unrelationship, although they had guessed Liu and Dani's status from the lack of information.

When it came time for the traditional kiss at the end of our marriage ceremony, Charlie pecked my cheek like he had done sixteen years earlier and started to run. But he came back when I smirked at his joke. Mum on my shoulder thought it was hilarious. Danielle, Mom, and Dad seemed to get the joke, too, but the rest of our guests looked confused. He then gave me a proper kiss.

"What did I tell you?" Mum said as I walked to the reception, hand in hand with Charlie. Danielle walked close by.

For a moment, I was alarmed at the thought that Charlie could hear what Mum was saying, but I quickly remembered that of course only I could hear her words. Danielle gave me a knowing look and I had the momentary thought that maybe Danielle *could* hear her.

"Yes, you *were* right," I replied to Mum.

Danielle smiled.

"Who was right?" Charlie asked.

During her fourth year as president of China, the United States was once again engaged in an epic congressional battle between left and right on tax policy and spending. The dysfunctional process for resolving these matters had itself long been an issue and caused difficulty with the US holding onto its AA+ credit rating,[231] which had already been downgraded from AAA. Growth rates in the US hovered between one and two percent. Danielle offered to mediate a solution and, desperate for a way out of what had become a political quagmire, Democrats and Republicans reluctantly accepted her offer.

She flew to Washington and held a joint session of Congress,[232] and unlike most sessions of Congress where almost no one actually attends, everyone was there. She declared the issue would be "resolved today, even if today ends three days from now. Why take months to reach an agreement that can be reached in hours?"

She interacted from the podium with senators and representatives of Congress, calling on various members to explain incongruities in things they had said, chastising anyone who lapsed into partisan rhetoric.

"I'm only eighteen; I can outlast you all. That's my strategy, actually. You'll get so tired that you'll accept anything I put forward."

At 6:00 AM she achieved a consensus on a plan that cut expenses while promoting economic growth, and did not raise tax rates yet still enhanced tax revenue by closing exceptions and loopholes put in years earlier by industry lobbyists based on rationalizations whose validity had long since lapsed.

She insisted they were going to vote on it that morning.

"As it so happens, I have this already written up," she said, taking a thick document out of her briefcase. I thought how odd it was the US Congress still used paper documents.

Each party was split, but Danielle's proposal received a small majority from each party. President Obama, who was approaching the end of his second and final term, signed the bill.

"I've accomplished what I came here to do," Danielle said, and we flew back to China.

"It seems your country is calling for you," Zhao confided to Danielle as he rode back with the two of us in the presidential motorcade from the airport.

"I'm pretty sure the politicians in China are just waiting for me to leave. I've been a transitional object. They give me lip service, but everything will revert to the old patterns when I leave power."

"Oh, I don't know about that. I think we've crossed a Rubicon, Danielle. We have a real chance now to make a lasting difference."

"After all that work, just a chance?" I asked.

"A chance, yes, but what's wrong with that?" Zhao asked. "History is made up of chances. Chances that are recognized. Opportunities that are seized upon. Or not. It will be up to us not to squander the opening your sister has given us."

AGE NINETEEN:
WE ARE FALLIBLE, ARE WE NOT?

I have mixed feelings about this," Danielle confided to me in one of our late-night tête-à-têtes in her presidential suite.

"Running for US president?"

"Yes," Danielle replied. "I won't have time for Danielle."

"The foundation or the girl?" I asked.

"Precisely," Danielle replied.

The stimulus for our discussion was a news flash that Ohio had become the sixth state to pass the "Danielle Amendment"[233] permitting a one-person exception to the rule that the president of the United States must be at least thirty-five years old.

Over the next several weeks, given her performance before Congress, her successful term as Chinese president drawing to a close, and the US president being a lame duck as Danielle had anticipated years earlier during her brief stint in jail, the trickle of states approving the amendment became a flood. President Obama signed the amendment and it became law.

Within a day the Republican Party held what it called a "Flash Convention" and nominated Danielle for president. There was consternation in the Democratic Party that the GOP got the jump on them, but they quickly nominated Hillary Clinton which suited Danielle just as well.

The *Slate* headline read "Pick a Gal for President."

Danielle finished her four-year term as president of China and reported that she had received a B- on her "China" social studies project. "I was a bit too distracted with my businesses, rolling out the cancer cure, and laying the political groundwork in the US," Danielle explained.

Danielle and Liu shared a Nobel Peace Prize for bringing democracy to China. "Well I'm just going to have to get used to it," she told me.

"Used to having three Nobel Prizes?"

"No, having Liu continue to be in my life."

In their first televised presidential debate, the candidates met at Stanford University.

When asked why the nation should select her to be the next president, Clinton replied, "Danielle has been a great contributor to our country and to the world. But she is still a teenager and will have plenty of time yet to serve. And to learn."

"I'll acknowledge that Mrs. Clinton is not a teenager," Danielle replied with a smile. "But I dare say she is getting younger every day and will also have plenty of time to serve. I look forward to supporting her candidacy as I wrap up my presidency of the United States."

Secretary Clinton's appeal to experience fell flat as Danielle's presidency of China was widely regarded as having been successful.

Clinton's next criticism was that Danielle loved China more than the US, but polls showed that two-thirds of the voting public appreciated the growing friendship between the two nations. "Our exports to China have increased fourfold," Danielle pointed out.

Clinton's next and final criticism of Danielle achieved greater traction: Danielle would have a conflict of interest between her duties as president of the US and running Danielle, her foundation, whose budget now exceeded a billion dollars a year, funded mostly by profits from her cancer cure. This challenge put pressure on Danielle to give temporary leadership of the foundation to someone else in a blind trust which was how these conflicts were usually dealt with, but she refused.

"My goals for the presidency and the foundation are the same: a more just and charitable world," Danielle explained. But polls showed that a majority in the US didn't see the presidency as primarily promoting a charitable world, but rather serving American interests.

"There's no conflict between American society and the betterment of humanity," Danielle said, but this proved to be a controversial formulation, and the polls tightened.

On election night, Danielle, Mom, Dad, and I watched the election night coverage in our living room. The election came down to Michigan. Danielle's support for self-driving cars[234] had been controversial. It wasn't clear to Detroit voters whether this would help or hurt the American car industry.

When Danielle pulled ahead by a half a percent in Michigan, Mum cheered from my shoulder. Mom and Dad remained on the edge of the couch. Danielle calmly sat in an arm chair with her arms folded.

At 6:00 AM, CNN called Michigan for Danielle.

She had been elected president of the United States.

At her inauguration, Danielle sang and danced at all the major balls until four in the morning. She wore a dark blue evening gown that fell to the top of her four-inch heels. Her bodice was decorated with dark orange and yellow marigolds.

Liu made an appearance by himself at one of the balls. He caught Danielle's eye, took a few long strides in her direction, and bowed solemnly at the waist. She told me later this reminded her of the first time they met in person, how they'd bowed to each other, her hair got caught in his glasses, and they ended up tripping over each other.

At six in the morning, she issued four ultimatums and took off in Air Force One for Afghanistan. The United States had left Afghanistan earlier in Obama's term, but with the recent resurgence of the Taliban,[235] the US had returned, albeit discretely, with an emphasis on special operations forces.[236] However, the definition of special operations was stretched as there were again 50,000 Americans in Afghanistan involved in the fight, and there were again strident calls for the US to withdraw.

One of Danielle's ultimatums was to the newly elected president of Afghanistan to turn over to the Afghan government the billions of dollars his family had stashed away. Through back channels she made it clear that she knew exactly where the money was and had documented the trail of how it got there.

Another ultimatum was to Pakistan to permit her special operations forces relatively free rein there to finish off al-Qaeda[237] and the Taliban or she would remove their nuclear weapons.[238] She made it clear that she knew exactly how to do this.

The third and fourth ultimatums were to al-Qaeda and the Taliban to turn themselves in. As she expected, the Afghan and Pakistani leadership agreed to her terms, since she had given them no real choice. Also, as she expected, she received no reply to the last two ultimatums.

Prior to her inauguration, Danielle had perfected a new microbot[239] technology which was able to locate people based on incomplete DNA identification.[240] She was concerned with the privacy implications of the technology and kept it top secret, but used it anyway.

It worked like this: Swarms of essentially invisible micro-robots were released by an unmanned aerial vehicle. They were able to maneuver with their microwings and locate people within an area of a few hundred yards. Without being noticed, the bots performed a DNA test on a piece of hair and sent a coded message with the result, which was transferred from bot to bot, back to the aerial vehicle. Although DNA hair analysis is not as definitive as a full DNA test, it is sufficient to identify human targets with over 99 percent reliability.

The White House Legal Counsel concluded the technology constituted a privacy infringement, but the chairman of the Joint Chiefs of Staff shot down that line of reason, arguing the information would be kept secret, and in any event national security trumped privacy. The discussion reminded me of Danielle's argument to Mom about Life Bits.

The CIA had narrowed down Osama bin Laden's[241] location to a few hundred possible locations, which was sufficient to use this approach. The microbots reported back with 99 percent reliability that Osama bin Laden was hiding in a comfortable compound in Abbottabad,[242] which surprised her team. She instructed Seal Team Six to capture him alive, which generated strong resistance from the military.

"He will be a hot potato," the chairman of the Joint Chiefs of Staff[243] objected. "There will be no end to the outrage if we are actually holding him." But capturing him alive was critical to Danielle's plan.

The operation to capture him went smoothly as there was virtually no resistance at his compound. He had apparently been hiding in plain sight although not actually going outside the building.

She intended to interview him on live television.

"This is insane. We emphatically veto this plan," General Petraeus,[244] the Director of the CIA told Danielle.

"The last time I checked I was the president," Danielle answered firmly.

"With all due respect, Miss President, you are providing a direct communication channel for the head of al-Qaeda to trigger a massive terrorist attack on the United States."

"First of all," Danielle said, "he had no trouble broadcasting to the world through the Internet. Secondly, I know the al-Qaeda trigger codes, both verbal and gestural. There will be a time delay and I'll cut off the transmission if he uses one."

"My understanding was that the CIA would be in control of interrupting the transmission," the general responded.

"I appreciate your offer, General, but I will be in control of the transmission. You guys can't think fast enough anyway."

"I'm afraid I need to give you this document, Miss President." General Petraeus handed Danielle his resignation.

"I don't recall asking you for this, General."

"I cannot be associated with something this irresponsible," he replied.

"Thank you very much for your consideration, General." With that, Danielle ripped the resignation into little pieces, a signature Danielle move.

"I'm sorry I don't seem to have a fan handy, so I would appreciate if you would carefully file this for me," Danielle said. She picked up the pile of torn paper and deposited it in his hand. "I think we're finished for now. Thanks for stopping by. I'll be sure to keep you posted."

ее

Danielle was stern as she approached bin Laden in an undisclosed location. She wore a dark blue floor-length dress that covered her arms and shoulders. He wore his traditional freshly pressed white robe and white head covering.

He rose and said that he welcomed a dialogue with someone who had lived a pure life. He behaved like a world leader at a summit meeting. He had an air of smugness, confidence, and disdain for his capture.

They spoke in Arabic while the world watched with real-time translations in many languages. She said she wished to discuss the justification for the tactics used by al-Qaeda. Bin Laden eagerly took the opportunity, extensively quoting from the Qur'ān,[245] with his own commentary. He went on for an hour without interruption from Danielle, who listened patiently.

When bin Laden had finished, Danielle said that she would like to comment on his quotations and discussion. She signaled for a Muslim cleric to bring out a copy of the holy book. She did not handle the Qur'ān herself because she did not want to distract the conversation with issues about proper handling, especially since she is female. The cleric wore white gloves and he rested the book carefully on a proper surface, opening it to different pages for bin Laden to follow along as Danielle spoke.

"It is true," she began, "the Qur'ān is remarkable and unique among holy books in that it has not changed since its conception."

"It is literally the word of He who shall not be named, and was directly conveyed to Muhammad,"[246] bin Laden responded.

Danielle nodded. "By way of the angel Jibril."[247]

"Yes, a reliable messenger," bin Laden said. "And we of the Muslim faith have preserved its every sacred letter for 1,400 years."

"A remarkable feat," Danielle acknowledged.

"Which reflects the purity of the faith, a purity we must protect with our lives if necessary," bin Laden said.

"It is true that the words have remained unchanged, and that other holy books cannot make this claim. There are indeed many versions and translations of the Old and New Testaments of the Jewish and Christian Bible,"[248] Danielle acknowledged.

"That is why we must be steadfast," bin Laden said.

"Nonetheless, we need to understand and interpret those words," Danielle pointed out.

"Hence the need for total devotion to the pursuit of truth through this sacred text," bin Laden said.

"But we are fallible, are we not?" Danielle said.

"The words are infallible. We must relentlessly seek perfection through them," bin Laden said.

"Yet we cannot hope to achieve that," Danielle responded. "We cannot attain the flawlessness of God. That is what the Qur'ān says, does it not?"

"For that reason, we have been gifted with this infallible guide," bin Laden replied.

"The guide may have been impeccably preserved, but we are unable to follow it precisely. We have to understand and interpret it, and our ability to do that as mortal beings pales in comparison to the wisdom we seek," Danielle said.

"We can get very close to ideal understanding through rigorous study, dedication, and integrity of heart," bin Laden said.

"Is it not arrogant to think that we can know the mind of God?" Danielle asked.

"We have His very words in front of us, unsoiled by centuries of human imperfection," bin Laden argued.

"Yes, but being so much lesser than God, we cannot hope to correctly understand them," Danielle said. "Furthermore, Arabic is a living language and has changed a great deal in 1,400 years. We cannot simply apply today's meanings to words and phrases that have changed meaning during that time."

"That is why we study as meticulously as we do," bin Laden said.

"But we inevitably make mistakes despite that study," Danielle replied. "You have made mistakes."

"It is true that I would not be a prisoner had I made no errors."

"I am referring to your pronouncements, to your philosophy, to the thoughts that you have shared with me today."

"I do not think you will find inaccuracies there, Miss President."

"Take your interpretation of the word 'jihad,'"[249] Danielle explained. "Yes, the Qur'ān describes jihad as a holy struggle, and commands a righteous Muslim to commit himself totally to this exertion, but the fight is primarily with oneself to rid oneself of evil, to follow a righteous path."

"There is also society to be concerned with," bin Laden replied.

"Muhammad preached the pursuit of justice in society through words and nonviolent actions," Danielle said. "When he was asked 'what is the ideal form of jihad,' he replied it was 'a word of truth in front of an oppressive ruler.'"

"And if that fails?" bin Laden challenged.

"The Qur'ān commands that if you are persecuted and oppressed, you should move to a more peaceful and tolerant land. 'Let those who believe emigrate to escape persecution and strive in the way of Allah,[250] these have hope of Allah's mercy.'"

"And if that is not possible?" bin Laden asked.

"As a last resort," Danielle replied, "the Qur'ān does permit defense of one's rights, but still implores that one not transgress against those who are innocent. As Chapter 2, verse 190 says, 'Fight in the cause of Allah those who fight you, but do not transgress limits; for Allah loves not transgressors.'"

Soon, bin Laden seemed to become less dismissive of their dialogue and increasingly impressed with her deep knowledge and respect for the Qur'ān.

"Your understanding is commendable," bin Laden admitted. "But we have had these debates many times. We are in that special circumstance of defending ourselves and the honor of Islam from the vast evil influences of infidels."[251]

Danielle continued persistently pointing out extensive inconsistencies in bin Laden's interpretation of the Qur'ān. "You've described Jews and Christians as apes and pigs, but there is no such reference in the Qur'ān."

"There is such an implication in the fifth Sura," bin Laden replied.

"I believe you are referring to Sura 5:60 which states, 'Say, shall I inform you of him who is worse than this in retribution from Allah? Worse is he whom Allah has cursed and brought His wrath upon, and of whom He made apes and swine, and he who served the Shaitan; these are worse in place and more erring from the straight path.' I don't see a reference to Jews or Christians."

Bin Laden did not respond. "Here is a word in the ancient Arabic," Danielle continued, "that you interpret in two of your speeches as 'embrace,' but you then interpret this same word in eleven of your speeches as 'crush.' These two concepts—'embrace' and 'crush'—do exist on a continuum, but have very different intentions. The word can in fact be used either way, but the meaning becomes unambiguous when you consider the context. I have studied ancient Arabic so that I may understand these passages. It is properly 'embrace' in the context used."

Watching with Mom and Dad in our living room, I felt the tide had shifted, but I was concerned about how the public was responding to the tone of the dialogue.

Finally, Danielle made one last point. "Why have you allowed yourself to be used as a tool of those who oppose Islam?" she asked.

"Al-Qaeda's alliance with the CIA was entirely tactical," bin Laden pointed out, "just as you made a pact with Stalin[252] to fight Hitler.[253] I severed all ties with your intelligence community when the Russians left Afghanistan," bin Laden replied.

"That's not what I was referring to," Danielle clarified. "Your twisting of the meanings of the Qur'ān, your persistent deformations in the direction of intolerance, and promotion of violence and the violation of the rights of the innocent have been a great tool for those who hate Islam and wish it harm. The Islamophobes have tricked you into acting as their accomplice. You have been under their mind control. If you did not exist, the enemies of Islam would have had to invent you."

At this point in the conversation, bin Laden had lost the swagger of his stance. "I am not convinced, Miss President, but some of your words are undeniable. I am left with uncertainty."

"How can you justify your actions," Danielle said, "if you are uncertain as to the meaning of God's words?"

"I thought that I was certain."

"Is that not a crime, to carry out such acts when you are confused as to what the Qur'ān commands?"

"I have gotten closer than ever before to the meaning of the words of He who shall not be named, thanks to this meeting," bin Laden said.

"Can you justify your actions now?" Danielle asked.

"I am left in a state of doubt. I acted in haste without full understanding. I have thereby sinned against He who shall not be named, and I deserve to die," bin Laden said. "In accepting this punishment, I should not be regarded as a martyr. I am deserving of the ultimate punishment."

"We are not here to discuss your punishment, and that will not be up to you, or even to me for that matter. I wanted to talk to you about truth."

"And that you have done."

"I am also asking for your cooperation," Danielle continued.

"What is it that you ask?"

"I need you to tell your followers that you were wrong; that al-Qaeda is wrong. That all plans and organization should be abandoned."

Bin Laden bowed his head and went on to speak at length fulfilling Danielle's request.

As Danielle left, she faced him, stood erect, and said "May God have mercy on your soul."

After the telecast, the CIA still worried that coded messages for terror attacks had been issued. "I didn't notice any such messages," Danielle told General Petraeus, "but why don't you check it out."

"I'll do that," Petraeus replied, "but my bigger concern is that as a result of your dialogue with Mr. bin Laden, a faction of al-Qaeda, with

forces in Iraq and Syria, has broken ties with al-Qaeda and is now going in its own direction. They appear to be even worse than bin Laden's followers."

"We'll just have to deal with one problem at a time," Danielle replied.

The biggest controversy about her meeting with bin Laden concerned the apparent deference she showed to him. Polls showed a high level of discomfort with the tenor of her discussion.

"You treated him like a world leader, politely debating esoteric issues," Craig Michaels said in an interview with Danielle on his show *Hot Seat*.

"I treated him as someone who is still influential and who has something we need," Danielle replied.

"He is a vile mass murderer responsible for the deaths of thousands of innocent Americans and many others," Michaels countered.

"And your point is what?" Danielle asked lifting her eyebrows.

"Polls show you were too respectful."

"I got what we needed. The crumbs can fall where they may. Anyway, I was respectful to Islam and the Qur'ān, not to bin Laden."

"Would you have shown the same respect for Hitler?" Michaels asked.

"If it would have saved the life of a single victim of Nazism, then yes."

"So, if we had captured Hitler after World War II and you were president, you would have engaged in a patient dialogue to convince him that Nazism was wrong?"

"Probably not—the Germans had grown disillusioned with Hitler and the Nazi movement was already a spent force when Germany surrendered. There would have been little point."

"There were still ex-Nazis prowling around," Michaels pointed out.

"They were not significant at that point. But al-Qaeda is still potent, although I believe with bin Laden's recantation, that movement will soon be swept into the dustbin of history."

"He was not completely certain of his disavowal at the end of your meeting," Michaels pointed out.

"So much the better. He recognized that having doubt was an unacceptable basis for the evil deeds he carried out."

"And you think his followers will accept this repudiation? He was a prisoner after all. Many are calling you naïve."

"Oh, they'll believe it," Danielle countered. "At least many will. They will see his sincerity. It was not the sterile renunciation of someone in captivity forced to make a false confession. His uncertainty gives it credibility. And they will be convinced themselves by the logic of our discussion."

Danielle used the intelligence gained from the capture of bin Laden to capture the other al-Qaeda leaders in the first and second tier of leadership including Al-Zawahiri,[254] insisting they be captured and not killed. She dialogued with a few of the other leaders in a similar manner as her meeting with bin Laden.

By then the third-tier leaders of al-Qaeda were in charge. With the decimation of the leadership, the convincing repudiation by bin Laden, and the infiltration of their ranks by Danielle's agents, the new leaders called for their groups to disband. There was push back within al-Qaeda by purists and hard-liners, but their cause imploded as their internal debates became riddled by the same doubts that bin Laden expressed in his dialogue with Danielle.

The CIA, however, became concerned with a new group that had broken off from al-Qaeda and was organizing in Iraq and Syria.[255] They appeared to be even more ruthless and brutal than al-Qaeda.

Danielle presented presidential medals to the members of Navy Seal Team Six.[256] The presentation was televised, but the faces of the commandos were all blurred out.

Afterwards, she tweeted *"I just hugged each of the 73 members of Seal Team Six. OMG!!"*

She followed this with another tweet: *"Correction: There is no such thing as Seal Team Six."*

AGE TWENTY:
ONLY SOMETIMES, WORDS STORM

Miss President, it is my pleasure to present the Honorable Amukusana Mwanza, president of the Organization of African States,"[257] the White House sergeant-at-arms announced.

Danielle and Amu broke into big grins and flew into each other's arms. Amu gave me a hug, too, and they went off holding hands as Danielle gave Amu a tour of the Rose Room.

"Tippecanoe and Tyler Too,"[258] Danielle said in a singsong voice as she held up a medal and put it around Amu's neck. "President Harrison[259] gave this to Alexander Ross[260] for writing the theme song for Harrison's election."

"What does it mean?" Amu asked.

"Tippecanoe and Tyler Too? Nothing as far I know. That's why I like it. According to historians it was the song that sang Harrison into the presidency," Danielle explained.

"You sang yourself into the White House, too," Amu observed with a smile.

I saw a wicked gleam emerge in the two young women's eyes. I looked to where they were staring and there lay two eighteenth century

French pillows that had been presented to George Washington by King Louis the Sixteenth of France[261] to congratulate the United States on its independence.

Danielle took the first swing while Amu ducked. Amu returned fire.

I saw a look of terror come into the eyes of Jeremy, one of Danielle's elite Secret Service[262] agents. His training was focused entirely on reacting instantly to any attack on the president of the United States and here he was witnessing just such an attack, albeit with a two-hundred-year-old silk pillow. I caught his eye and mouthed the words, "It's okay."

A few swings later, Danielle got Amu with a direct hit to the head which caused the pillow to explode, sending a million feathers ascending into the air, before covering the floor with a blanket of white. I felt like we were standing on a snowy field with a gentle winter storm descending in all directions, carved figures in a shaken snow globe.

"Wow, they sure pack a lot of feathers into a small pillow," I exclaimed.

"They're in pretty good shape for two-hundred-year-old feathers," Danielle said.

Danielle and Amu got on their hands and knees and attempted to pick up the feathers. I fetched two maids who ran out to help, joined by me and the Secret Service agent.

"It is okay, Miss President, this is our job," one of the maids implored.

Danielle and Amu, still covered in white feathers, retreated to the Oval Office[263] to talk about Africa.

Danielle let Amu sit in her presidential chair—a large black leather swivel chair—and put her feet up on her Oval Office desk—a massive brown wood structure carved with the Presidential Seal.

"The glass is now fifty percent full," Amu said proudly.

"Wow, you mean all of Africa?" Danielle exclaimed.

During her second year in office, Danielle introduced a radical tax simplification plan. People were skeptical at first as they had seen proposals like this before.

"I want to see all the tax planners doing something productive," was an oft-quoted Danielle line.

"What about IRS agents?" she was asked at a press conference.

"Yes, them, too," she replied.

She came out strongly for low tax rates on the one hand but with no exceptions or loopholes on the other.

"It's just not possible to tax the rich more than we're doing in areas where they actually pay taxes," was another well-known Danielle line.

"You can't just take last year's taxable income levels and apply higher rates to them as if the higher rates would have no effect on economic decisions. The moment that tax rates change, all of the decisions immediately change, too, as do the levels that you are applying the tax rates to. If you increase capital gains taxes,[264] then the wealthy will reduce the amount of security transactions that result in capital gains, thereby locking in investments in unproductive businesses. Increase dividend taxes and corporations reduce the level of dividends. Increase tax rates on investment income and the money moves off shore, and so on. It's just like a company. It does not directly control its revenue, only its prices. Increasing prices may or may not increase revenues. Often it decreases them."

She introduced a more sophisticated model that she had developed that properly reflected these feedback loops.

"The true path to revenue enhancement," she pointed out, "is to close loopholes and exceptions put there by lobbyists years or decades ago with rationalizations that have little to do with today's world."

She succeeded in passing a tax simplification[265] plan that essentially had no exceptions, even for home ownership. "Why should we favor the class of people who happen to own homes? Renting a house or apartment is a perfectly rational economic decision. Let the market work out what is best for each person."

She introduced a small negative income tax,[266] which went a long way in gaining the support of the left. The government would now pay low income earners twenty percent of the first $20,000 of their income. "I'd rather pay people who work than pay people not to work," Danielle explained.

"And this will be a first step in addressing the employment impact of future automation from AI," Danielle added.

She made one exception to her otherwise convincing plea for simplification: tax breaks to encourage investing in new enterprises, and for being an entrepreneur.

She also brought entrepreneurship to the schools. "If college kids like Silver, Bhutto, Zuckerberg, Page, Brin, Gates, Jobs, and Wozniak can start revolutions, why not high school and junior high school kids?"

Economic growth rates jumped quickly after Danielle took office just from the optimism she brought, stimulated by the enormous success she had running China. With her economic policies, US GDP[267] annual growth rose to five percent by the middle of her term.

$$\sim\!\ell\,\ell\!\sim$$

I paid one of my regular visits to Ambassador Liu at the Chinese Embassy in Washington, DC. He was always very solicitous of me and we went through a litany of routine issues. We worked on software transparency to address the continued suspicion that the countries were stealing each other's trade secrets. A colleague of Liu's came in—a beautiful Chinese woman wearing a trim black skirt and a red jacket embroidered in black with intricate Chinese characters. We caught each other's eye. *I've seen that woman before,* I thought. *But where?*

They walked down the hall and disappeared into a private office. While they were out of sight, I wandered carefully into an annex of Liu's office where I understood he worked when alone. There was a half-filled cup of Starbucks coffee which Liu always drank, and his reading glasses lying atop a report. Of course, I couldn't linger there for more than a few moments, but something significant caught my eye, and I made a mental note, so I could report it back to Danielle.

Liu and his colleague, Jinghua Liang, had a conversation which I subsequently learned about from Danielle.

"It's fate, don't you think?" she said.

"Fate?"

"Fate, destiny, something meant to be," Jinghua clarified.

"I suppose every day and every detail fulfills our destiny," Liu responded, not entirely clear what she was getting at.

"I worked in the Intelligence Ministry and now I am here working with you. That is destiny, is it not?" Jinghua said.

"Well I'm glad you are here, Jinghua."

"I am, too," Jinghua replied. "I very much enjoy when we work together, sometimes late into the night."

Liu was at a loss for words so there was a silence which Jinghua broke. "What do you think of me?"

"You're a wonderful researcher, Jinghua, probably the best I've worked with."

"Thank you, sir. I was asking perhaps a bit more personally."

Liu thought for a moment and responded, "You are a beautiful, intelligent and purposeful woman. You will make some gentleman very happy."

Jinghua hesitated and replied, "You are a gentleman."

Liu also hesitated, smiled, looked at her, and said, "You are very kind, Jinghua, but I have already given my heart away."

"Oh, that is good, sir, very good. I am happy that you will be happy. And the keeper of your heart, too."

Liu betrayed a forlorn look, looked away and said, "I wish that it were so, but I took my heart back. Well, that was actually not my intention, but it is what I clumsily managed to do, and now I've lost it."

"Your heart, sir? That is not a good thing to lose."

"Yes, I don't recommend it."

"Perhaps you would like me to help you find it?"

"I wish that were possible, Jinghua. But that is something I will have to do myself."

Liu returned to his meeting with me. We got through a couple of the issues on my list, but there was more to discuss.

"Okay if I return tomorrow at two and we can continue?" I suggested.

"That will be great, Claire."

⁓ℓℓ⁓

The next day, I watched on Life Bits while Liu waited for my arrival. Instead it was the other Calico sister who strode into his office. Liu's embassy staff nearly fell over themselves at this sudden unannounced visit by the president of the United States, not to mention that she was also their former president. Not quite sure of the correct protocol under the circumstance, a few stood up, others knelt down, one bowed, and one appeared to fall over.

Danielle and Liu retreated to his meeting office.

Liu was circumspect, not wanting to say the wrong thing, which he felt he had done consistently with Danielle.

Looking uncharacteristically nervous, Danielle drew in a slow breath. "It's hard to know where or how to begin."

Liu attempted to break the ice with a poem. "'Starting is the hardest thing.[268] Only sometimes, words storm ...'"

Danielle finished the first stanza, "'... like a March flood hurls a kayak down the Allagash.' That was the first poem we shared."

"I remember it well," Liu said.

"Liu ..." Danielle cleared her throat and started again. "As I said when we met, I'm a little slow sometimes, but I finally figured out why you, uh, dumped me six years ago."

Liu looked at her intently.

"You wanted me to experience relationships with other boys ..."

Danielle continued, "But you felt I would regret having given my heart away so early if I didn't open myself to other relationships while still young. And our love, if it was strong and true, would survive, and we'd come together again in the end."

Liu gave her a wry smile. "That's eloquent, Danielle, I should have you speak for me in the future—especially when I'm talking to you."

Danielle took a deep breath. "Why didn't you tell me what was going on, what you had in mind?"

"There was a lot that I wanted to say, but for whatever reason ..." Liu shook his head.

As he spoke I wondered if the primary reason Liu had been unable to explain six years ago was Danielle's overwhelming silence to his first words about changing the relationship.

He continued, "I found myself unable to speak."

"Yes, I remember our extreme silence that evening. I think about it all the time."

"Although I wanted to provide a clearer and more comforting perspective," Liu explained, "I didn't want to put the burden on you. I wanted you to have the opportunity to open your heart to others."

"I understand, I'd just be waiting for you," Danielle added to his explanation, "My explorations would just have been a dating game."

"So to speak," Liu said.

"Unlike the wonderful dates I did manage to have," Danielle said with a smile. "Still it would have been good to know that I was participating in this, uh, experiment."

"It wasn't an experiment exactly," Liu said. "You deserved the opportunity explore relationships with an open heart."

"What I deserve," Danielle replied, "or what I *desire* to deserve is love. I thought I had that."

"You said yourself in our first meeting, that true love will conquer any obstacle."

Danielle sighed. "That was an awfully big chance to take. You sent your true love out into the wilderness—and forced me to do the same with you—and then relied on my romantic notion about love conquering all?"

"The immediate motivation, Danielle, was my strong feeling that you would regret not having had this chance, this freedom. It would have followed us forever."

Danielle looked down at the floor. My Life Bits perspective at this point was through her eyes so I started to count the floor tiles Danielle was looking at, reminding me again of when I was waiting for her to be born.

Danielle finally said, "You were supposed to date other people, too."

"Yeah, well, I did try. I did."

"But was it real? Did you really give yourself to others or did you always know we'd end up together?"

"I feared I had lost you. The uncertainty I'd caused by rejecting you also forced me to consider other partners, which only solidified my commitment to you."

"So doubt is the only path to certainty?"

"Yes. Something like that."

"I understand," Danielle replied. "So, did I pass the test?"

"Yes," Liu said.

"What was my grade?"

Liu laughed. "It was pass-fail. Oh, and did I pass *your* little test?"

"With flying colors, Liu." Danielle started to cry.

"Kind of a delayed reaction," Liu said, and started to cry as well.

She nodded. "I never properly cried from when you told me to go away. I guess I didn't know what to make of it. I told you I was a little slow. I do need to say," Danielle continued, "please don't ever do this again. I mean if you express your love to me the same way again, I … I don't think I could survive it." Danielle smiled now while still crying.

"Maybe we should kiss," Liu said.

"Hey, hold your horses, what kind of girl do you think I am?"

"It's not like you've never kissed a boy before."

"There've only been five. Well, I only kept track of kisses on the lips. But we have an agreement, don't you remember?"

"Yes, of course."

"I didn't make that agreement with the other boys," Danielle clarified. "The agreement you and I have, on the other hand, is still in effect. But it won't be long now, Liu."

AGE TWENTY-ONE:
THAT FRESHLY KISSED LOOK

Russian president Putin[269] walked into the oval office with a birthday cake for Danielle's 21st birthday. The frosting had an image of a family of stacking Matryoshka dolls,[270] each looking like Danielle.

She had just started to cut the cake when her cell phone beeped. She squealed and ran out of the room. She then ran back in, hugged Mr. Putin and ran back out again.

"It's a guy," her vice president told Mr. Putin.

"Ah ha; Good for her," President Putin said with a smile.

Danielle and Liu met in the private sitting room. They had both brought their Danielle and Liu dolls.

Danielle's Liu doll was the worse for wear. Her eyes were wide with anticipation. "Maybe we should do our curtseying and bowing thing," she suggested.

They started to kneel down, lurched, banged their heads together and broke out laughing.

I felt my face turn red, a feeling I recalled from when Charlie stole his first kiss almost two decades earlier. I quickly turned off Life Bits Share and let them have a private moment.

An hour later I gingerly reconnected to Life Bits.

"Oh my god, I left the president of Russia waiting," Danielle said.

"I wouldn't worry about it, I'm sure he can take care of himself."

"Maybe he also found someone to kiss," Danielle said. "Was it worth waiting for?"

"It would have been worth waiting a thousand years for," Liu responded.

"RT!" Danielle said in mock horror.

Liu responded, "I don't think we need to worry about that anymore."

"Isn't it surprising," Danielle said, "the world hasn't noticed us yet? I mean they know we work together, but ..."

"There was that blogger," Liu pointed out, "who found it remarkable you never hugged me or even shook my hand when we got together publicly. He found that suspicious."

"I guess we overcompensated," Danielle admitted, "but, really, no one seems to know. I'd better pull myself together," she said, looking in the sitting room mirror. "I have that freshly kissed look."

That weekend, Danielle held a State dinner for President Zhao in the State Dining Room in the White House. This time she brought an official date. It was the first time that the world saw Liu in this role.

She held his hand and went around introducing him. Of course, the guests already knew the Chinese ambassador, but this was the first time they had met him as "my boyfriend," as Danielle put it. It was also somewhat of a family reunion as Mom, Dad, Charlie, and I were also guests.

Danielle had Congress pass special legislation to provide dual citizenship for Liu. He would keep his role as ambassador but also work for Danielle's administration promoting democracy and human rights around the world.

I was scanning Facebook when I found *The Daily Beast's* latest cartoon about Danielle—showing her with a ghostly image of President Reagan.[271] The caption read, "Mr. Reagan, are you there? Speak to me." They were alluding to the most controversial aspect of the first half of Danielle's term, a massive program to build an arsenal of anti-missile missiles.[272]

A strong economy blunted some of the criticism but the Center for American Progress,[273] an influential liberal think tank attributed the GDP growth to Danielle's spending on the missiles—which had reached a trillion dollars a year.

"I know this isn't popular," Danielle said on CNN, "but the value will become clear before long."

During the second half of her term, economic growth rates approached six percent. She focused on a new project to eliminate nuclear weapons from the world. She felt this would be a worthy use of the growing worldwide political influence of the Daniellites. Liu and I were pressed into service for this initiative. Even Charlie helped out with a special Bombs Away art exhibition.

Danielle was able to secure Israel's agreement through a promise to provide them with an advanced military technology which she had been involved in developing which deployed AI and nanotechnology.[274] India and Pakistan agreed if it occurred simultaneously for both nations, and if all other nations agreed. Russia agreed if India, Pakistan, and China would agree. She got China's agreement due to her strong continued influence there, but it was contingent on Russia and the United States. France had agreed early on that they would end the possession of nuclear weapons if all of the aforementioned nations agreed, which they never expected to happen.

"No one likes to talk about the specter of nuclear annihilation, and ever since the end of the Cold War[275] the issue appears to have dropped out of sight. But the weapons themselves have not disappeared. There are still enough thermonuclear weapons[276] to wipe out all human life ten times over. And the weapons remain on a hair trigger[277] due to the insane logic of mutually assured destruction."[278] So began one of Danielle's many speeches to the American people on the topic. But it was indeed an unpleasant topic to talk about and Danielle's approval ratings started to drop.

The complex web of contingent agreements was dependent on agreement by the United States, but that was the one nation where she drew a complete blank. Both houses of Congress voted strongly against her proposal.

So, it was back to the drawing board, and she sent Liu as an emissary to renegotiate all of the agreements. In the end Danielle managed to get approval of all nations, including the US, for a treaty requiring a thirty percent across the board reduction.

"Great. We now have only seven times as many weapons as we need to kill all humans," Danielle confided to me. Her social studies grade for the "get rid of nuclear weapons" project: C+.

"Your grades are getting worse, Danielle," Liu told her.

"That's true, and I can't say the problem sets are getting any harder. Maybe I'm past my prime."

"Oh, I don't think that's true."

"Well then, I must be spending too much time kissing you."

A few months later, Mom called and said she wanted us all to come over for dinner the next evening at their second home in Georgetown. I told Mom that I had a 3D conference with the Haitian Governing Board that day, but she insisted, saying it was a celebration and everyone needed to be there. Not wanting to be a bad sport, I rescheduled my meeting and arrived at home wondering what award Danielle had won this time. Everyone—Mom, Dad, Danielle, Liu, Charlie, and I—showed up, which gave me a very warm feeling, as it was a rare occurrence these days.

There was another gentleman there, but he was not the guy from the Nobel Award Committee whom we had all come to know quite well. We excitedly caught up with each other, and Charlie passed around his tablet showing how he was continuing his Bombs Away art project, but everyone was getting increasingly curious as to what it was we were celebrating.

Finally, Dad asked us all to sit on the couches in the living room.

"This gentleman, Donald Pritchker, came around looking for a Calico sister, so I thought we would all gather to hear what he has to say," Dad said.

"You don't need an excuse to get us together, Dad," I replied.

Danielle put her hand on my knee. "Dad's up to something. Let's see what he has to say."

"I'm Donald Pritchker," the gentleman began. "I have a letter here that I would like to deliver personally. It's to you, Claire. It reads, 'The Pulitzer Prize[279] Committee is greatly pleased to inform you that your book, *Danielle: Chronicles of a Superheroine, Part One: Dancing on Quicksand,* has been selected for this year's Pulitzer Prize for Non-fiction.'"

"Oh my god," I said. "I didn't even know I was nominated."

"To the master storyteller!" Dad said as he raised his glass. We toasted enthusiastically, spilling our champagne on each other.

Tears of pride welled up in Danielle's eyes as she gave me a big hug. I could see what people saw in these hugs from Danielle. The hugs from Mom and Dad weren't bad either. I shed a few tears myself.

Dancing on Quicksand was my account of Danielle's and my adventures together in the Middle East. *This won't be at all bad for sales of* Part Two: Bounding the Great Wall, I thought. Danielle convinced me to wait on releasing *Part Two* until the public knew about her and Liu. The timing worked out pretty well, after all.

I got a lot of praise for my illustrations. My favorite was of Danielle and me burying the evidence of a crime in the sand in Zambia when she was seven.

Danielle asked that I not reveal that it was she who had sent Jinghua to test Liu's love for her, but she relented when Liu said he was fine with

247

me including it. I also described what I had seen in Liu's private office annex when I'd looked in while Liu talked to Jinghua: the doll of Danielle sitting on his desk holding a fresh white rose.

I was back in *The Look* green room. I thought, *I've been here before, seated on this same sagging sofa.* There was the large unframed picture of Wanda Rossberg wearing her green shapeless blouse. And the faded picture of Sandra Winters with her co-hosts, had been in the same spot ever since I first came on *The Look* with Danielle thirteen years earlier. If you looked carefully someone had drawn a mustache on Sandra's face, and the attempt to remove it had not been completely successful. Like most green rooms I've been in, there was very little green there. Aside from Wanda Rossberg's smock, there was a spindly ivy plant in the corner. I don't think it had benefited from the rapid turnover of interns on the show.

"Shock at Olga Walker's Move to *The Look*," read a recent *Variety* headline taped to the surface of the coffee table which had a few more nicks and stains each time I saw it. Actually, Olga rarely showed up, but I understood she planned to be here for my song. They were expecting something big from me.

I figured the timing might be a little tricky. I planned to say, *"I would like to sing a song dedicated to my sister, Danielle."* Then I would just stare at the hostesses. But how long should I smile and stare before finishing my sentence and completely blowing everybody's mind?

I tried to think this through, but like a singer losing her timing, posture, and pitch, my practice did not work very well. I wasn't sure why I was pacing; I suppose I hadn't fully absorbed the announcement myself. I mean it was good news, but my relationship with Danielle was about to change yet again.

I picked up my coffee cup—okay, it was green, too—and the room started to shake. The hot coffee spilled on my hand, and I dropped the cup. It smashed on the hardwood floor. I thought a truck must have driven by, but shaking rooms and breaking coffee cups still terrified me. It took me back to 23 years earlier, sitting on that dirt floor in a Haitian factory.

I gathered my wits and decided to focus on my routine. Before I knew it, they were urgently calling me to come out on stage. As I walked out I thought that my voyage with my sister had just begun.

I was struck by the bright lights. I don't think it was any different than the previous times I was on the show, but I had never noticed them before. I felt perspiration on my brow.

"I'd like to sing a song dedicated to my sister ..." I said.

The hostesses smiled and waited for me to sing.

I sat there with my guitar, staring back at them and saying nothing further for what seemed like forever. It reminded me of the concert at the Country Music Association Festival thirteen years earlier when I introduced Danielle.

Finally, I finished my sentence.

"—and her fiancé!"

The hostesses' faces lit up, and so did the audience as they all realized I had just announced the engagement of Danielle and Liu.

At that moment, Danielle and Liu came out of the wings and there were hugs all around and the traditional exclamations about her engagement ring. Liu wore a slim blue suit with a striped white shirt and black tie. Danielle wore a beige spring dress patterned with pink roses and an open button-up white sweater.

"So, tell us about your relationship," Olga asked. "When did you first become a couple?"

"Uh, well, almost ten years ago," Danielle said.

The women were a bit stunned but tried to keep their composure.

"But we had our first kiss only eight months ago, on my twenty-first birthday, and we didn't touch each other until then." Danielle said. "Well, except for two times."

"Actually, it was three times," Liu corrected her. "There was the time we met when we fell over each other and became entangled like manifolds and membranes."

"Manifolds and membranes?" Wanda Rossberg asked. "Hey, if you love each other, you could be bungee jumping together in your birthday suits for all I care."

Everyone laughed.

"We actually do want to explain our relationship which, of course, is hard to do for any couple."

"Tell them about the movie, Claire," Liu said.

"I'm making a movie called *The Story of Danielle and Liu,* about how they met, and how they got to where they are now, which of course is them sitting here on *The Look* with me and all of you and Danielle wearing this beautiful ring."

"Claire is certainly the right person to tell the story," Danielle said.

"I want to play you, Danielle," Wanda said. The audience laughed.

"Actually no one plays us," Danielle replied. "Claire and I have been doing Life Bits since I was born. So, it will all be original footage."

"Yeah, it's quite an editing job," I said. "We each have 87,000 hours of footage. Of course, a lot of that is of us sleeping. There were security concerns to deal with, but we've got all of that worked out. Mr. Rothstein has offered to help with the editing." I grinned. "He's Assistant Editor."

"You mean we'll actually see the two of you—Danielle and Liu—meet?" Sandra Winters exclaimed.

"And your first kiss?" Olga beamed.

"That's the idea," Liu said.

"We're kind of interested in seeing that ourselves," Danielle added.

"I just watched those scenes," I said. "But you'll have to wait until the movie comes out, which will be in about a month assuming Rothstein and I can finish this crazy editing job. We've got a hundred people helping us."

Finally, I got to sing my ballad to my sister and future brother-in-law:

The girl who came into my life
when I was eight
leaped over seas
and valleys
with me dearly
holding on
She had a schoolgirl crush
on a master
of time and space
of liberty and peace
of sacrifice and waiting
for a kiss ...

AGE TWENTY-TWO:
FOREVER HOLD THE PEACE

"How did Danielle get to be so, uh, special?" I asked Dad, as I sewed the finishing touches on my pink matron of honor dress.

"She's always been that way, as you undoubtedly recall," Dad replied.

"That doesn't really answer my question, Dad. You seem to know something."

"Well, someday perhaps it will become clear," Dad replied. "Come on, we don't want to be late for the wedding."

Danielle and Liu were married on her twenty-second birthday on the South Lawn of the White House. Liu was then not quite twenty-six. It was the first White House wedding of a sitting US president. Now six months pregnant, I was the Matron of Honor. Zhao was best man and Charlie was a groomsman. Amu, Annie, Meredith, Baylor Sweet, and Martine Rothblatt were bridesmaids.

Our proud dad walked his younger daughter down the aisle. Mom was relieved that all the arrangements were working and that she

wouldn't have to talk to the White House Social Affairs Department anymore about the snafus with the white lilies or questions about how many people were needed to hold up the *chuppah*.[280]

Danielle's dress reminded me of her "coming out" gown at the Grammys six years earlier although it was all white and her bodice was an elaborate embroidery of white roses with white flower lace across her shoulders. And the small white and yellow iris on her left breast; it was indeed the same one from six years earlier.

Presiding was a female Unitarian[281] minister. Religious leaders of all the major religions, including Rabbi Schneerson, participated in the ceremony to offer their blessings on the newlyweds.

The Unitarian minister began, "A rabbi, a minister, a priest, and an Imam preside over a wedding …"

We all danced late into the night. Danielle refused to change into another dress as many brides do and danced for hours in her wedding gown.

Annie, Amu, and Baylor Sweet all jumped up to catch the bridal bouquet but it was Amu who caught it. Tony, Ben, and Elliot applauded.

Uncle Eric admired the seven-tiered chocolate wedding cake. Chairman Zhao appeared tipsy from the champagne. Baylor Sweet danced exuberantly to Dustin Siever's latest hit, while Mom and Dad tried to waltz to it. Charlie eyed my stomach.

As the guests were leaving, the head of the National Security Council[282] urgently got Danielle's attention and beamed a message to her lens display:

"Level 9.5 alert: An atomic bomb has exploded in a remote area of Ohio. Casualties unknown. A message has been decoded: 'Madame President, most sorry to interrupt the festivities. This is just a demonstration of our capability for now. More to come.'"

THE END

OR

JUST THE BEGINNING

Read on to learn how YOU can become a Danielle.

How You Can Be a Danielle

How You Can Be a Danielle

As I point out in the Preface to *Danielle: Chronicles of a Superheroine*, for all the quandaries we face—business problems, health issues, relationship difficulties, the great social and cultural challenges of our time—there exists an idea that will enable us to prevail. We can and must find that idea. And when we find it, we need to implement it.

That is Danielle's philosophy. And it can be your philosophy, as well. If you see a problem, big or small, you can apply your mind—and your courage, creativity and tenacity—to solve it. We can all be Danielles regardless of age and situation. If Danielle's exploits seem remarkable, I would point out that each of her accomplishments are achievements that a person, even a child, can do today. Indeed young people are already changing the world. The major tech companies—Microsoft, Apple, Google—were started by students barely over twenty. We see students in high school and earlier grades creating transformative ideas.

This is also the best way to learn. "Learn by Doing" is the philosophy of Singularity University, of which I am cofounder and Chancellor, where students self-organize into teams to take on grand challenges. Whether these projects succeed or fail, the students will succeed in learning a myriad of skills and ideas. Learn by Doing is also the philosophy of the school founded by Danielle's Dad, and that Danielle and her sister, Claire, attend. Danielle's adventures represent her school projects. If I think back on my own life and what I have managed to learn, it is all from my projects, not from school.

This is a guide—for all ages—to help you contribute to solving the kinds of problems Danielle takes on. If everyone did this, the world would become a far better place.

One aspect of today's technology is that it allows children and adults to magnify their reach exponentially in a way never before possible. An idea can spread virally on social media regardless of the age, background, status, title, or accomplishments of the originator. It is only the power of the idea that matters.

I do need to strike one note of caution: Danielle is a superheroine and none of us has all of her super powers, not yet anyway. For example, you might admire Superman and Wonder Woman and it would be commendable to emulate their dedication to truth and freedom, but I would advise you not to jump off your garage thinking you could fly.

Similarly, as you seek to be a Danielle, please use reasonable caution to stay safe. Although Danielle's parents struggle with her independent ways, they do review—and approve—each of her ambitious ventures. She is always supervised by an adult—Uncle Eric, Aunt Ellie, Mom, Dad, and Claire (when she becomes an adult). So if you are a child, I encourage you to do the same: seek the guidance of adults who can steer your efforts while keeping you protected. For example, you can press for democracy and freedom in other lands, but it's best to do it from a country that already enjoys these liberties and from which you can carry out your efforts safely.

These entries provide ideas and suggestions for activities and organizations that you can join and assist. Since organizations and websites are constantly changing, please consult with the updated version of this guide at this site: DanielleWorld.com/resources. All of the numbered notes in these sections correspond to resources on the website.

Your efforts will be multiplied by others following in your footsteps and being inspired by your ideas. The following conversation Danielle has with Mom, Dad, and Claire after six-year-old Danielle has returned from helping with the drought in Zambia illustrates this idea (written from Danielle's sister Claire's perspective):

"We didn't do much," Danielle said at the dinner table.

"Hey that's an improvement over 'we didn't do *anything*,'" I noted.

"It sounds like thousands of people who were drinking contaminated water before now have clean water," Mom said. "That's something to be proud of, not mope about."

"Danielle is always looking at the glass half-empty rather than half-full," Dad observed.

Danielle sighed. "By my calculations, the glass is now about one third of one percent full."

"That's a lot, Danielle," Dad countered. "The Talmud says 'whoever saves one life has saved the whole world.'"

She perked up slightly. "The Talmud says that? Okay, but a million people in Zambia are still without clean water."

"Danielle, you can't solve all of this by yourself. Anyway, you've contributed more than just some machines," Dad pointed out.

"Like what? Amu's and my instructional video?"

"You gave them the most valuable thing of all, a good idea," Dad explained. "Others can follow in your footsteps."

"We'll see," Danielle said. "Mao once said he felt he was only moving a few deck chairs around on a sinking ship. He didn't feel he was having much impact."

"Too bad Mao didn't stick to moving deck chairs around," Dad replied. "Impact is not as important as having the right ideas. If one percent of the world did as much as you, there would be no suffering."

Footnote links at
DanielleWorld.com/resources

and Learn to Program Computers from a Young Age

O ne of Danielle's most important skills in the novel is computer programming. This allows her to create the Danielle Music service to revolutionize the distribution of music, develop a new quantum encryption system to protect her "life bits" stream (which is recording every moment of her and her sister Claire's lives), and write software to help rebels in Libya and overcome dictator Muammar Qaddafi's military.

But Danielle's fictional story has many real-life inspirations, where young people changed the world through computer programming. The most famous examples include Bill Gates starting Microsoft by creating software for the first personal computers, Larry Page and Sergey Brin creating the first truly effective search engine in their Stanford University dorm, and Mark Zuckerberg, who wrote the code for Facebook in his dorm room and turned it into one of the world's most valuable and innovative companies.

Coding has countless practical applications. You can use programming skills to share information with people around the globe, form new communities, discover and learn from data, entertain others, and develop new inventions. The possibilities are limited only by your imagination.

But you don't even have to be in college to have a big impact through programming—for example, at age 14, Daniel Singer created an anonymous messaging app called YouTell that attracted over three million users. If you learn how to code, you can join Danielle, Zuckerberg, Singer, and many others like them in changing the world.

Whether you're in grade school, middle school, high school, college, or even older, there are dozens of great ways to get your start in computer programming.[1] So how do you begin?

One of the best ways to start learning programming as a beginner is to take an online course. There are many options, ranging from simple instructional videos, to full classes with projects, quizzes, and graded assignments. Here are some of the best:

- Osmo Coding[2] is a game system for iPads that's perfect for young kids in elementary school. It helps you learn about logic and the basic concepts of programming, but without formal lessons. Instead, you learn by doing—experimenting with a set of physical blocks that represent code elements, and seeing how they control Awbie, a cartoon character on the app. Even if you're older, you might want to see if your family or school can get Osmo for a younger sibling or friend. Helping them learn with the app can help you understand coding better, too.

- Tynker[3] has free tutorials and games that teach basic coding and are specially designed for kids. If you're in elementary school or middle school, you might want to check out this fun site first before moving on to more advanced options.

- Khan Academy[4] has a wide selection of high-quality introductory courses, available for free. You watch videos which explain new concepts and then experiment with interactive tools to get more experience. The lessons come in bite-sized chunks that you can work through at your own pace, and are a fantastic way to learn JavaScript, which is one of the easiest and most useful programming languages. Whatever your age, within just an hour or two, you can be writing simple programs.

- edX[5] is a platform that allows you to take online courses from top universities for free. Top instructors from schools like Harvard, MIT, and Caltech teach many of the classes, and others are taught by professionals from tech companies like Microsoft. These courses are more in-depth than Khan Academy and often take several weeks to complete, but are good for advanced high school students. Some edX courses can be used to earn college credit.

- Udacity[6] and Coursera[7] are two of the most popular for-profit providers of Massive Online Open Courses (MOOCs). Some of their classes are free, and others charge fees which go toward paying instructors to individually evaluate your work and give you feedback on how to improve. Both companies offer a broad selection of programming courses and can help you master more specialized skills.

Although online courses can be really helpful, many people prefer face-to-face interaction with a teacher as they're learning how to code. Fortunately, a rapidly growing number of schools now offer classes on computer programming. If your school is one of them, you're lucky! If not, you can think like Danielle and encourage your school to teach computer programming.

- Code.org[8] is an organization dedicated to giving all students access to programming classes. If you or your parents contact them, they can work with your school to set up courses for you and your fellow students. This will not only benefit you, but it also helps other young people who come after you. Another similar organization is Codesters[9], which focuses on a powerful but accessible programming language called Python.

- Code.org also sponsors a project called Hour of Code,[10] which partners with companies like Khan Academy to create simplified 1-hour programming tutorials. Starting with no previous experience at all, you can learn all the basics of computer programming in just one hour!

Other options for getting coding experience as a young person:

- **Take community college classes.** Many community colleges let interested young people take classes while they are in high school or even earlier. These classes are often free and let you learn programming in a hands-on environment with teachers and other students of different ages and backgrounds.

- **Start a programming club.** Learning a skill like programming is easier when you're learning together with friends. If you start a programming club at your school, everyone can practice their skills at the same time, and help each other work through challenging projects. You might even be able to get sponsorship from local businesses to pay for courses and bring in guest speakers who work in programming. If you're a girl, getting other girls interested in programming can help overcome the stereotype that coding is just for boys. For help with this, <u>Girls Who Code</u>[11] is a nonprofit dedicated to helping schools, churches, or other community organizations start coding clubs for girls in grades 6-12.

- **Volunteer with a nonprofit.** Once you have some basic coding skills, you can gain more experience by using those skills to help good causes. There are probably nonprofit organizations in your community that could expand their positive impact if they had websites or mobile apps to connect them to the people they are working to serve. When you volunteer to help them, everyone benefits!

- **Find a mentor.** Danielle learns a lot from mentors like Martine Rothblatt, but your mentors don't have to be famous. With the guidance of a parent or teacher, brainstorm with people you know who already have experience in programming and might be willing to give you advice on developing your talents further. A mentor can share their experiences of learning to code, teach you tricks and shortcuts, and show you how to avoid mistakes they made when they were younger.

- **Experiment on your own.** The greatest pioneers of computing have all done a lot of experimenting on their own. Once you've learned some simple coding, you can start thinking about how to try new ideas. Don't be afraid to put in hours tinkering around with code and trying to solve problems for yourself. Figuring out these challenges without help from anyone else can be one of the most rewarding parts of programming.

Becoming a computer programmer at a young age takes hard work, but brings a lifetime of benefits. These include:

- **Understanding logic better.** Computer programming teaches your mind to think carefully and logically. This makes it easier to analyze problems, make good decisions, and find what's wrong with the arguments other people make.

- **Becoming a clear communicator.** In real life, programming is usually collaborative. You'll work with a group of other people on your projects, which means you have to understand each other's code. Writing code that's easy for other people to understand trains you to express your ideas clearly and to "get to the point."

- **Using computers more fully.** Computers (which includes smart phones and tablets) have many features that the average person never uses. Learning to code helps you understand these functions and take better advantage of them.

- **Building websites and apps.** Communicating with large groups over the Internet requires platforms like websites and apps. Programming skills give you much greater control over this process. Much like Danielle with Danielle TV, you can build followers this way and create new online communities.

- **Unlocking insights.** The past several years have seen an explosion in so-called Big Data. We now have access to huge amounts of raw information, but programs are needed to sift through all that data and figure out the patterns. Writing these programs can uncover important insights no one could have otherwise figured out.

- **Simplifying tasks.** Many daily tasks require lots of time. Programming lets you put computers to work, saving some of that time so you can put it to a better use. For example, you might write a program that helps you study by picking out relevant information from an e-book and quizzing you on the content until you've learned it. Or you could write a program that sorts through your emails or tracks the money you're saving.

- **Implementing new ideas.** One of the biggest obstacles to innovation people face today is finding someone to translate their ideas into code. If you can write code yourself, you have a huge advantage. When you have an idea for a new service, network, or machine, you can design at least a basic version of it to get the concept off the ground.

Finally, if you're like Danielle, you may be thinking about how you can use computer programming skills to help others while you're still a young person. Fortunately, there are many options for how you can make a difference.

- **Volunteering for charity.** As mentioned above, there are lots of opportunities to volunteer for nonprofit organizations that support good causes. Social Coder[12] is a website that connects volunteer coders with charities in need of programming help. This can take many different forms. Some charities need someone to create or redesign an appealing website to attract donors and raise awareness. Others may need a mobile app to connect them to people who use their services. Sometimes, programmers use data to figure out how a charity can provide its services more effectively.

- **Entrepreneurship to solve a problem.** Some people talk about nonprofit volunteer work as though it is the only socially valuable use of your programming skills, but this isn't true. If you think of a specific problem in the world that can be solved by software, go for it! Danielle realized that there was a need for a better way of keeping communications secure, so she created a quantum encryption system. In real life, Larry Page and Sergey Brin used their programming knowledge to create the Google search engine and turn it into one of the world's most valuable companies. But Google has also made vast amounts of information available for free to billions of people. Even if your own entrepreneurial project isn't as big as Google, you can still have a positive impact by identifying a need people have and developing a product to fill that need.

- **Teaching others.** Even as a student, as soon as you have developed your programming skills, you can start teaching them to others. When Danielle is in Libya, a young orphan girl asks her to be her adoptive mother, but Danielle points out that she is still a kid, too. In a similar way, it's easy to feel that you're too young and inexperienced to teach someone else coding. But the opposite is true. Research shows that learning from peers has major benefits, and it is very rewarding to pass on your new skills to others. Not only does this bring them the benefits of learning how to code, but it also deepens your own mastery.

For more information, please see the following entries in the companion book A Chronicle of Ideas: A Guide for Superheroines (and Superheroes): Analytical Engine, Ada Lovelace, C++ Compiler.

Footnote links at

DanielleWorld.com/resources

and Help Eradicate Female Genital Mutilation

Female Genital Mutilation (FGM) is one of the great human rights violations of our time. The latest estimates say that at least <u>200 million women and girls</u>[1] around the world have had parts of their genitals cut off, usually without their consent. Even at age eleven, Danielle stands up to this injustice by speaking out against FGM at the United Nations and working with the King of Saudi Arabia to ban the practice. But you don't have to have a platform as big as Danielle's to move the world closer to an FGM-free future.

Most of the victims of FGM are in a nearly powerless position. They are typically children born in countries that are poor, where most people don't have much education, and human rights aren't strongly protected. They are growing up in societies where women are widely seen as inferior to men, so they can't safely speak out for themselves. The people with the power to end FGM—the leaders of the countries where it is practiced—have not made it enough of a priority, so the practice remains. Changing this will require ordinary people around the world to speak on behalf of those without power.

So how can you do this? One of the biggest obstacles to ending female genital mutilation is that it is a taboo subject. Because it is associated with sex and female anatomy, most people aren't comfortable talking about FGM. As a result, many people in Western countries never hear about it and don't even know that it exists. You can change that by making a decision to educate yourself about FGM and talk about it with others, even if those conversations feel a little awkward.

Educating yourself includes not only learning the medical facts about female genital mutilation, but also learning about the reasons people do it, learning about the campaigns to end it, and hearing what FGM survivors say about their experiences.

Here are some useful resources to start you off, but the Internet has hundreds more articles, videos, and podcasts to deepen your knowledge:

- The World Health Organization's basic information about FGM,[2] with facts and statistics that are useful to know when talking about it.

- The UN's answers to frequently asked questions about FGM[3] and the efforts to stop it.

- More detailed information about different types of FGM,[4] what they involve, and where they are practiced.

- An essay by Ayaan Hirsi Ali,[5] a Somali survivor of FGM who has become a prominent activist against genital mutilation. She argues, like Danielle does in the novel, that much of the discussion about FGM hides the brutal reality of this procedure.

- A powerful and emotional talk by an FGM survivor[6] from Sierra Leone who came to Australia as a girl and struggled with the trauma of what had been done to her.

- Once you've educated yourself about female genital mutilation, it's important to break the taboo and share with others what you've learned. When your friends are talking about injustice, human rights, or women's issues, you can be like Danielle by being the first to bring up an awkward subject and tackle it directly. Ask friends what they know about FGM, and point them to resources that can give them more information.

When you're talking with other people about female genital mutilation, you'll often hear the argument that FGM is an important rite of passage in some cultures, and that it is intolerant to oppose or criticize it. Some people even say it is racist (and an example of "Western imperialism") to condemn FGM, because most of the people doing it are from Africa and the Middle East.

To change people's minds, you'll need to be able to listen to them carefully and then answer their concerns with good logic and facts. Here is some more advanced reading that can help you do that better:

- An interesting article by philosopher James Rachels[7] on cultural relativism. This is the idea that we don't have any right to judge the practices of another culture. Rachels shows why this view doesn't make sense in this instance.

- Explanation by ethicist Karen Musalo[8] of the view that human rights are universal. This means that whoever you are, or whatever society you're born into, you have the same human rights as anyone else— and that culture doesn't allow other people to violate those rights.

- BBC summary of how human rights relate to FGM.[9] Includes information on the harms and pain caused by different types of FGM.

There are a few key tips to keep in mind when you're working to convince people why they should work to stop FGM:

- Universal human rights apply to everyone everywhere, even if the local culture doesn't actually recognize all those rights. Since almost all experts agree that FGM is a human rights violation, it's essential to uphold women's and children's human rights by ending FGM.

- Some cultural practices that offend Western culture, such as leaving dead bodies out to be eaten by animals, do not cause anyone real harm. Cultural relativism can explain why those people do those things. But FGM causes girls and women excruciating pain, brings risk of serious side-effects, can lead to a lifetime of health problems, and interfere with a woman's ability to engage in sexual relations.

- The focus of anti-FGM activists in America and the rest of the developed world should be on how to protect girls, not on judging the cultures they came from.

- Even though <u>FGM has been illegal in the United States since 1996, it is still happening here</u>[10]. Doctors believe that over half a million women and girls in the US are at risk for FGM, with some of these being subjected to the cutting every year. Some are mutilated in secret in America, while others are taken overseas to undergo FGM in their home countries. So far, only one person has been prosecuted under the federal FGM ban. Making people aware that this is happening in their own community is a powerful driver to action.

Once you've made people aware of the hidden reality of FGM, and convinced them it's a problem that's worth their concern, what's the next step? One of Danielle's greatest talents is mobilizing people to work together, and you can do the same. Even though students usually don't have the opportunity to travel to FGM-practicing countries and work directly with victims, you can collaborate to raise money and awareness for charities and advocacy organizations that provide the help women need.

Some ideas you might try:

- Arranging to make a presentation for students at your school.

- Forming a club for people who want to end FGM and inviting inspiring guest speakers. Holding bake sales or other fundraisers to get money for donation.

- Finding a Guinness World Record to break and using the resulting media interest to draw attention to FGM and the charities working to stop it and assist the victims.

When selecting FGM-related charities to support, it's important to make sure that they are reputable and doing effective work. These are some of the most respected:

- <u>The Ayaan Hirsi Ali (AHA) Foundation</u>[11] focuses on education and advocacy to end FGM, and also deals with forced marriage and "honor killings," where young women suffer violence due to perceived immorality, or because they have been the victims of sexual violence.

- The Daughters of Eve[12] takes an approach focused on the needs of girls and women—especially those who have already suffered female genital mutilation.

- 28 Too Many[13] provides support for organic activism within societies where FGM is common. It also offers some great suggestions for how you can get involved and have a real impact in support of this cause.

In addition to raising support and awareness for anti-FGM organizations, you can also:

- Share information about FGM on social media, connecting people with the right mix of talents to work together and have an impact.

- Sign petitions calling on politicians to be more aggressive in fighting genital mutilation.

- Write to your elected representatives and urge them to make protecting people from FGM a higher priority.

- Conduct research to expand your knowledge and awareness of this practice and the efforts to eradicate it.

For more information, please see the following entries in the companion book *A Chronicle of Ideas: A Guide for Superheroines (and Superheroes)*: Female Genital Mutilation (FGM), Female Circumcision.

Footnote links at
DanielleWorld.com/resources

and Promote Democracy in China

✻ ✻ ✻ ✻ ✻

One of the causes closest to Danielle's heart is promoting freedom and democracy in the People's Republic of China. She recognizes that the communist government is restricting the freedom of its 1.3 billion citizens and makes up her mind to create positive change. You can do the same. Even if you're not elected president of China like fifteen-year-old Danielle, you can still have a meaningful impact on the lives of the Chinese people.

Like all activism, it's important to educate yourself about the issues. With a curious mind and an Internet connection, you can learn a lot about the human rights situation in China, and discover the specific ways that people there need your help.

Here are some helpful resources to expand your knowledge and point you toward deeper learning:

- A short summary of human rights infringements by China's communist government.[1]

- Brief timeline[2] of pro-democracy activism in China.[2]

- A more detailed report on how the Chinese government infringes human rights and civil rights,[3] and denies citizens political freedom.

- A short video on the lack of democracy in China[4] and how the government there represses political opposition to one-party communist rule.

- An interview with Chinese pro-democracy activist and Nobel Peace Prize winner Liu Xiaobo (1955–2017),[5] recorded shortly before he was arrested and jailed by the authorities until his death.

Because the great majority of Chinese people do not speak English, Danielle learns Mandarin to be able to connect with them directly. If you put in the effort to learn Mandarin (or another Chinese language) yourself, you'll be able to not only communicate with Chinese people, but also understand Chinese culture more deeply.

Your best options for learning Mandarin include:

- **Immersion programs.** The most effective way to learn a new language is to put yourself in an environment where it's all around you. There are opportunities for students of all ages to travel to China and learn Chinese by immersion with native speakers. For example, the China Institute runs programs[6] for high school students to spend a summer learning Mandarin and staying with a Chinese host family. If some of your school friends are also interested in studying Mandarin, the institute can also work with your school to organize[7] a special trip for you and your classmates.

- **Online courses**. Maybe you don't have the time or money to travel to China for an immersion program, or your parents say you're not ready to go. Luckily, there are many courses you can take for free online, and allow you to study Mandarin at your own pace:

  - ChinesePod[8] is a language-learning platform that's designed for mobile devices, and focuses on learning words and phrases that will be useful in conversation right away. ChinesePod has thousands of self-contained lessons that you can study in whatever order you like. If you're too busy with school and other commitments to take a more formal course, you can probably find a few minutes a day to use ChinesePod on your phone or tablet while you're waiting in line, riding in the car, or eating lunch. For a monthly fee, you can also work 1-on-1 with a Chinese tutor.

- Coursera offers a great 6-hour Mandarin[9] course for beginners that can teach you the basics and get you ready for more advanced courses later. This is much like the start of an introductory Chinese course you could take at college.

- Chinese Learn Online[10] is a system designed to take you from a beginner all the way up to a fluent speaker. In contrast to the self-contained lessons of ChinesePod, Chinese Learn Online uses progressive lessons, which you study in sequence and which build on each other to help you develop a deep mastery of Mandarin.

- Beijing Language and Cultural University[11] offers formal Mandarin courses with 1-on-1 personalized instruction. These courses are not free, but are pretty affordable, and can give you the feedback you need to perfect your pronunciation and command of the language.

● **Rosetta Stone**. One of the world's most popular and trusted language-learning systems is available as easy-to-access software lessons.[12] They're one of the more expensive options for learning Mandarin, but you can download a free trial to see if it's a good fit before you commit to paying for it.

● **Local Classes**. Many community colleges now offer Mandarin classes, taught by experienced language teachers. These are sometimes free, and or usually have very low prices. They often allow curious and motivated students in high school, or even younger, to enroll. A growing number of cities also have classes or camps, such as these in New York[13] just for kids who want to learn Mandarin.

The Communist Party of China gets much of its power by shaping and censoring the information that citizens can access. Journalists in China face strict censorship, and government-run news agencies put out propaganda designed to make the leaders look good and hide their failures from the public. As a result, many people there don't fully understand how the government is limiting their freedoms or what democracy is like in Europe or the United States.

There is an unwritten, and largely unspoken, covenant between the communist-controlled government and the people that the government will provide economic growth and the people will essentially stay out of politics. The government has indeed provided enormous economic growth, so this pact has worked for the most part. Many observers, including this author, believe, however, that in order for economic growth to continue at the same rate as in recent decades, there will need to be a liberalization of access to information and democratic decision making.

Although the government mostly blocks Internet access to Facebook, Twitter, and Google, there are other ways you can form relationships with Chinese people. By making these direct contacts, you can be an independent source of information.

Some of the best ways to communicate directly with Chinese people include:

- **Travel to China**. The best way to meet Chinese people and form lasting relationships with them is to travel to China. If your family goes to China for a vacation, try to learn some Mandarin beforehand so you can start conversations with people outside the major hotels and tourist areas. An even better opportunity for connecting with Chinese people is to participate in educational programs like the China Institute.[14] There, you not only meet Chinese students your own age, but stay with a host family. These often become lifelong friendships. The goal is not to directly proselytize in China, but, hopefully, as more Chinese citizens see the freedoms enjoyed by other countries, they will encourage change from within.

- **WeChat**. The most popular messaging service in China is an app called WeChat.[15] It isn't very good for meeting strangers, but if you get to know some people while you're in China, it's a great way to have conversations with them after you come home. Additionally, they can introduce you to their own friends via WeChat, and you can get a wider range of contacts that way.

- **Matching Services**. Decades ago, pen pal services connected students in different countries so they could exchange letters by snail-mail. Today, sites like ConversationExchange.com[16] pair you up with Chinese people for conversations via email, text chat, audio, or video. You can find lots of partners this way, and talk to people of diverse ages, genders, and geographic locations in China.

When you're talking with people who live in the People's Republic of China, you don't need to criticize their government to promote democracy. In fact, such direct criticism would probably make them feel uncomfortable, and might get you in trouble. Instead, you can best promote democracy just by forming an honest human connection with them. As they learn more about your life and the political freedoms that you have, they may start to see through their government's propaganda, and ultimately start demanding political change.

It's hard for any one person to match Danielle's change-making powers as a superheroine, but groups of people working together can amplify their impact. Several organizations work tirelessly to document and expose human rights violations in China and to promote freedom and democracy. If you support these groups and encourage other young people to get involved in their work, you can achieve results beyond what you could do on your own.

The best of these organizations includes:

- Human Rights in China,[17] an organization that supports pro-democracy activists within China and brings international attention to Chinese voices advocating greater political freedom.

- Human Rights Watch,[18] one of the world's top watchdogs monitoring human rights abuses and violations of civil liberties. They work to get reliable sources documenting offenses by the Chinese government, which can build international support for Chinese pro-democracy movements.

- Freedom House,[19] which does research and advocacy about threats to freedom and democracy around the globe. They report on how the Chinese government uses censorship, arrests, and intimidation to undermine the free press and prevent citizens from getting accurate information.

You can support these organizations in several ways:

- **Education**. You can hold an education session at your school to spread the word about the struggle for democracy in China. Show videos of talks by Chinese activists, invite guest speakers who have lived in communist China, or write letters to elected officials urging them to support China's democracy movement more strongly.

- **Fundraising**. You might organize a fundraiser at your school or in your local community. This could be donations tied to an education session, or something like a bake sale or car wash that donates the proceeds to the organization.

- **Volunteering**. If you're old enough, you can intern for pro-democracy organizations, or volunteer for them. Volunteering may include contacting people on the organization's behalf to solicit donations, handing out printed information about the work it does, or assisting at events that raise public awareness.

When twelve-year-old Danielle gets 100 million Chinese people into the streets on short notice for her dance celebration (celebrating her Middle East peace agreement), she demonstrates to China's communist leaders that they no longer have complete control over what their citizens do. Once the people see that they can organize for fun purposes like dancing, they realize that by acting in unison, they can promote important democratic reforms.

In real life, true democracy might be achieved in China because of a similar innovation. The Arab Spring revolutions of 2011, although the results were mixed, occurred as a result of Facebook and Twitter, which allowed activists and protesters to share information and make plans in real time. What the Chinese people need is a platform that gives them accurate and reliable information about what is going on in their own country and around the world—and that allows them to coordinate communication and sharing ideas. The communists have created a "Great Firewall of China" to censor the Internet and keep tabs on citizens. You can help create ladders to climb over the wall.

If you know computer programming, you can start to create new democracy-promoting tools yourself. If you haven't studied how to code yet, it's easy to learn! See the entry "How You Can Be a Danielle and Learn to Program Computers from a Young Age" for more information on how to do so.

There are plenty of areas where there's need for a Danielle-style innovator to help people in China reach democracy:

- **Getting around censorship.** Due to government control of the Internet, it is currently difficult for the average person in China to access social media sites like Facebook, and censored news sources like *The New York Times* and *The Wall Street Journal*. A creative new platform might be able to let Chinese users access wider sources of information.

- **Sharing information.** In order for democracy to work, citizens need to be well informed. One of the main goals of the communist government is to keep its citizens in the dark about what is really happening in their country. There's need for technology that makes it easier for people to share accurate information, photos, and videos without interference by the government.

- **Organizing large groups.** Authoritarian governments fear mass protests more than almost anything else. Technology that makes it easier for people to organize protests in a decentralized way and react to government crackdowns would make it harder for the Chinese Communist Party to suppress the pro-democracy movement.

- **Reducing isolation.** Because so few Chinese people speak English, and so few foreigners speak Chinese, there is a big natural barrier to integration with the outside world. If a platform integrated AI-assisted translation into ordinary communication, it would give Chinese people much greater access to ideas from democratic countries. This would naturally make it much harder for the communist government to stay in power.

See how many more innovations you can think of!

For more information, please see the following entries in
the companion book, *A Chronicle of Ideas:
A Guide for Superheroines (and Superheroes)*:

Kuomintang, Mao's Long March, Mao Tse-Tung, Forced

Collectivism, China's One Child Policy, Tiananmen Square, President Hu, The 17-Point Agreement, The 1959 Uprising, One Country Two Systems Policy, Central Committee of the Chinese Communist Party, Chinese Communist Party, Chiang Kai-Shek, Chairman of the Communist Party of China, Mandarin, Zhongnanhai, Ming Dynasty, Forbidden City, Deng Xiaoping, Shanghai, Power From the Barrel of a Gun.

Footnote links at
DanielleWorld.com/resources

HOW YOU CAN BE A DANIELLE

and Promote Nuclear Disarmament

Of all the challenges our species currently faces, the threat of nuclear war is the only one currently with the potential to wipe out human civilization. This could happen in a matter of a few hours. Although the number of nuclear weapons in the world has declined by about 75% since its peak during the Cold War, there are still about 15,000 warheads in the arsenals of the United States, Russia, and several other countries. These weapons could be used as a result of deliberate war, an international misunderstanding, malfunctioning technology, or cyber-attacks by hackers. Or they could be stolen by terrorists and used against a major city somewhere in the world.

Danielle makes it one of her highest priorities to achieve nuclear disarmament—a world where all nations peacefully give up their nuclear weapons. Even though Danielle is not fully successful in the novel, she does make progress in this endeavor. Like Danielle, you probably won't be able to eliminate nuclear weapons on your own, but there are some things you can realistically do to bring a nuclear-free world closer to reality.

To learn more about nuclear weapons and why they are such a danger, you can check out these resources:

- Interesting list[1] of 50 facts about nuclear weapons, compiled by the well-respected Brookings Institute.

- United Nations list of resources[2] for students to learn more about nuclear disarmament and the risks of nuclear war.

- Illustrated explainer video[3] by AsapSCIENCE about the effects of nuclear weapons, a background for students and curious young people.

- Short animated video[4] by former US Secretary of Defense William J. Perry about the consequences of a nuclear attack by terrorists, and an interview[5] with Perry explaining his views.

- Informative and intentionally humorous video[6] by John Oliver explaining the danger from America continuing to have a stockpile of thousands of nuclear weapons that are hard to keep safe.

Even as a young person, you can take several concrete actions to promote nuclear disarmament:

- **Advocate to friends.** At present, a majority of citizens in America and the UK still support their countries keeping stockpiles of nuclear weapons. Achieving disarmament will require changing a lot of people's minds. By talking to your friends, classmates, teammates, and neighbors about this issue, you can gradually shift public opinion toward supporting disarmament. Take the time to become familiar with the key arguments[7] for disarmament, and think of ways to answer potential objections.

- **Start a club.** Groups of people working together for the same goal are usually more effective than activists working all alone. Find a group of young people in your community who share the goal of global nuclear disarmament, and start a club to unite your efforts and share suggestions. In planning your group's projects, read this useful guide[8] by the International Campaign to Abolish Nuclear Weapons (ICAN) on activities students can do to promote nuclear disarmament. The guide includes important facts, information resources, and creative ideas for activism by young people. Because changing many people's minds requires lots of hard work, you should also take a look at ICAN's suggestions[9] on how to build collaboration between a wide range of groups in support of nuclear disarmament.

- **Organize an event.** Holding an event at your school or in your neighborhood is a great way to introduce your fellow students to the issues around nuclear disarmament. You could organize discussions, bring guest speakers who work for anti-nuclear organizations, or show videos like those mentioned above. One unusual activity that can be the focus of a school event is a group effort to fold 1,000 paper cranes. In Japanese culture, this represents peace and nuclear disarmament. Once you've folded the cranes, send them to a politician who you want to send a powerful and symbolic message to about the passion and commitment of the disarmament movement. Here's an example[10] of how such projects can have great impact in the media, raising vital awareness about the urgent need to reduce nuclear stockpiles.

- **Write publicly.** Whenever you see newspapers or online publications publish articles in favor of nuclear weapons, that's a great opportunity to write a letter to the editor[11] arguing for disarmament. This will expose large numbers of readers to arguments against nuclear weapons that they may never have heard or considered before. You can also use your social media accounts or blog as a platform for sharing your views about nuclear disarmament with a wider audience.

- **Support pro-disarmament policies.** Most politicians in nuclear-armed countries continue to oppose disarmament. One major reason for this is that nuclear weapons bring jobs and economic benefits to the places where they are based. A second reason is that politicians wrongly believe that their national pride and prestige depend on having huge stockpiles of nuclear warheads. To change their minds, ordinary people like you need to contact them regularly and encourage them to work in favor of nuclear disarmament. Specifically, call on them to support the Treaty on the Prohibition of Nuclear Weapons,[12] a landmark treaty first signed in 2017, which is essentially a total ban on all nuclear weapons. More than 135 nations are already participating, and when 50 of them have formally approved the treaty, it will be legally enforceable. A working treaty would make it more likely that nuclear-armed countries like the US and Russia would eventually sign and consider giving up their stockpiles or at least significantly reducing them. Make sure to tell your elected officials that if they won't work toward disarmament, you'll give your support to another candidate who will.

You can also directly support organizations that have done good work campaigning for nuclear disarmament over many years. You could hold fundraisers for them through a school club, or volunteer for them if you're old enough. These organizations include:

- ICAN:[13] The International Campaign for the Abolition of Nuclear Weapons focuses on educating people about the practical risks and dangers of nuclear weapons.

- Greenpeace[14]: A large non-governmental organization dedicated to a wide range of environmental and anti-war causes, which prominently includes nuclear disarmament.

- Campaign for Nuclear Disarmament:[15] A UK-based advocacy group that opposes all weapons of mass destruction, but with a focus on nuclear weapons. It provides helpful educational materials[16] for students and teachers.

In the longer term, nuclear disarmament might become politically possible because of some new technology that makes warheads or missiles obsolete. You might be the person to invent it! For more information on how to put yourself in the best position to achieve new breakthrough technologies, see "How You Can Be a Danielle and Encourage Women in the Workplace and Girls to Pursue STEM Careers"; "How You Can Be a Danielle and Learn to Program Computers at a Young Age"; and "How You Can Be a Danielle and Become a Physicist."

Securing the world against the threat of nuclear weapons depends on several technological advances:

- **Detection**: Creating new methods of scanning that can more effectively detect radioactivity from nuclear weapons. This is necessary to prevent terrorists from smuggling a nuclear bomb into the country, and to prevent theft of radioactive material from the many sites it's stored at all over the globe.

- **Missile Defense**: If it becomes possible to reliably shoot down any nuclear weapons that are fired, an international body like the United Nations could use this technology to make nuclear weapons obsolete.

The more complex aspect of this would be to shoot down cruise missiles which fly close to the ground.

⊛ **Cybersecurity**: There are currently far too many vulnerabilities in America's nuclear weapons program. If hackers broke into the system, they could potentially trigger a nuclear war. As long as some nuclear weapons remain on alert, there will be a need for better cybersecurity techniques to prevent this from happening.

You could be the one to figure out the solution to these problems.

For more information, please see the following entries in the companion book *A Chronicle of Ideas: A Guide for Superheroines (and Superheroes)*: Atomic Bombs Exploded in Japan, Thermonuclear Weapons, Hair Trigger, Mutually Assured Destruction.

Footnote links at

DanielleWorld.com/resources

and Record Your Life

O ur memories of events from our past are very partial and fragmentary. Even for events that we recall, our memories consist of impressions and features, not precise recordings. As I wrote in *How to Create a Mind*, when we recall an event we essentially hallucinate our recollections by filling in many blanks. We do not retain videos of past experiences. Even these tenuous remembrances are lost when people suffer from dementia or die.

Danielle realizes that technology can solve this problem, and begins recording her life with a system called Life Bits. Although the technology in the novel is slightly more advanced that what's available today, it's already possible to record amazing details of your life. You are part of the first generation in human history with the ability to create a complete multimedia record of your life and use it to recall experiences from your past, allow future AIs to access it to provide insights into your own mind, and to pass it on to the generations that come after you.

To understand why recording your life digitally is so important, it's important to think about the two main problems with our natural memory.

- **Memory is incomplete.** We often think of our minds as recording everything going on around us, but science shows that this is far from the truth.[1]

- Our minds naturally remember moments and information that are important or stressful, but most everything else never makes it into our long-term memory. Details that seem unimportant at the time may be unavailable to your memory if you try to recall them later.

- In addition, memories tend to decay if we don't think about them periodically. Events that you can recall in detail now might be reduced to just a few impressions when you're older.

● **Memory is unreliable.** Even the things we think we remember are often not totally accurate. They can be changed[2] and influenced[3] by external factors.

- One reason for this is that our senses are limited, and our brains are constantly supplying information to fill in the gaps. For example, your peripheral vision is mostly in black and white, but your brain creates the illusion that everything you see is in color. When you see a stop sign out of the corner of your eye, it will seem red to you because your brain knows that stop signs are red. Most of the time, this effect makes life easier, but if this happened to be a green stop sign, you would wind up with an inaccurate memory of a red sign.

- Another problem is that recalling memories in our brains isn't like pulling up a photograph as a file on your computer. It's more like sketching a drawing based on a very brief description. Each time you remember an experience, your brain "recreates" it in your mind's eye, which can cause the memory to change over time.

- Our brains are also lazy. They love stereotypes because they save brainpower. If you're walking down the street and see a fight suddenly break out between a tough-looking man with tattoos and a young woman in business clothing, your brain may tell you that you saw the man start the fight—even if it was really the other way around. This is a big problem for law enforcement, because eyewitness testimony is often influenced by stereotypes the witnesses don't even notice.

- Memories can be influenced by things other people tell you, or things you read. If you see a car accident, and another witness says to you that she saw a lot of broken glass, you might later remember seeing broken glass yourself, even if there really was none.

- Our subjective perceptions, emotions, and wishes can influence how we remember things. It's common for people giving speeches to remember their awkward pauses as much longer than they really are, or to remember their own role in arguments as being more innocent than in reality.

With clever use of technology, you can begin to correct all of these problems. Although your own memory is incomplete, you can get more complete information by recording lots of data about your experiences. And even though your own memory is unreliable, making objective recordings gives you an alternative not influenced by your brain's weaknesses. This is known as "lifelogging."

Lifelogging was pioneered by Microsoft researcher Gordon Bell, as part of a project called MyLifeBits.[4] You may be interested to read Bell's fascinating book[5] about his experience and vision for the future. Here's a short interview[6] with Bell about the project.

There are many different options for the kinds of information to record about your life, and how intense your lifelogging efforts can be. Some people take a single webcam video every morning, while others are constantly filming themselves. What you do is up to you. But the earlier in life you start, and the more of your life you record, the more will be available to you in the future.

In general, here are the main aspects of life that you can record, along with some tips for how to do so:

- **Experiences.** One of the most popular forms of lifelogging is for people to constantly record video and audio of their daily lives. In the novel, Danielle and Claire have this technology embedded in contact lenses, but that's still several years away. Later they also have tiny cameras hovering in the air recording their images from different angles. In the meantime, you have a few different choices for how to record the things you see and hear.

  - Wearable cameras, such as the Perfect Memory[7] device, can be worn around your neck, and constantly record whatever is in front of you. When something interesting happens, you can tap the device to highlight the past few minutes of video so you can find it easily later, as <u>shown in this demo</u>.[8] <u>This video</u>[9] shows a time-lapse of someone's day from her own point of view. These wearable cameras are small and lightweight, and not very noticeable. But you should still be careful about what and who you are filming. In some states you may have to notify people that you're filming them if you're not in a public place.

   — In some cases, you may want to get a view that more closely matches your own eyes—a camera at eye level that follows your head as you look around. For example, if you're going skydiving, whitewater rafting, or scuba diving, the sensation of looking around is a key part of your experience. The most popular option for capturing this is mounting a small, durable camera like a <u>GoPro</u>[10] to your helmet or goggles.

   — In addition to views from your own perspective, some people like to have views of themselves from the outside. Some lifeloggers set up webcams, like the <u>Google Nest</u>[11] system, around their homes and upload the footage to the Cloud.

   — Sometimes, you can record footage of yourself in public from a drone. Companies like <u>Cape</u>[12] have developed software that allows drones to follow you around outdoors and capture high-quality video footage. This could be useful to record your athletic activities, a speech you're giving, or a musical performance. It could also provide proof of your actions during a tense situation like a protest.

- **Conversations.** One of the most important parts of life is the conversations we have with other people. Some conversations are major milestones, like asking someone to marry you. There are others that we only realize are important later, like valuable advice from a mentor, an insightful discussion with a friend, or a last talk with a relative who dies soon after. Recording your conversations through lifelogging lets you preserve them perfectly and recall them whenever you want.

   — **Video.** If you lifelog with a wearable camera, conversations you have in person will be preserved. As artificial intelligence becomes more advanced in the future, this footage will become even more useful. For example, you can already generate automated transcripts from video and search them for keywords, but in the near future you'll be able to tell the AI to do more abstract searches. You might ask it to pull up every conversation of serious life advice, and the software will be able to find them for you. Please note, though, that when you record personal conversations with others, you should make sure they're aware and agree to be recorded. Sometimes, you might decide that it's better to turn off your video recording so someone can speak to you about something private.

- **Chats and text messages.** Regularly back up your chats and text messages to the Cloud. You can use this information to see how your relationships change and develop, and better understand what subjects you like to talk about. If you preserve this data now, you'll be able to learn even more from it in the future, when AI can analyze it more deeply. You can even create an AI chat-bot that talks like you!

- **Social media posts.** Even though sites like Facebook and Twitter do a good job protecting your data, it's always possible that you could unexpectedly lose something you post on social media. There might be a technical malfunction or an attack by hackers. Or maybe you'll accidentally delete something yourself. By copying old posts and archiving them yourself—ideally both in the Cloud and in offline storage—you'll always have this dimension of your life recorded. The most reliable form of backup is full incremental Cloud storage—this means archiving every version of every file. There are software attacks that can encrypt or otherwise destroy your files, even those you save in the Cloud. Incremental storage means that the Cloud system prevents any change to a file that might destroy it and you can always go back to versions of your files that are intact.

- **Ideas.** Cameras and message archives are good for recording your experiences and conversations, but that doesn't preserve the ideas in your mind. If you get in the habit of writing down thoughts and ideas that come to you, you can avoid losing them. This can include big things like goals and aspirations, all the way down to how you were feeling on a given day. Some lifeloggers like to keep a physical notebook or journal with them and then scan those notes onto their computers. Many of history's most famous thinkers have been faithful about writing in a daily diary, from US President John Adams, to philosopher Ralph Waldo Emerson, and author Lewis Carroll. By preserving your ideas in this way, you can go back later and analyze how your writing and personality evolved.

- **Health data.** It's now possible to collect lots of data about your body and habits that it wasn't practical to measure in the past. This is sometimes known as "quantified self." Companies like Fitbit[13] make wearable devices that constantly collect information about your health. You can see how much time you're sleeping, how many steps you take in a day, how your heart rate changes throughout the day, and more. Apps like Exist[14] and Instant[15] connect your health and fitness data with data from your other apps and devices to help you discover patterns between them. For example, you might find that a particular music playlist inspires you to hit higher exercise goals. Or that you're more productive with your work and ideas when you take a short nap before starting. Like with other areas of lifelogging, you'll be able to get even deeper insights as AI gets more powerful.

- **Physical objects.** Many of our most precious possessions are physical objects. From old family photos to handwritten letters by our ancestors, these items are vulnerable to decay, loss, or destruction. If you scan or photograph (or record) all the objects that are meaningful to you, you can make them safe against these risks. For written documents, digitizing them also lets you convert the text to a searchable form, which makes them more useful. For example, if you upload military service records about your grandfather to Ancestry.com,[16] you might get to meet an elderly man who served with him in war and has stories about him to share with you.

Recording your life has many benefits:

- **Memory preservation.** As explained above, lifelogging lets you use technology to make up for the weaknesses in our own memory. You can document your life in an objective and permanent way, and review it whenever you like.

- **Documenting facts.** Many arguments happen because people remember things differently. If you can pull a video right up and confirm what actually happened, those arguments can be settled. Similarly, if you're ever accused of doing something you didn't do, your lifelogging can prove your innocence—and if someone commits a crime against you, you can prove their responsibility.

- **Self-improvement.** Recording lots of data about yourself lets you get a better understanding of your own habits, strengths, and weaknesses, as explained in this interview[17] with psychology professor Seth Roberts. With this knowledge you can plan how to improve your life. You can then set specific goals and track your progress. This applies to diet, exercise, study performance, and many other areas. You can even use lifelogging to keep track of your friendships so you can stay in touch with people and be a better friend. In this video,[18] Blaine Price gives a talk on the insights he's gained from quantified self. And in this video,[19] Gary Wolf explains how extremely detailed data can unlock new understanding.

- **Making discoveries.** Lifelogging creates data more accurate than scientists can duplicate in a laboratory. You can use this data to make breakthrough discoveries that advance human knowledge. For example, in this TED talk,[20] MIT scientist Deb Roy explains how he set up a video recording system around his home to study how his baby son learned language. Over three years, he collected about 250,000 hours of footage of his son growing up, transcribed over seven million words, and then analyzed that data to figure out the process of how babies learn language from their caregivers. In a similar way, you may be able to make new discoveries based on the data you collect and analyze.

- **Forming connections.** As Danielle discovers, lifelogging can be a powerful way to connect with other people around the world. In the past few years, social media has expanded opportunities for broadcasting live video of yourself over the internet, and connecting with other people in real time. If you're on a vacation or trip, you can stream video of yourself to friends back home so they can better understand what the experience is like for you. When people see the world (almost) through each other's eyes, there's more room for empathy and compassion.

- **Creating a legacy.** To learn about your parents' lives, you can watch old home movies, and they can tell you stories based on the small percentage of their experiences that they actually remember. To learn about your grandparents' lives, you might just have still photos and their memories from long ago. To learn about your great-grandparents' lives, you might only have a few letters and black-and-white photographs. For even earlier generations, many people know almost nothing of their ancestors except their names and when they lived. But recording your life in digital format means that your own children will have access to most of the same memories that you do. And because digital files can be preserved and copied, even your great-great-great grandchildren will be able to learn about you in all that detail (and given the accelerating advances in life extension, you are likely to still be around to share it with them). All the most meaningful parts of your life—your successes and failures, and the lessons you learned—can be shared with future generations.

Here are some more ideas[21] for how to start your own lifelogging project like Danielle, but the only real limit is your creativity.

For more information, please see the following entries in the companion book *A Chronicle of Ideas: A Guide for Superheroines (and Superheroes)*: Life Bits, Life Bits Share.

Footnote links at

DanielleWorld.com/resources

HOW YOU CAN BE A DANIELLE

and Advance Critical Thinking

When eleven-year-old Danielle speaks to a world audience from Yad Vashem, Israel's Holocaust museum and memorial, she talks about the ideas of historian Hannah Arendt.

In her speech, she says,

> Death is an eternal tragedy whether it stems from hatred or from indifference. The Shoah resulted from both. When Hannah Arendt went to interview Adolf Eichmann, the architect of the Holocaust, she expected to descend into the bowels of human loathing. Instead she encountered an ordinary and prosaic bureaucrat whose malevolence resulted from his failure to question the values in his midst. The Shoah resulted at least in part from this failure of critical thinking, from this "banality of evil," to quote her deservedly famous phrase.

Thus Danielle's conclusion is that the Holocaust resulted at least in part from a failure of critical thinking, and she works to advance critical thinking as a way of preventing future atrocities.

Critical thinking is a mindset of questioning ideas and testing them to see if they are true—and questioning actions to see if they are morally right. Instead of just believing whatever they are told, critical thinkers seek to confirm it for themselves. They regularly reflect on their own assumptions and values to see whether they are consistent with their deeper ideas about truth and morality. From the 1920s to the 1940s, there was a major failure of critical thinking in many European societies that resulted in the catastrophic tragedies of World War II. Charismatic leaders told people what they wanted to hear, and without critical thinking, the people believed them. This enabled the rise of totalitarian dictators like Hitler, Stalin, Mussolini, and, later on, Mao Tse-tung.

Today, there is concern about contemporary failures of critical thinking. On the Internet, people can easily choose the content they want to see, and it's tempting to block out information that goes against one's worldviews. Moreover, social media now contains "fake news"—deliberately untrue stories meant to mislead people for political purposes. These phenomena can distort public discussion and subvert democratic processes.

First, you should learn more about what critical thinking is, and how to develop it more in your own life:

- Simple <u>animated video</u>[1] explaining a five-step process for thinking critically.

- More detailed <u>article giving you nine strategies</u>[2] for critical thinking in everyday living.

- <u>Fascinating video</u>[3] on how "filter bubbles" can turn your social media feeds into an echo chamber where you only hear opinions that reinforce your existing beliefs.

- How to <u>develop your mental habits in stages</u>[4] to become a more rational person.

- Some helpful <u>do's and don'ts for how to criticize your own thinking effectively</u>[5].

- <u>Collection of TED Ed lessons</u>[6] on critical thinking.

- Series of <u>videos by the Foundation for Critical Thinking</u>[7] aimed at explaining critical thinking to younger kids.

Your mental habits are a lot like your diet. Just as exercising and eating healthy foods will make your body strong and healthy, consuming well-founded information from reliable sources will equip you to be a critical, independent, and objective thinker.

Here are some useful principles for maintaining a healthy information diet:

- **Draw from diverse perspectives**. No single source of information is completely right all the time. Every newspaper, television commentator, blogger, and author has their own strengths and weaknesses. The best solution is to seek out a wide range of contrasting views on important topics. If you see the best arguments for an idea and the best arguments against it, you can make an informed judgment about which arguments are backed up by better logic and evidence.

- **Seek original sources**. Many factual claims you see online simply aren't true. Many pundits on television and online make false claims, and there is no "referee" to correct them. So whenever you hear a dramatic statement—an improbable fact, an extreme number, or a surprising explanation—see if you can trace it back to a reliable source. For example, if you read an article from a site called PatriotEagle4USA.com claiming without proof that two million refugees have entered the US from Syria, search on Google for independent confirmation. Is that number reported in respected news sources like the *New York Times* or *Wall Street Journal*? Or official government statistics? If not, you should not believe it (for the record, that's about 100 times the real number).

- **Avoid false equivalencies**. When you're thinking critically about what a leader is telling you, you'll often find that they have made misleading statements. You'll naturally be tempted to be angry about this, but their supporters will say: "Well, what about the lie that his opponent told?" It's hard work to figure out the truth, so it can be very tempting to just conclude that all politicians are liars and it doesn't matter who's in charge. This is a dangerous lapse in critical thinking. In trying to find who is more trustworthy, remember that not all lies are equivalent. An exaggeration of a true fact (e.g. saying that a policy saved $10 million when it really saved $8 million) is not nearly as bad as fabricating events that never happened at all, or denying provable facts that can be verified with a 5-second Google search. Since nobody in politics is 100% faultless, critical thinking is required to separate the "ordinary lies" from the "big lies" and focus your energy on opposing the most dangerous falsehoods. One of Hitler's techniques was called the "big lie," for example blaming all of society's ills on the Jews.

- **Consider alternatives**. When you think you're starting to figure out the truth about something, it's easy to suffer what's known as "confirmation bias." When you see information that supports an idea you already like, your mind naturally wants to accept it. This may lead you to the wrong conclusion. To fight against confirmation bias, you have to make extra effort to consider other possible explanations. For example, if you are an advocate of equal justice for racial minorities, you should be careful about assuming that all unequal outcomes are the result of racism. In each case, ask yourself what role might be played by other important factors like poverty, education, and bad policies. This can make you a more effective advocate against actual racism.

- **Take responsibility**. Adolf Eichmann's problem was that he didn't take any moral responsibility for his actions. As long as his superiors ordered him to do something, he felt that wiped away any guilt for what he was doing. Thinking critically requires taking moral responsibility for what you do and what you say. The best way to avoid going along with injustice is to not pass off your moral choices to anyone else. If something is right, you should be able to explain why it's right—and if it's wrong, you should be able to explain why it's wrong.

To learn more about what happens when lots of people fail to think critically, you should take a look at these short videos:

- <u>An introduction to the history of the Holocaust</u>,[8] by Yad Vashem in Israel.

- <u>Animated explainer on how Hitler came to power</u>[9] in Germany.

- A summary of <u>how Mussolini became dictator</u>[10] in Italy.

- <u>An informative video on Stalin's crimes</u>[11] in the Soviet Union.

- A fact-filled video about World War II,[12] from John Green's *Crash Course* series.

- A brief history of ISIS,[13] which shows what happens when people fail to think critically in modern times.

It is important to practice critical thinking yourself, but Danielle also sets an example of how young people can show leadership. Consider these ideas for how you can advance critical thinking in your wider community:

- **Start a club.** Bring together a group of friends, neighbors, or classmates, and pledge to help each other become better critical thinkers.

  - Bring in speakers from your area who can talk about critical thinking and rationality. Potential guests include journalists, scientists, judges, or philosophers.

  - Hold debates about controversial issues, and then switch sides. Seeing difficult questions from different perspectives builds your critical thinking muscles.

  - Take an online course together, maybe on rhetoric, the Holocaust, or critical thinking[14] itself.

- **Speak out on social media.** Some people criticize social media activism as "slacktivism," saying that it is too easy and doesn't really make a difference. It's true that you shouldn't let online activism replace other efforts to solve global problems, but speaking out on social media can have an important impact.

As humans we are very social creatures and heavily influenced by what we think the other members of our community are doing. When leaders like Hitler and Mussolini came to power, they tried to create the illusion that everyone in society supported what they were doing and saying. This helped suppress critical thinking, because if people don't hear anyone around them speaking out against an idea, there's a tendency to think that the idea must be correct.

Because so much of our social lives now take place on social media, by using your critical thinking and speaking out against injustice, you can shift your friends' perception of what other people in their community think. This can positively influence those around you and make them more likely to think critically themselves. This action can take many forms:

- **Starting a blog** to express your views.

- **Recording videos on YouTube** applying critical thinking to important issues.

- **Engaging respectfully with people** on Facebook and Twitter and encouraging them to use better critical thinking, while speaking out against injustices yourself.

- **Volunteer for pro-critical thinking politicians.** Don't let yourself get cynical. Although there are some politicians who try to manipulate public opinion with dubious claims and arguments, there are also many people in politics who are trying to advance critical thinking. Do some research on the politicians in your area, and see if you can find one whose statements show a commitment to truthfulness and critical thought. Even as a student, you may be able to volunteer for them— whether in their campaign office, or knocking on doors in the community to spread their positive message.

- **Program tools to teach critical thinking.** Apps and games have the potential to make learning fun and intuitive. If you've learned programming, you could create a platform designed to help people distinguish fake news from real news, or train their ability to overcome confirmation bias. If you haven't learned coding yet, see the entry for "How You Can Be a Danielle and Learn to Program Computers from a Young Age."

- **Meet survivors.** One of the most powerful reasons to care about critical thinking is the very real human suffering that happens when people don't think critically. Reading about the Holocaust is sad, but the history gets a completely different emotional power when you talk to someone who actually lived through it. You can <u>arrange to meet with a survivor and bring them to your school</u>[15] so their stories can impact a bigger audience. You should act quickly because the generation of actual survivors won't be alive much longer.

———————————————

For more information, please see the following entries in the companion book *A Chronicle of Ideas: A Guide for Superheroines (and Superheroes)*: Hannah Arendt, Banality of Evil.

———————————————

Footnote links at
DanielleWorld.com/resources

and Combat Totalitarianism in the World

✳ ✳ ✳ ✳ ✳

During the 20th century, totalitarianism led directly to the deaths of well over 100 million people. Totalitarianism isn't defined by any particular philosophy, but rather by the ambition of a government to control every aspect of its citizens' lives. In Germany, this took the form of National Socialism, also known as Nazism. In Italy, it was Fascism. In the Soviet Union and China, it was communism. When Danielle becomes president of China at fifteen in the novel, the country had already had some reforms, but was still suffering from the lingering effects of totalitarianism.

You can combat totalitarianism yourself in two main areas: helping those currently ruled by totalitarians, and making it harder for totalitarianism to come to your own society in the future.

So how can you do this? First, make sure you understand the basics of the problem. Here are a few helpful videos on totalitarianism:

-  An advanced high school-level talk on totalitarianism[1] and how it works. Focuses on the World War II era.

- A fast-paced, fact-filled <u>video on totalitarianism in China</u>,[2] from John Green's *Crash Course* series. Although China is no longer totalitarian, the influence of totalitarianism there still influences the world's most populous country.

- <u>A short explainer by Vox about North Korea</u>,[3] the world's only remaining classic totalitarian regime.

In addition to the totalitarian government of North Korea, the terrorist group known as the Islamic State of Iraq and Syria (also ISIS, ISIL, IS, or Daesh) also rules its territory with a system like totalitarianism. Over 25 million people live in North Korea, and at its peak, eight million people lived in ISIS-controlled areas, although most of them have now been liberated. These people have no political freedom, their rulers torture and kill anyone who opposes them. Widespread shortages of food and medicine sicken men, women, and children, and the rulers try to brainwash everyone into hating people in the outside world.

It is difficult and sad to confront the terrible suffering experienced by our fellow human beings in totalitarian controlled areas, but it is also frustrating, because it seems difficult for people thousands of miles a way to make a difference. Yet there are some important ways you can help these people.

It is too dangerous to travel to war zones to help directly, but many young people are raising money and awareness to support the brave work of several relief organizations making a positive impact in the lives of those suffering under totalitarianism. These include:

- <u>Liberty in North Korea</u>.[4] The policies of the North Korean government caused about 1 in 10 of its people to starve to death during the 1990s, and the population still suffers from serious malnutrition and food shortages. Yet the government blocks most foreign relief organizations from the country, which makes it hard to help the people there. North Korea's leaders have banned most citizens from leaving, so each year thousands of people risk their lives trying to escape. Those who successfully get out of the country are known as defectors, and face great challenges as they try to make new lives in

South Korea or the United States. They are without their families, lack education and money, and have never had access to the Internet or accurate news about the world. It is a very difficult adjustment. Liberty in North Korea provides aid to defectors and also raises awareness about the struggles of those left behind inside North Korea. You can request a speaker to come to your school, [5] and bring together your friends to raise funds and make donations.[6]

- International Rescue Committee.[7] The International Rescue Committee provides crucial help to the people affected by ISIS totalitarianism. Millions of people have been displaced from their homes, lost all their possessions, and been separated from their families. The IRC focuses on supporting health, safety, education, economic wellbeing, and equal rights for these people. You can raise awareness and support for their work by sharing videos[8] like these within your social networks, or having them shown at your school or place of worship. Over 92 percent of all donations go directly to helping those in need.

- Doctors Without Borders.[9] One of the most serious problems for victims of ISIS is that many of them have lost access to even basic medical care. Doctors Without Borders sends medical teams into high-risk areas to help those who need it most. This includes women and girls who have been injured by religiously-motivated violence and female genital mutilation. They also provide life-saving treatment to those tortured by ISIS or wounded in the fighting. Learn more about their work here,[10] and share this information in your community. These doctors work for a small fraction of the money they could make elsewhere, which allows the charity to make the most of all the donated money it receives.

- Save the Children.[11] The population ruled by ISIS has a very high proportion of babies and children. They are especially vulnerable, and many have been orphaned by the fighting. Save the Children provides emergency relief services to these children, and also campaigns to raise awareness about their suffering in countries like the United States. The goal of this is for citizens to insist that their politicians work harder to find solutions to the crisis and protect children at risk of violence. This charity is a particularly good choice for young people to support, because it is easy to ask yourself: "What if I had been born in another part of the world?" This connection to suffering people your own age is emotionally powerful. Some students hold car washes and other drives to collect direct donations,[12] while others set up fundraisers with special athletic activities,[13] like races and triathlons.

- Yazda.[14] ISIS is an ultra-extremist group within Sunni Islam, and it commits horrible acts of violence against anyone who doesn't share their religious views. But they have been especially brutal to a small minority group in majority-Muslim Iraq called the Yazidis, who follow a religion that combines influences from Zoroastrianism, Islam, Christianity, and Judaism. In 2014, ISIS conquered the small area where the Yazidis lived, and tried to commit genocide against them. Many Yazidis escaped, but lost their homes and their families, and are struggling to put their lives back together. Your support of Yazda can help this ancient community recover.

Although totalitarianism has been ended in most of the world, it would be wrong to think that it is impossible for it to return. Really, totalitarianism is just a more extreme form of authoritarianism. There are many authoritarian governments still in power, such as Russia, China, and Saudi Arabia. There are also authoritarian movements within many democratic countries, including the United States. Sometimes these movements are based on ideas of racial supremacy, or hatred for a certain religious group. They all share the idea that some people don't deserve full rights in society. Like Danielle, all citizens should vigorously oppose these ideas.

Here are some concrete ways you can combat the ideas that might lead to totalitarianism:

- **Practice and promote critical thinking.** Totalitarianism only gets power when millions of people buy into it. Totalitarian leaders use dramatic, emotional language and images to discourage people from thinking independently and logically. They also try to create the illusion that everyone in society is united in support of their extreme ideas. When people feel like everyone else is supporting the movement, this makes them less likely to question whether it promotes immoral ideas.

This is why it is so important for you to think critically—questioning what you are told, to test whether it is correct and ethical. If other people see you questioning injustices, they will be more likely to stand up to those injustices too. For more information on how to build your critical thinking skills and encourage critical thinking in your community, see the entry for "How You Can Be a Danielle and Advance Critical Thinking."

- Support good journalism. Because totalitarianism is so harmful, people will only go along with it if they are fed lies and propaganda. Brave journalists inform citizens about abuses by their government and expose truths the government wants to keep hidden. For this reason, totalitarian governments try to shut down independent journalism (often by arresting or killing journalists who do not follow their ideas) and force people to rely on official propaganda. In less extreme cases, leaders may try to intimidate journalists, or discredit them with the public by claiming they are biased.

In many countries, journalism is also under threat for economic reasons. Because so much free content is available on the Internet, high-quality newspapers and investigative news magazines have seen their paid subscriptions fall dramatically. This means there is less money to hire talented journalists, and more pressure to churn out simple articles quickly instead of working slowly and patiently on more important stories. You can fight this trend by finding a publication doing good work on issues you care about, and investing in a paid subscription. Many have student discounts available.

- **Create pro-freedom technology.** Totalitarianism requires that a government be able to control the lives of its citizens. In the 1930s, this was easy because people got most of their news from newspapers and radio stations. If a government sent soldiers to seize control of the printing presses and radio transmission towers, they could control the information available to the people.

Today, though, information is much more decentralized. The Internet now links billions of devices that can talk to each other directly. So, to control the flow of information, authoritarian leaders have to develop new technologies that can censor the Internet and monitor what citizens are doing. In response, people have used platforms like Facebook and Twitter to communicate, and technologies like Tor[15] to protect their privacy.

But oppressive governments are still finding new technologies to control people's lives. With hard work and creativity, you could create the next pro-freedom technology that makes totalitarianism impossible. The best way to get started is to learn programming. For more information on how to do this, see the entry for "How You Can Be a Danielle and Learn to Program Computers from a Young Age."

———————————

For more information, please see the following entries in the companion book *A Chronicle of Ideas: A Guide for Superheroines (and Superheroes)*: George Orwell, From Each According to His Ability, To Each According to His Need, Totalitarian, Trains Leaving On Time in World War II Italy, Stalin, Hitler.

———————————

Footnote links at
DanielleWorld.com/resources

HOW YOU CAN BE A DANIELLE

and Promote Racial and Gender Equality

�֍ �֍ ✷ ✷ ✷

Prejudice based on race, gender, or other characteristics is as old as humanity. Most of human history was characterized by severe scarcity of resources so a primary motivation for discrimination was the concern that another group would deprive your own group of its material resources. Scarcity is still an issue in today's world, but prejudice is also motivated by ancient ideas of the "proper" role of different groups as implied by the word itself: "pre" "judge."

That all humans are entitled to respect and opportunity is a fairly recent ideal, having only emerged in the last couple of centuries, along with the idea of democracy. But true equality is even more recent. For example, in the United States, one of the first true democracies, many African Americans were held as slaves until the mid-nineteenth century, and women only got right to vote about a century ago (in 1920).

Danielle recognizes the goal of equal rights from an early age, when she tells a CNN reporter at age five that undocumented immigrants face an "American apartheid." Later, Danielle breaks down gender stereotypes, from achieving great success as a girl in science to accepting a Grammy for Best Male Singer. But even if you're not a Grammy nominee, you too can fight prejudice and promote equality.

The most basic step in solving a problem is taking the time to understand the issue. To promote racial and gender equality, knowledge is one of your most powerful tools. Take a look at these resources to learn more about prejudice and how to fight it:

- **Racism.** Science tells us that there's really no such thing as different races. Some human populations tend to have different physical features—like skin color, hair color, height, and eye shape. For centuries, people with certain groups of features have been artificially classed into races, mainly based on skin color. When people treat other people negatively because they perceive them as being of a different race, that's racism. Here's more information:

  - Introductory article for students[1] summarizing what scientific research has discovered about racism, its effects, and how to address it.

  - Helpful explanation of hidden bias,[2] which is unintentional prejudice that can influence our behavior without us even knowing it. For example, many white Americans don't feel any hatred for African-Americans, but still tend to associate them with crime and poverty because of old cultural stereotypes and the stories they see in the media. Hidden bias can also be unconsciously adopted by the groups being discriminated against.

  - The Implicit Association Test.[3] This is a simple test you can take on your computer that measures how much hidden bias about race you might have. Notably, even African-Americans often have hidden bias against other African-Americans, because stereotypes are so strong. Note that finding hidden biases does not make you a bad person. It is courageous to make a conscious effort to figure out the areas you might have biases and work to overcome them.

- **Sexism:** Unlike race, gender isn't just a set of made-up categories. Biology determines that the great majority of humans will be either male or female, but there are lots of misleading stereotypes about what this means. In most societies, these stereotypes led to discrimination that makes it harder for women to fulfill their potential. For example, many people think that because most men are usually stronger than most women, physically demanding jobs like firefighters and soldiers are not for women. No matter how strong an individual woman is, she will have to overcome the biases in the minds of other people. Women also face higher rates of sexual harassment at their jobs. These biases and behavior are sexism. Here's some further information:

- A quick summary from the University of California, Berkeley[2] that gives more basic facts about what sexism is, how it causes harm, and things students can do about it.

- If you're a male, it can be especially hard to understand what sexism is like because you haven't experienced it firsthand. This essay explains sexism from the perspective of women studying to be doctors. [5]

- A powerful video that shows girls and women repeating sexist things people have said to them.[6]

● **Transphobia.** Sometimes, people experience a mismatch between the biological sex indicated by their DNA and what they feel like inside, known as gender. They may have been born a boy but experience life as a "woman trapped in a man's body." In other cases, people are born with genitals that are not clearly male or female, or feel that their gender is neither male nor female. When these people live these identities openly, they often face discrimination and prejudice known as transphobia. These are a few starting points for learning more about transsexuality and transphobia:

- An introduction to the idea that gender exists on a spectrum, [7] and what life is like for people who do not identify as the biological sex they were born as.

- A clear and concise summary from the University of Cambridge about transphobia[8] and the harm it causes to trans (also known as transsexual or transgender) people.

- A fascinating TED Talk[9] by my friend Martine Rothblatt, an entrepreneur, business executive, futurist, and author who was born male but is now a transgender woman. Martine's talk shows you that many transgender people live exciting and fulfilling lives, and do not let prejudice define them or hold them back. Her book, *The Apartheid of Sex* clearly articulates this issue.

Prejudice based on disabilities is another important category of bias. I have worked closely with the National Federation of the Blind (the largest organization of blind people in the United States) for over forty years, having partnered with them on the Kurzweil Reading Machine, the first print-to-speech reading machine for the blind. Even in these four decades, there has been enormous progress in overcoming prejudice against the blind and other disabilities, but, again, ancient ideas that people with disabilities are unable to contribute to society continue to be a powerful and negative influence.

Maybe the most important way to educate yourself about prejudice is to get to know people with diverse backgrounds. If there are students at your school with backgrounds different from yours, try to listen to their experiences with open ears. You may learn that prejudice impacts their lives in ways you hadn't even imagined.

Similarly, you may have experienced or witnessed prejudice in ways your friends can learn from. You could also encourage your school to invite adults to come speak to students about their own experiences facing and overcoming racism, sexism, transphobia, and other forms of prejudice.

But education is only the first step. What can you actually do to promote racial and gender equality?

For more information, please see the following entries in the companion book *A Chronicle of Ideas: A Guide for Superheroines (and Superheroes):* Apartheid, South African Apartheid, Nelson Mandela, Martine Rothblatt, *The Apartheid of Sex.*

Footnote links at

DanielleWorld.com/resources

and Prevent Future Genocides

G enocide is the most severe crime that humans can commit. It involves the deliberate attempt to wipe out a group of people based on their race, religion, or ethnic identification. The violence committed by European settlers against the Native Americans has been called a slow genocide, with millions of deaths over about four hundred years. But during the 20th century, technology, such as the telegraphs, the machine gun, and many others, allowed governments to organize and conduct much more intense killings.

From 1932 to 1933, in the Soviet Union, the "Holdomor" occurred, which was a famine that killed five to ten million people in Ukraine. Historians have debated whether this was intentional, in which case it would qualify as genocide, or the result of misguided Totalitarian extremist policies of forced collectivism.

During World War II, Nazi Germany exterminated about 15 million people they saw as "subhuman," including about six million Jews. After this, the world vowed: *Never again!* But several genocides have nonetheless happened since then. For example, the Cambodian genocide killed about two million people in the 1970s, and the Rwandan genocide killed around 800,000 people over just 100 days in 1994. In 2014, the ISIS terrorist group killed thousands of people from the tiny Yazidi religious group. In the novel, eleven-year-old Danielle gives a speech at Yad Vashem, Israel's Holocaust Museum and Memorial to a worldwide audience, calling on people everywhere *never again* to let genocides happen.

So how can you answer Danielle's call? First, make an effort to learn more about genocide and understand why it happens. These resources can be a starting point:

- Basic facts about genocide[1] and its history over the last century or so.

- The Ten Stages of Genocide,[2] a model that describes how prejudices gradually escalate from ideas to killing. By recognizing that a society is moving through these stages, the international community may be able to stop it before a genocide happens.

- I recommend reading Night,[3] a short but powerful book by Elie Wiesel about his experiences during the Holocaust. The subject matter is upsetting, but it is important to learn about this history to truly understand why everyone must work together to prevent future genocides.

- A fascinating and heartbreaking talk by scholar and diplomat Samantha Power[4] about the Rwandan genocide, and why nobody stepped in to stop it before it was too late.

- Key information on the Armenian genocide,[5] of which Armenians were victims over a century ago. To this day, the Turks and the Armenians bitterly disagree about the facts of the genocide, with Turkey denying responsibility.

- Additional articles about genocide and genocide prevention,[6] compiled by Genocide Watch.

Evil leaders do not commit genocide by themselves. It takes thousands, if not millions, of ordinary people going along with it— following orders to kill innocent human beings without questioning those orders. As Danielle puts it in the novel, this is a failure of critical thinking. When people don't think skeptically about the ideas they hear, and don't take moral responsibility for their actions and those of the people around them, they are more likely to go along with unjust actions.

Education can give people the tools to be better critical thinkers. Yet in some parts of the world, people don't even have access to basic education. They may not know how to read. This means they have to rely on the leaders for their information, and can be easily misled. You can help make genocide less likely by supporting organizations that provide education to people in the developing world. The more ordinary people have access education and achieve literacy, the harder it is for leaders to commit genocide. Here are some good options:

- The American University's list of 10 innovative organizations[7] providing education to poor young people around the world.

- The World Literacy Foundation[8] works to ensure that all children learn to read, including with the use of innovative technology. The foundation uses a solar-powered tablet called Sun Books to let children read in areas that don't have access to electricity.

- United World Schools[9] educates some of the most vulnerable children in Southeast Asia, and connects them with sponsors in developed countries to support them.

Sometimes, education is not enough to prevent genocide. German citizens in the 1930s, when Hitler was coming to power, were highly educated. If leaders convince enough people that a minority group should be destroyed, violence can begin very quickly. So, it is important to monitor situations of prejudice all over the world and sound the alarm long before a genocide begins. If the danger is identified in time, the international community can step in to prevent it. The United Nations, supported by the United States and other powerful countries, can put political and economic pressure on the people thinking of committing genocide. If this doesn't solve the problem, they can send peacekeeping troops or other military forces to protect the vulnerable group.

This process relies on organizations that keep a lookout for potential genocides and give warning when signs of danger appear. These include:

- Genocide Watch[10] focuses on anticipating genocides before they happen and raising global awareness before it is too late. This mission has five main components. The first is educating people about the problem of genocide, both in general and regarding particular high-risk areas. The second is using predictive models to forecast possible genocides. The third is prevention, suggesting how the international community can stop genocide before it starts. The fourth is intervention—rallying support for military intervention to stop genocides once they begin. The fifth is campaigning to ensure that people who have committed genocides are brought to justice.

- Stop Genocide Now[11] is a grassroots movement that uses technology and media to tell stories about genocide and make people care more strongly about preventing genocide. It suggests concrete ways that ordinary people can take action to prevent future genocides.

- STAND[12] is the world's largest student anti-genocide movement. STAND provides support and training for students who found local chapters of young people dedicated to preventing genocide. These resources show students how they can make their voices heard, both on how to raise awareness among their peers and achieve major political change.

Genocide never happens without warning. There is always a period of months or years when a group realizes it is under threat, as the society around them goes through the Ten Stages of Genocide. People who know a genocide might happen often try to escape. During the 1930s, Jews in Germany realized they were in danger before the mass killings began. Many left behind their property and careers and tried to flee to other countries that seemed safer, such as France, the United Kingdom, and the United States. My parents and their families were amongst those who fled. My Aunt Dorit Whiteman (my late mother's sister) wrote a book about this experience, titled _The Uprooted_.[13] But most of these refugees were denied safe haven and had no other way to escape.

To provide a safe haven before genocides occur, it is important to help refugees find safe places to go long before killing starts. These organizations play key roles in assisting refugees:

- UNICEF[14] is the United Nations organization that helps children fleeing war and violence, like that in Syria, Iraq, South Sudan, and the Central African Republic. This includes supplies and life-saving aid, as well as programs to provide education and stability.

- The International Rescue Committee[15] provides a wide range of services to refugees, and tries to make sure they get fair treatment by governments. The IRC is known for its innovative programs and for collecting information about its own performance. It uses this information to increase its effectiveness.

- The Office of the UN High Commissioner on Refugees[16] works to increase cooperation among countries on solving refugee crises. Before the Holocaust, other countries had plenty of room to take in Jewish refugees, but they generally acted like it was someone else's problem. The UNHCR aims to prevent this by promoting international collaboration.

One common way students support organizations like those above is starting anti-genocide clubs at their schools. These clubs can hold meetings to watch documentaries about genocide, invite genocide survivors to give talks, and see videos about the work that charities are doing to prevent future genocides. Club members can then raise money for anti-genocide organizations or assist directly by facilitating research, communication, and efforts to oppose oppressive actions that can lead to genocide.

In addition to supporting anti-genocide organizations, students can also have an impact by contacting politicians directly. The average elected official has dozens of priorities all competing for her time and attention. Powerful donors want her to spend time on projects they think are important, and her priority is to keep donors happy so she can raise money for reelection, but at the same time keep ordinary voters happy as much as possible. The key to getting politicians to act is either by recruiting their donors to care about genocide, or showing them that large numbers of voters care. Even if you're too young to vote, contacting politicians will have an impact. For one thing, they are likely to believe that older members of your family likely agree with you.

Students can write letters and make phone calls, either to the politician directly or to their biggest donors, whose names are usually publicly available. Explain, based on what you've learned, why stopping genocide in time is of critical importance both morally and to contribute to a more peaceful and just world. Figure out a specific action the politician should take, such as voting for an intervention to halt an ongoing genocide. Many politicians hold "town halls" or other local meetings where you can make your voice heard publicly.

Finally, genocide prevention always has room for improvement through new technology. If you know how to code, see if you can brainstorm some ways to create a tool that could make genocide less likely. If you haven't learned coding yet, see the entry for "How You Can Be a Danielle and Learn to Program Computers from a Young Age" for more information. Here are some areas where there's need for new innovation:

- Better tools for people to document atrocities on video and share them with a wide audience.

- A platform for people in developed countries to more realistically experience what life is like as a group that is at risk of genocide.

- More accurate methods of measuring the impact of charity programs in improving the lives of refugees.

- Equipment that makes it easier for refugees to survive while fleeing dangerous situations.

- Software that helps refugee children deal with the trauma of their experiences.

For more information, please see the following entries in the companion book *A Chronicle of Ideas: A Guide for Superheroines (and Superheroes)*: Hitler's "Final Solution,"

Yad Vashem, Holocaust, Eternal Flame, Hall of Remembrance, Shoah, Hall of Names, Adolf Eichmann, Never Again.

Footnote links at

DanielleWorld.com/resources

HOW YOU CAN BE A DANIELLE

and Harness the Wisdom of Crowds

❋ ❋ ❋ ❋ ❋

The "wisdom of crowds" is the observation that groups of people often make better decisions collectively than even the smartest single member of the group. For example, a crowd of ordinary people at a county fair betting on the weight of an ox can, through the result of this simulated market, be more accurate than even trained cattle experts. Or a group of amateur chess players voting on what moves to make could beat a much more experienced player. Why do things like this happen?

One way of looking at it is that there are usually more ways to be wrong than ways to be right. Imagine a large group answering a difficult multiple-choice question, with options A, B, C, D, and E. Most people do not know that the correct answer is C. But of the 30% who know this, everyone will choose C. The remaining 70% of the crowd will have a mix of wrong answers and perhaps by accident the correct answer— some will have a hunch and other will just guess randomly. On average each choice from the 70% of the crowd who do not know answer will get about 14% each, which is a total of 44% for the correct answer versus 14% for each of the wrong answers. It can be even higher because people may be able to narrow down their choices to less than all five choices. The correct answer stands out even if only a minority of the crowd knows it.

Using market mechanisms allows people to use probabilistic knowledge and contribute to an answer even when they are not sure of the answer because there is meaningful information in hunches and intuitions.

Another reason crowds can be so smart is that individual members of the crowd often have pieces of information that no one else in the crowd has. No single member has all the pieces of the puzzle, but when crowds make decisions as a group, all the information from different members can be taken into account. For this to work, there needs to be some method for everyone in the crowd to communicate and integrate these disparate hints.

In the novel, ten-year-old Danielle recognizes the wisdom of crowds when she asks her Twitter followers a hard question about a pattern in the jazz pieces she plays at her Lincoln Center Concert. She guesses it will take 20 minutes to figure out that the time signatures use prime numbers instead of the usual powers of two, but the online crowd forms a correct consensus in just 15 minutes. Later, Danielle uses the wisdom of crowds when using her followers to solve problems and create positive change in places like Libya and China. You can harness the wisdom of crowds, too!

To get more familiar with how the wisdom of crowds works, take a look at this talk by James Surowiecki,[1] who literally wrote the book on it: *The Wisdom of Crowds: Why the Many Are Smarter Than the Few and How Collective Wisdom Shapes Business, Economies, Societies and Nations* (Doubleday, 2004).

Here are some areas where you can put these ideas into practice:

- **Crowd-sourcing opinions.** Danielle keeps in close communication with her millions of social media followers, and they give her important insights about what is going on in the world. In the same way, you can use social media to get answers that harness the wisdom of the online crowd.

Let's say you hear conflicting stories about water pollution problems in Africa and want to learn the truth from people on the ground there.

If you just asked a lot of people individually, you'd get many different answers, but no information from the crowd about which ones are more reliable. However, sites like Reddit fix this problem by giving people the ability to up-vote or down-vote answers they think are good or bad. Over time, these votes reflect the collective judgment of the crowd.

As a less serious example, when you read user reviews of products on Amazon, you're using the wisdom of the crowd. Amazon lets people rate the reviews they read, and the software prominently displays the reviews that most people found useful. This mechanism gives you information that's more reliable than any single expert review on its own.

Other ideas for seeking opinions that use the wisdom of the crowd include:

- Have your Facebook friends recommend books to read or movies to watch, and ask them to "Like" the other suggestions they think are good ones.

- When considering what colleges to apply to or jobs to seek, look for reviews or testimonials that many people have already up-voted, liked, or rated as helpful.

- If you're curious about an interesting or difficult question in an academic subject or about the creative arts, ask for help understanding it on Stack Exchange.[2] This website pools information from knowledgeable people, and the best answers to your question will get voted to the top.

- If you're wondering how likely a major world event is, take a look at prediction markets (discussed further below), because they reward people for using good information and making accurate predictions.

- **Collaborative problem-solving.** Everyone has their own unique set of mental strengths and weaknesses, and their own base of knowledge and experiences. Solving hard problems often requires many different kinds of problem-solving abilities, and no single person has them all. Harnessing the wisdom of crowds can help solve problems that even top experts can't figure out.

In biology, one important set of difficult problems concerns figuring out how proteins fold into different shapes. This is important for designing new medicines and curing disease. So scientists at the University of Washington created an online game called <u>Foldit</u>,[3] which turns the process of figuring out protein folding into a fun puzzle. 57,000 players tackled these puzzles, using all their diverse problem-solving skills. The game gathered the insights they figured out, and the solutions from the players outperformed what individual experts or the software algorithms could do.

You can use the wisdom of crowds to solve problems in many ways, including:

- **Collaborative engineering**. If you're working on an invention or trying to create something new—either as a physical device, or in computer programming—it can be a big help to get suggestions from a large group, such as on a <u>specialized forum</u>.[4] Each poster will have their own skills and experiences and can comment on each other's ideas. This is why software companies do beta testing. Large numbers of users talking with each other and the developers can find problems more effectively than a small number of experts.

- **Networking**. To make a difference in the world, you'll often need to find a certain type of person to help you—maybe an expert who you can trust in a certain subject, or a person who's mastered a certain skill. Even if you don't know someone like this, there's a very good chance that among the people you know, some know the types of people you're looking for, but you don't know who to ask for an introduction! Instead, it can be helpful to ask your social media contacts an open question: "Who is the best roboticist you know?" If several of your friends suggest the same person, that is a good indication that they are genuinely good at what they do.

- **Tip of the tongue**. Sometimes, it can seem like the most pressing problem in life is remembering something that's on the "tip of your tongue." It can be agonizing! Maybe you're trying to recall the name of a show you used to watch on TV when you were younger, or identify a familiar-looking face in a historical photo. You may not know a single person who's likely to know, but asking a large and diverse crowd, like the people on the Tip of My Tongue[5] subreddit, often brings up the correct answer very quickly.

- **Forecasting the future.** It is not always clear who has information that will help predict a future outcome. For example, a candidate in an election might have a major scandal that is about to emerge, but only a few people know about it. Prediction markets are a way to bring out this wisdom from the crowd in a way that people can use.

Here's how they work. The people who run the market set up a prediction, for example: "Jane Smith will win the 2020 election for mayor of Jonesville." The organizers then set up a way for people to buy "shares" in different possible outcomes. If Smith wins the election, every share for her winning gets a dollar, and every share for her losing gets no money. Knowing this, people can buy and sell shares based on how likely they think she is to win. If you think there's a 50% chance that she will win, you should be willing to pay $0.50 for a share that would pay $1.00 if you're right. People who are very confident will have incentive to bet more money on the outcome, which affects the trading price.

If someone knows a scandal is about to ruin the chances of Smith's election opponent, that means the odds of her winning will be higher. As a result, they will be willing to spend more money on shares for her winning—maybe $0.70 or $0.80 each. This will drive up the overall price of those shares. When you see the price rising like that, that can be a signal that people are betting based on information you don't yet know. With many people participating in such a market, the best information tends to be revealed. This makes prediction markets often significantly more accurate than individual experts, or polls.

Whenever you try to harness the wisdom of crowds, it's important to remember that crowds don't always show their wisdom. Sometimes crowds act irrationally, usually because they all start thinking alike. According to James Surowiecki, wise crowds show the following four features:

- **Diversity of information.** Each person should have their own knowledge, experiences, or skills to contribute.

- **Independence.** Each person can form their initial opinions on their own, without having them determined by other people in the group.

- **Decentralization.** People should all be free to make their own decisions based on their own particular knowledge.

- **Aggregation.** There needs to be a mechanism like buying shares in a prediction market, voting or careful debate that allows the best ideas to rise to the top.

For more information, please see the following entries in the companion book *A Chronicle of Ideas: A Guide for Superheroines (and Superheroes).* Wisdom of Crowds.

Footnote links at

DanielleWorld.com/resources

and Help Promote Peace in the Middle East

At age eleven, Danielle works to promote peace in the Middle East, meeting with the king of Saudi Arabia and other leaders in the region. She understands that achieving peace must start with a solid foundation of human rights and greater freedom for all people there. Even if you don't travel the world and meet with heads of state like Danielle does in the novel, you can still make a difference, bringing the goal of peace closer to reality.

There are currently four main sources of conflict in the Middle East: the struggle between the Israelis and the Palestinians, the violence by the ISIS terrorist group and its self-proclaimed caliphate in Syria and Iraq, the conflict between the Sunni and Shia branches of Islam including the civil war going on in Yemen, and the ongoing oppression and violence affecting citizens in many Middle Eastern countries in the wake of the Arab Spring. Let's take a look at each of these areas in turn, focusing on what you yourself can do to promote peace in the Middle East.

Israeli-Palestinian conflict. The ongoing struggle between the Israelis and the Palestinians is probably the conflict most closely associated with efforts to achieve peace in the Middle East.

- **Background.** People often talk about this problem as a religious feud that has been going on for "thousands of years," but this isn't true. Jews and Muslims coexisted peacefully for centuries in the area that's now Israel and Palestine. During much of that time, the Ottoman Empire ruled almost all of the Middle East. But when the empire collapsed after World War I, both the Jews and the Palestinian Arabs wanted independent states. The creation of the State of Israel in 1948 led to the first of several bitter wars between the two sides, which Israel won. Since then, there have been decades of Israeli military occupation and Palestinian terrorism, and many attempts at peace have failed. Now, the question is mostly about land, identity, and justice.

  - **Land.** The Jewish and Palestinian ethnic groups are not neatly divided into two regions. Instead, they are mixed among each other across the whole area. Everyone considers the land sacred to their own people and don't want to move as part of a peace settlement. This makes it difficult, but not impossible, to figure out a "two-state solution" for splitting the land into two separate permanent homelands.

  - **Identity.** Israelis see their country as an essential refuge for the Jewish people, who were without a state for nearly two thousand years. During that time, they were persecuted and murdered in many parts of the world, culminating in the massacre of six million Jews by the Nazis, known as the Holocaust. They see it as essential that Israel be a Jewish state. On the other hand, Palestinians also have a strong national identity, and want a free and independent state where they can decide their own destiny. This means that neither side really wants a "one-state solution" for a single country that includes both groups. A key issue is that the two groups representing the Palestinians, the Palestinian Liberation Organization (PLO) and Hamas, do not accept the idea of Israel as a Jewish state.

  - **Justice.** Hundreds of thousands of Palestinians fled their homes during the 1948 violence, and want a peace settlement to give them the right to return, along with their descendants. Meanwhile, Israelis want to keep their policy of allowing Jews anywhere in the world to move to Israel, especially if they are being persecuted. There has been a long cycle of revenge and anger, and everyone wants their grievances to be settled in the peace process.

Here are some short videos that can start you going deeper into understanding the conflict:

- A fast-paced and fact-filled <u>video on Israel and Palestine</u>[1] from John Green's *Crash Course* series.

- <u>A short documentary from National Geographic on Israeli settlers and Palestinians living close to each other</u>[2] in the occupied West Bank.

- <u>An introduction to Combatants for Peace</u>,[3] an organization that brings together people from both sides to end the fighting.

- <u>A fascinating talk about the challenges to peace by former US Secretary of State Condoleezza Rice</u>,[4] who was involved in the negotiations.

- **Action.** The great majority of people on both sides want peace and are willing to make some sacrifices to achieve it, but there is a lot of mistrust that has built up between the two sides. Promoting peace involves helping people break down those barriers and trusting each other enough to make peace possible. Many non-governmental organizations are doing great work in this area.

  - <u>Alliance for Middle East Peace</u>.[5] You could bring together your friends and schoolmates in raising money to donate to this group, which creates cooperation between over 100 organizations dedicated to achieving peace between Israelis and Palestinians. Look through the list of members to learn more about their work and consider supporting those that most inspire you.

  - <u>Seeds of Peace</u>.[6] This is a leadership program for young people from areas affected by war and violence. Israeli and Palestinian teens come to a special summer camp in Maine, USA where they can meet each other, interact face-to-face, and get to better understand each other's perspectives. When they go home, they can be voices for peace in their communities, reminding people of the humanity of those on the other side. Watch <u>this video</u>[7] about their work, and <u>read</u>[8] about ways to get involved!

- **Travel.** If you can visit Israel and Palestine, it's a great opportunity to understand the conflict up close. You can learn a lot by meeting Israeli and Palestinian young people in person, getting to know them, and talking about how your lives are similar and different. Seeing your commitment to peace can inspire them to keep working for peace themselves. If you have a Jewish background, you can travel to Israel free of charge with <u>Birthright Israel</u>,[9] and if you have a Palestinian background you can go on a similar trip to Palestine called <u>Know Thy Heritage</u>.[10]

- **Innovate.** Technology has incredible potential to connect people and help them understand each other in new ways. If you know computer programming, you can create tools to build trust between people and help make peace possible. For example, you could create an app that matches Israelis and Palestinians for chat conversations and provides translation. Or a service that helps Palestinian children access high quality education that promotes peace. Or a project for getting reliable information into Gaza, because it is ruled by the Hamas terrorist group, which spreads anti-Semitic propaganda. If your talents are in the arts, you might create a new multimedia platform to let both sides experience "a day in the life" of the other. Use your creativity, and talk to Israeli and Palestinian people to learn more about what they need.

ISIS violence. The most virulent threat to peace in the Middle East in recent years was ISIS, which occupied a large region of Syria and Iraq. ISIS conducts brutal terrorist attacks in the Middle East. ISIS has recently been removed from virtually all of this area. It continues to spread its radical ideology around the world via the Internet, although having lost its territory, its ability to organize attacks has significantly diminished.

- **Background.** For many decades, Muslim terrorist groups have been carrying out attacks in the Middle East and Europe, but religion was usually a secondary motivation. However, in the last twenty years or so, more dangerous groups have killed thousands of people for primarily religious reasons. Based on a warped interpretation of Islam, they believe that they are commanded by God to kill those who don't agree with their religious views, even other Muslims. Osama bin Laden and al-Qaeda perpetrated dramatic and devastating attacks, like 9/11, but following bin Laden's death, a new group called ISIS became the most dangerous radical Islamic terrorist group. ISIS uses online propaganda to recruit young people all around the world—therefore young people can play a major role in stopping them.

Here's some further information about the threat of ISIS and movements like it:

- A quick summary of facts about ISIS,[11] including a timeline of how it formed and conquered so much territory.

- A helpful video explaining al-Qaeda[12] and the danger it still poses after bin Laden's death.

- A brief explainer from Vox on the Syrian conflict[13] and how that allowed ISIS to take power.

* **Action.** Defeating ISIS in Syria and Iraq is a job for the large international military alliance that is working to liberate all the territory they have captured. But there is also an online battleground, and that's where your efforts can make a difference.

  - **Counter-radicalization.** Numerous organizations have gotten involved in counter-radicalization work—like Muflehun,[14] which counters radical messaging by showing how the authentic message of Islam forbids terrorism. They also help people who are tempted to become violent, and have respected community leaders guide them back onto a peaceful path. One interesting project is called ViralPeace,[15] and uses interactive workshops to train young people on how to "push back against hate, extremism and violence." By spreading the word about these organizations, volunteering for them, and supporting them financially, ordinary citizens can meaningfully contribute to the fight against hateful ideology.

  - **Language learning.** If you want to work in a more direct counter-radicalization role as you get older, language skills are a big help. ISIS and organizations like it do a lot of their messaging in Arabic, but also other languages, like Farsi, Turkish, Urdu, Pashto, and Tagalog. People who learn these languages are in high demand for jobs at counter-radicalization think tanks, charities working with terror victims, and organizations that provide education to vulnerable populations. These language skills can also be a big boost for careers in diplomatic service, the military, or intelligence agencies. The earlier you start learning, the better! There's a wide variety of apps[16] to choose from that can be a fun and easy way to learn Arabic and other languages, and if you prefer a more structured course you could use a trusted system like Rosetta Stone.[17] Many community colleges also offer in-person classes in Arabic, and will often let younger students enroll as well.

- **Building new tools.** Just like with the Israeli-Palestinian conflict, there are lots of opportunities for innovation and creative thinking to bring positive change. This video shows college students working together on a challenge[18] to design new tools for counter-radicalization, with 45 teams taking part. There are new challenges and competitions like this frequently, and such projects are a great way to collaborate with friends with diverse skills and create something useful that none of you could have created on your own. If you haven't learned programming yet, see the entry for "How You Can Be a Danielle and Learn to Program Computers from a Young Age." Better software can assist in identifying people vulnerable to radicalization, and make it easier to send the messages most likely to change their minds.

- **Stand against prejudice.** There is no justification for violence and terrorism like the acts committed by al-Qaeda and ISIS. But when young Muslims in Western countries experience prejudice and hatred due to their religion and ethnicity, it is easier for radical clerics to convince them that killing is the answer. When young Muslims feel socially excluded and don't have many non-Muslim friends, it is easier to see people of other faiths as "the enemy" instead of as individual human beings. For this reason, your actions to form friendships with Muslims in your community can undermine the extremists and prove them to be liars.

Sunni-Shiite conflict. There are two main branches of Islam in the Middle East: the Sunnis and the Shiites. Violence and resentment between them is a major cause of instability in that part of the world. Healing this divide can go a long way toward establishing peace.

- **Background**. There is a long history of violence between Sunnis and Shiites, stretching back centuries. Both sides have grievances and remember injustices that they still resent. Today, most of the Muslim world is Sunni, with mostly Shiites in Iran. Iraq has high numbers of both, which is a cause of tension due to the lingering distrust between them. In the politics of the modern Middle East, the government of Saudi Arabia is the most powerful representative of Sunni interests. The two holiest places in Islam, Mecca and Medina, are both controlled by the Saudis. Meanwhile, Shiite interests all over the world are represented by the government of Iran. Unfortunately, both of these governments follow extreme versions of their religious traditions. The Saudi leaders follow Wahhabism, which is a fundamentalist form of Sunni Islam, and the Iranian leaders practice a fundamentalist version of Shia Islam with clerics controlling the government. The Saudis and Iranians don't fight directly, but encourage their allies to fight each other in places like Syria, Iraq, and Yemen.

Although the fighting in Syria gets most of the headlines, the violence in Yemen is also especially violent. Since 2015, there has been an ongoing civil war between the forces of Yemeni president Abdrabbuh Mansur Hadi, who is backed by the Saudis, and a Shia rebel group called the Houthis who are supported by Iran. al-Qaeda-linked groups have also taken over large areas of the countryside. All sides have targeted civilians, and more than 10,000 innocent people have been killed so far, with no end in sight.

To start learning more, take a look at these resources:

-   A short video introduction to the divide between Sunnis and Shiites[19] and what the differences are between the two groups.

-   A helpful summary of how the Sunni-Shia struggle has become a rivalry[20] between the rulers of Saudi Arabia and Iran.

-   A thought-provoking and informative explanation from John Green's *Crash Course*[21] about the history of revolutions in Iran.

-   Fast facts about Yemen[22] and the civil war there, including a timeline of major events.

– A clear and insightful <u>video explainer about the conflict in Yemen</u>,[23] focusing on its causes and the motivations of the different sides.

– Dramatic <u>footage from on the ground in Yemen</u>,[24] by VICE News. The video shows the period leading up to the civil war, and features Yemeni people talking about their experiences in their own words.

● **Action.** Promoting peace in the conflicts between Sunnis and Shiites will require improving human rights for everyone, as well as creating greater political freedom for women, who often lack basic rights and have little control over their own lives. Even though the war zones are too dangerous for you to visit yourself as a young person, you can organize your community to support some great charities doing valuable work in high-risk areas.

– <u>Iraq Foundation</u>.[25] This group is working both on short-term humanitarian relief projects and long-term efforts to rebuild human rights and democracy in Iraq. One of the main reasons ISIS was able to conquer so much of the country in 2014 was that its civil society was weak. People from different tribal groups did not trust each other, and Sunnis and Shiites looked out for themselves instead of putting the good of the country first. Establishing that trust and a strong belief in democracy can prevent a group like ISIS from ever returning to the country. The Iraq Foundation puts special focus on training women to be leaders in their communities, and helping them fight for full equality in society.

– <u>Amnesty International</u>.[26] A disproportionate amount of the human rights violations in the Yemeni civil war are committed against women and girls. They are often denied the educational opportunities that boys get and are forced into marriages while they are still children. Female genital mutilation (FGM) is also very common in some parts of Yemen. Amnesty International documents these abuses for the world to see, and puts pressure on government leaders to stand up for the rights of victims. For more information on what you can do to end FGM, see the entry for "How You Can Be a Danielle and help Eradicate Female Genital Mutilation."

- Doctors Without Borders.[27] The fighting in Yemen caused a breakdown in sewer systems and disrupted the people's access to clean water. As a result, around a half million people contracted cholera, a deadly disease that is almost nonexistent in developed countries. Around 2,000 died in this epidemic, and more deaths are still happening. Other diseases are spreading, too, and the lack of medical care is causing people to die unnecessarily from minor illnesses. Doctors Without Borders sends physicians into the war zone to provide much-needed care and save lives.

Arab Spring aftermath. Following the failure of revolutions in several Middle Eastern countries, violence and instability are making it difficult for ordinary people to live their lives. Extremist groups and dictators are battling each other, with innocent civilians caught in the crossfire.

- **Background.** In 2011, revolutions broke out in several majority-Muslim countries around the Middle East and North Africa. People were frustrated with living under harsh dictators, and flooded the streets with massive protests. Authoritarian leaders were forced from power in Tunisia, Egypt, Libya, and Yemen. The protesters wanted more freedom, and many demanded a transition to more democratic systems of government. At first, there were major successes. But despite early reasons for hope, everywhere but in Tunisia, serious violence soon returned. The protests also sparked the Syrian civil war, and prompted a brutal government crackdown in Bahrain. And so, there is tension throughout the Middle East. Many people got a taste of freedom during the Arab Spring, but now they are caught in the middle of ongoing violence and are desperate for positive change.

Watch these short videos to get a deeper understanding of how the Arab Spring happened and why it matters:

- Another *Crash Course* video from John Green[28] about the relationship between Islam and politics.

- A fascinating segment from PBS about the Arab Spring[29] and its significance.

- An analysis from *The Economist* about how the Arab Spring[30] and its aftermath is affecting Egypt, which has the largest population in the Middle East, with nearly 100 million people.

● **Action.** You can help people in Arab Spring countries build a better future for themselves by supporting pro-democracy organizations, and also through working on innovations that make it harder for dictators to control people's lives.

  - Project on Middle East Democracy.[31] Known as POMED for short, this group uses a three-pronged approach for supporting freedom in the Muslim world. They conduct research aimed at finding what policies are most effective at promoting democracy. They also engage in advocacy in countries like the United States, urging the government to take an active role in strengthening democracy in the Middle East. Finally, they collaborate with organizations working in the region to help them be better change-makers. This includes training, leadership workshops, and expert advice.

    ▪ National Democratic Institute.[32] The NDI focuses on helping activists in these countries create institutions and traditions that most people in America and Europe take for granted. You can't have a healthy democracy if minorities aren't included in political parties, if elections are threatened by violence, if nobody holds debates where candidates can talk about important issues, and if young people don't think that voting matters. NDI has studied how pro-democracy societies have been created in the past, and trains local activists with those lessons, so each country doesn't have to make those same mistakes.

    ▪ Technology. As discussed above, your creativity can have a major impact on people's lives in the form of new innovations. Dictators can only hold onto power when they can confuse and frighten their citizens. Technology allows people to share information with each other without the government being able to stop them. In 2011, Facebook and Twitter were hugely important platforms for helping the protestors coordinate their activities. In watching videos about these conflicts and hearing the people speak about their problems, think of ways how new online platforms might be able to help them. For even more on how technology can be the best friend of democracy and human rights, see the entry for "How You Can Be a Danielle and Combat Totalitarianism in the World."

For more information, please see the following entries in the companion book *A Chronicle of Ideas: A Guide for Superheroines (and Superheroes)*: King Abdullah, Saudi Arabia, Madrassa Schools, General Assembly, Benjamin Netanyahu, Kadima, Likud, Palestine, Terahertz Frequency, Knesset, Quartet of Nations and Institutions, Nobel Peace Prize, Shiite, Sunni, Sunni Terrorist Groups, the Taliban, al-Qaeda, Osama Bin Laden, Abbottabad, Qur'ān, Muhammad, Angel Jibril, Jihad, Allah, Infidels, al-Zawahiri, Breakaway Group From al-Qaeda.

Footnote links at

DanielleWorld.com/resources

HOW YOU CAN BE A DANIELLE

and Combat Drought and Polluted Water in Poor Nations

Water is essential for human life. In addition to our need to drink water, we use it for bathing, cooking food, and carrying away waste. We also need water for our animals to drink, and to water crops. So, it's a life-threatening problem when people have inadequate supplies of clean water, either because there is no rain, or because the water they do have is contaminated.

In the novel, Danielle recognizes this problem when she is six, and travels to Zambia to help the people overcome a drought, where she uses new technologies created by famed inventor Dean Kamen. Fortunately, this doesn't have to just be fiction. New technologies and ideas are making it easier than ever before to help communities suffering from water deficiencies and pollution.

Droughts are a normal part of climate patterns, where a year or several years go by with much lower rainfall than normal. This can be a problem even for developed countries, but it isn't life-threatening there. This is because they have large infrastructure projects like artificial reservoirs to store excess water from high-rain years, so they can use it during droughts. In poorer countries, though, people don't have much ability to store water from the periods when there's more rain than usual. As a result, when a drought strikes, people quickly find themselves without the water they need for survival.

In 2017, for example, large parts of Africa (especially in the eastern and southern parts of the continent) are suffering from the worst drought in over 60 years. This sparks a spiral of problems that makes each worse. With less water available, people have to travel longer distances to obtain even a small amount of water. Since children are often in charge of getting water for their families, this means they have to leave school and their education suffers. Without enough water, crops die, leaving people with too little food. As famine sets in, people get weaker and suffer from more diseases.

Here are some resources that can help you start learning more about droughts and their impact on poor people around the world:

- A report from CNN about the drought in Africa and resulting famine,[1] which has left 20 million people at risk of starvation.

- Facts about how the drought and famine affected Djibouti in 2011,[2] around the beginning of the crisis.

- An update on the famine's impact on Somalia as of 2017.[3]

- A closer look at how the drought is affecting South Africa in 2017.[4]

There are several highly effective aid organizations working to combat the effects of this Africa drought, and the impact of drought in poor nations more generally. Raising money for them in your community can directly allow them to save more lives, and is a great opportunity to develop your leadership abilities and get young people working together for a vital cause.

- Oxfam[5] is one of the world's most respected famine relief organizations. They help drought victims through emergency support, like temporary food and water supplies, sanitation equipment, and cash grants to replace income lost when crops wither and animals die.

- UNICEF[6] focuses on providing aid to children, who are especially vulnerable to famine and malnutrition. Those who grow up malnourished may not have proper brain development, so it is crucial to make sure they have enough food and clean water while growing up.

Even though technology is unable (for the near future, at least) to change weather patterns to eliminate drought, there's lots of room for innovations that can help minimize the harm droughts cause to humans.

- **Water storage.** A big need in drought-affected countries is water storage. If a community can store all the extra rain from years when they get more than they need, and keep it clean, they can use that water when droughts hit. Unfortunately, people in poor countries either don't have large enough storage systems, or don't have the means to keep water clean until they need it. The Africa Sand Dam Foundation[7] is a non-governmental organization in Kenya that helps communities make creative use of local rock formations and other geographical features to store water.[8] Young people can come up with new solutions, too. For example, a 16-year-old South African girl named Kiara Nirghin[9] invented a promising new material for storing water by experimenting with natural substances found in orange peels and avocados!

- **Drought resistance.** Many of the people most vulnerable to droughts are poor farmers. Even if there's enough rain for them to have drinking water, there may not be enough for their crops to grow. Without crops, they have no income, and can't get food or medicine. That's why there's a lot of research being done into how to create plants that are more resistant[10] to hot and dry conditions. This TED Talk by biologist Jill Farrant[11] shows how this is done through genetic engineering. If you study science and agriculture, you may be able to achieve new breakthroughs in this yourself

- **Water pollution.** An even bigger worldwide problem than drought is polluted water. When the drinking water is unsafe, it causes serious diseases. Children are particularly vulnerable to water-borne illnesses. In some cases, this water is dirty-looking, and people are so desperate they drink it anyway. But in other cases, water can be harmful without it looking or tasting dangerous. Major causes of this pollution include chemicals that contaminate the water from factories or mining, pesticides or animal products that get washed from farms into lakes and rivers, and contamination from human waste. When people don't have sewers to take away their waste, bacteria from feces can get into drinking water, causing deadly diseases, like cholera.

Take a look at these links for a fuller understanding of why so many people lack clean drinking water, and how that causes disease:

- Facts[12] about how unsafe drinking water is the world's leading cause of premature deaths. It is especially tragic because these deaths are all completely preventable with current technology.

- A BBC investigation[13] into the scale of the worldwide problem with unsafe drinking water. The crisis is much larger than many people thought.

- A powerful and emotional animated video[14] about the impact of cholera.

Purifying water in poor nations is one of the world's most important and difficult challenges. Here's the problem: The water treatment systems used in developed countries are large and expensive projects. It takes many years and billions of dollars to build purification plants, pumping stations, and large pipes to carry the water to where people need it. Poor countries can't afford to build those systems, and people without clean drinking water can't wait years for them to be built anyway. Also, in war zones and unstable countries, big water treatment systems can get damaged in the violence. For this reason, clean water technologies need to satisfy three conditions:

- **Affordable.** The technology has to be sufficiently inexpensive for poor communities to buy, or for charities to install for them.

- **Simple.** In countries that are poor or affected by violence, there may not be many trained engineers with the skills to build and maintain very complicated systems. And when they break down, it may be hard to bring in unusual parts to repair them. This means it's better to use technologies that are simple, reliable, long lasting, and easy-to-fix.

- **Decentralized.** Since it's not practical to build big centralized water systems for thousands or millions or people, there's need for decentralized systems that can be installed for hundreds or dozens of people at a time, or even individuals!

There is a wide range of very promising new water purification technologies being developed and tested. If these can be made cheaply enough and distributed to the communities that need them, millions of lives will be saved.

- Summary of information[15] on six intriguing water purification technologies that might be good for poor countries.

- The SlingShot,[16] created by pioneering American inventor Dean Kamen, can run on almost any fuel, and take virtually "anything wet" and turn it into safe, drinkable water. As explained in this video,[17] it is a breakthrough because it can do this using far less energy than other methods. And because it uses a Stirling engine, poor people can power it with whatever fuel they have available. In the novel, six-year-old Danielle uses the SlingShot to help alleviate the drought in Zambia.

- The Stirling engine[18] is a technology that's more than 200 years old. Unlike the internal combustion engine, like what we have in our fossil fuel-powered cars, there are no explosions inside a Stirling engine. Instead, when the engine's two sides have difference in heat levels, it turns that difference into useful mechanical work that can generate electricity and operate machines. This means that even very simple fuel sources, like campfires or piles of trash, can be turned into power just by building a fire next to the Stirling engine—and that power can be used to purify water. In the novel, Danielle uses Stirling engines to power the SlingShot water purification machines she has ordered for Zambia.

- The Lifestraw[19] is designed for use by individual people. You can stick it into a glass of unsafe water, and as you suck it up through the straw, it filters the water so it's safe by the time it gets to your mouth. Here's a somewhat unpleasant, but eye-opening, video[20] of two popular vloggers demonstrating how well the Lifestraw works by using it to drink lots of horrible liquids, including their own urine!

- This amazing TED Talk by Michael Pritchard[21] about his invention called the Lifesaver filter, which is designed for use by a single person or family. You can put foul water into it, and after you pump its handle with your arm a few times, safe and clear water comes out.

- The Janicki Omniprocessor[22] is a larger water purification system that could be good for a whole village. It takes in raw sewage and turns it into electricity and purified drinking water. Bill Gates and his wife Melinda have used their charitable foundation to fund development of this invention and others like it. For some laughs, watch Bill on *The Tonight Show* drinking water purified by the Omniprocessor[23] with host Jimmy Fallon!

But water technology breakthroughs don't require a Bill Gates-sized budget. Passionate and curious young people around the world have come up with impressive innovations of their own.

- 17-year-old Cynthia Sin Nga Lam invented a device called the H2Pro,[24] which takes dirty water and sunlight and can turn them into clean water and power.

- 18-year-old Perry Alagappan noticed that waste from electronics is leaving toxic metals in many water supplies, so he invented a filter made from graphene[25] that can purify water up to five times more cheaply than previous technology.

- 14-year-old Lalita Prasida Sripada Srisai developed a new water filter that uses discarded corncobs.[26]

If you study chemistry, think creatively, and experiment persistently, you may be able to come up with a similar invention yourself! If your interests lie elsewhere, you could raise money to buy purification devices and send them to people who need them, through charities like Water is Life.[27] If you're old enough, you could even go on a special trip with your school, your religious group, or a charity, and give out water filters yourself and train people in how to use them.

In many cases, people in poor countries have access to clean water, but before they can drink it, it gets polluted by bad sanitation practices.

If they don't know about the danger of drinking contaminated water, even if they had the right technology, they might not use it. The answer is education programs that take into account the local culture and explain to people how diseases spread and what they can do to prevent their water from becoming contaminated. Supporting these programs can have a great impact, because once a community keeps its water clean, disease lessens, which helps many other problems.

- Like with famine aid, UNICEF[28] focuses its clean water programs on helping children, especially in schools. This is because unsanitary conditions in schools can force students to leave school, especially girls when they begin menstruating.

- Organizations like Lifewater[29] focus on community education. They go into villages and local communities and educate people face-to-face about how to keep their water clean. If feces are getting into the drinking water, they build latrines that keep human waste at a safe distance from the water supply. It's then important to work with a community to create safer bathroom facilities and practices. As Ronnie Kaweesa of Compassion Uganda[30] says, "The poor are intelligent and resourceful. It's just a lack of experience."

- Many people are surprised to learn that in some developing nations, poor people get access to smartphones before clean drinking water is available. This means that education campaigns can use compelling and memorable videos to make their points, like this one from UNICEF, [31] which teaches people in Ghana about preventing cholera.

As you learn more about the problem and speak with people from those countries, you'll understand more about the problems they face, and may get new ideas for projects you could start to help them.

For more information, please see the following entries in the companion book *A Chronicle of Ideas: A Guide for Superheroines (and Superheroes):* Zambia, Zambian

Drought, Slingshot Water Machine, Stirling Engine, Decentralized Water Purification Cells.

Footnote links at

DanielleWorld.com/resources

and Become a Physicist

Physics is the study of the physical laws that govern the universe—from the smallest subatomic particles up to clusters of galaxies and distances of billions of light-years. All other sciences rest on the foundation of physics. For example, biology studies the application of the laws of chemistry to the complex molecules that make up living cells. But the laws of chemistry are themselves an application of the laws of physics to different kinds of atoms interacting with each other. Understanding physics allows us to understand the world we live in as well as create new technologies, and thereby shape our environment more effectively.

In the novel, Danielle recognizes this at age four, when she realizes that everyday reality is made of "machines within machines within machines." This inspires her to study physics, where she later comes up with her "n-dimensional membrane" theory to describe the smallest scales of the universe, and wins a Nobel Prize at fifteen for her "hidden gear" experiment about uncertainty in quantum physics. But accomplishments such as this aren't just for fictional superheroines. The tools exist today to conduct serious science experiments at a young age.

The first step to become a physicist, or any type of scientist, is getting inspired. Great physicists are motivated by a passion for learning about how the universe works. Many have described the way these rules work as elegant and beautiful, and inspiring awe. Let some of these great minds share with you their inspiration:

- Nobel laureate Murray Gell-Mann[1] on the beauty of physics, and the wonder he still experiences from unlocking its mysteries.

- Stephen Hawking,[2] (1942 – 2018) one of the world's most famous scientists on the "big questions" that are still unanswered about the universe.

- University of Cambridge physicist Harry Cliff[3] on a fascinating question: "Have we reached the end of physics?" Or is there still a lot left to discover?

- Renowned physicist and science author Brian Greene,[4] pondering the question of whether there are multiple universes, and why the laws of physics are what they are.

- Footage from old TV documentaries with the late Richard Feynman,[5] one of the greatest physicists of the 20th century, talking about why science can be so exciting and interesting, and why he finds doing physics his most enjoyable activity.

- Episode of the *Vsauce* series on YouTube, hosted by Michael Stevens,[6] asking the sort of question young kids argue about on the playground: "What would happen if every single person on earth jumped at the same time?" It shows how you can apply scientific logic to all kinds of problems.

- Physics for Future Presidents,[7] an excellent book by Richard A. Muller that explores intriguing and relevant questions in physics in accessible language.

If the physics classes at your school are not challenging enough, many community colleges allow younger students to enroll in courses if they can show that they're ready for it. Other organizations in your community can also support and reward your physics study—for example, the Girl Guides[8] and Girl Scouts[9] are developing special merit badges to recognize achievements in science-related fields. The Boy Scouts[10] have several badges for these areas, too.

Yet some people find that classroom education isn't the best way for them to learn physics. It can be a big help to study at the times that are most convenient for you, when you can focus your full attention on the subject, and to work at your own pace. There is a wide range of websites and mobile apps you can use to help you improve your physics skills:

- Brain It On![11] (Android). Lets you solve physics puzzles, and has you use games to get a better intuition for how the forces of physics work.

- Monster Physics[12] (iPhone). This one is aimed at younger kids, and encourages creative thinking to understand how things work. Create your own virtual machines from a range of parts, and watch how the parts work together.

- Pocket Physics[13] (Android). Simple explanations for a wide range of concepts in physics, including illustrations. Good for all ages from primary school up to university.

- High School Physics – Free[14] (Android). High school-level physics lessons, including problem-solving exercises and calculator functions.

- Physics Full Course[15] (iPhone). An all-inclusive course with school-style lessons and exercises to practice your skills.

- Complete Physics[16] (Android). Includes advanced physics over a wide range of topics, with quizzes to help you test your knowledge.

- Physics Classroom[17] (Web). Website with lots of different exercises and simulations to see the forces of physics in action.

If you're looking for a more structured and intensive method of learning physics, online courses can be a great solution. These are taught by some of the best professors in the world, and many give you the option to work collaboratively and discuss the subject with fellow students or even to receive personalized feedback from instructors. Some of the best offerings in physics include:

- A Khan Academy course that provides an introduction to physics[18] from the very beginning, and works up to more advanced concepts. Based on video lectures and animated demonstrations.

- A slightly more advanced course from Udemy,[19] with more focus on learning problem-solving techniques. Includes about 1.5 hours of video lectures, with problems to solve in between.

- "How Things Work,"[20] a popular University of Virginia course available on Coursera. The course includes videos and graded assessments, and focuses on learning physics in the context of everyday objects. Takes about 11 hours to complete. After you finish, take a look at Coursera's many other options[21] in physics.

- Yale University offers open-access free online courses based on its college-level physics classes. The introductory physics course comes in Part I and Part II.[22] In total, there are 49 lectures of about 75 minutes each, along with problem sets and quizzes. This is a good option for advanced physics students looking to stretch their knowledge and improve mastery of the subject.

If these courses excite you, and you feel a calling to become a physicist, you should give some thought to what aspects of physics seem most exciting. Broadly speaking, there are three kinds of physicists, divided by what role their work does in the context of science.

- **Theoretical physics** is concerned with figuring out what laws govern the universe, and coming up with theories that can explain the phenomena that scientists observe. Often, these theories are given in the form of mathematical equations. If the theory is correct, observations about the real world will follow those equations. The big challenge for theoretical physicists is coming up with equations that describe real life as accurately as possible, but in the simplest possible way. Theoretical physics requires a combination of creativity, persistence, logic, and abstract thinking. Probably the most famous example was Albert Einstein performing simple thought experiments which led him to devise his special Theory of Relativity. This theory resulted in unexpected and strange conclusions, including that the passage of time for you relative to another object would be affected by your speed relative to that other object. Einstein's theory has been confirmed by countless experiments over the past century. In my book *How to Create a Mind*, I describe the simple thought experiments that Einstein performed to come up with his theory. These experiments required no equipment or resources other than a rich imagination and a willingness to "not fall off the horse"—meaning a willingness to stay with the implications of a thought experiment even if it led to apparently bizarre conclusions. These thought experiments require no substantial understanding of physics and very elementary math.

- **Experimental physics** is the work of testing physics theories in the real world and collecting data that can be used to create new theories. Experiments were how early scientists like Galileo, Isaac Newton, and Michael Faraday first figured out the laws of physics. Famous experiments were used to discover effects like electricity and radiation, which have countless practical applications in the modern world. Experimental physicists use the scientific method to attempt to find evidence that disproves a current theory, or demonstrates the existence of something previously unknown. Successful experiments involve coming up with novel ways of testing physical laws, and then carefully making sure that the experiment isn't thrown off by unexpected factors. Thus, to be a good experimental physicist, you should work on improving your ingenuity, patience, and organization.

- **Applied physics** is the use of physics knowledge to solve real-world problems. Thus, it has a lot of crossover with inventing and engineering. The challenge of applied physics is figuring out how known theories can be used to make new technologies possible. Thus, it requires both understanding how physics works and imagining how those principles could be applied in innovative ways. To do this, applied physicists need to be good at "lateral thinking," which is approaching problems from unexpected and original angles. They also need to develop good analysis skills—for looking at big, difficult problems and breaking them down into smaller, simpler problems that can be solved more easily. Applied physicists often have a "hacker" mentality, and get a thrill from figuring out how to do things that are seemingly impossible.

Hundreds of years ago, science was primitive enough that some people could master everything there was to know about physics. But now, so much has been learned already that people only have time to master a small part of it. So they specialize, which has become true of every area of science. Thus, physicists—whether theoretical, experimental, or applied— usually focus on one or two sub-fields within physics. Here are the main branches of physics, along with college-level online courses that can help you explore them more deeply to see if that's where you'd like to specialize:

- **Mechanics** is the study of how objects behave when in motion or when forces are acting on them. Mechanics usually focuses on objects at the scale that we can see and interact with in everyday life. When people are trying to invent new machines or vehicles, they use mechanics to figure out how they will work. Mechanics can also be used in the creative arts—for example, people making video games or computer-animated movies use mechanics to make sure that the objects onscreen behave accurately and therefore look "convincing." A course from the University of New South Wales in Australia[23] provides a solid introduction to mechanics.

- **Quantum physics** studies the tiniest scales of the universe, from individual atoms down to subatomic particles, and even smaller objects called strings that we can study through math but can't observe directly. Unlike classical mechanics, where the interactions of objects can be perfectly modeled and predicted if you know all their properties, quantum physics features uncertainty. No matter how much information you have about a given subatomic particle, you can't say for certain how it will behave—you can only talk about it in terms of probability. A major question in quantum physics is how the properties of particles at these tiny scales relate to the properties of larger objects. A course from the University of Maryland, College Park[24] lets you explore the basics of quantum physics and prepares you to go deeper. Danielle questions the probabilistic nature of quantum mechanics. She postulates a "hidden gear" mechanism that cannot be observed, but determines the outcome of quantum events. She gets a Nobel prize for conducting an experiment confirming this "gear," but she discovers that the action of this mechanism is still indeterminate.

- **Chemical physics** focuses on the link between the most basic laws of nature and the chemical properties of atoms and molecules. Why is it, for example, that chemical bonds between atoms work the way they do? Why do certain molecular structures show some properties instead of others? This area of study can reveal the deeper mechanisms that drive large-scale chemical reactions such as what might occur in a chemistry class. This understanding can lead to creation of new materials and molecules that are useful in medicine, science, computing, and other fields. The University of Manchester has a highly-rated course[25] that will introduce you to the intersection between physics and chemistry.

- **Electromagnetism** is an area of physics central to most of the technologies we use today. Electricity, magnetism, radio waves, visible light, x-rays, microwaves (and other kinds of waves) are all effects of the electromagnetic force, which is one of the four fundamental forces of physics. A video from the *SciShow* with Hank Green[26] explains in more detail. Scientists who study this force uncover insights that may be helpful in areas like computing, communication technology, and sensor devices. An open MIT course[27] lets you get a better understanding of electromagnetism-related physics.

- **Astrophysics** is the branch of physics dedicated to planets, stars, galaxies, and the universe itself. Astrophysicists study how these heavenly bodies form, and how they evolve through their life cycles. They also study the origins of the universe itself, from the effects from conditions right after the Big Bang to what the universe might be like billions, or even trillions, of years from now. Other topics in astrophysics include research into the workings of exotic objects like black holes, neutron stars, and quasars. Astrophysics also investigates unusual concepts like dark matter, wormholes, time travel, and parallel universes. The University of Tokyo provides an excellent course[28] for beginners on astrophysics.

- **Materials physics** concerns how the basic laws of physics shape the properties of liquids and solids. It includes substances like crystals, and investigates why some molecules assemble into crystalline shapes and others do not. It also documents how matter behaves when it is transitioning between different phases, such as when liquid water freezes into ice. Materials physics opens opportunities for the creation of new materials and new technologies that make use of them. The National University of Science and Technology MISiS in Russia offers an informative course[29] on this.

- **Mathematical physics** is the development of new mathematical techniques for modeling physical phenomena, or for creating new theories. Often, ideas in pure math that at first don't seem to have any practical applications are later discovered to be helpful in solving unexpected kinds of problems. <u>A series of lectures by physicist Carl Bender at Washington University in St. Louis</u>[30] is a very popular introduction to the techniques of mathematical physics.

- **Particle physics** is the branch of physics that covers how different kinds of subatomic particles behave, especially the 61 types of elementary particles that make up all known matter. It uses many ideas from quantum physics, but puts more emphasis on experiments, such as the Large Hadron Collider at CERN. These particle accelerators smash subatomic particles apart at incredibly high energies to study what they're made of. <u>The University of Geneva offers a rigorous course</u>[31] for people first getting into particle physics.

Finally, growing your skills and knowledge of physics requires hands-on experience of how these laws work. Since large-scale experiments in the real world are time-consuming and expensive, a great alternative is learning about physics through simulations. The simulators available below let you get a practical feel for many of the phenomena you'll be studying.

- <u>A wide variety of interactive physics simulations,</u>[32] covering topics like buoyancy, electric charges, density, and projectile motion.

- <u>Another large group of simulations</u>[33] to choose from, mainly focusing on the interaction of simplified objects like springs and pendulums. You can adjust all the properties of these objects, like size and mass, and see how those changes affect the simulation.

- <u>A set of sophisticated physics simulations</u>[34] on chemistry, biology, and physics. Accessing these simulations costs money, but your school may be able to purchase them for you.

For more information, please see the following entries in the companion book *A Chronicle of Ideas: A Guide for Superheroines (and Superheroes):* Orbits of Celestial Bodies, Quarks, String Theory, Multi-Dimensional Manifolds, Quantum Probability Fields, Terahertz

Frequency, Hidden Variable, Probabilistic Nature of Quantum Mechanics, Falsifiable Experiment, Collapse of the Wave Function, Presence of an Observer, Entangled Membranes, Curled Dimensions, Anti-matter, Hidden Dance of Pairs, Entangled Particles at a Distance, Speed of Light, Heisenberg's Uncertainty Principle, Gaussian Distribution, Muons, State Information in a Quantum Field, Quantum, Hidden Quantum Variable, Indirect Measurements in Physics, CERN Accelerator, Multi-Dimensional Folds, Probabilistic Elements in Physics, Indeterminate Nature of Quantum Mechanics, Nanotechnology.

Footnote links at

DanielleWorld.com/resources

and Help Cure Cancer

❁ ❁ ❁ ❁ ❁

Before you can follow in Danielle's footsteps to help cure cancer, you should seek a deeper understanding of what cancer is and how it works. Then, we'll take a look at how you can support the world's most innovative cancer researchers, the steps you can take to prepare for a career working to find cures, and what you can do right now to start searching for a breakthrough yourself.

In developed countries, cancer is the number two cause of death, behind heart disease. It is common wisdom to say that cancer is not a single disease but rather a family of more than 200 diseases. However, there are common threads to all cancers. For one thing, when cancer is deadly, it is due to metastases, which are cancer colonies, that develop throughout the body. It is rarely the original tumor that causes the most destruction.

Another commonality to virtually all cancers, according to the cancer stem cell hypothesis, is their origin from cancer stem cells. Chemotherapy drugs are effective at killing cancer cells, but according to the cancer stem cell thesis, the cancer tumor returns because chemotherapy drugs are not effective at killing the cancer stem cells which created the cancer cells in the first place. Cancer stem cell research has been an active focus of cancer research since the early 2000s.

A stem cell is characterized by being able to undergo both symmetric reproduction (to create a copy of itself and therefore another stem cell) and asymmetric reproduction (to create a differentiated cell, such as a colon cell or a lung cell). In the case of cancer stem cells, asymmetric reproduction creates cancer cells which then form the bulk of a cancer tumor. They are the originators of cancer. Moreover, there appears to be a link between the growth of organs in a fetus and the growth of cancer.

MIT scientists Elena Gostjeva and Bill Thilly wrote in a 2006 paper:

> For more than a century, cancer researchers have seriously considered tumors to reflect characteristics of embryos… Adenocarcinoma [such as colon cancer] looks as if it were embryonic tissue simply growing at the fetal rate to form embryonic colon. In addition, metakaryotic nuclei can divide both symmetrically and asymmetrically, a capacity generally reserved for stem cells.

In other words, it appears that due to certain genetic errors and mutations, cancer tumors are actually fetal organs growing inappropriately in a grown person. For more information, please see the entry for Cancer Stem Cell in the companion book, *A Chronicle of Ideas: A Guide for Superheroines (and Superheroes).*

See these links for more information about the nature of cancer:

- Informative TED-Ed video explainer[1] on what makes cancer cells different from healthy cells.

- Answers to key questions about how cancer works,[2] from the Science Museum in the United Kingdom.

The mutations that cause cancer stem cells to create cancer cells can have a variety of causes. Sometimes the cells are damaged by external radiation, like from ultraviolet rays in sunlight, x-rays, or a nuclear reactor leak. This radiation sends high-energy particles through the body, where they smash into the DNA inside cells and corrupt the genetic instructions for how the cells should replicate. In other cases, viruses, which are essentially pieces of DNA or RNA, can cause cancerous mutations. Toxic chemicals can get into cells and disrupt their normal reproduction processes. Genes can affect the way cells are copied during their reproduction, making certain types of errors more likely. Drugs and alcohol can irritate the body's tissues, forcing them to repair themselves such that errors—mutations—occur. For more detailed explanations of how these mechanisms work in the body, see:

- What happens when cells start reproducing uncontrollably.[3]

- The effects of failure of apoptosis,[4] or programmed cell death.

- The action of tissue invasion,[5] where a tumor generates "pioneer cells" that spread to nearby structures and start new cancerous growths; a process called metastasis.

- How angiogenesis,[6] or growth of blood cells to feed tumors, lets cancers establish themselves more firmly in the body.

We've made progress on combating cancer in recent decades. In America for example, the cancer death rate has dropped about 25 percent since the early 1990s, and millions of cancer deaths have been prevented, both through treatments and prevention programs like anti-smoking campaigns and environmental regulations. Yet, so far, the progress has not been evenly distributed among cancers. For example, leukemia was a death sentence sixty years ago, but now the great majority of patients survive it. By contrast, other forms like pancreatic cancer are almost as deadly today as they were back then. In the novel, this motivates Danielle to search for a more complete way of curing cancer. Here's more on the challenges of achieving major cures:

- Hank Green of *SciShow* with a clear, fast-paced video[7] on why we haven't cured cancer yet.

- A short guide by the Cancer Treatment Centers of America[8] on how to understand cancer and why it's so challenging to treat.

Today, most cancer treatments still focus on surgery, radiation, and chemotherapy. Surgeries cut tumors out of the body, but damage healthy tissue and might leave tiny remnants of cancer behind. Radiation shrinks tumors but can cause cancer to recur later. Chemotherapy puts powerful drugs in the body that suppress production of fast growing cells—slows cancer growth—but also harms normal tissues like the hair, skin, and digestive tract. More significantly, they do not work against cancer stem cells. Some chemotherapy drugs actually create conditions (called anaerobic conditions, which means "without oxygen") that encourage the growth of cancer stem cells.

Newer approaches involve creating drugs with specially engineered molecules that can target cancer cells more specifically, without causing so much collateral damage to the rest of the body. A very exciting emerging trend in cancer therapies involve treatments that actually reprogram the body's immune system, which ordinarily is not effective against cancer, to target the cancer cells and destroy them.

The challenge for doctors is to kill all the cancer cells as soon as possible. If the first round of treatment just kills 99.99% of these mutated cells, the surviving .01% will be those with a natural resistance to the treatment. The cancer can then come roaring back, stronger than before. This is known as the asymptoting logarithmic response curve. Also, as discussed above, cancers get their start with malfunctioning stem cells. These work differently from other cancer cells, so treatments that kill most cancer cells leave cancer stem cells unharmed. An MIT team working on cancer stem cell treatments has discovered several drugs that appear effective at killing cancer stem cells or preventing them from reproducing. In the novel, Danielle succeeds in curing most cancers with two cocktails of drugs, one attacking cancer cells, and the other attacking cancer stem cells.

Here are some helpful explanations of a range of new approaches to fighting cancer:

- A video by the science journal *Nature* about immunotherapies,[9] which stimulate a patient's immune system to fight cancer more effectively.

- Another explanation by *Nature,* on approaches that fight cancer by targeting the metabolism[10] that cancer cells use to get the energy they need.

- A summary of the cancer stem cell theory[11] and how these cells serve as starting points for cancer.

- An explanation of therapies[12] based on cancer stem cell theory, including anti-cancer vaccines, from Oxford cancer researcher Robert Rees.

- Dr. William Li on the role of angiogenesis in cancer, and how diet[13] can suppress it.

- More TED Talks[14] to help you understand different theories about cancer and proposed treatments.

One way you can help cure cancer is by supporting organizations doing innovative research into the therapies above. You can volunteer to help them raise money, or if you're old enough and have the right skills, you might be able to get an internship assisting in their research. Otherwise, you can start a fundraiser in your school or community—showing people videos about why this work is so important and why their donations can have a big impact. You might organize athletic activities to fight cancer, where people make donations to participate, or where they get sponsorship from friends and family who pledge to donate a certain amount of money for every mile run, lap swum, or pushup completed. Take a look at these organizations to see what kind of mission you'd most like to support:

- Memorial Sloan Kettering Cancer Center,[15] one of the top cancer research hospitals in the world, with an extremely broad range of therapies being tested.

- The MD Anderson Cancer Center[16] at the University of Texas supports several ambitious "moon shot" programs aimed at achieving breakthroughs with approaches like immunotherapy, genomics (therapies related to genes), and proteomics (related to proteins).

- The Cancer Research Institute[17] has been widely praised for the effectiveness of the research they support, and for the very high percentage of total donations that goes directly to research.

- The Breast Cancer Research Foundation[18] is ranked as one of the most effective cancer charities in America. It funds research into new ways of preventing, detecting, and treating the cancer that kills more women than any other.

- St. Jude Children's Research Hospital[19] provides care for young people with cancer, especially those with rare cancers who can't get treated anywhere else. These treatments provide researchers with valuable information into how pediatric cancers work and what approaches are most effective at beating them.

- Resources from the American Lung Association[20] on how to quit smoking. The research they support is shedding new light on the science of addiction, and how people can stop using tobacco more easily. This can greatly reduce deaths from the lifestyle-related cancer that kills more than any other.

- Action on Smoking and Health[21] (ASH) does similar things in the UK. ASH opposes the tobacco industry and supports more regulations on their activity.

In addition to supporting organizations working toward cures and prevention, you can also have a positive impact by supporting campaigns to fight pollution from cancer-causing substances. For example, the particles emitted as smoke from coal-burning power plants can get trapped in people's lungs and cause cancer. Citizens working together in local communities can help minimize the presence of these chemicals in the environment. Technological innovation can also save lives indirectly, by finding ways to make emissions cleaner, so fewer people get cancer in the first place.

If you are interested in a career as a cancer researcher, you should seek the most challenging biology, chemistry, and math courses your school offers. In addition, you can get a head start on college-level study with online courses about cancer medicine:

- Introduction to the Biology of Cancer,[22] a college-level Coursera course from Johns Hopkins University. Takes one to four hours per week for six weeks.

- Another Johns Hopkins course focusing on how cancer spreads, Understanding Cancer Metastasis.[23] Takes 1.5 hours per week for three weeks.

- Genomic and Precision Medicine,[24] from the University of California, San Francisco, about personalized approaches to fighting cancer that are tailored to the patient's individual genetics. Takes about two hours per week for seven weeks.

- Understanding Clinical Research: Behind the Statistics,[25] a University of Cape Town course that can help you understand published medical studies as you research more about cancer and how it can be cured. Takes two to three hours per week for six weeks.

But you don't have to wait until you have a PhD or medical degree to work directly on curing cancer. Even young people are able to work on experiments that can save lives. For inspiration, here are some teens who have done meaningful cancer research already:

- At 17, Lauren Bendesky[26] interned at the MD Anderson Cancer Center research lab to help analyze the same cancer that she had beaten.

- A TED Talk by Eva Vertes[27] on how research she did at 17 started with curiosity, and led her to emailing research professors with questions, making connections between ideas, and forming promising theories about how cancer might be defeated.

- While in high school, Angela Zhang[28] became curious about new methods of fighting cancer, and started reading papers and attending talks about the subject. This led her to design a nanoparticle targeting system for delivering drugs to cancer cells.

- A group of high school students calling themselves Burlingame Cancer Research,[29] who get together to study the latest science on cancer from journal articles and other sources. The group used its knowledge to organize a conference to bring together a variety of researchers on blood cancers and stimulate new ideas about potential cures.

- A TED Talk by Jack Andraka,[30] a teen who invented a potentially useful new test for pancreatic cancer, which would make it easier and cheaper to detect in the early stages, when it can still be treated successfully.

These stories show that there are several common ingredients to success for young people who want to help cure cancer:

- Read academic journals about medicine, and look for a novel way to connect the problems you read about to ideas from other subjects, like chemistry, biology, or engineering.

- Build your skills at doing lab experiments. MIT OpenCourseWare offers helpful online courses on experimental biology[31] and laboratory chemistry.[32]

- Look for professors or labs in your area who can mentor you. Ask them questions based on your reading, and suggest ideas for experiments they could help you with.

- Think about whether you have skills not usually applied to treating cancer, which might be an opportunity for innovation. For example, if you've learned computer programming in areas like artificial intelligence and machine learning, consider how those techniques might make it easier to detect or treat cancer.

For more information, please see the following entries in the companion book *A Chronicle of Ideas: A Guide for Superheroines (and Superheroes)*: Asymptoting Logarithmic Response Curve, Logarithmic Scale, DNA Replication Errors, Drug Cocktail, Cancer Stem Cell, Orthogonal Approaches, Reproductive Enzymes, Anaerobic Conditions, Chemotherapy Drugs, Eukaryotic Cancer Cells, Food and Drug Administration, Mayo Clinic.

Footnote links at

DanielleWorld.com/resources

and Start Your Own Company

Entrepreneurship is the process of finding opportunities to provide products or services that people will want, and then starting businesses to provide them. These startup businesses vary tremendously in their purpose and ambition. Entrepreneurship ranges from kids in elementary school starting lemonade stands in their front yards, up to technology companies that hope to transform whole industries and change the way billions of people live. Some startups are about creating new products or services that never existed before. Others are about providing existing products or services in a smarter, easier, faster, or less expensive way. In the novel, Danielle recognizes the power of entrepreneurship, and creates several companies including Danielle Music, Danielle TV, and Danielle Stem Cell to make her ideas a reality. You can do the same!

If you have an idea for a product or service that doesn't exist yet, but should, starting a company is one of the best ways to make it happen. If your idea is successful, you can receive not only financial benefits, but more importantly, you can have a large positive impact on the world. Let's look at the concrete steps you can take to make that happen:

- **Identify a need or problem.** The first step to building a successful company is finding a need in your community or the world at large that you can fill, or a problem you can solve. These opportunities could be very local, like kids in your town wanting someone to tutor them in math, or global, like people needing inventions for detecting cancer more accurately or less expensively. Try thinking of this in terms of what someone might wish for. Here are some wish-statements, along with the companies they might inspire.

- "It's a hot day. I wish I could have some cold lemonade right now." [Neighborhood lemonade stand]

- "My lawn needs mowing, but I don't have time to mow it myself." [Yard-work business]

- "Lots of people want to buy and sell items like they do at garage sales, but there isn't a good way for them to connect online." [eBay][1]

- "I wish there were an app that could summarize news stories so I could save time." [Summly app][2]

- "It's hard to get a taxicab at the places and times I want one." [Uber][3]

- "It would be great to have a more realistic and immersive virtual reality system." [Oculus][4]

Here are some other resources on finding the need that your company will fill:

- 5 tips from the Young Entrepreneur Council[5] on identifying a market for your company.

- 14 ideas from Patrick Bet-David[6] on how teenage entrepreneurs can make money.

- TED Talk by Simon Sinek[7] on why having a sense of vision and purpose is so important to being a successful leader. If you have a crystal-clear understanding of why your company needs to exist, that will make people want to help you and follow you.

Once you have found a need you're excited about filling, you should practice explaining it in just a sentence or two, so you can communicate clearly what you're hoping to do.

- **Come up with a solution.** The next step is thinking of a specific answer to the question you've found. This might be opening an online store, manufacturing and selling an invention you create, or programming an app. Note that there may be multiple potential solutions to your problem. For example, you could solve the problem of thirsty people in your neighborhood by opening a lemonade stand, or starting a lemonade shop in a storefront, or founding a lemonade-by-courier business where people order lemonade by an app and you hire people to deliver it to their houses on their bicycles. The solution you choose should be based on what you think your customers will want, and how much you think they will pay for it.

- **Figure out what you need to deliver that solution.** When you decide how you want to solve this problem, you'll next have to think about how to put that solution into practice. In terms of time, money, and skills, what do you need to do so you can actually begin serving your customers? Here are some specific questions you might want to ask yourself, and do research on if you don't know the answer already:

  - If your idea is an invention, have you built a prototype yet? If not, how much time and money will it take to build one? If you already have a prototype, how much would it cost to have a factory mass-produce it for you?

  - Do you need to buy any equipment or supplies before the business opens? If so, how much will this cost?

  - If you are creating something with computer programming, how long will it take you to do the coding? Do you need to learn a new programming language to implement your idea in the best way? What computer equipment do you need?

  - Will you be your company's only employee, or will you need partners or employees with different skills to work with you?

  - Do you need any special licenses, inspections, training, or approval in order to legally operate the business in your community? You can look up the laws and regulations in your area online, and if you're in doubt, you can contact the local government and ask. If the legal questions are extensive, you may need to consult with an attorney.

- **Decide how you will make money.** In order for a company to stay in business, it needs to make money. Even if you intend to donate all your profits to charity, or provide your products to customers without making a profit, you'll still need to bring in enough money to pay your own costs in running the business. For many kinds of companies, this is a pretty simple question to answer: you'll sell products at set prices, or charge set fees for your services. In some cases, though, the question requires outside-the-box thinking. If your business makes it easier for buyers and sellers to find each other, you might charge a commission on all transactions. If your business involves time slots or tickets, you might maximize sales by offering special discounts for people who take the less-desirable ones. Many businesses now operate through ad revenue. If your company produces how-to videos and shares them through YouTube, you would get a share of the money that Google (YouTube's parent company) makes from selling ads on your videos.

- **Make your business plan.** This is a short document stating all the key elements of your idea for the business, along with research you have done on the market. What other companies are already doing something similar? What makes you different? How much money could the business realistically expect to make in its first and subsequent years? Creating a business plan serves three purposes. First, it helps you get clear in your own mind on how the business will work, how you plan to overcome potential obstacles, and how you intend to develop the company over time. Second, it helps people you trust understand your idea so they can give you constructive feedback. And finally, it can convince potential employees and investors that your company will be worth their time and money. Here are <u>some tips from the Young Entrepreneurs Forum</u>[8] on how to write a business plan that will stand out from the competition.

- **Find collaborators.** Your company might just be you working all by yourself; many businesses are. But every company needs a network of people in the community who believe in it and help it succeed. Your job is to find those people and get them excited about your idea. There are several different kinds of collaborators:

  - **Partners.** Starting a company can be a very ambitious project, and it can be a big help to have partners willing to share the load. They start the company with you, and share both in its expenses and its profits. It's often best to pick partners who have different skills from your own. If it's a food-related business, it's better to have one person with a talent for food preparation and another with a talent for sales than to have two great chefs but no one to find customers for them.

- **Employees.** As your business grows, you won't be able to handle all the work yourself. You can hire others to work with you, either on a full-time or part-time basis, depending on your needs. Hiring employees requires good judgment. You want to find people who are trustworthy, work hard, and have a positive attitude. If you already have other employees, you want to be sure new ones will fit in well with the team.

- **Contractors.** There are some tasks you won't be able to do yourself, but it doesn't always make sense to hire an employee for specialized tasks. For example, if your company only has three employees, you shouldn't hire a full-time lawyer because you won't have enough work for them to do yet. Instead, you'll hire an outside lawyer to serve as a contractor whenever you need her. Other kinds of contractors businesses often have to find include: accountants, web designers, IT managers, artists, and equipment repairpersons. Before hiring contractors, read reviews of their businesses, and ask people you trust for recommendations.

- **Vendors.** In some kinds of businesses, you'll need to buy a steady supply of goods—either products to resell, or materials you use to make your own products. If you're opening an online toy store, you want to find which toy companies' products you want to sell. If you're selling baked goods, you'll have to decide on which grocers or food supply companies can give you the best ingredients at the best prices. If it's a factory making parts for you, it's important to confirm that they have high enough quality standards, and can deliver the parts on time.

- **Mentors.** Many small-business owners already have decades of experience working in their industries. They've had many failures and successes, and learned something from all of them. As a young person, you have advantages like creative ideas and a fresh perspective, but it is important to also be humble and recognize that you can always learn from other people. Mentors are experienced entrepreneurs who can share what they have learned with you, so you can avoid the mistakes they made, and follow the accomplishments they've done well. Ask your parents or teachers for advice on people who could serve as mentors, and if you're under 18, always make sure your family understands who is mentoring you and that they approve your contact with them.

- 9 tips for finding a potential mentor,[9] contacting them, and turning them into an actual mentor.

- Ideas from Patrick Ben-David[10] on how young people can find great mentors.

- Mentorship expert Ellen Ensher[11] on connecting with mentors and forming strong relationships with them.

- **Advisors.** Mentors give you general advice about entrepreneurship, leadership, and life. By contrast, advisors provide more specific advice about your business and the market you are entering. They can advise you about unexpected problems that similar companies have encountered and tell you how they solved them. They may also have enough experience in your industry to be able to refer to you vendors, contractors, and employees you can trust. Some advisors provide guidance for free to startups, especially by young entrepreneurs, but as your company grows you should expect to pay a fee for their expertise.

  - Advice from OpenView Venture Partners[12] on finding great advisors for your startup company.

  - 7 tips from First Round Capital[13] on getting the most out of the advisors you bring on to help your business.

- **Investors.** Some businesses need significant funding right at the beginning to get started. In other cases, you'll need a big chunk of money to grow your company and expand into new markets. If either applies to you, you'll need investors willing to write you checks in exchange for partial ownership of your company. Investors who come in before your company is actually doing business are often called seed investors, while those who give you money to expand are called angel investors. Once a startup has already become successful, subsequent investment is known as venture capital. Attracting good investors requires a solid business plan, and an outstanding "elevator pitch"—a polished verbal summary of what your company is about and why it's worth their investment, short enough to fit into a 30-second elevator ride.

- **Influencers.** In almost every market, there are some people who are seen as authorities about which companies people should do business with. For restaurants, these are dining critics and food bloggers. For gadgets, these are tech magazine editors and YouTube reviewers with lots of subscribers. Your job is to find those influencers and convince them why your product or service is better than the competition. If your company can get respected influencers to recommend you to their followers, you'll have a much greater chance of success.

- **Start your company!** Once you've made the proper preparations, open your virtual or literal doors and start doing business. Remember: not everything has to be perfect right away. It's more important to just start than to wait for absolutely perfect conditions. This can be one of the most exciting, frightening, and rewarding experiences of your life—try to enjoy and appreciate the highs, and learn from the lows. A successful entrepreneur and friend of mine, Harry George, compares this to walking on a mountain ridge. You see the grand mountain peaks ahead of you as well as the potential falls all around you. Take the time to listen to some of the world's top experts and biggest entrepreneurs (and a teen entrepreneur!) on how to start your business, and what will make it succeed:

  - 10 steps to start a business, from Rhonda Abrams[14] for *USA Today*.

  - TED Talk by entrepreneur Bill Gross[15] on the key factors that allow some startups to succeed while others fail.

  - Fascinating thoughts from billionaire Elon Musk[16] on how to start a business, drawing from his entrepreneurship experience in online payments, electric vehicles, solar electricity, and rocketry.

  - Candid advice for entrepreneurs from Richard Branson,[17] founder of the Virgin business empire, covering industries like music, airlines, telecommunications, and private spaceflight.

- TEDx Talk by entrepreneur Jan Bednar[18] on what college students in particular need to know before starting a business.

- Tips from teen entrepreneur Alyssa Ruby[19] on starting your own online business.

- An outstanding book on how to approach the starting of a business in the broadest and most optimistic way is *Bold, How to Go Big, Create Wealth and Impact the World*[20] by Peter Diamandis (my cofounder of *Singularity University*) and Steven Kotler.

There are a few additional issues to think about as you plan for starting your company:

- **Setting up an online presence.** For almost all businesses, you'll want to have a website. First, you should decide on the right domain name, then register it at a site such as GoDaddy.com.[21] This is usually quite inexpensive. Then, you can use a platform like Squarespace[22] or Wix[23] to create a website on your own—with no need for special programming skills. Or, if you'd prefer, you can pay a web designer to create a custom website for you. Many businesses find it's helpful to have a presence on social media platforms like Facebook, Twitter, and Instagram, but it really depends on what the business is. If your company revolves around something like local business networking, it makes sense to be active on many social media sites. But if you just have your own dog-walking business for people in your neighborhood, you might only need a Twitter feed.

- **Protecting your intellectual property.** Depending on your business, you may be creating intellectual property, and it is very important to make sure that it is protected. Often, this means creating your company as a corporation, which gives it special status under the law. Corporations can own property, file lawsuits, and do other things that normally only people can. The process for establishing a corporation varies a bit from place to place, but here's a good starting point for forms[24] from each of the 50 United States. If you are inventing something new, you should consider filing for patent protection,[25] which will give you exclusive rights to your creation for a set number of years (about twenty years from when you file your patent). You can also apply for trademarks[26] to protect your logo, product names, and creative designs. You can protect creative works such as books, documents, and designs with copyrights. You should get advice from a lawyer on these applications. Some lawyers may provide legal advice for free or at discounts for young entrepreneurs, so contact a few business law offices to see if they can help you.

● **Bootstrapping versus investment.** In the business world, "bootstrapping" refers to starting a business with little or no money, and then investing the profits back into the company so it can gradually expand. Especially for the small businesses that young people start, this is often the best approach. You can grow at your own pace, and don't have to worry about keeping a group of investors happy who are looking to make money from your company. Many entrepreneurs like the feeling of freedom that comes from bootstrapping. On the other hand, getting investors can help you grow faster and be more competitive in crowded markets. For ideas with very high startup costs, investment is necessary. Also, investors in a company have an incentive to help it succeed, and can often provide very helpful advice and connections to young entrepreneurs. Consider carefully which approach fits your idea and personality best.

● **Entrepreneurship competitions.** There are lots of organizations out there working hard to encourage young people to start their own companies. Competitions give you a chance to practice pitching your idea to investors and answering their questions. This experience is very valuable. You can also win money to fund your startup, along with other support, like mentorship, consulting services, and help prototyping your products. The money you might win in the competition is the least of the benefits. The distinction of winning can propel your business to attract the resources it needs to take off. A friend of mine won MIT's $50K competition (now $100K). He won $50,000, which attracted venture investors, and a few years later, he sold his business for $300 million. Take a look at these entrepreneurship competitions to see if you find a good fit:

   - Hatchpad[27] gives info on several top entrepreneurship competitions aimed at high schoolers.

   - U.Pitch[28] is aimed at students currently in college. It focuses on a 90-second pitch to judges.

- MIT $100K[29] is open to the public for the initial stage of the competition. To progress, you'll find a collaborator who is a current MIT student.

- New Venture Competition[30] requires collaboration with one Harvard Business School student, but offers great resources for prizewinners.

- **Incubators.** Incubators are programs designed to help entrepreneurs turn great ideas into great companies. An incubator can give you seed money, mentorship, office space, and many other kinds of support. The incubator can also pair you up with other entrepreneurs with skill sets that complement your own. When your company is ready to grow, they can find you great employees. Here are some incubators for you to consider:

  - Info on 10 top incubators,[31] and what features make them stand out. For example, some incubators focus on Internet technology, while others are better for biotechnology or robotics.

  - Technovation Challenge[32] is a Google-sponsored tech entrepreneurship program for girls ages 10-18.

  - Catapult[33] is a summer incubator program for high schoolers that provides a focused and intensive experience to learn the entire startup process.

Never let yourself think that young people can't be successful at entrepreneurship. Here are some inspiring examples of kids and teens who've built great businesses:

- 10 young entrepreneurs[34] who've already achieved notable success.

- 20 self-made teenage millionaires,[35] and how they made their money.

- 8-year-old Evan[36] generated $1.3 million in annual ad revenue (in 2014) from his YouTube channel[37] reviewing toys.

- 10-year-old Mikaila[38] started the Bee Sweet (now called Me & the Bees)[39] lemonade company with her great-grandmother's lemonade recipe. It started with a neighborhood lemonade stand when she was four, but she expanded the business into a company that sells to Whole Foods and other large grocery stores.

- 11-year-old Asia[40] (AKA "Super Business Girl") created a business selling homemade candles to buy clothes and food for needy children in 2014.

- 15-year-old Thomas[41] created a 3-D printing company called Carrot Corp[42] in 2014.

- 16-year old Ben Pasternak[43] developed Flogg, an app for buying and selling things within your social network in 2016.

- 17-year-old Nick D'Aloisio[44] created the news-summarizing app Summly and sold it to Yahoo! for $30 million in 2013.

For more information, please see the following entries in the companion book *A Chronicle of Ideas: A Guide for Superheroines (and Superheroes)*: Securities and Exchange Commission, Chief Operating Officer, Incentive Stock Options, Black Scholes Valuation, Long-Term Capital Gains, Series A Investment, Simple Preferred Stock, Ratchet Downside Protection, Nonstatutory Stock Options, Bond Offer, Silicon Valleys, Capital Gains Taxes.

Footnote links at
DanielleWorld.com/resources

HOW YOU CAN BE A DANIELLE

and Advance Artificial Intelligence

Artificial Intelligence, or AI, is the single most important technological trend in history. As I explained in my book The Singularity Is Near[1] (Viking, 2005), thousands of years of gradually accelerating progress is leading toward a point in time when a computer can provide greater overall intelligence than a human (who is not herself enhanced by AI). I have consistently put that threshold at 2029.

In the 2030s we will merge our neocortex (the outer layer of the brain where we do our thinking) with AI in the Cloud (computation available through wireless communication) thus increasing our intelligence. According to my calculations, we will then multiply our intelligence a billion-fold by 2045, a prospect so transformative that we have borrowed a metaphor from physics and call it the Singularity. The metaphor is to compare this future historical event to the event horizon of a physics singularity (that is, a black hole) where it is difficult to see beyond the event horizon. The Singularity will profoundly transform every aspect of civilization—and we are among the lucky five percent of humans who ever lived who will have this happen within our lifetimes. It will, in turn, vastly increase our life spans.

Even before the Singularity, AI will have greater and greater impact on the way we live. Artificial intelligence follows my Law of Accelerating Returns, which observes that the price-performance, capacity, and impact of information-based technologies improve by a roughly constant percentage every year, thus expanding exponentially. This means that actual progress is slow at first, but builds up "momentum" over time, and finally progresses at explosive speed. We are just now reaching the point where progress in AI is becoming noticeably faster, often surprising AI scientists.

For an overview of how AI works and its history, please read the entry on Artificial Intelligence in the companion book, *A Chronicle of Ideas: A Guide for Superheroines (and Superheroes)*.

In the novel, Danielle uses artificial intelligence in her computer programming, in her effort to combat tyranny in Libya, to analyze crowd images and provide security during her flash mob celebrations, and to capture Osama bin Laden. You can follow her example by using AI in your daily life now and helping bring about the Singularity in the future.

To start on this path, you should make an effort to learn more about artificial intelligence, how people use it, and where it's going. Here are some explanations you'll find useful:

- A quick two-minute intro to artificial intelligence[2] by Murray Shanahan, a roboticist and futurist who studies the Singularity.

- A more detailed explainer video about artificial intelligence by Frank Chen,[3] who studies AI at one of the top investment firms in Silicon Valley.

- 10 interesting applications of AI[4] in products that are already available.

- TED Talk by Google star computer scientist Jeff Dean[5] on how AI will affect your life in the coming years.

- My own fuller discussion of the Singularity[6] and what it means, recorded for the Big Think series.

- Animated video by the Future of Life Institute[7] with commentary by AI researcher Max Tegmark on myths versus facts about superhuman AI, or superintelligence.

- A key question about superintelligent AI is whether it might try to destroy humanity. Here are two thoughtful perspectives on this question, from ethicist Sam Harris,[8] and risk expert and philosopher Nick Bostrom.[9]

- My TED Talk on why we shouldn't look at superhuman AI as a danger that will be separate from humans, but rather an extension of the abilities of our own species, due to the coming merger[10] between artificial intelligence with human intelligence.

- Two outstanding blog posts by Tim Urban at *Wait But Why* (*Part I*[11] and *Part II*[12]), explaining in conceptual terms what steps will be necessary for AI to reach superhuman levels. Tim uses amusing stick-figure graphics and does an excellent job explaining complex ideas in ways that are easy for anyone to understand. He also discusses the disagreement I have with some other futurists about how best to think about risks from AI. Here's Tim's Talk at Google[13] expanding on the ideas in the blog posts.

- Billionaire entrepreneur and innovator Elon Musk has begun early development work on a project to develop one approach to the brain-computer interface that I predicted in *The Age of Spiritual Machines* (Viking, 1999). Called Neuralink,[14] it involves putting a many-lead connector in your brain that can link it with the Internet. Musk's design will be appropriate in the near term to provide a brain-to-machine interface for people with serious neurologically based disabilities, such as quadriplegia. My own vision is for this interface to be provided by nano-scale machines (that is by medical nanorobots) to provide direct access to almost unlimited knowledge in the Cloud, and enable direct brain-to-brain communication with other people. *Wait But Why* has a long but highly worthwhile blog post about Neuralink[15] and its implications.

One of the most important areas of artificial intelligence is machine learning: the ability of an AI system to learn and to adapt and improve performance based on its own experience. Machine learning is based on rough models of how the brain works and learns by being exposed to many examples of a situation (for example, many images of different categories such as cats and dogs, or many examples of movies in a game). Take a closer look at machine learning here:

- A basic intro to what machine learning is,[16] why it is different from other kinds of computer programs, and how it is used.

- This clear explainer video by Android Authority[17] digs deeper into what machine learning is and how it works.

- Udacity's half-hour intro to machine learning,[18] including some useful examples that help you see how these concepts are applied in the real world.

- A short video about machine learning[19] from the perspective of Google, featuring interviews with the company's AI engineers.

- HubSpot's animated video explaining machine learning[20] and the idea that AI and humans shouldn't be seen as in competition against each other, but rather as working together to solve problems.

- The *Jeopardy!* match between an IBM artificial intelligence system named Watson and the two top human players in the show's history, Ken Jennings and Brad Rutter.[21] Notice that although Watson's first choice guesses are usually correct, her second and third choices, displayed at the bottom of the screen, are often not even using the right category of the key word. This shows that although the machine learning used to train Watson gets to similar final answers as human intelligence, Watson's "thought process" is often different from that of a human player.

Machine learning is probably the best way to get started on learning how to apply artificial intelligence yourself. The first step is getting some experience with the basics of computer programming in general. For more information on this, see the entry for "How You Can Be a Danielle and Learn to Program Computers from a Young Age." There are also some very helpful resources available that can specifically help you build your skills in machine learning:

- An excellent overview from HackerEarth[22] on how you can start from scratch and get good at coding machine learning. It includes information on how to learn programming languages that are good for machine learning, especially Python. It also gives you pointers on the specific coding techniques you should master, and walks you through learning how to build your first AI bot. Once you've created your first simple artificial intelligence, you'll better understand the possibilities of more complex AI.

- If you already have experience at computer programming, this detailed guide from Machine Learning Mastery[23] can be very useful on how to dive deep into machine learning techniques and develop advanced skills.

- Another advanced tutorial on machine learning,[24] which is good for students who have already taken some college-level math.

As your skills improve, you'll start getting more ideas for ways to use machine learning to solve problems you see in the real world. Fortunately, you don't have to build those programs from scratch. Google has created a free, open-source library of machine learning AI called TensorFlow.[25] TensorFlow has a wide range of pre-built tools you can use, modify, and expand to meet the needs of your project.

Here's more on neural networks, the primary tool used in deep learning:

- An explainer video about Google Deep Mind,[26] the project that built AlphaGo, an AI system that mastered an ancient board game called Go and defeated the world's best human players. This was an important breakthrough because the usual method of AI game playing (logical analysis of move-countermove sequences) doesn't work for Go because there are too many possible moves at each point in the game. The Deep Mind team used neural networks to learn subtle pattern-recognition insights. It originally trained the neural nets using transcribed online games and then greatly augmented this data with simulated games of the program playing itself.

- A closer look at neural networks[27] in general, how they work, and why they have so many advantages over other approaches to AI.

- A video on how to build a simple neural network in four minutes.[28] A good intro for those who already have basic programming knowledge.

To apply neural networks to problem solving, there's a whole set of related skills that it's helpful to learn. If you intend to study AI in school, or pursue a career in this area, you can get a great start by taking some online courses:

- A free college-level course on artificial intelligence from MIT.[29] Covers topics like reasoning, neural nets, and visual object recognition. And here's a lecture from another MIT course, Intro to Machine Learning.[30]

- A highly popular introductory machine learning course from Stanford,[31] available for free through Coursera (though for a fee you can get a certificate verifying your mastery of the concepts). Covers a broad range of topics, and includes graded assignments to test your skills.

- Deep learning refers to AI that uses "hidden" layers in its neural networks between the input and output layers. The use of many hidden layers is the key to deep learning being able to make subtle and abstract judgments. If you already have solid coding experience, take a look at this series of five Coursera courses,[32] created by Deeplearning.ai in partnership with Nvidia and the Deep Learning Institute. Includes projects and case studies about real-world applications.

- A Udacity course on Artificial Intelligence for Robotics,[33] by Georgia Tech. This free advanced course takes about two months to complete and covers AI programming techniques relevant to robots that interact with the real world.

Another great way to develop your skills in artificial intelligence is through competitions and "hackathons." These are events that bring people together for a short period of intensive collaboration to solve a particular problem or group of problems. Here are options you can look into:

- The FIRST Robotics competition[34] is an international high school robotics competition started by legendary inventor Dean Kamen. Teams of students, coaches, and mentors build and program game-playing robots weighing up to 120 pounds. In 2017 there were over 6,000 teams. Kamen created FIRST to encourage young students to become excited about high tech careers. Participation is about equal between boys and girls. Regional competitions lead to a national competition. These competitions have all of the excitement of national sports competitions.

● Battlecode[35] is MIT's annual programming competition, which is open for anyone to enter. People compete to design AI systems that can outperform their rivals at a game called Battlecode. Prizes are over $50,000 dollars. More significant than the money is the credential of winning competitions such as this.

● The AI Games[36] are a set of online competitions to build the best possible artificial intelligences to play games like Connect Four and Texas Hold 'Em.

● Vindinium[37] is an ongoing AI programming challenge, where players can use the programming language of their choice to win an online fantasy game.

● RobotChallenge[38] is an annual robotics competition that promotes innovative artificial intelligence systems. If you're interested, get a team together with like-minded friends and compete!

● There are also one-off events, like the Global AI Hackathon,[39] which brought together programmers, designers, neuroscientists, data scientists, and idea generators of all skill levels, and had them work together for three days in 15 major cities around the world. There are often events like this—see what's coming up in a place near you, and sign up! For example, New York City had the NYC Artificial Intelligence Hackathon,[40] with the satirical theme of creating technologies that "advance the robot apocalypse." By thinking about those problems carefully and collaboratively, you can help make sure a real robot apocalypse never happens.

● The General AI Challenge[41] is co-Sponsored by Microsoft, and includes a range of challenges for anyone who can achieve milestones on the way to human-level artificial intelligence. This is a very high-level challenge, which will give out $5 million in prizes over time.

In the coming years, especially if you focus your career on artificial intelligence, you'll have to start thinking more seriously about the ethical implications of AI. If you start learning about those questions now, you'll be able to become a leader in society's debates about how to use AI safely. Look over these links as a starting point for going deeper on these issues:

- My thoughts at SingularityHub[42] on how to keep artificial intelligence "friendly," through human integration with AI. As our abilities become more heavily augmented by AI, humans will have to place new emphasis on how to limit conflict between people. Democracy, liberty, and compassion will discourage humans from using superintelligent AI in destructive ways.

- When you code artificial intelligence, your biases and worldview can shape the way the AI works. The data you give an AI to train its machine learning algorithms will affect the lessons the AI learns. So it is important to keep this risk in mind and take active steps to prevent negative human biases like prejudice from being reflected in the AI we create. This short video by Google explains.[43]

- An animated explainer by WhyFuture[44] about the road to superintelligence and the ethical questions we'll face in trying to steer AI toward positive outcomes for humanity.

- This engaging and informative video about AI personhood by Hank Green from the *Crash Course*[45] series on philosophy. Personhood is the question of whether a human-level AI could have true consciousness like humans do, and whether it might be entitled to rights like humans have. For example, if an AI tells us that it is conscious and deserves freedom, should we believe it? This is a theme of my movie The Singularity is Near,[46] which is a companion film to my book of the same name.

- OpenAI,[47] a project co-founded by Elon Musk, which facilitates international collaboration toward the goal of achieving friendly superintelligence that integrates well with humanity. OpenAI takes inspiration from the (mostly successful) international efforts to regulate nuclear energy and prevent such potentially destructive power from falling into the hands of terrorists.

- MIRI,[48] the Machine Intelligence Research Institute focuses on figuring out how to design AI in ways that can make it naturally safer. For example, they study how advanced AI can be made more transparent so programmers can better understand why it makes the decisions it does. That way, problems can be identified and fixed before they get out of control. You might consider donating to MIRI, or starting a fundraiser with friends who also care about the future of AI.

As you become more proficient at building and applying artificial intelligence, think of how it might be able to solve some of the difficult problems in your community and the world. Consider the areas where AI has natural advantages: making fast computations, processing huge amounts of data, following complex logical rules, and recognizing patterns. How could those abilities boost and complement areas where humans still have advantages, like social skills, abstract reasoning, interpreting complex situations, and hand-eye coordination? The innovations you create this way can bring great benefit to society and bring us closer to a beneficial and safe world of integrated AI and human intelligence.

For more information, please see the following entries in the companion book *A Chronicle of Ideas: A Guide for Superheroines (and Superheroes)*: Artificial Intelligence, Society of Mind.

Footnote links at

DanielleWorld.com/resources

and Help Cure Heart Disease

Heart disease (or cardiovascular disease) is the number one cause of death in developed countries. It includes a number of problems that can develop with the heart and the circulatory system. Heart disease is generally caused by a combination of genetic dispositions in combination with unhealthy lifestyle factors especially food choices. Unlike many other diseases, the risk of heart disease can be dramatically reduced by people making healthier choices in terms of nutrition, exercise, weight control, and stress management.

The primary process underlying most forms of heart disease is atherosclerosis. Atherosclerosis is a condition in which the arteries' inner walls thicken and harden due to deposits of substances called plaques. This is a primary feature of coronary artery disease and can lead to heart attacks, strokes, claudication of the limbs, impotence in men, and other negative effects.

If plaque builds up in the coronary arteries, the blood vessels that feed the heart, the muscle of the heart can be gradually weakened and damaged. When this happens, the heart may start to beat irregularly, and become unable to properly pump blood to the rest of the body's organs. In some cases, a plaque can break open, spilling material that lodges deeper in the artery, triggering blood clotting that can block the artery entirely. If this happens to an artery feeding the heart, the tissue beyond the blockage will be suddenly starved of oxygen and begin to die. This is known as a myocardial infarction, or heart attack. This can be fatal, but even if a person survives, the heart tissue killed in a myocardial infarction does not grow back, leaving the heart permanently injured and more vulnerable to another heart attack in the future. Recently developed experimental therapies using stem cells injected directly into the heart have shown an ability to reverse this damage.

Another risk is blockage of blood vessels supplying oxygen to the brain. When this happens, brain cells quickly start dying. This is the most common form of stroke.

The main form of atherosclerosis involves the buildup of a soft type of plaque known as vulnerable plaque. This may be triggered by excessive levels of low-density lipoprotein cholesterol (LDL-C, or "bad" cholesterol) in the blood. As LDL accumulates, it oxidizes and attracts white blood cells. White blood cells that have consumed fatty LDL until "stuffed" are known as "foam cells." The presence of foam cells can trigger the immune system to begin a cycle of inflammation that causes more vulnerable plaque to accumulate. The immune system will create a fibrous "cap" over the vulnerable plaque to wall it off from the bloodstream and contain the problem. The cap is primarily made of collagen and calcium. This capped plaque is called an atheroma.

Yet formation of a fibrous cap over a plaque does not end the danger. As the plaque grows on the artery's inner wall, it makes it harder for blood to flow through. Over time, the arteries stretch and expand to accommodate this blood flow, and in the process harden. This makes them less flexible to expand and contract with each heartbeat. If someone has high blood pressure, such as when doing strenuous work, the extra tension can cause a fibrous cap to rupture. The contents of the plaque then travel through the artery and cause a blockage, or spur formation of a blood clot, called a thrombus, that comes loose and causes a blockage itself. Depending on where the blockage occurs and how severe it is, this can result in fatal heart attacks and strokes.

See these links for more on atherosclerosis:

- Basic overview of heart disease from the Mayo Clinic.[1]

- Quick two-minute visual intro to atherosclerosis.[2]

- More in-depth explainer video about atherosclerosis and related conditions,[3] including key terms and complications caused in other parts of the body.

- Detailed animated view of how atherosclerosis works.[4]

High blood pressure (or hypertension) is another common condition. This can be aggravated by smoking cigarettes and excess weight. Hypertension can cause or worsen a related problem, arrhythmia. This is where the heart beats abnormally, which can cause clots to form and trigger a heart attack or stroke. Congestive heart failure is where the heart becomes too stiff or too weak to pump as much blood as the body needs. This can be worsened by high-stress lifestyles, or by being overweight or obese. For more on the causes of heart disease, see these informative videos:

- Dr. Caldwell Esselstyn[5] on the idea that heart disease is a food-borne illness, explaining the role diet plays in cardiovascular health.

- Short CNN clip[6] on the links between stress and heart disease. Includes practical tips for reducing stress.

- Dr. Rhonda Patrick[7] speaking on the Joe Rogan show about the causes of heart disease, described in clear and understandable language.

All these conditions can be improved or eliminated by maintaining an active lifestyle. People who exercise regularly have lower blood pressure and are less likely to develop atherosclerosis; the heart muscle stays healthy, and it is easier to stay the right weight for a person's body type. When exercise is combined with a healthy diet, no smoking, and no more than moderate alcohol consumption, a person's risk of cardiovascular disease is likely to be greatly reduced.

If you take a leadership role in encouraging people to follow healthier lifestyles, you can have a great impact in lowering the likelihood of heart disease. As a young person, three ways to do this are bringing groups together (for example, starting a club), creating tools (programming an app), and motivating action (telling stories that inspire people to change their habits). Here are some ideas for how you might do this to influence dietary factors:

- **Start a club.** Becoming a champion for healthy eating habits in your community is a perfect place to begin. Start a healthy eating club[8] at your school. Together, you can watch videos about the science of food and wellness, ask for more nutritious options in the cafeteria, or learn to cook heart-healthy snacks on your own.

- **Build an app.** If you know computer programming, you could design an app that helps people establish good eating habits. Think of how you could make it easier for people to find healthy foods at reasonable prices, set good diet goals, and hold each other accountable for eating things that will keep your hearts healthy. If you haven't learned to code yet, check out the entry for "How You Can Be a Danielle and Learn to Program Computers from a Young Age."

- **Tell a story.** If your talents lie in the arts, you could create series of videos or a documentary to show people in a creative way why it's important to have a good diet. Or you could work with other students, sharing your experiences with them and mentoring them on healthy food. If your parents and family members don't have health-promoting habits, encourage them to make a commitment to wiser eating, such as explained by Dr. Maya Adam[9] in this video.

The same principles apply to exercise, and getting people to spend more time outdoors and moving their bodies:

- **Start a club.** Becoming more active is easier when you're doing it with friends. Action for Healthy Kids[10] is an alliance of organizations that encourage young people to stay active and fit. They provide resources that can guide you on starting a fitness club at your school.

- **Build an app.** There's lots of room to be creative in designing fitness apps, and many different kinds of exercise. Think of how you could make physical activity more enjoyable, and how you can help people set goals and feel gratified when they accomplish them. One of the best motivators to exercise is when it doesn't feel like a chore. For example, in 2016 the augmented reality game Pokémon Go got hundreds of millions of people to go out walking and jogging—not just to meet fitness goals, but for the fun of finding and catching digital monsters in public places. Take a look at ARCore[11] by Google, which recently released a new set of tools to help people develop augmented reality apps of their own.

- **Tell a story.** The American Heart Association[12] has lots of resources to help you inspire people in your community about healthy living—from diet and exercise to ways to quit smoking and reduce stress. This includes the stories of real people who have transformed their lives for the better. The Healthy for Good movement[13] helps people get motivated to make healthy choices and keep making them.

In addition to healthy lifestyle campaigns, there is also cutting-edge medical research being conducted to better understand how heart disease works and how to cure it. The best of this research is highly innovative, and gets ideas from unexpected fields. Here are just a few examples:

- This TED Talk by biomedical scientist Nina Tandon[14] on how tissue engineering can help people get the right treatments for their own organs, such as the heart.

- A fascinating story by engineer Tal Golesworthy[15] on how he repaired his own heart, using creative thinking from outside medicine.

- Consider supporting the British Heart Foundation,[16] which funds key research into the molecular-level factors driving heart disease, which may ultimately make cures possible.

- Another organization worth your support is the Children's Heart Foundation,[17] which drives research on congenital heart problems that affect children.

If you want to obtain a deeper understanding of heart disease, or pursue a career researching ways to cure it, you should take the most challenging biology, chemistry, and math courses you can. If you're ready, you can also start college-level study with online courses related to heart disease and heart health, such as these introductory options:

- Easing the Burden of Obesity, Diabetes, and Cardiovascular Disease,[18] a 5-week course by the University of Sydney. It is a college-level course, but does not require any prior background in medical science.

- Science of Exercise,[19] a 4-week course from the University of Colorado Boulder, covers how exercise works in the body, and the benefits that result. It is aimed at beginners.

- Understanding Obesity,[20] from the University of Edinburgh, is a 4-week course on the effects of obesity on health, including heart disease, and how obesity can be prevented. No prior experience necessary.

- Introduction to Food and Health,[21] from Stanford University, is a 5-week course for beginners on how better diet can improve health and reduce problems like cardiovascular disease. Includes a focus on the relationship between lifestyle and diet, and covers practical ways to form and maintain healthier habits.

If you're motivated, you can start working on curing heart disease right now, even at a young age. Here are a few suggestions on how (which also apply to cancer research, as explained in the entry for "How You Can Be a Danielle and Help Cure Cancer"):

- Read academic journals about medicine, and look for a novel way to connect the problems you read about to ideas from other subjects, like chemistry, biology, or engineering.

- Build your skills at doing lab experiments. MIT OpenCourseWare offers helpful online courses on experimental biology[22] and laboratory chemistry.[23]

- Look for professors or labs in your area who can mentor you. Ask them questions based on your reading, and suggest ideas for experiments they could help you do.

- Think about whether you have skills not usually applied to treating heart disease, which might be an opportunity for innovation. For example, if you've learned computer programming in areas like artificial intelligence and machine learning, consider how those techniques might make it easier to detect or treat cardiovascular problems.

For more information, please see the following entries in the companion book *A Chronicle of Ideas: A Guide for Superheroines (and Superheroes)*: Arterial Calcification, Fetal Bone, Fetal Organ, Atherosclerosis.

Footnote links at

DanielleWorld.com/resources

HOW YOU CAN BE A DANIELLE

and Promote Peace and Understanding in the World

Contrary to what you might think from watching the news, we are actually living in the most peaceful era in human history. It doesn't seem like it, because media technology allows us to get more information, and more *vivid* information, about the violence that does happen. But in terms of the likelihood that the average person will die from violence, there has never been a safer time to be alive.

Still, there are many very real and deeply tragic conflicts going on around the world. Unlike in previous centuries, relatively few of these conflicts are fighting over resources. Rather, today's conflicts revolve around political power and identity—as expressed through religion, ethnicity, culture, and national identification. In order to achieve peace, whether through stopping these conflicts or preventing new ones from starting, people first need to understand each other better. Violence based on identity is only possible when people don't see each other as human beings deserving equal rights and dignity. Danielle understands this in the novel, and acts as a peacemaker in places like the Middle East, Tibet, China, and Libya. She also convinces Osama bin Laden to renounce terrorism and dissolve al-Qaeda. Here are some concrete things you can do to promote peace and understanding around the world:

- **Religious tolerance.** One of the world's worst causes of violence is a lack of religious understanding. When one group of people believes that another group isn't merely wrong, but enemies of God, it is much easier to justify opposing and harming them. Changing this requires religious tolerance—where even if different faiths disagree on philosophy, they can live together in mutual acceptance and harmony. Achieving this requires different religious groups to get to know each other directly, form personal friendships, and engage in dialogue. I grew up with a Unitarian religious education which stressed tolerance as expressed in the aphorism, "there are many paths to the truth."

  - You have the ability to promote these interfaith encounters in your local community. Take a look at the work of organizations like the InterFaith Conference of Metropolitan Washington[1] which sponsors events like a Unity Walk and InterFaith Concert to bring people of different faiths closer together. Similarly, the Interfaith Dialogue Association[2] in Michigan organizes speakers, conferences, and discussions that help members of all religions better understand what unites them. Think of what your own community is like. Which religious groups are the largest? How well do they get along with each other? Try reaching out to religious leaders like your local priest, minister, rabbi, or imam, and offering to help them start an interfaith dialogue program.

  - Although it is more difficult to promote interfaith dialogue thousands of miles away, there is extra need for it in places with ongoing religious violence. People living in America and Europe can play an important role by supporting the people in those communities who are trying to bring healing and understanding. The Center for Religious Tolerance[3] is an example of a small charity started by Americans who raise money for a range of interfaith peace-building projects in Israel and Palestine. CRT's founders were inspired by a trip they took to the Holy Land and meetings they had with community leaders there. If you have the chance to visit a part of the world where there are major religious tensions, consider raising money back home to help leaders committed to peace and understanding.

- In some cases, true harmony isn't possible in the short term. When one religious group is actively persecuting another, the first step is to stop the persecution. Consider supporting the International Association for Religious Freedom,[4] which advocates to the United Nations on behalf of persecuted religious minorities, in addition to its interfaith dialogue projects on five continents.

- If you know computer programming, you could create a platform online to facilitate interfaith dialogue. This could be an app that matches people of different faiths to chat with each other, a "day in the life" program to help people understand what life is really like for members of another group, or something totally different that you think of on your own. If you haven't learned coding yet, take a look at the entry for "How You Can Be a Danielle and Learn to Program Computers from a Young Age."

- Conflicts between religious groups usually aren't started by average members of those religions. Instead, extremists spread twisted and hateful interpretations of their faith, and distort the reality of religions that they oppose in order to recruit new followers. There is a great need for innovative "counter-radicalization" tools. Imagine you're a young Sunni being told by a radical cleric that Shiites or Jews are your enemies. Try brainstorming ideas for what you'd need to know to understand that this is wrong. Then, think of ways of getting that information to that vulnerable young person before they become radicalized by hateful messages.

- One of the best ways to reach understanding with people different from ourselves is to work together, especially in service of others. Talk to faith leaders in your community and see if you can start an interfaith service initiative, like a food pantry for poor people, or a volunteer project to clean up after a natural disaster.

● **Racism.** Another obstacle to peace and understanding is racism and ethnic prejudice. Almost everyone feels natural empathy for people in their own community who look like them. But in many societies, people feel like those from different backgrounds with different facial characteristics and skin and hair colors are the "other." This makes it possible for people to justify racist actions they would never take against someone they identify with. By taking a stand against racism, even in its early stages, you can prevent actual violence in the future. For more ideas on how to do this, see the entry for "How You Can Be a Danielle and Promote Racial and Gender Equality."

- Consider supporting the Let's Fight Racism[5] campaign, which is a United Nations project to get people of all races and ethnicities working together to stand up to racists and create positive social change. The campaign offers resources for how you can work with your school to bring lessons about fighting racism into the classroom.

- Another important campaign is Stand Against Racism,[6] sponsored by the YWCA of America. This project has involved more than 250,000 participants in activism and charitable giving. The campaign provides events and training to help people be more effective at stopping racism in their communities. You can participate no matter what your background is!

- Author and educator Jane Elliott offers a remarkable practical experience with racism that has open thousands of people's eyes around the world. She hosts a workshop called the Blue Eyes Brown Eyes Experiment,[7] which shows how easy it is for ordinary people to start mistreating each other based on differences in appearance. Watch a quick video of how her experiment went when she did it on Oprah Winfrey's talk show[8] in 1992. See if you can get your school or another local organization to invite Elliott to conduct the workshop in your community.

- To better understand racism and its impact, take a look at some or all of these nine TED Talks[9] that discuss racism in America.

- Make an effort to read articles by people who have experienced racism, and try to understand how that has shaped their worldview and their daily experiences. If you have experienced racism yourself, you can do a lot of good by going outside your comfort zone to share your stories with others who haven't had those experiences.

- **Education.** Another big obstacle to world peace is lack of education. Although literacy rates have improved enormously in recent decades, in some countries they are still low. When people can't read and evaluate the news for themselves, they are easier for hateful people to manipulate them into violence. Giving people access to education promotes peace and understanding by opening them to the whole universe of human ideas. It is only through education that ideals can outweigh prejudice and hatred. Thus, promoting education in your community and around the world is a crucial way to create peace and understanding. For more information on how to do this, see the entries for "How You Can Be a Danielle and Help the People in Developing Nations"; "How You Can Be a Danielle and Foster Learn by Doing"; "How You Can Be a Danielle and Help Promote Equal Rights for Women"; "How You Can Be a Danielle and Promote Racial and Gender Equality"; and "How You Can Be a Danielle and Encourage Women in the Workplace and Girls to Pursue STEM Careers."

— Save the Children[10] provides education to many of the poorest and most vulnerable children in the world. In 2016, its programs benefitted more than 13 million children around the world. These programs include art classes, training for teachers on how to educate more effectively, and coaching for parents on how to prepare young children for school.

— Libraries Without Borders[11] provides books and learning technology to refugees and people affected by war and conflict. They also create training tools designed to promote social entrepreneurship and innovation by those who wouldn't otherwise be able to start their own companies and nonprofits.

— Donors Choose[12] is a US-based nonprofit that matches donors with under-funded classrooms around the country. This allows them to get supplies and learning equipment that the kids couldn't have without charitable support. Donors Choose is ranked as one of the top education charities in the world, both in terms of its efficiency with the money it raises, and the positive impact it has.

— Because girls don't always have access to as much education as boys in many parts of the world, there is need for extra attention to helping them go to school. Consider supporting an organization like Educate Girls,[13] which works with local partners to improve girls' education in India, the world's most populous democracy. My own family has been involved in this idea as my great-grandmother and her daughter, my grandmother, founded and ran the first school in Europe that provided higher education for girls.

- The FIRST Robotics Competition[14] brings together students from around the world to work on creative problems in science and technology, through exciting competitions in robotics.

- Here are 10 more innovative non-governmental organizations[15] working in education around the world. Study them and see if you feel a connection to one of their missions as something you might become passionate about supporting.

- You could create an app to give young people in poor countries easier access to free education resources, or guidance on which ones might be right for them. Or you could create something aimed at adults who didn't get as much education as they wanted when they were children, to help them catch up more easily.

● **Freedom.** Authoritarian, and especially totalitarian, regimes try to control the way their citizens think. When people feel close ties of friendship and understanding to people of other religions, races, and nationalities, they naturally want peace with them. This means that if the totalitarian leaders want to use violence against those groups, their own people will resist. So the government controls the flow of information and tries to create barriers between groups, to make their citizens more obedient. For this reason, innovations that help people live in more open and free societies ultimately results in less conflict and violence. Here are some ideas on how you can encourage freedom around the world, but for more information, see the entries for "How You Can Be a Danielle and Combat Totalitarianism in the World"; "How You Can Be a Danielle and Help Promote Peace in the Middle East"; "How You Can Be a Danielle and Prevent Future Genocides"; and "How You Can Be a Danielle and Advance Critical Thinking."

- The Middle East is where much of the world's worst violence is currently happening, and where peace and understanding is most badly needed. The Project on Middle East Democracy,[16] or POMED, works with local organizations to equip them to stand up for democracy and human rights. They provide training and consulting, and engage in advocacy back in America and Europe in favor of democracy in the Middle East.

- The National Democratic Institute[17] focuses on building up the institutions and unwritten rules of civil society that allow democracy to function. The NDI trains pro-democracy activists, and helps them work together to increase freedom in their home countries.

- Many authoritarian and totalitarian governments engage in surveillance, where they monitor the activities of citizens, and use this information to punish people who oppose the regime. This has prompted a movement in response called "sousveillance" (since the word "surveillance" roughly "means watch from above" in French, "sousveillance" means "watch from below"). Sousveillance is technologies that help citizens monitor the government and hold it accountable. Watch this fascinating explanation by Anders Sandberg about sousveillance,[18] and think of ways you could create an innovative sousveillance system yourself. What could you do with ordinary equipment like a smartphone or camera to help citizens document abuses by their governments?

For more information, please see the following entry in the companion book *A Chronicle of Ideas: A Guide for Superheroines (and Superheroes)*: The Dalai Lama, Authoritarian, Totalitarian.

Footnote links at

DanielleWorld.com/resources

and Foster Learn by Doing

❀ ❀ ❀ ❀ ❀

There are many different modes of learning. People learn by reading, by listening, by talking and interacting with others, and by watching displays of phenomena such as scientific experiments. But one of the most effective ways to learn is by actually doing something you have a passion for. The goal of this "doing" may be directly related to what you are learning, or you may learn lessons that are only indirectly related.

If I think about what I have managed to learn in my life and career it is from my projects and not formal lessons. The educational paradigm of filling young (and not so young) minds with facts is obsolete—we carry that information in our pockets and on our belts. The goal of education should be to teach how to turn this wealth of knowledge into positive changes in the world, whether that means solutions to pressing problems, or artistic expressions that lift our spirits.

Learning by doing has several important advantages. First, it engages all your senses, which helps your brain retain what you learn. Second, it lets you make mistakes and discover for yourself the strategies to overcome them. This helps you recognize the underlying patterns of what you're learning about, which according to my "Pattern Recognition Theory of Mind" (which I articulate in my book *How to*

Create a Mind) is key to how we develop our thinking. Third, practical experience is more likely to stimulate your emotions. Whether it's the rush of satisfaction from succeeding or the frustration of failure, these emotions deepen your learning because you care about the lessons and their consequences.

In the novel, Danielle goes to the Stern School, which has the motto "learn by doing." The Stern School is inspired by the real-life Stern Schule, a progressive school founded by my great grandmother Regina Stern in Vienna in 1868. This was the first school in Europe to provide higher education for girls. If you were lucky enough to get an education as a girl in mid-nineteenth century Europe at all, it went through at most ninth grade. The Stern Schule went from Kindergarten to 14th grade— that is, through high school and the first two years of college. The idea was controversial and generated opposition and anger as it went against what many, actually most, people believed was the natural order of gender roles. The arguments then were similar to the arguments we hear today although support for women's rights was very undeveloped in 1868. My great grandmother's daughter, my grandmother, became an exemplar of her mother's philosophy and became the first woman in Europe to get a PhD in chemistry. She took over the school and between the two women they ran it for 70 years until fleeing Vienna and Hitler in the summer of 1938.

My grandmother wrote a book about the school and her experiences, called *One Life Is Not Enough*, a title that presaged my own interest in life extension. The book has been published in Austria. She wrote the book on a mechanical typewriter. She showed me the book and the typewriter when I was five. I was, at that time, more interested in the typewriter than the book. That typewriter played an important role in my deciding at a young age to become an inventor. That typewriter inspired me to collect mechanical linkages from the neighborhood with the idea that I could solve any problem by just figuring out how to put these devices together. It would take a number of years before these early inventions of mine got traction, but I learned a lot about science and engineering in the process.

Moreover, the school my great-grandmother and grandmother ran encouraged the philosophy of learning by doing to provide real-world experience for these young women.

In the novel, Danielle's assignments at the Stern School are directed at real-world problems, and many of her adventures result from her Stern School curriculum. For example, her Middle East peace mission is part of an assignment for her social studies class. As a result, she succeeds in negotiating a Middle East peace agreement, but due to ongoing violence in some parts of the region, she only gets a B+! You can follow in Danielle's footsteps by practicing learning by doing in your own life, and also by helping other people do the same.

First, take a look at these explanations of a few different examples of learning by doing:

- A short video explaining the importance of reflection to the overall learn-by-doing process.[1] The best kind of learning is about more than just directly using new skills and information, but actively thinking about that experience and trying to figure out what it can teach.

- A summary by Edutopia of the "Boss Level" program,[2] which engages young people in project-based learning. Projects give students a chance to apply several different areas of learning together with a single practical goal.

- A fascinating TED Talk by education scientist Sugata Mitra[3] explaining an experiment in India showing that kids encountering computers for the first time naturally teach themselves how to use them, using a learn-by-doing approach.

- A useful discussion between Engineered Truth's Matthew Tran and FreeCodeCamp founder Quincy Larson,[4] on the subject of how you can apply the learn-by-doing model to teach yourself computer programming.

- Engaging TEDx Talk by entrepreneur Robin Mansukhani,[5] on how learn-by-doing education is creating a revolution in how people build skills in engineering and other STEM subjects.

Here are some inspiring people who have been successful with learning by doing, from great pioneers from history to innovative teenagers in the present:

- British physicist and chemist Michael Faraday[6] (1791–1867) was one of the most famous scientists of all time. He had very little formal schooling, but learned science by working as a laboratory assistant and then by designing and conducting his own experiments.

- American inventor Thomas Edison[7] (1847–1931) did not have much education either, but had a great sense of curiosity. He solved problems by experimenting with potential solutions, trying many different ideas and recording the results. Edison received more than 1,000 patents during his career, and is credited with inventing the most pioneering inventions of the early twentieth century, including the phonograph, the motion-picture camera, and the modern light bulb.

- The Wright Brothers,[8] Orville (1871–1948) and Wilbur (1867–1912), were two bicycle mechanics from Dayton, Ohio. They dreamed of creating the world's first airplane, and learned aircraft design by trial and error. At the time, many experts said it was impossible. But in 1903, the Wright Brothers built a working model, and achieved the first-ever controlled powered flight in a heavier-than-air vehicle. That illustrates another advantage of "learn by doing." The Wright Brothers never learned from "experts" that what they were trying to do was "impossible."

- Kelvin Doe,[9] a 15-year-old from Sierra Leone who built his own radio broadcasting system from discarded parts and then ran a radio station for young people in his country.

- Santiago Gonzalez,[10] a 14-year-old computer programming whiz. Santiago built up his coding skills by actually creating his own apps, making them available to the public, and seeing what feedback they got.

Creating your own projects is one of the best ways to learn by doing. Whether you're writing a computer program, building a robot, or shooting a music video, keep in mind these suggestions for getting the most out of the experience:

- **Let yourself be ambitious.** When young people talk about their ideas and projects, some adults unfortunately like to tell them that these plans aren't realistic. If someone tells you this, it may be because they want to spare you disappointment if you don't succeed. This is a well-intentioned motive, but the learn-by-doing mindset says that even if the project doesn't turn out how you hoped, you can still learn a great deal that you could never have learned from classroom study. So don't be afraid to set big goals and undertake difficult projects.

- **Focus on serving others.** For most projects, you'll need the support of other people. This could be collaborators, financial sponsors, or journalists who spread the word about what you're doing. If the project is just for your own benefit, there isn't much reason for those people to help you. But if the project is intended to help people in need or solve a real-world problem, it's much easier to get a team of people on board and obtain other forms of support who are excited about your vision.

- **Reach out to successful people.** People who've already achieved big things in your field can be great mentors to you. But these people might get hundreds or even thousands of requests for help every year. So how can you stand out from the crowd? Ben Casnocha, who served as chief of staff to LinkedIn founder Reid Hoffman, suggests[11] that you look for ways you can offer successful people a perspective they couldn't buy "off a shelf." As a young person, you have insights that older executives and scientists don't have. This can be the starting point for relationships that genuinely benefit both sides, so you're not simply asking for favors.

- **Don't wait until you feel ready.** When you have a big project in mind, it's natural to feel uncertain. There is a lot that can go wrong, and the more you improve your skills, the more you realize how much you still have to learn. But the world's greatest innovators almost always dive into projects before they feel ready. A common saying is: "Entrepreneurship is jumping off a cliff and building a parachute on the way down." You will learn the most from experiences that stretch your abilities to the limit (of course, don't jump off a real cliff!).

- **Have an experimental mindset.** Even the world's most experienced engineers, programmers, and architects often modify their plans partway through a project. In trying to solve a hard problem, you'll

411

probably bump up against obstacles. So it's important not to fixate on one single solution. Instead, focus on experimenting with different approaches, and be willing to adjust your thinking based on what you learn. If you're trying to solve a problem that can be described with numbers, tools like the Wolfram software[12] and Brilliant.org[13] can help you explore, test, and visualize potential solutions. Regardless of how the project turns out, this will maximize your own learning.

- **Give yourself permission to fail.** Many people are afraid to start bold projects because they're afraid they'll fail. Sometimes they think that a failed project means that they failed as a person—or failed as a scientist, artist, or entrepreneur. Sometimes, people get their ego tied up in a project and will be embarrassed if it fails. In some cultures and traditions, failure is an embarrassment. If you feel these fears, you need to fight them. The essence of "Silicon Valley" is that failure is called "experience." Every great pioneer you've ever read about has failed. Usually, they've failed many times. Apple founder Steve Jobs was fired from his own company before making a triumphant return and making it the world's most valuable corporation. Bill Gates had a company called Traf-O-Data, which failed before he started Microsoft and became the wealthiest person on earth. According to Gates: "It's fine to celebrate success but it is more important to heed the lessons of failure." A similar idea is often attributed to Thomas Edison: "I have not failed. I've just found 10,000 ways that won't work." Learning from failure greatly helped all these figures succeed.

- **Find lessons in every experience.** You have opportunities to learn by doing even in unexpected activities. Whenever you talk to groups of people, you can learn about public speaking. Whenever you search for information online, you can learn about researching answers efficiently. Whenever you travel to a new place, you can learn about relating to people who've had different experiences. Also, make a point of learning from "near misses." When most people crash their bikes, they learn something about how to ride more safely. But the best learners try to learn just as much from the crashes that almost happened. Consider following writer Julia Galef's idea of keeping a "surprise journal"[14] to record every time your expectations are violated, and try to figure out why. This can help you discover hidden patterns in your own thinking.

For a better idea of how you or your school can apply the learn-by-doing philosophy, look over these organizations that are already implementing it around the world:

- Before schooling was common, learn-by-doing apprenticeships were the main form of education for young people. They learned skills in valuable trades by working under the supervision of an experienced master. Today, the Global Apprenticeships Network[15] connects young people with opportunities to learn job skills by applying them.

- Piper[16] is a kit that lets young people learn about computer science by building their own computer and programming it themselves.

- MEL Science[17] is a company that sends you chemistry experiments to do at home and safely learn science in a hands-on way.

- Here is a worthwhile report[18] with a lot of information on entrepreneurship education around the United States, including national programs that encourage learning by doing.

- Short explainer from the Buck Institute for Education[19] illustrating how project-based learning works. This approach lets students combine learning in several different subjects into work on a single project, using a learn-by-doing approach.

- Helpful overview of project-based learning by educator David Lee.[20] Describes the steps of the process, including how teachers can use this approach in the classroom.

- Clear and helpful diagram[21] comparing the normal direct instruction that happens in most classrooms to project-based learning.

- Interesting video[22] about a partnership between America's National Science Foundation and Pace University to help middle school students do marine science research with real-world environmental benefits.

- Expeditionary Learning,[23] a nonprofit affiliated with the Outward Bound movement, helps schools create in-depth learn-by-doing programs. Their focus is projects with practical impact that take kids out of the classroom and get them into their wider community.

- A closer look at how learn-by-doing can be applied[24] in elementary schools. Shows kids at Deer Park Elementary in Florida learning about science through a realistic problem: How can campers in the wilderness use light and sound to communicate at a distance?

- A quick video[25] on how learn-by-doing can be applied in high schools, focusing on Sammamish High School's transition to a problem-based learning curriculum.

- Information from the Nueva School (kindergarten through 12th grade) on their "Learn by doing, learn by caring" philosophy,[26] which focuses on hands-on exploration and social responsibility.

- Deep Springs College,[27] which applies learning by doing to college-level education. In addition to regular classes, the small student body runs a working farm and ranch where they put their skills into practice.

For more information, please see the following entry in the companion book *A Chronicle of Ideas: A Guide for Superheroines (and Superheroes)*: The Stern Schule.

Footnote links at

DanielleWorld.com/resources

and Encourage Women and Girls to Pursue STEM Careers

❀ ❀ ❀ ❀ ❀

Even in countries with relatively progressive gender equality, like the United States, women still face challenges in the workplace of certain industries. Especially in STEM (Science, Technology, Engineering, Math) fields, there is a large gender imbalance, with men holding the great majority of jobs at all levels.

My family's involvement in this issue goes back to my great-grandmother Regina Stern founding the first school in Europe that provided higher education for girls in 1868. See the entry "How You Can Be a Danielle and Learn by Doing," which shares this story.

The reasons for this disparity are controversial. One stereotype is that women cannot handle the stress and the technical content of STEM careers.

There is an important and very convincing historical trend that speaks powerfully to this issue. When I was growing up, doctors ... were men. To be more specific, 94% of all doctors in the early 1950s in the United States were male. At the time, this was attributed to two factors. First, that being a doctor was stressful, and that women, being more sensitive, were unable to thrive in such a stressful profession.

The first part of that assertion was certainly true—being a doctor *is* stressful. A doctor often needs to make decisions with very incomplete information, and often in a matter of minutes, sometimes seconds, that are life or death decisions. Consider the situation of an emergency room doctor which, as the name suggests, deals with emergencies and has to decide, often in seconds, which course of action to take with only fragmentary information. And if you make the wrong decision, your patient can be harmed or die, and you will be held accountable, and possibly sued. That's certainly high stress.

You might even say that being a doctor is more stressful than being a software engineer. In the software field, we have a name for mistakes—we call them bugs. The origin of this term was an actual bug—a moth—that Grace Murray Hopper found in the Mark I computer. She was, incidentally, the first programmer of a working computer. In fact, the first two computer programmers were women. The other was Ada Lovelace who wrote programs for the Analytical Engine in the nineteenth century. She never got to run her programs because the Analytical Engine never ran, but we have records of her programs and they have been assessed as being bug free. She was also the first to write about artificial intelligence. We have a name for the process of fixing mistakes in software engineering—it's called debugging. In medicine, doctors don't usually have an opportunity to fix mistakes without negative consequences.

The other factor was the assertion that women could not handle the large amount of technical information required to be a doctor. One estimate is that doctors learn about a hundred thousand chunks of knowledge, and this knowledge includes mastering a lot of scientific literature and math, and making complex technical inferences quickly.

Polls taken from that period show that the public—both men and women—were not comfortable with the idea of their doctor being a woman because of these two beliefs.

Today the situation is very different. 36% of doctors are women, but that includes the legacy of older doctors who are mostly men. With regard to the new doctors emerging from medical schools and residency programs, a majority are women. Even the highest stress specialties such as emergency medicine have a majority of the new doctors being women.

That's quite a shift. So how has that worked out? By every measure, very well. Polls today show that both women and men are very comfortable with having a female doctor and the idea that women cannot handle either the stress or the science of being a doctor has gone away.

Some observers say that women are attracted to medicine because of the emphasis on interpersonal interaction, but we see the same demographics in areas of medicine that do not involve interacting with a person, such as radiology where you interact with an image and pathology where you interact with a tissue sample.

This is not a university study involving hundreds of people. We're talking about hundreds of thousands of physicians in the United States treating hundreds of millions of patients. There has been a similar shift around the world with millions of physicians treating billions of patients. That should really put to rest the idea that women cannot handle professional stress as well as highly technical content.

There is a similar trend in the legal field. So why has software engineering and STEM fields in general lagged in terms of gender equality?

The good news from the history of the medical profession, which I just relayed, is twofold. First, it shows that the historical explanations regarding women's lower ability to handle both stress and scientific content are not correct. It also shows that cultural expectations regarding gender roles and actual diversity can be dramatically changed.

There is a gender-related factor that I believe does influence career choices, and that has to do with child rearing, the burden of which still falls more on women than men. That reality is itself cultural. It is changing, but has not changed as much as it could or should. There has been some change. In 1900, 31% of the US population had jobs. Today it is 44%, and the difference is largely due to women entering the workforce.

There are increasing examples of the traditional "housewife" role being reversed. And couples with young children share the work of child rearing somewhat more equally. But it is still far from an equal distribution.

One of the reasons cited for women's interest in being a doctor is the flexibility of hours. Although being an intern is notoriously demanding with very long shifts, once a doctor gets through that rite of professional passage, they have the flexibility to take a few years off, or work part time for several years—per child—without harming their career status. They can simply pick up working full time again when their children are older.

That flexibility typically does not exist in tech jobs for women or men. My own view is that we should move in that direction, for both genders. That would make tech jobs more attractive to women and also help couples more equally share the child-rearing role. Traditional maternity and paternity benefits, while generally progressive in the tech industry compared to some other industries, is not nearly sufficient to address this issue. Tech employees generally do not have the option to work part time for an extended period of time, and if they leave for more than a few months they are likely to lose their job.

I think a change in these policies would make engineering jobs more attractive to women and also facilitate more equal sharing of the job of child rearing. Trying to influence these policies is one way to change the STEM imbalance.

Another general recommendation is to address what is called the pipeline issue (the flow of girls and women entering STEM fields), and that needs to be addressed starting in elementary school.

In the novel, Danielle breaks down stereotypes in many ways. She encourages her followers to reconsider their fixed ideas about gender roles, encourages educational reforms, and excels herself as a scientist. Winning Nobel Prizes in Physics and Medicine sets a powerful example for girls and women all over the world. In real life, Facebook COO Sheryl Sandberg has taken a leading role in improving women's opportunities in the workforce, and in encouraging girls to study STEM.

Sandberg, who has served as Chief Operating Officer of Facebook since 2008, saw firsthand how women working in technology often struggle to get the same opportunities as men. In 2010, she gave a TED Talk[1] titled "Why We Have Too Few Women Leaders," which went viral. Women all over the world started sharing their stories in response, and Sandberg was inspired to write a 2013 book called *Lean In: Women, Work, and the Will to Lead.*[2] The book offered women practical tips on how to balance the demands of careers and families, and it soon became a #1 *New York Times* bestseller. The book led to a whole "Lean In" movement.[3] Here's how you can participate:

- **For women and girls.**[4] Based on her experiences, Sandberg observed that women pursuing leadership roles often fail to support each other. Some say they feel threatened by other women, or that older women in leadership roles are reluctant to mentor them and give them a "hand up" the corporate ladder. Lean In offers advice on how women can help each other succeed in several ways:

  - **Ally-ship.** Being allies to each other in the face of gender bias or mistreatment. Too often, women observe someone else experiencing sexism, and stay silent for fear of seeming oversensitive or humorless. By working together, women can make it much harder for abuse to keep happening.

  - **Mentorship.** For anyone to succeed in a competitive industry, they need mentorship from older and more experienced colleagues. Since it often feels more natural for men to mentor younger men, this leaves young women without the career advice, connections, and support that their male counterparts get. Women can break this cycle by acting as mentors to younger women and girls. You can be a mentor at any age!

  - **Positivity.** It can be very helpful to women to have a supportive group of peers who can encourage each other, share experiences, and exchange advice on how to deal with challenges in the workplace.

  - **Role modeling.** How young women act sets an example for girls who look up to them. By speaking with confidence, showing leadership, and being willing to take risks for what they believe in, women can model for girls how they can break down gender stereotypes.

- <u>For men and boys</u>.[5] Facebook COO Sheryl Sandberg recognizes that women can't achieve a level playing field in the workplace on their own. It requires men working with them proactively to create a fairer environment for everyone. Lean In has suggestions for concrete ways men can support women's careers. This ranges from showing husbands how they can better share parenting responsibilities with their wives to tips for male managers on how to fight sexism on their teams. Some of these ideas are applicable in school as well. For example, boys should be careful not to interrupt girls (or other boys either!) during class discussions. This helps create an environment where both boys and girls feel welcome.

- <u>Go deeper</u>.[6] Lean In offers lots of resources to help you learn what you can do about this problem. Whether you're a young woman starting a career, a girl interested in studying STEM, or a guy wondering how to make your school or workplace fairer for everyone, you can learn practical steps to have a positive impact. These resources include:

  - Videos of talks by experts on subjects like leadership, gender bias, negotiation, and balancing career with other priorities.

  - Essays and research articles that can help you understand this issue more deeply. They can also be helpful when you discuss gender bias with someone who does not agree that it is a problem. It helps to be able to point them to both scientific studies and firsthand experiences of women who experienced discrimination in the workplace.

  - Guides on how to form Lean In groups among your peers, and ideas for activities that can help young women connect and form relationships. If you'd like to find a Lean In group (known as Lean In Circles) to join in your local area, or want to start one of your own, here's <u>how you can make it happen</u>.[7]

  - <u>Lean In's 10 tips for recent graduates</u>,[8] with powerful strategies for young women to start their careers ready to break down stereotypes and achieve the success they want.

  - <u>Sheryl Sandberg's follow-up talk</u>[9] "So We Leaned In … Now What?" about reactions to her ideas and what has changed in response to the Lean In movement.

420

Usually, gender bias isn't the result of deliberate prejudice. In most cases, it doesn't happen because men hate women, or consciously want to make life harder for them. Rather, it comes from the way our brains naturally process information about the world. We instinctively use our own experiences to form generalizations. If children (and adults) rarely see women as CEOs, it's easy to assume that it's natural for CEOs to be men. The same is true for professions like engineers and mathematicians.

This means that one of the most effective ways of eliminating stereotypes is making people aware of people who have broken the stereotype. When girls grow up seeing female CEOs and STEM professionals, it will be easy to imagine themselves in those same roles. And when boys grow up seeing those examples, they won't see it as unusual for women to have leadership roles in the workplace, or to compete in previously male-dominated fields. Therefore, you can help end gender bias by learning about stereotype-breaking women, and sharing their stories more widely.

- 16 more TED Talks by strong women leaders.[10] Listen to their personal stories, think about how they overcame challenges and obstacles in their way, and consider how you can apply those lessons in your own education and career. If one has a strong impact on you, share it in your social networks to spread the message.

- Another 11 TED Talks, by brilliant women in STEM.[11] Watch what they've accomplished, and let your friends know about their achievements—most probably haven't heard about them!

- Not only is gender bias a problem in the workplace, but lingering racism can also affect women from minority groups. The combination of sexism and racism can make career success especially difficult for women from these backgrounds. For inspiration, take a look at these 33 black women[12] who have achieved great success despite those challenges. You can use these stories to refute the stereotype that minority women aren't driven or successful.

In addition to helping raise the profile of women role models in STEM, it's also important to be careful about the way we talk to young girls ourselves.

- **Focus on ideas instead of beauty.** Our culture encourages people to constantly tell little (and big!) girls how pretty they are. Of course, there is nothing wrong with being beautiful, but undue attention on looks unintentionally sends the message that girls' appearance is what people care about most. Lisa Bloom[13] has some great advice about how to focus instead on ideas—ask girls what books they are reading, what they are learning in school, and what they're curious about! This sends the message that people are interested in what they have to say and what they are thinking.

- **Support their interests.** Many STEM-related toys are marketed as being for boys. Unfortunately, this means that older people may discourage young girls who ask for those toys or want to play with them. As a result, they may be turned off the path toward STEM early in life. You can help break this cycle by encouraging girls who show STEM interests—buy them science toys that may be intended for boys, expose them to new STEM-related experiences, and talk to them about their interests and goals.

- **Encourage leadership.** In 2014, the Lean In movement launched a campaign called #BanBossy.[14] Sheryl Sandberg and her colleagues noticed that little girls who are confident and assertive are often called "bossy." By contrast, the same traits in boys are more likely to be seen as positive signs of leadership ability. #BanBossy doesn't refer to a literal ban, but encourages people to stop using language that sends girls the message that they should not be leaders.

Finally, although women are underrepresented in STEM leadership roles, the problem doesn't start there. There are too few women CEOs because there are too few women in the senior management jobs that CEOs are drawn from. And there are too few women in those jobs because they are underrepresented throughout the career pipeline, going all the way back to internships and first jobs. And it's hard to fix that as long as girls face stereotypes that discourage them to study STEM in school in the first place. For this reason, the best way to open women's opportunity in STEM careers is to give girls opportunity to pursue STEM interests while they're still students. Here are some great initiatives for girls in STEM that you should consider supporting or participating in:

- 1000 Girls, 1000 Futures[15] is a global project for girls ages 13–19 who are interested in STEM. It provides one-to-one mentoring from female scientists and engineers, along with special coursework to feed their curiosity, and networking with other like-minded girls.

- Girls Who Code[16] is a nonprofit that works to help schools, churches, or other community organizations start computer programming clubs for girls in grades 6-12. It also runs a 7-week Summer Immersion Program for girls in grades 10–11, which provides focused coding experiences and exposure to STEM jobs.

- Girlstart[17] is a Texas-based nonprofit that sponsors STEM education programs for girls in grades K–12. The local activities include summer camps, after-school programs, conferences, and community-based events, but Girlstart provides lots of useful free STEM education resources that you can access from anywhere.

- Girls into Global STEM[18] is primarily aimed at girls in Europe, but its resources are useful to STEM-interested girls everywhere. GIGS provides information and educational resources for teachers to help bring girls into STEM. The program focuses on how STEM skills can be used to achieve a positive impact around the globe on humanitarian issues.

- Girls Inc.[19] is a nationwide American nonprofit that does research on girls' education, advocates for expanded opportunities for girls in STEM, and offers competitive scholarships. It sponsors educational activities all around the United States and Canada, including Operation SMART (Science, Math, and Relevant Technology), which provides programs and resources for girls to develop skills and interests in STEM subjects. Find a Girls Inc. group near you!

- For more local options, take a look at the Connectory,[20] which lets you look up STEM programs in or near your ZIP code.

- Pathways to Science[21] provides a directory of STEM programs for young women, with a wide range of age ranges, subjects, and geographic locations.

You can find more tips to help you encourage girls and women in STEM and the workplace by looking at the entries for "How You Can Be a Danielle and Learn to Program Computers from a Young Age"; "How You Can Be a Danielle and Foster Learn By Doing"; "How You Can Be a Danielle and Help Promote Equal Rights for Women"; and "How You Can Be a Danielle and Promote Racial and Gender Equality."

Footnote links at

DanielleWorld.com/resources

and Help Promote Equal Rights for Women

W omen make up slightly more than half of the world's population, but they continue to face discrimination and disadvantages in societies all around the world. Women's rights is a complex issue with a long history. It was only about a century ago that women obtained the right to vote in England and the United States.

My family's involvement in this issue goes back to my great-grandmother Regina Stern founding in 1868 the first school in Europe that provided higher education for girls. See the entry "How You Can Be a Danielle and Learn by Doing," which shares this story.

This issue has roots that go back thousands of years in terms of ideas of proper gender roles. Gender stereotypes often portray women as less capable than men in areas such as technical subjects and leadership. The recent success of women in the medical and legal fields belie these stereotypes, but they continue to persist in such areas as engineering. In many parts of the world, girls have less access to education than boys. They may be discouraged from having careers outside the home, or limited to only a few "feminine" occupations like teaching and nursing.

In some countries, women have fewer legal rights than men. Millions of girls each year are subjected to female genital mutilation (FGM), which the United Nations recognizes as a human rights violation. See the entry on Female Genital Mutilation in *A Guide for Superheroines (and Superheroes)* for more details on this issue. These are just a few examples of the continued discrimination and repression of women around the world.

In the novel, Danielle is a passionate advocate for equal rights for women. Not only does she act as an inspiring example—a superheroine—she becomes politically active. She fights against female genital mutilation, supports entrepreneurship, and improves girls' access to education. Danielle understands that achieving equal rights for women requires advances in several different areas. Girls must have equal access to education and they must be safe from gender-based violence. They must have civil rights and the political freedom to shape their own destiny. And they must have the economic freedom to improve their lives through innovation and hard work. You can have a positive impact in each of those areas. Let's take a look at opportunities for each one.

- **Education.** In many countries, girls don't get the same educational opportunities as boys. In some cases, girls are formally prohibited from going to school, or if allowed to attend school, there are strong social pressures which cause many to drop out. In sub-Saharan Africa, disease and poverty force many girls out of school because they have to work and take care of their families. Even in Europe and America, gender stereotypes often discourage girls from studying STEM (Science, Technology, Engineering, Math) subjects. Here's some further information on the problem, along with ideas on how to support or create solutions:

  - A short animated video[1] on the difference between the lives of girls who go to school and those who don't.

  - Nobel Peace Prize winner Malala Yousafzai[2] on her campaign for girls' education in Pakistan, which caused the Taliban to try to kill her.

- Powerful TED Talk by Ziauddin Yousafzai,[3] Malala's father, reflecting on his family's efforts to improve women's rights despite threats and danger.

- The United Nations Girls' Education Initiative[4] provides country-specific information on parts of the world where girls have major barriers to education. This can guide your thinking about where your own efforts could have the greatest impact.

- The International Rescue Committee[5] is one of the world's top charities for providing education to children affected by war and poverty, factors that force many girls out of school. Last year, the IRC helped about 1.5 million children and provided training to 33,000 teachers. Donating to the IRC or one of the other organizations listed here allows them to hire more educators and purchase vital school supplies. Consider holding a fundraiser at your school, or starting a donation drive on social media. This is an outstanding cause for young people because it directly benefits people who are alike in so many ways, except where they happened to be born.

- Save the Children[6] is another excellent nonprofit that supports global education. Although it is not focused specifically on girls, that isn't a problem. Improving girls' education isn't about helping them win a race with boys, but rather a challenge to help everyone get the education they need. Save the Children helped educate more than 13 million children last year, and also provided teacher training, coaching for parents, and arts enrichment programs.

- It's often good to support charities that focus on one particular country or region. This is because there are cultural factors shaping the specific reasons why girls don't have adequate educational opportunities. Nonprofits that understand these issues better may have enhanced impact. For example, Educate Girls[7] creates community-led educational programs for girls in poor parts of India, which is the world's most populous democracy.

- CARE[8] is an international nonprofit working on a wide range of humanitarian issues, many of which directly affect women. According to CARE, women's rights depend on an interlocking set of improvements to health, education, and empowerment. On girls' education, CARE focuses on properly understanding the many individual barriers to success, which makes it easier to overcome each one. CARE provides lots of startling facts about girls' education, and gives you specific information about how your donations can improve girls' lives.

- Camfed,[9] the Campaign for Female Education, uses an innovative model that not only provides schooling to girls who wouldn't get it otherwise, but also provides leadership training and assistance to become economically independent.

- A list of another 10 innovative non-governmental organizations[10] working in education around the world.

- One of the major barriers to girls' education in poor countries is that access to electricity, sanitation, and the Internet is limited. You could provide a very meaningful boost to education by coming up with new innovations in those areas. For a look at how to apply a problem-solving mindset to big problems and create new solutions, take a look at some online innovation classes.[11] For example, Design Thinking for Innovation[12] is a 10–20 hour course from the University of Virginia on the process of observing something you want to change, generating ideas, and experimenting with them.

- If you know computer programming, you could create a new online tool to help girls in poor countries connect to better educational resources. For example, there might be need for a service to connect non-English-speaking girls with native English speakers to boost their language skills. Or maybe a service to help people translate educational materials from English into children's native languages. If you don't know coding yet, take a look at the entry for "How You Can Be a Danielle and Learn to Program Computers from a Young Age."

- **Gender-based violence.** In some traditional societies, girls are targeted for diverse forms of violence. Female genital mutilation is an extremely painful procedure that causes lifelong health problems and impairment. Forced marriage robs girls of control over their lives, and may involve sexual assault. Acid attacks are a brutal form of violence that permanently disfigures women—for example, as punishment against a domestic servant who protests unfair treatment, or revenge against a woman who rejects a man's romantic advances. Worst of all are "honor killings," when women are murdered for acting in ways that men in their family does not approve of, such as having a romantic relationship with a man of their own choosing, or dressing in Western-style clothing. Some women are even killed for being victims of rape.

Here are some resources and ideas for action on gender-based violence:

- 5 things to know about honor killings,[13] from *USA Today*, based on the findings of the US Department of Justice.

- The Honour Based Violence Awareness Network[14] provides more information you can share about honor violence to raise awareness among your friends.

- Inspiring talk by Pakistani activist Khalida Brohi[15] on how she works to combat honor killings.

- CARE provides some shocking facts about violence against women[16] around the world, and how large the scale of the problem is.

- Human Rights Watch[17] does crucial work monitoring gender-based violence. They keep track of honor killings, FGM, and child marriage, and produce country-specific reports[18] about the violence and about progress that's being made to stop it.

- The Ayaan Hirsi Ali Foundation[19] is an advocacy organization that calls on governments to act more aggressively to stop honor violence. The foundation also supports counseling for victims, and provides training for educators, social workers, and law enforcement officers to help them better protect girls and women.

- A more comprehensive guide[20] to non-governmental organizations working to end gender-based violence and to assist victims.

- Don't be afraid to speak out among your friends about the need for people around the world to work together to stop honor violence. Some people say that violence like FGM is just a cultural practice and that it is culturally insensitive to criticize it. But you will be standing on the side of universal human rights. Remember:

the girls and women who suffer gender-based violence cannot safely speak up for themselves, so you—whether you are male or female—can be an important voice for their rights.

- If you know coding, think of ways you could create an online platform for helping people in danger of gender-based violence. For example, an app could give people an easy way to report suspected abuse, or spread awareness about how women can discreetly signal for help from other females in their community. For more ideas, see the entry for "How You Can Be a Danielle and Help Eradicate Female Genital Mutilation."

- **Political and civil rights.** The core question of women's rights is whether women and girls have equal political and civil rights to those of men and boys. These are the rights to act as a free and independent member of society—for example, to leave the house by yourself, to drive a car, to choose your spouse, to vote in elections, and to run for office. When women have these rights, they can participate directly in decisions about how their communities will be run. Once women have political power, it is much easier for them to keep their other rights safe, and to expand opportunities for the next generation of young girls. Look over these links and suggestions—you can support the nonprofits below by fundraising, sharing their message with your friends, and volunteering to participate.

  - Short video of women from Burundi[21] explaining the need for them to have greater political rights to facilitate peace and stability.

  - Consider joining the Association for Women's Rights in Development,[22] which advocates internationally for women to have full political equality. AWID releases an ongoing series of reports on the global state of women's rights, and provides resources to help women fight abuse and oppression.

  - Women for Women[23] is a nonprofit that focuses on social empowerment for women, especially in countries that have been affected by war and terrorism. It offers job training, life skills education, and help developing business skills.

  - Adeso Development Solutions[24] is a highly respected aid organization that works to expand women's political rights across Africa. In many cases, women have full political rights according to the law, but cultural factors discourage them from participating in politics. Here's a video[25] about Adeso's project[26] on behalf of the European Union to encourage women's political participation in Somalia.

- UN Women[27] is the United Nations entity responsible for encouraging women's empowerment around the world. It provides training for women on how to run for political office, and supports efforts in individual countries to pass laws that give women more freedom. UN Women also works to educate men about how gender equality benefits them as well.

- USAID[28] is the US Agency for International Development, which does similar work to UN Women as part of its broader mission of helping people in poor or violent countries. It works to make it easier for women to enter fields like politics, journalism, and law. USAID also focuses on ensuring that women get equal access to their countries' court systems so they can defend their rights, and so people who abuse them can be punished.

- Here's a list of more organizations working for women's rights worldwide.[29] This includes both international charities and groups working in specific countries or regions.

- One of the obstacles to women becoming more active in politics, is that in some societies, they are discouraged from having large public meetings like political parties do. You might be able to create an online platform to make it easier for women to organize politically. Talk to women who have lived in repressive societies, and listen to their suggestions about what tools they wish they would have had.

- When deciding where to travel or spend your money, try to be conscious of which governments seriously violate women's rights. For example, women in Saudi Arabia were, up until very recently, prohibited from driving (this was reversed just as this book was being written!) and are denied many of the rights that men have.

- For more ideas, see the entry for "How You Can Be a Danielle and Promote Racial and Gender Equality."

- **Economic security.** Saving money and building wealth is a very important part of equal rights. Women with no money are totally dependent on the men around them, and don't have the freedom to leave abusive or unhappy living situations. In societies where women can't inherit property or start their own businesses, enormous amounts of human potential are lost. Women who might otherwise have cured cancer or achieved breakthroughs in artificial intelligence are instead so focused on survival that they cannot be innovators. As the American science writer Stephen Jay Gould put it: "I am, somehow, less interested in the weight and convolutions of Einstein's brain than in the near certainty that people of equal talent have lived and died in cotton fields and sweatshops." On the other hand, improving women's economic rights has been shown to be one of the most important factors in making countries healthier, richer, and better educated. Microfinance—small loans to poor people to help them climb out of poverty—is a powerful tool for building up women's economic security. Here are some suggestions for organizations worth supporting, and areas where you could have a strong impact with innovations of your own:

- Some important statistics on women's equality and economic participation from the World Bank[30] and the International Monetary Fund.[31]

- A short video on how microfinance works,[32] and how it improves economic opportunities for people who otherwise wouldn't have access to the money they need to start businesses or get job training.

- Nobel Peace Prize winner Muhammad Yunus[33] on the history of microfinance, and the positive impact it has had.

- CARE[34] does extensive work in poor countries to improve economic development for women. It publishes interesting and useful stats and facts about microfinance and the economics of poverty.

- FINCA[35] is one of the world's top microfinance nonprofits, and is active all over the world. FINCA is known for doing good research into how to improve the social impact of its lending, and on its advocacy around issues of economic justice.

- The Women's Microfinance Initiative[36] is a relatively new microfinance organization that focuses on setting up village-level lending hubs in East Africa. This helps communities become self-sufficient, and reduces reliance on external aid. WMI also works with women to transition them into the regular banking system.

- Even in wealthy countries, women's economic security is often limited by insufficient paid maternity leave. UN Women works to advocate better parental leave policies,[37] as explained in this speech[38] at the United Nations by actress Anne Hathaway.

- You could create an app to help connect women who are interested in entrepreneurship, so they could more easily share ideas, collaborate, and give each other advice.

- Many people around the world want to support businesses created by women, but there isn't a single directory that people can use to make that easier. If you build one, more money could flow to these businesses from people who want to support them.

- If you know a language spoken by many women in the developing world, you could create videos teaching them business skills in their native language. Otherwise, you could find someone in your community who knows one of these languages and work with them to create this educational content.

- For more ideas, see the entry for "How You Can Be a Danielle and Encourage Women in the Workplace and Girls to Pursue STEM Careers."

For more information, please see the following entries in the companion book *A Chronicle of Ideas: A Guide for Superheroines (and Superheroes)*: National Organization for Women, Terry O'Neill.

Footnote links at
DanielleWorld.com/resources

and Help the People in Developing Nations

❋ ❋ ❋ ❋ ❋

Throughout history, the great majority of people have lived in poverty. The Industrial Revolution began to change that in the 19th century, and by the end of World War II in the middle of the 20th century, prosperity was quickly expanding around the globe. Literacy rates soared and the world's new middle class got advances like electricity, medicine, automobiles, and television.

Unfortunately, many people in developing nations were left behind. Extreme poverty and starvation still affected many parts of Africa, Asia, and South America. With Asia's transformation from old fashioned agrarian economies to modern information industries, poverty in Asia has fallen by more than 90 percent in the past three decades. Economic progress is also beginning to assist Africa and South America. The international community has also been working together to reduce poverty in these regions. There has been a great deal of progress, and the proportion of people in extreme poverty has declined by more than half in the last twenty years. Over 3.8 billion people now have access to the Internet, which wasn't even available to kings and billionaires thirty years ago. Yet there is still a lot of work to do. 1.2 billion people live on less than $1.25 per day, and almost half of the world's population of 7.5 billion makes under $2.50 a day. More people have access to a mobile phone than a toilet or clean water. Solving these problems will require innovation and hard work, but progress is moving in the right direction.

In the novel, Danielle realizes that the world's poorest countries have several overlapping problems. A lack of safe drinking water causes conditions like cholera. Droughts cause famine and make people more vulnerable to disease. Without electricity, people use oil lamps that cause air pollution, illness, and fires. These conditions force many children to drop out of school to care for their families. Danielle works to solve several of these issues and improve overall quality of life in developing nations, starting with her efforts to help overcome the lack of clean water in Zambia at age six. Let's take a look at some of the most urgent problems in these countries, and what you can do to address each one—from nonprofit organizations you can fundraise for to innovations you can create on your own.

- **Food security.** Droughts and conflict have left many people in the developing world without enough nutrition to stay healthy. This can make people more vulnerable to disease, and when children grow up malnourished, they may suffer permanent cognitive and physical problems. Here are some famine-relief nonprofits worth your support, along with ideas to spark you own innovation:

  - Oxfam[1] provides a mix of food, water, equipment, and cash to the people hardest hit by famines. They not only help people survive during an acute crisis, they also focus on getting them back up on their feet so they can support themselves afterward.

  - UNICEF[2] is the UN's emergency assistance organization for children. It focuses on making sure that babies, children, and teenagers have the nutrition they need to get through famines and grow up healthy.

  - Action Against Hunger[3] is active in around 50 countries, and provides assistance to about 13 million people each year, with a focus on Africa. In addition to emergency food aid, they provide services like micro-loans, veterinary care for farm animals, and entrepreneurship training, all of which help prevent food insecurity from starting in the first place.

- People in extreme poverty typically can't afford enough food. Innovations that make food cheaper to produce make it easier for the poor to get what they need. For example, if you can figure out an inexpensive way to set up vertical farming[4] in developing countries where clean water is scarce, you could make fresh food more affordable. Study the factors that affect food production costs and think about how you could bring those costs down.

- Another problem is delivery of food. When famine strikes, international aid agencies try to send people the food they need, but roads are often poorly maintained or non-existent, and sometimes violence makes it difficult for supplies to get through on trucks to remote villages. Brainstorm some alternate means of sending food packages to remote areas, and consider the pros and cons of each. One innovative idea is to use small automated drones to deliver food and medicine.

- In some developing countries, millions of people live in dense urban slums. Even though they aren't starving, the only food they can afford is junk food. As a result, there has been an increase in obesity, heart disease, and diabetes in many of these places. Try designing a program for poor city-dwellers to grow fresh, healthy food right where they live. What are the obstacles they might face? And how could they overcome them?

- **Clean water.** Lack of sanitary drinking water causes cholera and other diarrhea-related conditions. Kids are especially vulnerable, and diarrhea kills about 800,000 young children every year. Here are some ways you can help people in developing countries access safe water and prevent waste from contaminating it:

  - To deal with the acute side of the problem, you can raise money to buy water purification devices and send them to people who need them through Water is Life.[5] About $10 buys a filter that will give a child clean drinking water for a year. Another similar technology is the Lifestraw[6] filter.

  - Lifewater[7] focuses on community education about good sanitation practices. They help people prevent feces from contaminating drinking water and causing diseases.

- The Africa Sand Dam Foundation[8] is a nonprofit that helps villages use their natural environment to construct safe water storage facilities.

- Several young people have designed innovative new water filtration systems, just by studying how filtration works and experimenting with potential solutions. Study existing filtration technologies and see if you can find an area you can improve on, or find gaps in functions you could fill. For more information, see the entry for "How You Can Be a Danielle and Combat Drought and Polluted Water in Poor Nations."

- Talk with someone native to a developing country with sanitation problems and learn from them how unsafe hygiene habits there lead to disease. Help them create videos aimed at changing these habits so people can prevent waste from contaminating their water.

- One problem with sanitation in the developing world is that toilets are still fairly expensive to build and install, and sewage systems are often inadequate. Take a look at these eight innovative toilet designs[9] that are more practical for developing countries, and try to think of a way of improving on them. How could they be cheaper, simpler, or easier to install?

- For more information, see the entry for "How You Can Be a Danielle and Combat Drought and Polluted Water in Poor Nations."

- **Disease.** Infectious diseases are one of the greatest burdens on human prosperity in developing countries. Disease kills people early, makes many others sick, and forces people out of school and into poverty. Here are some ideas for tackling disease:

  - The Against Malaria Foundation[10] is one of the most efficient lifesaving charities you can donate to. For the amount of money that's considered cost-effective to save a single life in America, the insecticidal mosquito nets they distribute can save almost 2,700 lives in developing nations.

  - Doctors Without Borders sends physicians into poor and dangerous areas where people otherwise couldn't get medical care. In addition to treating illnesses and injuries, they provide vaccinations that prevent deadly diseases, like tuberculosis.[11]

- Several common diseases in developing countries cause blindness, but can be cured relatively cheaply and easily with proper medical care. Sightsavers[12] is an international charity that has provided vision treatment to almost 350 million people, including 6.1 million sight-restoring cataract operations. If you're looking to support an organization with a country-specific focus, the Aravind Eye Hospital[13] in India is known as the developing world's top center for curing blindness.

- Although few women in wealthy countries die from childbirth anymore, maternal death is still common in many developing countries. CARE[14] provides a range of services to pregnant women in poor communities to lower their risks and reduce the danger of medical problems from pregnancy and childbirth.

- People with AIDS still face shaming and shunning in many parts of the world. You can find a group or organization working to reduce the social stigma of AIDS, and work with them to create videos and memes that share a message of caring and acceptance with young people. Contact students living in a developing country for suggestions on how you can tailor this message to people living there.

- Mosquitoes are one of the main carriers of disease in many developing countries, especially in Sub-Saharan Africa. There can be huge benefit from new technologies for repelling or killing mosquitoes. Insecticidal nets are already very good at protecting people while they're sleeping in bed, but there's need for better anti-mosquito technology that can protect people during the day. Read about mosquitoes' biology to see if you can think of a better way to disrupt their breeding, or to make them avoid contact with humans who are outdoors.

- Although anti-smoking campaigns have greatly reduced lung disease in wealthy nations, smoking is still a major killer in developing countries. What do you think could be done to reduce smoking and save lives? Break down the problem into smaller parts. How could people be convinced to not start smoking in the first place? What could help them quit? How could ex-smokers form healthier habits? Talk to a smoker or former smoker to learn from their experiences.

- For more information, see the entry for "How You Can Be a Danielle and Promote World Health."

● **Electricity.** In much of the developing world, rural communities don't have access to electricity. This puts people at a huge disadvantage, because electricity is so vital to modern society—from lighting, to healthcare, to Internet access. Consider how you can help bring electric power to those who need it.

  - SELF,[15] the Solar Electric Light Fund finds communities without good access to electricity and installs photovoltaic grids and solar-powered devices like refrigerators and cell phone charging stations. Supporting SELF can create a positive cycle of electricity, health and education, and growing wealth.

  - The Janicki Omniprocessor[16] is a breakthrough technology that turns raw sewage into both electricity and pure drinking water. The Omniprocessor is too expensive for you alone to buy for communities that need it, but you can raise awareness about the technology on social media and encourage governments to pay for their installation in developing countries.

  - There is always need for new methods of generating electricity from trash or waste material. The Janicki Omniprocessor is a great innovation, but it's very large and expensive. Ask someone who has lived in a developing country what kinds of waste is generated in poor communities. Study what chemical compounds they contain, and look for potential reactions that could be used to release energy that can be turned into electricity.

  - When communities in developing countries lack electric lighting, they often use kerosene lamps to work at night. These lamps give off smoke that causes lung disease and other breathing problems. Their emissions even contribute to climate change. Solar Aid[17] is a nonprofit that provides solar-powered lights to help people see in the dark without the need for dirty lamps.

  - One obstacle to installing photovoltaic systems in remote areas is that they require special training to install and repair. If you could design a solar electricity system that villagers could install without any training, and that they could easily maintain in working condition, it would be much easier for these communities to access inexpensive, clean energy from the sun.

- In wealthy countries, we use expensive batteries to power devices like cell phones, radios, computers, and e-books. But in the developing world, people may not have access to those batteries, or convenient electricity sources to charge them. Human-powered electricity might be a helpful solution. Using your knowledge of physics and engineering, you could design a more efficient system for powering hand-held electronics by turning a crank, pedaling a wheel, or something similar.

⚫ **Environment.** Developing countries are at high risk for harm to the environment. Pollution and deforestation combine to cause long-lasting damage. Not only does this disrupt natural ecosystems, it can also cause major health problems in people living there. Here are some ways to help prevent and reverse environmental damage in developing countries:

- It's common for people in developing countries to cook their food over dirty stoves that damage their lungs over time. The Global Alliance for Clean Cookstoves[18] provides cleaner stoves that people can use safely.

- Many kinds of pollution can easily cross national borders. Air pollution from one country can make people sick in a neighboring country. Polluted water circulates from one nation into the waters of another, killing the fish that people rely on for food. Since no nation can solve the problem alone, UN Environment[19] is the United Nations group that helps countries work together to fight pollution.

- The Union of Concerned Scientists[20] uses scientific evidence to advocate policies that protect the environment. This is particularly important to the welfare of people in developing countries.

- A great tragedy of the developing world is that people often have to sacrifice their long-term future to meet their short-term needs. For example, during famines, farmers kill the dairy cows they use to make a living, because they need meat. Deforestation is a similar problem. In order to get more land for grazing animals or farming, people burn down forests, which damages the environment for decades and causes harmful air pollution. There is a need for social innovation that provides incentives to not deforest the land. You can pick a developing country and research who owns the forested land there. Think of ways to create incentives for them to protect the environment.

– Millions of people in developing countries die because of air pollution. This is due to a mix of dirty electricity-generating technology, old gasoline-powered cars, sooty cooking stoves and heating fires, and cheap kerosene lighting. Clean energy technology can solve all of these problems. You could raise money to install photovoltaic panels in needy communities, or if you're old enough, organize a volunteer trip of young people to install photovoltaics yourselves.

● **War and conflict.** Many developing countries are affected by terrorism, war, ethnic cleansing, or other forms of violence. When people don't have the sense of security to know that they will be alive next year, basic survival becomes an all-consuming priority. This leaves little time for education, political development, or economic education. Take a look at these opportunities to help people in violent areas stay safe and get the help they need:

– The International Rescue Committee[21] works to provide emergency services to refugees and people displaced within their own countries. They also advocate policies by the world's governments to provide more help to victims of violence.

– Because young people are disproportionately impacted by violence, Save the Children[22] focuses on providing services like nutrition, education, and healthcare to children in conflict zones.

– Preventing or stopping genocides requires good information about crises to be shared with the world before it is too late. Genocide Watch[23] monitors areas where genocides might happen and sounds the alarm about what outside governments and organizations can do to help.

– Millions of people have been displaced from their homes due to war and terrorism in developing countries. Unfortunately, much of this suffering is hidden. Conflicts like the civil war in the Central

African Republic get very little news coverage in English-speaking nations—and while there is a lot of news about the fighting in Syria, not much of it shows the stories of refugees in a way that people can relate to. You could create a media app interviewing victims of conflict and helping them share their stories with the world. If you make it easier for people in wealthy countries to empathize with them, these citizens will be more likely to demand humanitarian action from their governments.

- People in conflict zones often struggle to get reliable information about how to keep themselves safe. Cell phone networks go down, or radio broadcasts may not have information relevant to a particular person's situation. Think of alternate ways people could get safety updates in a chaotic area. What would it take to reestablish cell service with drones? Or make satellite communications inexpensive enough for victims of violence to access?

- Genocides happen because people forget the lessons of history. If people kept in mind how easy it is for terrible atrocities to happen, they would be much more insistent about preventing them. Find survivors of past genocides in your community—such as the Holocaust, the Bosnian genocide, or the Rwandan genocide—and interview them about their experiences. Share their stories on social media to help young people around the world understand, on an emotional level, why it is so important to prevent genocides.

- For more information, see the entries for "How You Can Be a Danielle and Promote Peace and Understanding in the World" and "How You Can Be a Danielle and Combat Totalitarianism in the World."

● **Democracy and rights.** Many developing countries are governed by authoritarian regimes. They do not allow the people to freely choose their own leaders, and often violate the human rights of their citizens. Supporting democracy in these countries can have great benefit, so here are a few ways you can make a difference:

- Healthy democracy isn't possible without a wider framework of traditions and unwritten rules that let people trust each other and work together. The National Democratic Institute[24] is a nonprofit that works with local pro-democracy activists to help them lay the foundations for freedom in developing countries.

- Some of the worst violence and political repression in the developing world has been in Sub-Saharan Africa. The Centre for Democracy and Development[25] helps countries in this region make the transition from authoritarianism to democratic governance, especially in Nigeria, Africa's most populous country.

- Because women don't have the same rights as men in much of the developing world, the Association for Women's Rights in Development[26] (AWID) focuses on promoting the rights of girls and women. In addition to fighting for full legal equality, AWID also works to improve economic, political, and educational opportunities for female citizens.

- Authoritarian regimes usually try to manipulate their citizens with propaganda. As a result, even if those countries have elections, the people can't truly make a free choice because they have been given false information. An app or website that makes it easier for people in developing countries to find accurate information about their governments, in languages they understand, could make it harder for non-democratic regimes to stay in power. If you haven't learned computer programming yet, take a look at the entry for "How You Can Be a Danielle and Learn to Program Computers from a Young Age."

- When governments violate people's rights in developing countries, it often goes unreported. If someone doesn't have a video camera or an easy connection to YouTube, it's hard for them to show the world what is really going on. Even if they upload video of abuses to YouTube, if it is captioned in a non-English language or categorized improperly, it might go unseen. There's a need for simple, affordable technology—whether hardware or software—to help people document abuses by their governments and then share them with the international community in a way that gets enough attention.

- Countries can't say they support human rights if they don't support women's rights. Women and girls are half the population of developing countries, but face many disadvantages. They own a small fraction of the property, get much less education, and suffer a disproportionate share of sexual violence. You could start a campaign among young people to put pressure on governments to protect women's rights in developing countries. Authoritarian regimes get a lot of their money by selling resources to wealthy democratic countries, but if students convinced those democratic governments not to buy resources from governments that oppress women, there would probably be reform.

- **Education.** Economic wellbeing naturally follows when people are able to get the education they need. Poor children who go to school are much less likely to stay in poverty, and this increase in wealth is what lifts developing countries up to developed status. Yet it is hard to expand education when communities don't have electricity or Internet access, or when violence or remote location makes it impossible for kids to get to school. Consider these options for promoting education in developing nations:

  - The World Literacy Foundation[27] works to expand access to reading materials, using a solar-powered tablet called Sun Books. This is a much more efficient solution than sending individual books to remote regions.

  - If you'd like to support a nonprofit that focuses on a single region, take a look at United World Schools,[28] which builds schools and provides education to extremely poor children in Southeast Asia. Many of their schools cost less than $1 per child per week.

  - Libraries Without Borders[29] provides books and educational materials to people affected by poverty and conflict. In addition, they train people in entrepreneurship, so they can put their innovative ideas into action to help their communities.

  - In many developing countries, few people grow up speaking English, which is the common language of the Internet. As a result, those people don't have access to the vast wealth of educational materials available online. Instead, they speak hundreds of relatively small languages with few educational materials. You could create a platform for connecting people fluent in both English and another of these languages with students in the developing world, to translate for them the resources they need.

  - Similarly, you could design a simple and social language-learning platform, to connect students in developing countries with

English-language tutors. Live interactions between people allow for faster and deeper learning than these students could get from books alone.

— A common reason for students to drop out of school in developing countries is that walking to class is not safe. Bandits might rob them, terrorists might kidnap them, or government soldiers might harass them. Many girls worry about the risk of sexual assault. You could create a distance-learning system for people who cannot safely go to school. Think of all the things it would need—like electricity and an Internet connection—and try to figure out how your learning system could provide them. Then, consider what educational resources and features it should include. Try to bring together a team of teachers, programmers, and engineers to support your idea and make it a reality.

For more information, please see the following entries in the companion book *A Chronicle of Ideas: A Guide for Superheroines (and Superheroes)*: The Haitian Earthquake, Vertical Agriculture, Three-Dimensional Printing of Building Modules, Organization of African States.

Footnote links at

DanielleWorld.com/resources

HOW YOU CAN BE A DANIELLE

and Promote World Health

❀ ❀ ❀ ❀ ❀

Around the world, billions of people suffer from diseases that reduce their longevity and quality of life. Of these, hundreds of millions have severe illnesses, and over 50 million die every year. Most of those deaths are from a set of well-known causes that are preventable. In other cases, although cures have not yet been developed, they are within reach of exponential health technologies (such as biotechnology and nanotechnology) within the next one to two decades. So, if people can make it ten or twenty years in reasonably good health, they will be able to take advantage of new health breakthroughs that will dramatically extend their lives.

Also, the types of diseases that people suffer from differ between wealthy nations and poor nations. In developed countries like the United States, people often suffer from heart disease and diabetes caused in part by eating too much saturated fat, sugars, and starches, and not exercising enough. In developing countries like Haiti and Zambia, people get diseases such as cholera because they don't have access to clean drinking water. Improving health in wealthy nations mainly requires advances in medical technology to develop new treatments and cures, and campaigns to encourage people to practice healthy lifestyles. In poor nations, it requires new technologies and distribution strategies to help people access sanitation and basic medicine, as well as educational programs to integrate those technologies into the communities.

In the novel, Danielle promotes world health in several ways. She develops ingenious therapies for cancer and heart disease, and encourages her followers to be physically active. For developing countries such as Zambia, she arranges for innovative water filtration systems to be installed in communities so they can avoid polluted-water diseases, such as cholera. For example, she introduces the Slingshot water purification technology (see below) to Zambia when she is six years old. There are many opportunities for you to follow Danielle's example, either advancing medical innovation, or helping create healthy conditions around the world.

Let's look at a range of the most serious problems for world health, and what you can do about each of them—ranging from organizations that you can support, to areas where you might be able to create valuable innovations.

- **Heart disease.** Heart disease and related diseases of the cardiovascular system are the leading cause of death in developed countries. A combination of unhealthy diets, lack of exercise, and high obesity rates lead to atherosclerosis (the clogging of the arteries with plaque) which is the primary cause of heart disease. This can cause chronic problems like pain and heart failure, as well as acute problems such as heart attack and stroke. By forming healthier habits, most people can greatly reduce their risk of heart disease. Here are some ideas for how you can work to reduce heart disease:

  - My health books (coauthored with Terry Grossman, M.D.), Fantastic Voyage[1] and TRANSCEND,[2] provide extensive descriptions on how to dramatically reduce your risk of heart disease and related problems.

  - To refresh yourself about the problem, take a look at this Khan Academy introduction[3] to heart disease, heart attacks, and atherosclerosis. It explains how these processes work, in clear language with examples.

- The American Heart Association[4] runs some excellent programs to encourage healthy living, through a combination of diet, exercise, managing stress, and not smoking cigarettes. You could organize a fundraiser, or use the online resources they offer to start activities at your school promoting fitness and good eating habits. Their Healthy for Good[5] campaign offers tips and resources that can help both kids and adults form lifestyles that prevent heart disease.

- You can also consider donating to the British Heart Foundation,[6] which is more closely focused on funding innovative research that looks at the molecular-level causes of heart disease. With these insights, it is easier to design drugs that keep the heart healthy, and with a minimum of side effects elsewhere in the body.

- If you know computer programming, you can create apps that encourage healthy habits. Think of ways you could make it appealing and exciting to set goals and achieve them. If you don't know coding yet, take a look at the entry for "How You Can Be a Danielle and Learn to Program Computers from a Young Age."

- Another area of need is for apps that can help people understand their risk factors for heart disease, and warn them when they should seek treatment. Right now, too many people wait to see a doctor until their heart disease has already caused their body permanent damage. Often, the first symptom of heart disease is a heart attack, and a third of first heart attacks are fatal. If someone's phone or computer could detect risk based on their behavior, it could get them to medical attention much sooner.

- Unhealthy eating habits aren't just the result of laziness or not knowing that junk food is harmful. Unlike in developing countries, poor people in rich countries find junk food to be the most affordable way to obtain enough calories. In some high-poverty neighborhoods, there are few, if any, sources of fresh, healthy food available. These are known as food deserts,[7] as explained in this TED Talk by Ron Finley. Innovation could solve this problem. Think of ways healthy food could be made available less expensively in food deserts. Many different subjects could be helpful in finding a solution—biology, chemistry, robotics, artificial intelligence, and more. For more information, see the entry for

"How You Can Be a Danielle and Help Cure Heart Disease."

● **Cancer.** Cancer is the second most prevalent cause of death in developed countries. Reducing this toll will take a combination of lifestyle changes, such as anti-smoking campaigns, and medical breakthroughs, such as drug cocktails that can destroy cancer stem cells. Here are some ideas for how you can promote world health by fighting cancer:

-   To review the basics, take a look at this <u>three-minute animated summary of what goes wrong in the body when cancer develops.</u>[8]

-   The <u>MD Anderson Cancer Center</u>[9] is one of the world's most advanced cancer research programs. The doctors and scientists there are working on several ambitious "moon shot" programs to develop advanced therapies that could greatly reduce deaths from hard-to-treat cancers. Consider raising money for them, volunteering, or raising awareness about their work on social media.

-   The <u>Cancer Research Institute</u>[10] gets outstanding ratings for the quality and impact of its research. They find the most promising scientists and projects and give them the funding they need to generate innovative breakthroughs. They're another worthy organization for fundraising.

-   The <u>American Lung Association</u>[11] provides resources to help people quit using tobacco, which is the main cause of lung cancer, which kills more people each year than any other type of cancer. They support research into new methods for fighting addiction more effectively and sponsor campaigns to persuade young people not to try cigarette smoking in the first place.

-   One of the reasons why some forms of cancer are so deadly is that they do not cause major symptoms until the disease has metastasized (spread to multiple locations). For this reason, many lives could be saved by more advanced screening tests that could detect cancer more cheaply, more accurately, and sooner. Even as a young person, you can do meaningful research on cancer detection, and maybe invent a revolutionary new approach. For more information, see the entry for "How You Can Be a Danielle and Help Cure Cancer."

- Because people carry their phones with them almost all the time, mobile apps offer a new opportunity to give people trying to quit smoking the support they need, when they need it. Think of ways you could develop an app to make quitting easier. If you know someone who smokes, ask them what the hardest parts about quitting are, and see if you can find a solution to these problems.

- Most current approaches to fighting cancer are very blunt tools. They combat the cancer, but also harm healthy cells in the body. In the future, cancers will be removed from the body with specially engineered molecules or nano-scale machines put into the body for that purpose. To be part of those breakthroughs, you should study this field as soon as you can. Consider taking an online course such as Nanotechnology and Nanosensors (Part I[12] and Part II[13]), a 60-100 hour class from the Israel Institute of Technology that gives beginners a solid and detailed introduction to nanotech.

- **HIV/AIDS.** AIDS and the virus that causes it, HIV, cause about a million deaths a year. Although smaller numbers of people in developed countries have AIDS, most of the victims are in poor parts of the world. Preventing and treating AIDS for these people would be a huge boost to world health. Consider these ideas for actions you can take:

  - For inspiration, take a look at some or all of these 11 TED Talks on innovative ways people are working to end HIV and AIDS.[14]

  - Population Services International[15] has a network of 50 health organizations in poor countries around the world. They are known for creating effective programs to stop the spread of HIV/AIDS, such as contraception, education, and special help for drug users. PSI has an excellent focus on achieving positive impact and measuring its results based on good evidence. In the most recent year reported, their work on AIDS and other sexually-transmitted infections prevented patients from losing a combined 10.5 million years of healthy life. By raising funds for PSI, young people in wealthy countries can make a big difference in the lives of some of the world's most disadvantaged young people, because so many children are made orphans by AIDS.

  - UNAIDS,[16] the Joint United Nations Program on HIV/AIDS, helps coordinate efforts by many different groups to fight this problem.

Donations to UNAIDS help them improve the medical services available in poor countries, and ensure that AIDS patients have access to care even though the disease has a negative stigma.

- Take a look at these <u>five ways technology is fighting HIV and preventing AIDS</u>. [17] Notice that these innovations draw on fields such as computing, psychology, and telecommunications. In a similar way, your best chance of making a contribution to the fight against AIDS is by applying fresh and unusual ideas.

- The arts are another opportunity for impact. In most parts of the world, AIDS patients face severe stigma. Some people associate the disease with behavior they perceive to be immoral, and there are widespread myths saying that someone can catch AIDS by casual interaction with someone who has the disease. As a result, people with AIDS are often shunned and isolated. That's why there's a need for art, videos, and music that show people a more positive view of people living with AIDS. This can create a more inclusive community and reduce prejudice. For inspiration, take a look at this <u>video about Alan Brand</u>,[18] an AIDS survivor who is working to break down the stigma about the disease.

- A likely avenue for a cure for AIDS would be the creation of a vaccine for the HIV virus. There has been progress in this direction, but no final breakthrough yet. <u>Learn more about work on an HIV vaccine</u>,[19] and see if there are any scientists in your area working on this who you could assist in their research.

- **Clean water.** In the developing world, 780 million people don't have safe drinking water, and 2.5 billion people don't have sanitary toilets. This results in diseases like cholera that cause diarrhea and other intestinal problems. Children and elderly people are particularly vulnerable. Diarrhea causes dehydration that is often fatal, resulting in the deaths of around 800,000 children younger than five years old each year. Giving people access to safe drinking water and good sanitation can prevent almost all of those deaths. Here are some ideas to start you thinking about ways to accomplish that:

  - To understand the problem better, take a look at <u>journalist Rose George</u>[20] explaining the relationship between sanitation and disease. For further information, take a look at the entry for "How

You Can Be a Danielle and Combat Drought and Polluted Water in Poor Nations."

- For inspiration, watch young scientist Deepika Kurup[21] explain her efforts to find new clean-water solutions, which started when she was only 14 years old.

- One of the most outstanding non-governmental organizations for healthcare is Partners in Health.[22] Its cholera program provides treatment, education, and prevention in some of the world's poorest countries. This not only helps the people directly spared of disease, but also the many children who would be orphaned or have to drop out of school because polluted water made their parents sick. Raising money for Partners in Health helps them provide clean-water solutions on the ground, which saves lives quickly and inexpensively.

- Other organizations worth your support include Lifewater,[23] which builds clean water systems in poor communities, and provides education on good sanitation practices to keep that water clean until people use it, and CARE,[24] which puts special focus on women's role in community sanitation.

- There's always need for better water purification systems and better well technology. Learn more about Dean Kamen's SlingShot[25] invention, and try brainstorming ideas about other ways to help communities get clean water and keep it sanitary. This is the technology that Danielle introduces to Zambia when she is six years old.

- Create an app or website that can help people find clean water or judge whether the water they have is safe to drink. It is worth noting that many people who don't have healthy drinking water or sanitary toilets do have access to the Internet via mobile phones.

- If you're interested in media, you could work with a clean-water charity to help them spread their message more effectively among young people. What do you think might make more people your age care about clean water for people thousands of miles away?

- **Infectious diseases.** Although AIDS gets more attention than any other infectious disease in the developing world, far more deaths are caused by other conditions. Every year, more than two million people die of malaria or tuberculosis. Occasionally, there are epidemics of diseases like Ebola or SARS. Fortunately, there are often inexpensive and effective defenses against these conditions, such as mosquito nets for malaria and vaccines for tuberculosis. Stopping outbreaks of diseases like Ebola requires a strong response from doctors and nurses to treat victims before too many people get infected. Look over these ideas to get you thinking about ways to make a difference combating infectious diseases:

  - First, take a look at this <u>talk by Bill Gates</u>[26] on mosquitoes, malaria, and education. The charitable foundation he started with his wife Melinda has taken a lead role in fighting malaria around the globe.

  - <u>The Against Malaria Foundation</u>[27] provides insecticidal nets to communities vulnerable to malaria. People can put these nets over their beds, so mosquitoes don't bite them while they're sleeping and spread disease. According to the charity evaluator GiveWell, this is perhaps the most cost-effective lifesaving donation you can make in the world. For about $100, you can save a person an entire year of healthy life—and for about $3,340, you can save a life. To put that in context, in America, some policy makers consider it cost-effective if someone's life can be saved for about $9 million!

  - <u>Fast facts about tuberculosis</u>[28] and its impact on world health. This includes information on the two main types of tuberculosis, and a timeline of efforts to treat it.

  - <u>Doctors Without Borders</u>[29] does essential work in poor countries vulnerable to tuberculosis. This lung condition kills about 1.8 million people a year, but can be prevented with vaccinations, and be successfully treated with powerful antibiotics. Raising money for Doctors Without Borders helps them provide these services as early as possible to those who would otherwise have no access to care.

  - Animated <u>TED-Ed lesson</u>[30] on what we know and don't know about Ebola.

- Doctors Without Borders made crucial contributions to containing the 2014 Ebola outbreak in Africa. Read more about their inspiring work here.[31]

- The US Centers for Disease Control and Prevention Foundation[32] provides training, equipment, and logistics to developing countries to help them fight diseases like Ebola. Donations to this program make it less likely that future epidemics will get out of control and kill large numbers of people around the world.

- In addition to the direct harm from infectious diseases, they are also the subject of widespread rumors and superstition. People in vulnerable populations sometimes incorrectly believe they can make themselves immune to a disease by ingesting unusual substances or performing certain ritual actions. Sometimes, rumors spread saying that real cures, like vaccinations, will poison people and make them sick. There could be great benefits from a new online platform that helps give people accurate information about disease outbreaks and explains why the rumors are wrong.

- It is often difficult to get enough trained medical personnel to remote areas of poor countries. It takes training to be able to deliver vaccine injections, screen people for malaria, or give medicine from IVs. This is an opportunity for innovation. Talk to someone who has worked in medicine in these parts of the world, and ask them how their training helped them do their job. See if you can think of ways that medical equipment could be made simpler, so people without specialized training can use it safely.

- The sooner doctors detect an outbreak of infectious disease, the easier it is to contain and prevent it from spreading to large numbers of people. There is, therefore, a need for better technology to inexpensively screen people for these diseases. If there's a university near where you live, see if any researchers there are studying infectious diseases. You might be able to assist in their research and contribute ideas about how to create better disease tests.

- **Diabetes.** In rich countries, diets high in "high-glycemic" foods such as sugars and starches have led to a large increase in type 2 diabetes. Diabetes is a major world health problem, because it can lead to deterioration of many parts of the body. It is a leading cause of blindness, nerve problems, and organ damage. It can substantially increase the likelihood of heart disease. Fingers and toes, or even whole limbs, can become so diseased that they must be amputated. A combination of modern medicine and good diet habits can keep diabetes under control, but treatments are still very expensive, and do not fully restore people's quality of life. Here are some ways you can get involved:

— The best way to find solutions is to start by thoroughly understanding the problem. Take a look at these fast facts about diabetes,[33] but you might wish to go deeper with Diabetes—A Global Challenge,[34] a 12-week online course from the University of Copenhagen, which gives students a fuller understanding of the impact of diabetes on world health, and what is being done to fight it.

— The Juvenile Diabetes Research Foundation[35] funds pioneering medical research into how to better treat, and eventually cure, type 1 diabetes (diabetes caused by an auto-immune destruction of the pancreatic islet cells of the pancreas). They provide funding to doctors and researchers with creative and daring ideas, some of which might not be able to get funding in the corporate world. At present, there is no cure for type 1 diabetes, and the best doctors can do is manage the condition so patients don't get worse. Raising funds for the JDRF is one of the best ways to assist this research. As a positive side-effect, you could use a fundraiser at your school to help fellow students with diabetes feel more included and supported by the community.

— Although diabetes is a huge problem in wealthy countries, many people in poor countries also suffer from this disease. And unlike your friends and neighbors with diabetes, they lack access to good treatments and may not have learned how a good diet can manage their condition. The World Diabetes Foundation[36] focuses on diabetes prevention and treatment in developing countries, where donation dollars go farther than in America or Europe. If you're looking for immediate impact on people's lives, this is an excellent organization to support.

— When people don't manage their diabetes properly, their elevated blood sugar levels can cause a variety of types of damage to their bodies. A major reason why some people don't monitor their blood sugar better is that most tests require them to poke their own skin and draw blood, which is uncomfortable and inconvenient. If you could create a more painless way to test blood sugar, more people would keep their diabetes under control. Talk to someone with diabetes and see if they have any special tricks to facilitate this process. This might give you some ideas about how a better test might work.

- Another problem with diabetes is that it can be difficult to keep track of which foods someone should avoid if they have the disease. In general, patients need to limit their sugar intake, but many foods that aren't even sweet still have a lot of sugar added to them. You might not guess how much sugar is in items like salad dressing, dipping sauce, or bread rolls. Equally problematic is high levels of simple starches. If you could design an app or other smart technology for warning people about the sugar and starch in their food, this would make it easier to keep diabetes under control.

- The best way to treat type 2 diabetes is to prevent people from getting it in the first place. If you create media or memes encouraging healthy eating habits among young people, you can reduce the number of people in your generation who will eventually develop diabetes.

- **Alzheimer's.** Alzheimer's is a degenerative disease of the brain that gradually causes people to lose their memory and mental abilities. Although some people get it while still in midlife, it mainly affects the elderly. With the Baby Boomer generation entering its 60s and 70s, experts predict that the number of people with Alzheimer's worldwide will skyrocket from 5.1 million in 2015 to 13.5 million in 2050—unless a cure is found. Here are some things you can do to understand this disease, support research for a cure, and help people who currently suffer from Alzheimer's:

  - First, take a look at this <u>short and informative video summary of what Alzheimer's disease is</u>[37] and how it works in the brain.

  - <u>TED Talk by scientist Samuel Cohen</u>[38] on potential progress toward a cure for Alzheimer's.

- Another talk, by neuroscientist Lisa Genova,[39] on steps people can take to reduce their likelihood of getting Alzheimer's.

- Consider supporting the Fisher Center for Alzheimer's Research Foundation,[40] one of the leading groups spearheading medical research into how Alzheimer's might be cured. There has already been encouraging progress toward understanding what goes wrong in the brain to cause Alzheimer's symptoms, and what general sort of therapies might be needed to cure it. If you raise funds for this organization, they go toward this long-term goal.

- On the other hand, the Alzheimer's Foundation of America[41] is more present-focused. The foundation works to support good care for people who are already suffering from Alzheimer's. Caring for people with memory problems takes a lot of skill, and the Alzheimer's Foundation is dedicated to increasing the standard of care that these people receive as they face this terrible disease. If supporting the foundation appeals to you, you might also find it rewarding to volunteer in your community with people who have Alzheimer's.

- Although there is no cure yet for Alzheimer's, there is good reason to believe that people who keep their minds active can reduce their risk of getting it, or slow the progression of the disease if they already have it. If you create an app to help senior citizens train their brains more effectively, you could help keep their minds sharper and give them a better quality of life. If you have the coding skills and a creative mindset, a psychologist or nurse who works with memory-loss patients might be able to advise you on what forms of mental training are most effective at fighting Alzheimer's.

- There's also a need for apps or inventions that help people with the early to moderate stages of Alzheimer's cope and function in daily life. For example, Alzheimer's might make someone forget where they left their keys, but this would be less of a problem if they could press a button on their phone and activate a noisemaker attached to the keychain. Check out these items for some inspiration,[42] and try to imagine other ways that technology could help people with memory problems.

- **Obesity.** Especially in developed countries, obesity is one of the prime causes of health problems. According to the World Health Organization, the global obesity rate has more than doubled since 1980. More than 1.9 billion adults around the world are overweight, and of these, over 600 million are obese, which means seriously overweight. This amounts to about 13% of the world's adult population. Being obese can lead to many other conditions, including heart disease, stroke, type 2 diabetes, and some kinds of cancer. Look over these ideas for ways you can encourage healthy lifestyles and reduce obesity:

  - Think about the provocative <u>ideas of healthy food advocate Jamie Oliver</u>,[43] who describes obesity as an epidemic among children, and proposes innovative diet solutions.

  - Study the publications of <u>the Center for Science in the Public Interest</u>,[44] which is a strong voice in favor of healthy food and balanced nutrition, and backs up its analysis with strong science. If you organize a fundraiser for them, you can support their mission to improve public health through improved diet.

  - Support <u>the Alliance for a Healthier Generation</u>,[45] which focuses on good nutrition for young people and advocates healthy food in schools. If your school doesn't offer enough healthy food, they can provide guidance to help you achieve positive change.

  - Another organization worth supporting is <u>Action for Healthy Kids</u>,[46] which works with schools to encourage more exercise for young people. They have resources to help teachers organize more physical activity during the school day.

  - Check out this <u>list of 18 top childhood health and nutrition nonprofits</u>,[47] as ranked by the charity evaluator GuideStar, and see if one of them appeals to you to support—whether for fundraising, volunteering, or sharing their message online.

  - Think about your own diet and exercise habits. What do you find difficult about sticking to those habits every day? Then, consider what might make those things easier. Can you imagine an app that might help? If so, the odds are that other people would feel the same way, so start coding!

— Some of the easiest and most enjoyable exercise happens when we think of it as play instead of exercise. The 2016 augmented reality app Pokémon Go attracted hundreds of millions of players by making exercise a natural part of a fun, addictive, and exciting game.

To get an even deeper understanding of the major problems in world health, and what you can do to help fix them, you should consider taking an online college-level course on the subject. Take a look at some options:

- Global Health and Humanitarianism[48] is a 6-week course from the University of Manchester about the relationship between challenges to world health and proposed solutions to resolve them. The course is aimed at beginners, doesn't require any prior background in the subject, and is a fairly modest time commitment.

- Essentials of Global Health,[49] a course from Yale University covering key topics in public health and providing more detail than a short course could. This is a more intensive course, lasting 10 weeks and taking 5-7 hours per week.

- There's a wide range of other online courses about public health,[50] with options for many different interests and levels of commitment. Look through the list and see if any catch your interest.

For more information, please see the following entries in the companion book *A Chronicle of Ideas: A Guide for Superheroines (and Superheroes)*: World Health Organization, Ribavirin, Cholera, Drug Cocktail, Cancer Stem Cell, Arterial Calcifications.

Footnote links at

DanielleWorld.com/resources

Acknowledgments

Thank you …

To all the Danielles who have inspired this book.

To my talented daughter Amy Kurzweil who was my deeply insightful fiction writing coach and who drew the inspired graphic novel style illustrations for *Danielle*.

To my devoted partner and wife, Sonya Rosenwald Kurzweil, for her love, guidance and insight into the interpersonal world.

To my sister, Enid Kurzweil Sterling, for her ideas, creativity, and work on our family heritage.

To my brilliant publisher Kevin J. Anderson and his pioneering publishing company WordFire Press. Kevin is one of the best-selling science fiction authors in the United States, with over 50 bestsellers and 23 million books in print. He has provided outstanding editorial guidance. WordFire Press represents many bestselling authors and has been immensely innovative in its approach to literature and publishing.

To my outstanding editor Rebecca Moesta whose exceptionally skillful editorial feedback has guided *Danielle* to be the best it (and she) can be. She is also one of the inspired leaders of WordFire.

To the devoted and talented staff at WordFire Press who guided this project to completion, including Master Editor Mia Kleve, Editor Pat Oliver, Production Manager Michelle Corsillo, book layout expert Quincy J. Allen, and publisher's assistants Chris Mandeville and Marie Whittaker.

To Celia Black-Brooks, for her guidance, encouragement, detailed work on photo permissions, and inspired efforts to let the world know about *Danielle*.

To my talented researcher John-Clark Levin who helped gather and shape the information in the nonfiction companion books, *A Chronicle of Ideas: A Guide for Superheroines (and Superheroes)*, and *How You Can Be a Danielle*.

ACKNOWLEDGMENTS

To my devoted book agent, Nick Mullendore, for his dedication, encouragement, and outstanding editorial guidance.

To my brilliant editor of KurzweilAI.net, Amara Angelica who provided invaluable guidance and ideas.

To my devoted and outstanding managing editor of KurzweilAI.net, Sarah Black, who provided precious detailed editorial feedback.

To Harry Kloor, a brilliant and enormously creative polymath, who provided guidance, encouragement, and ideas (and an introduction to WordFire Press!).

To Nanda Barker-Hook for her editorial guidance and for making sure I'm in the right city at the right time.

To Laksman Frank, for his creative book design and assistance with the illustrations and images in *A Chronicle of Ideas.*

To Tim Garrigan and the team at the Garrigan Lyman Group for their inspired and enthusiastic efforts to tell Danielle's story to the world.

To Allen Kurzweil, a brilliant novelist, for his outstanding editorial ideas.

To my son, Ethan, for his love and outstanding guidance in the entrepreneurial world.

To Rebecca Hanover Kurzweil, my daughter-in-law, for her love and outstanding editorial guidance and feedback.

To Rick Kot, my editor for four of my nonfiction books, for his encouragement and expert editorial guidance in the world of fiction.

To Aaron Kleiner, devoted best friend (for over fifty years) for his encouragement and guidance.

To Barry Ptolemy, for his invaluable editorial feedback, for teaching me the "Christian Arc" in story-telling and character development, and his outstanding work directing the *Danielle* virtual reality book trailer.

To Amy Kurzweil and Jaya Frank for the color illustrations.

To Terry Grossman, devoted friend, coauthor of my health books, and guide in the world of health.

To Martine Rothblatt, for being an outstanding role model and for her brilliant leadership in the world of entrepreneurship and biotechnology, two of Danielle's passions.

To Mickey Singer, devoted friend, and inspired intellectual and spiritual guide.

To Joe Polish, for his masterful insights for sharing Danielle with some of the most influential people on the planet, those that are helping to create the Danielles of the future.

To Tony Robbins and Deepak Chopra, for their insights into the most important human attributes: motivation and creativity.

To Steve Flier, for his guidance in the world of health.

To Martin Miller, for his guidance in the worlds of emotions, relationships, and the mind.

To my Aunt Dorit Whiteman, for her love and outstanding remembrances (including several books) on my family's heritage including my great-grandmother's "Stern Schule."

To Jacob Sparks, my daughter Amy's boyfriend, for his insights into the world of philosophy.

To Megan Fenwick, the first reader of draft one of this novel, who has inspired me with her love of books.

To my good friend, Charlie Kam, for his ideas, encouragement, and insights into our exponential future.

To and in memory of:

My mother Hannah, who was my first fan and to whom I credit my confidence.

My father Fredric, who inspired me and all those around him with his music and his kindness.

My grandmother Lillian Stern Bader, who showed me her mechanical typewriter when I was five, which inspired me to become an inventor.

My great-grandmother Regina, who in 1868 founded the Stern Schule, the first school in Europe to provide higher education for girls (which is the model of the Stern School, which Danielle attends).

Marvin Minsky, the father of artificial intelligence and my mentor.

And Loretta Barrett, my book agent through seven books, who guided me in the power of the written word, and who encouraged me with *Danielle*.

~ℓℓ~

To my mentees, who have provided many ideas and are emerging Danielles including Jessica Byington, David Dalrymple, Laura Deming, Lucy Flores, Danielle Kurzweil, Erica Lee, and Izzy Swart.

My brilliant colleagues at Google who have provided many ideas, including John Giannandrea, Brian Strope, RJ Mical, Jonni Kanerva, Chris Tar, Anna Patterson, Jeff Dean, Larry Page, Fernando Pereira, Corinna Cortes, Amarnag Subramanya, and many others.

To Peter Diamandis, my brilliant exponential cofounder of Singularity University who has provided deep insights and optimism into our abundant future, and my other inspired colleagues at Singularity University including Rob Nail, Gabriel Baldinucci, Salim Ismail, Neil Jacobstein, Emeline Paat-Dahlstrom, and others.

My devoted colleagues who have provided invaluable resources and support including Bob Beal, Maria Ellis, Ken Linde, Sarah Reed, Denise Scutellaro, Marylou Sousa, and Joan Walsh.

To my devoted readers who have provided invaluable feedback and who have been dedicated dialogue partners including Melanie Futorian Baker, Jasmine Boussem, Vint Cerf, Bonnie Amanda DeAngelo, Amelia Eakins, Salina Espinosa, Robin Farmanfarmaian, George Gilder, John Gregg, Audra Hardt, Sasha Helper, Arianna Huffington, Doug Katz, Kayce Laine, Goedele Leyssen, Paul Mahon, Cindy Mason, Marc, Mauer, Cyrus Mehta, Susan Monson, Margaret Moor, Rosy Moreno, Amiee

Mullins, Dean Ornish, Jackie Parker, John Parmentola, Felicia Ptolemy, Steve Rabinowitz, LeAnne Rumbel, Suzanne Somers, Kamila Staryga, Rachel Tayeb, Tim Thompson, Vivek Wadhwa, Lily Whiteman, Nadine Whiteman, and Stevie Wonder.

About the Author

Ray Kurzweil is one of the world's leading inventors, thinkers, and futurists, with a thirty-year track record of accurate predictions. Called "the restless genius" by *The Wall Street Journal* and "the ultimate thinking machine" by *Forbes* magazine, he was selected as one of the top entrepreneurs by *Inc.* magazine.

Ray was the principal inventor of the first CCD flat-bed scanner, the first omni-font optical character recognition, the first print-to-speech reading machine for the blind, the first text-to-speech synthesizer, the first music synthesizer capable of recreating the grand piano and other orchestral instruments, and the first commercially marketed large-vocabulary speech recognition.

Among Ray's many honors, he received a GRAMMY® Award for outstanding achievements in music technology; he is the recipient of the *National Medal of Technology*, was inducted into the *National Inventors Hall of Fame*, holds twenty-one honorary Doctorates, and honors from three US presidents.

Ray has written five national best-selling books, including *New York Times* best sellers *The Singularity Is Near* (2005) and *How to Create a Mind* (2012). He is co-founder and Chancellor of Singularity University and a Director of Engineering at Google heading up a team developing machine intelligence and natural language understanding.

If You Liked ...

If you liked *Danielle: Chronicles of a Superheroine* Complete Edition, you might also enjoy:

Star Challengers Omnibus
by Rebecca Moesta and Kevin J. Anderson

City of Angels
by Todd J. McCaffrey

Crystal Doors Omnibus
by Rebecca Moesta and Kevin J. Anderson

Also by ...

Ray Kurzweil

How to Create a Mind: The Secret of Human Thought Revealed
Transcend: Nine Steps to Living Well Forever
The Singularity Is Near: When Humans Transcend Biology
Fantastic Voyage: Live Long Enough to Live Forever
Are We Spiritual Machines?
*The Age of Spiritual Machines: When Computers Exceed Human
Intelligence*
The 10% Solution for a Healthy Life
The Age of Intelligent Machines

Amy Kurzweil (Illustrator)

Flying Couch, A Graphic Memoir

Our list of WordFire Press authors and titles is always growing.
To find out more and to see our selection of titles, visit us at:

wordfirepress.com